McAlister's Trail

Richard Marman

Cover Art, Design and Graphics by Richard Marman

McAlister's Trail

Copy right © 2015 Richard Marman

Published in London by Abela Publishing Ltd.
23 Firtree Close, Sandhurst, Berks, GU47 8HU 8NG, England

Email: author@RichardMarman.com

Website: www.RichardMarman.com

ISBN 13: 978-1-925833-0-10

Republished in 2018 with Ocean Reeve Publishing

First Edition, 2014

**Books by Richard Marman
available from Abela Publishing**

<u>The McAlister Line</u>
(In historical order)

McAlister's Trail
McAlister's Way
McAllister's Hoard
McAlister's Siege
McAlister's Spark

<u>Web and Wave Adventures</u>
(Illustrated books for children of all ages)

A Tale of Two Turtles
A Whale's Tale

Cananadian North West Territories
Vancouver
Pacific Ocean
United Staes
Rocky Mountains
Pacific
San Francisco
California
Grand Canyon
Colorado River
Arizona Territory
New Mexico Territory
Fort Mohave
Tucson
Fort Wendell Pierce
Nogales
Hacienda O'Conor
Baja
Mexico

For Judy

<u>Acknowledgments</u>

I would like to thank my wonderful wife, Judy to whom this book is dedicated, for never minding the hours I spent in front of a computer screen.

My charming daughters Sally and Elizabeth were a great support and keen proofreaders, I'm pretty sure this is the first western they've read.

Also a big thank you to three special young ladies: Brooke Bowtell, Lauren Jones and Camille Moroney, my art school and university buddies, for all their friendship, encouragement and feedback during the writing of this manuscript.

Foreword

My name is Zach McAlister and I have been tracking down my ancestry with my Grandpa Danny's girlfriend, Angela Holyman. Grandpa's a widower now, so Angela came to live with him at his place outside Merimbula in Southern New South Wales. They'd known each other when they were young, but drifted apart and Grandpa married my Nan. I've written about Angela and Grandpa's adventures in previous books — check them out.

Angela's super-smart and used to be a hot-shot doctor in London. She talked Grandpa into upgrading his computer and even bought him a Smart Phone. So now we can surf the net at a decent speed. We found a tonne of neat genealogical stuff and even downloaded heaps from London University where Angela used to do her research.

We tracked down much of our particular branch of the McAlister clan, many of whom left Scotland in the 16th, 17th and 18th Centuries. I was surprised how well documented their adventures were, but then many of them were remarkable journal keepers and often got mixed up in events that interested historians.

They mainly wanted to escape famine, war and oppression and spread all over the world. So far we've found links to my past relations in just about every continent.

Grandpa Danny mentioned he'd passed a McAlister ranch in Arizona during his adventures with Mad Monty. Angela has a squillion contacts and seems to know just about every geeky egg-head in the world. She got in touch with a history professor from the

College of Arts and Science at the University of New Mexico in Albuquerque.

With the professor dude's help we dug up this interesting little historical sideline from a series of letters and journals written by a prolific early 20th Century American soldier-chronicler called Cletus Mellow. Hanging out with Grandpa and Angela and writing their stories has improved my English about a million percent. Who'd have thought I'd use a word like 'prolific' a couple of years ago. Mature or what..?

Some of the information is now online, but a lot of the original hard-copy material was stored in the UNM archives. Twisting the history prof around her little finger was child's play for Angela. She persuaded him to copy ALL the stuff and upload into her Dropbox account. It must have taken him ages, because there was a heap of it, but he was a history nerd and assured us he enjoyed nothing better than digging into the past.

Anyway here's part of the piece old Cletus's wrote which includes one of our wandering McAlister Clan. It's a ripper yarn too.

Zack McAlister

January 2015

Prologue

Everyone thinks Fort Marcy was the first US outpost in the New Mexico Territory in eighteen and forty-seven at the beginning of the Mexican War, but that's not so. Fort Wendell Pierce started up back a couple of years before that. Old Wendell wasn't even US military, but a captain in the Texas Rangers out of El Paso. He'd been chasing Comanches who were chasing Apaches and generally causing mischief for white folks in south-western Texas at the time.

Wendell found water and a good place to defend, and set up a supply camp there. He thought he was still in Texas, but he was way off. The territorial boundaries were all up for grabs back then. They were still squabbling over the borders years afterwards.

Wendell got himself killed by guerrillas down on the Veracruz Line during the Mexican War in forty-seven, so the Army just kind of took over the fort and that turned out to be a pretty good move in light of how things were with the Apaches and Navahos. It was plum central with Apache tribes to the southwest and Navahos to the northwest.

The Navahos weren't such rascals as the Apaches and were treated pretty sternly by Kit Carson in my opinion, shunting them about from their home in the Arizona and New Mexico Territories to the Pecos River Salt Flats and back again. Ben Grierson didn't think much of Kit, opining he spent too much time during the War Between the States bothering Indians instead of fighting Rebs. You can't blame Kit entirely though. By and large he got on well with the

Navahos, but he allowed himself to be bamboozled by Star Chief Carleton and his Manifest Destiny hokum.

Anyway Fort Pierce grew more by accident than design. Grierson's Ninth and Tenth Buffalo Cavalry were there from time to time after the Civil War. They sure did a lot of Apache hunting over the years. An artillery-training unit that used the wide-open spaces as a firing range was still there when I rode through the gates in nineteen and seven.

I was just a young fellow then, a brand new Captain full of grit and good intentions. I'd been with the Tenth Cavalry since graduation and I'd only served with black troops. That suited me fine. They were easy to get along with and generally did what they were told. White troops were sometimes easy to get along with and did what they were told sometimes.

At the time I had a sergeant and a couple of troopers with me. Dane Cooper was the sergeant's name and I remember him as a right sporting soldier if ever I met one. I recollect he fought with the 369th Harlem Hellfighters in France back in eighteen. Killed a parcel of Germans and got a medal for it too. Joshua Billings and JP Shelton were the other two but I don't rightly know what became of them in later years. We'd all been together foot-slogging in Cuba at Kettle Hill and San Juan Hill back in ninety-eight.

Now that was a hot fight. The way you read it you'd think Teddy Roosevelt won the day all by himself, but that wasn't the gist of it. He nearly had to try mind, I recall him looking real bashful after ordering the first charge and no one followed. Why, he got maybe fifty yards up the hill and found out he was alone. He had to go back and chivvy up his *Rough Ridin'* boys, who said they didn't hear his order. But they did pretty well the second time. Got up there after being shot to bits.

The black troops worked damned hard too. John J Pershing, who got his nickname '*Blackjack*' for serving with Negros, was with us and didn't he go on to bigger things. But Teddy was good with a story and knew the editors of *Harpers* and *Colliers* and that painter fellow, Freddy Remington. My, did he dress the boys up well. But I'll allow he was a mighty tolerable artist.

Ben Grierson was long retired, he had a stroke soon after and that pretty much finished him off. But he knew my Pa from back during the War Between the States when they rode together on that Mississippi raid in eighteen and sixty-three. General Grant was mighty pleased by the way that turned out. Colonel Ben was always friendly to me, helping my early Army career with a good word here and there. He got me a post in the Tenth.

He said he had an interest in an incident at Pierce because a fellow he knew was involved and wrote to the Judge Advocate at Fort Wingate asking him to send me down to see what I could make of it. He was writing his memoirs at the time and maybe didn't want any unwanted skeletons jumping out at him.

Fort Pierce was still remote even then. There were automobiles and electric lights in the streets of Albuquerque and Santa Fe, but it was still a tough horseback ride up steep tracks to Pierce. It was looking a bit down at the heel. I reckon generals had stopped coming by and they didn't see the need to spruce things up. The duty sentry was sharp enough though, and gave a snappy salute, pointing the adjutant's office out to me across the parade square. One of General Crook's cannons from his wars with Geronimo and

Chato was at its centre, and the stars and stripes drooped from a flagpole. There wasn't a lot of activity about.

Dane Cooper and the troopers took my horse to arrange quarters. I told them I didn't need them for the rest of the day. They knew the drill and would find a snug billet with food and maybe a drop of whiskey, but they'd report sober and alert in the morning. I heaved my saddle panniers over my shoulder, climbed the porch steps and opened the door.

The adjutant's office was a mess of papers and a couple of harassed clerks. To me it seemed a lot of activity for a small backwater post, but I've spent my entire career as a line officer and have scant knowledge of army administration. The adjutant was Jimmie Granger, a fellow I'd known a little at the Point and he jumped up to meet me like a long lost pal, although I hadn't seen him for maybe ten years. That's what an isolated post does, I suppose. And he'd been there for quite a while.

'Well Cletus Mellow, my dear fellow,' he gushed, thrusting out his hand and shaking mine like I was the last human on the face of the earth. 'How great to see you. I got the message from Wingate. You're here to interview our prisoner I believe.'

'That's the size of it, Jimmie,' I replied, all business and efficiency. 'The Judge Advocate wants to know if there's enough prima facie evidence to make any sort of case out of it. Maybe you can fill me in on the details?'

He sent one of the clerks for a pot of coffee and dragged an extra chair over to his desk. He added some red-eye to the coffee, which was considerate.

'It's strange,' he began. 'I mean I couldn't really see the point, but we don't have the whole story. What we do know is that Sam McAlister killed a man in cold blood and he isn't inclined to tell anyone why he'd do such a thing. He's been behind bars ever since, but doesn't seem to mind.'

'This all happened about six weeks ago, didn't it?' I asked because the dates had been scratchy. I don't know how Colonel Grierson heard about it. He lived back east and was getting on in years, but he kept dozens of contacts in the Tenth. After all he formed the regiment forty years past when people like Sherman and Custer were dead set against Negroes serving in the army.

'Pretty close to that,' Jimmie said. 'A small bunch of Chiricahua Apaches turned up about fifty miles south of here, not far from the border. That's probably odd in itself, because I thought they were all long gone and hiding from Fedarales up in the Western Sierra Madre with the Mescalero. Anyway, we got some complaints from local farmers about sheep stealing and Major Bevan, the CO here, ordered a squad to go out, round them up and ship 'em over to the Fort Sill Reservation.

'Now Sam, who'd been scouting for us ever since he left the regular army years ago, goes out with them. A green shave-tail is commanding, but he's got a sound top soldier and that's about all you need. It doesn't take long for them to locate the camp around nightfall and the lieutenant decides to wait until just before dawn to take them by surprise and hopefully avoid any shooting. It sounded like a good plan, so they posted sentries and hunkered down for the night.

'At dawn they moved in, but Sam McAlister's missing. They figure he's just off somewhere and they don't need him anyway. As they enter the camp they hear a shot. Well, that gets everyone mighty agitated, but it's the only shot fired. The troopers have their handguns out, but there's nothing to shoot at. The Apaches have gone. Slipped into the night and vanished.

'Still they searched all the lean-tos and found no one except Sam McAlister. He's holding his old Schofield .44 revolver and there's a dead Indian in front of him. He's ancient, probably as old as Sam who must be way past sixty.'

'What did Sam have to say about it all?' I asked.

'Well, that's the strange part he said he'd know when to tell his story and who to tell it to. He did say it was something that had to be done, and he was glad it was finally over. He snuck into the camp after everyone was asleep and cut a deal with the Chiricahua. As much as we can gather, he tipped them off about the troopers and let 'em go, so long as they left this one, old Indian behind. I guess the Apaches decided that pragmatism was the order of the day and skedaddled. I'm not sure whether the major's madder about Sam killing an Indian or because he allowed the others to escape. I think the only reason anyone is bothering at all is because New Mexico and Arizona are vying to see who will get Statehood first, and law-and-order must be seen to prevail.'

Well, New Mexico won that one by a month and they sure had swelled heads about Arizona coming last.

'I wonder if he'll talk to me.' I said. 'I suppose there's only one way to find out.'

'Do you want to see him now? It's a bit late,' Jimmie asked.

'Now's fine. It's an hour or so to supper, he should have told me all he wants to by then.'

But I was wrong there. I never got to supper at the officer's quarters, but wound up sharing tortillas, chilli beans and beer in a prison cell with an old westerner from a time that was slipping into history.

Jimmie led me across the parade square to the provost marshal's building. It was next to the sutler's store where a raging fire was kept and the two cells were quite comfortable even as the chill of evening closed in. A bored sentry got to his feet, but Jimmie waved him down. Fort Pierce didn't stand on ceremony unnecessarily. Behind the bars Sam McAlister lay on a cot reading a dime novel. He was in no way remarkable, about normal height and build. He was clean-shaven and apparently no worse for wear considering he had spent nearly two months in a cell. Major Bevan insisted that he take daily exercise and he seemed well fed and hygienically acceptable.

I was admitted to the cell. Sam sat up, swung his feet to the floor and nodded.

'Evenin',' he said civilly. He had a deep western growl that sounded as if he was chewing something while speaking.

'Good evening, sir,' I replied. Civility deserves civility in return. 'I'm Captain Mellow. The Judge Advocate sent me from Fort Wingate.'

'I see you're from the Tenth,' he observed, indicating my shoulder patches depicting a buffalo with the motto, '*Ready and Forward*' written on a scroll beneath it. Of course he would know regimental insignia. We all wore khaki by then. The Army'd finally seen the sense of it back in Cuba and now we kept our dress blues for ceremonial occasions.

'Yes, sir, I am.'

'And Colonel Grierson sent you?'

'In a way. He especially asked the Judge Advocate's department for me. I'm not sure how I can help – I'm not a legal officer. I have been seconded from the Tenth to come and see you. Why do you think Colonel Grierson sent me?'

'Because I wrote him a letter and the gentleman yonder who now guards me was good enough to post it.'

'I know Mr McAlister from scoutin' days with Gen'ral Crook and Gen'ral Miles,' the guard informed us. 'It ain't right he's in here. One dead Injun more or less don't make no difference in anyone's reckoning.'

'Thank you for your enlightenment, Corporal Beaufort,' Jimmie said, 'but we're here to interview Mr McAlister.'

Beaufort was smart enough to hold his tongue.

'Now, why would Colonel Grierson have any interest in who you shoot way out here in the New Mexico Territory?' I asked.

'Because one of his Buffalo Soldiers was involved. He really cared about all his men, which is a rare thing for a senior officer to do. In the early days he knew all the men in the Ninth and Tenth. And this story starts in the early days. I hoped he might have come himself.'

'His health isn't the best, he would have liked to, but you can be sure I will relate everything you say.'

'Then you're the person I've been waiting for. It'll take some telling too. You got time, Captain Mellow?'

'Take all the time you want, Mr McAlister.'

'I'd be pleased if you called me Sam, I ain't one for airs and graces.'

It was odd how this accused felon, a man I thought had murdered in cold blood could inspire such an aura of serenity and normality. You simply could not help liking him. It was almost hypnotic.

'Then please address me as Cletus. I'm at your disposal,' I replied.

It was Corporal Beaufort's suggestion to visit the sutler's store for victuals and beverages, and it turned out to be fortuitous as we were to be up far into the night.

'You know, it's funny,' Sam drawled, 'but the story starts right here in this room. What I'm going to tell you I learned from that Indian before he died and my own part in it all.'

And what follows is the story Sam McAlister told me of his adventures in the old days of the Wild West concerning a half-breed Indian, a black cavalry sergeant, three beautiful Mexican women and culminating in that prison cell in a remote outpost of New Mexico.

We commandeered a couple of large notebooks from the Provost Marshal's stationery supply, and used one of those fancy, Lewis Waterman patented fountain pens Jimmie's Ma had given him for his birthday. It was really fine to write with, but ran out of ink after a bit, so Corporal Beaufort produced several pencils from his desk drawer and I was able to record every detail.

Chapter 1

Billy Songbird was born at Fort Pierce sometime in eighteen and forty-nine, or thereabout. His mother, Shadow Woman, was from a Kiowa tribe up in Kansas. She was given to a bunch of Comanches as a bribe to stop them raiding. The Comanches only kept their word for about a week and then the Kiowa had to toughen up and beat them off, as they should have done in the first place. There was no getting Shadow Woman back then, but the Kiowa thought of lots of clever ways to niggle the Comanche who soon got fed up and bored and moved south.

By this time it was maybe nine or ten years after General Sam Houston beat Santa Anna at San Jacinto for the territory of Texas, and then beat Stephen Austin for the Republic's presidency. Despite his Cherokee connections, Houston didn't think much of Comanches mostly because they were so damn warlike and uncontrollable. So he encouraged the Texas Rangers to continue what they'd been doing for years, and that was to chase all the Comanches they found out of Texas and make sure they didn't come back.

Shadow Woman was with just such a Comanche band on the run from Rangers when they passed by Fort Pierce. She had been handed around to several of the braves, but either they or their other wives didn't seem to take to her even though she was fair in anyone's eyes and hard working. But, she did have a harsh tongue and that might have been off-putting, although she needed to stick up for herself living with the Comanches. The army had stationed a detachment of infantry at the fort and they weren't quite as bellicose towards Indians, being preoccupied with Mexican guerrillas. A sutler named Thaddeus Bean had set up a store at the fort and the Comanches traded Shadow Woman for supplies that would keep them going for a couple of days.

Shadow Woman did the chores and Sutler Bean made some extra cash hiring her out to the soldiers for a dollar. He made quite a deal of money and Shadow Woman was pretty much resigned to the way things were. Bean carried a massive Bowie knife and said he didn't want his valuable merchandise damaged, making it clear that anyone abusing Shadow Woman would be without the equipment to enjoy her in the future. So generally the soldiers treated her reasonably.

Ultimately of course she became pregnant and Billy Songbird was born. Nobody knew who his father was, and nobody was going to claim responsibility. After the birth, Shadow Woman took the baby to a Hopi Shaman who lived at a high mesa pueblo in the Arizona Territory. He knew of medicines and charms that would prevent such events reoccurring.

She certainly loved her son, but Shadow Woman knew the logistical difficulties of a large family. Sutler Bean appeared to tolerate one baby, but may not be so well disposed towards more. The shaman, a fine baritone himself, predicted a musical gift in the infant even though he was only a few months old. So his mother named him Songbird before returning to Pierce. She came back simply because, off-hand as Thaddeus was, he treated her far better than the Comanches.

Over the years the fort developed from a row of tents to adobe and timber buildings with an outer stonewall that was continually being upgraded by successive commanding officers. A small community emerged around it, consisting of several Indian and Mexican families who found varying employment at the fort. Mostly they did the menial tasks the soldiers would rather avoid and were prepared to pay for.

The outpost was briefly taken over by Confederates in 1862, but they quickly abandoned it when Union forces under Colonel Canby advanced from Texas. These adventures didn't really affect Shadow Woman who lived in the sutler's store. In time she became Thaddeus's woman rather than anyone else's, especially after he bought a pair of teenage Mexican girls from some Apaches who'd kidnapped them south of the border. They proved more popular than Shadow Woman because of their youth. It was Thaddeus who considered Songbird too ethereal a name for a growing lad, and decided that *William* had a good, sound ring to it, and so he became *Billy*.

As he grew Billy preferred to spend his time in the outer village or roaming the surrounding hills. He learnt to hunt game and gather edibles from the land. Some things he picked up from others, some things he discovered by trial-and-error. Most importantly he learnt to divine water from animal spoor, subtle changes in vegetation and the very smell of it.

He also embraced elements of the white man's world that interested him. Miss Virginia Pritchard had come west to save the savages from their bestial paganism and reveal true Protestantism to their black hearts. And, possibly enlighten the idolatrous Mexican Papists into the bargain. She set up a school and conducted her classes from a single room at Fort Pierce.

Billy rejected Miss Pritchard's notion of Christianity, believing it was a poor god indeed who allowed his son to have nails driven through his hands, let alone be strung up on a cross. Gods should do better by their kin if they were of any worth. He did however learn reading, writing, mathematics and even a decent slab of science, history and geography from that worthy missionary. In these subjects Billy was an avid and receptive student between bouts of truant wandering in the mountains.

Despite her scholarly nature, Miss Pritchard was a passionate woman and eventually abandoned her calling for an East Texas rancher touring remote army forts to arrange beef supplies for their troops. He admired her fine, womanly figure and impious behaviour in the back of his supply wagon. While his forthright, manly bearing and fifty thousand acres of prime, longhorn-stocked, Texas real estate took her fancy. Not to mention a lucrative contract driving herds along the Sedalia Trail to the Missouri-Pacific railheads for shipment to abattoirs at the northern, industrial cities and their burgeoning markets.

That conscientious educator left Billy and a few other village waifs adequately informed, for which she was justly proud even though the Indians and Mexicans remained disappointingly unaware of true Protestantism.

The shaman's prediction proved correct and Billy developed a true tenor voice. He regularly earned a few dollars singing for the soldiers in their canteen. They were particularly fond of the way he sang in Apache and Navaho dialects to the catchy tunes of Stephen Foster and songs from the Civil War. He knew dozens of Spanish songs and even learnt a little guitar and banjo to help the melody along.

Unfortunately soldiers' canteens and young, impressionable Indian boys weren't an especially good mix. Billy didn't hold liquor well and was always getting into squabbles and sometimes fights. He spent a good deal of time cooling off in the fort cells.

And that's right where he was when a dust-covered, exhausted company of the newly formed Tenth Cavalry rode into Fort Pierce early in 1867. Major George Wheeler Schofield was their commander. Impressively handsome and sporting a flowing moustache and side-whiskers, he looked every part of the Civil War hero he was. Captain Eugene Bellamy was commanding a couple of infantry companies at Pierce then. He greeted Schofield tentatively as he eyed the column of black troopers behind him.

'My, my, you sure are a long way from home, Major,' Bellamy observed, knowing that the Tenth was currently based at Fort Leavenworth, Kansas.

'You have it in a nutshell, sir,' Schofield agreed. 'Been chasing down a pack of Comanchero bandits through the Texas Panhandle to the Rio Grande and then up this way. Some of the scoundrels escaped into Mexico, but we've sure made life powerfully disagreeable for 'em over the last couple of months. Blackest hearted bunch you'd ever meet. Mostly secesh trash who can't abide the War being over. Been butchering and raping homesteaders in the mid-west. We've done all we can, so we'll be heading back to Leavenworth after we've rested up for a couple of days.'

'Don't rightly know how we'll fit you all in,' Bellamy said dubiously.

'We'll bivouac out yonder along the trail,' Schofield said undismayed, but space wasn't Bellamy's only worry, as he explained to Schofield and his officers that evening over a drink in the officer's mess common room.

'I've got mostly Galvanised Yankees here at the moment,' Bellamy said. 'Reb prisoners-of-war who volunteered to come out here for Indian fighting to get away from Camp Douglas, Elmira and Rock Island, and I can't say as I blame them for that. We've got a parcel of Georgians with nothing to go home to so they've stayed on, but they have chips on their shoulders you couldn't crack with a sledgehammer. Now I've got nothing against black troops myself, we all know what the 54th Massachusetts did at Fort Wagner, but it may be a good idea if we keep 'em out of the fort while you're here.'

That might have been sound advice, but it came just a little late and may not have been heeded, as Schofield despised discrimination and was loathe to make special arrangements for his troops. There were three white officers with the Cavalry column, Major Schofield, Captain Ezra Maloney who was second in command and *A* troop leader. *B* troop leader was nineteen-year-old Lieutenant Sam McAlister, a young graduate straight from West Point, new but proving able and enthusiastic. All the non-commissioned officers and troopers were black. Schofield knew he could confidently leave the bivouac details and sentry rosters to his sergeants and corporals, so he'd had no qualms about accepting Bellamy's invitation for drinks.

Indeed the column organised tents, latrines, supper and corralling their mounts with efficient alacrity. Finding their duties complete Sergeant John W Hawken of *A* troop and Sergeant Jubal

Quinn of *B* troop decided to use up some of their poker winnings at the sutler's store. Both men were tough ex-runaway slaves who had served during the Civil War and found army life to their liking. Hawken had a wife and family back at Leavenworth, Quinn was single. Both men had been field hands before escaping along the Underground Railroad and both men had learnt to read and write.

They pushed open the sutler's door. Thaddeus Bean held no racial prejudice, allowing that one man's money was just as good as another's whatever his colour. He poured two stiff whiskeys and nodded for his Mexican girls to get friendly with the customers. Hawken and Quinn had the resources and the inclination to enjoy the sutler's facilities and the evening progressed well until a group of maybe half-a–dozen soldiers from the fort came in for a nip after duty. They were Georgia boys in a rambunctious mood at having to abide so many coloured troops nearby.

They were quiet enough at first, biding their time, and sitting around the store's only table playing cards. But, it didn't take long for the liquor to take effect and the situation could no longer be ignored. Private Travis P Kincaid, a spiteful ex-plantation overseer, was the leader of the pack and there was nothing he would like more than to give a couple of niggers a savage beating, just for the pure sport of it.

'Hey, Thaddeus,' Kincaid bawled across the room, 'looks like you're gonna have to get a couple of new sportin' gals after this. Ain't no respectin' white man gonna poke no whore after them niggers're through with 'em.'

'They ain't done nothing yet, and I don't know if they will,' Thaddeus replied. He could see how trade might be affected, but the two buffalo soldiers were cashed up and eager. Kincaid's crew were a long way between paydays and by the time they had the funds to afford the girls, Schofield's column would be long gone. By then lust would probably have dulled Kincaid's memory in any event. Hopefully Kincaid was just blowing off steam. Indeed his argument lacked validity seeing as he'd bragged about sporting slave girls back in his plantation days often enough. But, here was a situation that needed to be handled with care and discretion.

'You boys planning on usin' them gals any time soon?' he asked Hawken and Quinn.

'We just might,' Quinn replied with his heckles up and feeling contrary, 'but I ain't rightly decided.'

Hawken reckoned he could wait until he got back to Leavenworth, which seemed a much safer option.

'Yep, I think I will after all,' Quinn said, flipping a silver dollar to Thaddeus. 'Fact is I think I might try 'em both.' And he dropped another dollar onto the counter.

He gathered the girls up and headed for the back room.

'Now you ladies might never have been with a black man, but we have a certain reputation in that department,' Quinn said which seemed to amuse the girls hugely.

Kincaid sprang from his chair, sending it clattering to the floor and blocked Quinn's path. They were about the same size and pretty evenly matched, Kincaid carrying perhaps a little more bulk and a little less muscle, but he exuded the rat-cunning of a vintage bar room campaigner.

'There ain't no filthy nigger gonna poke our whores,' he hissed into Quinn's face, stinking of stale tobacco and a couple of rotting teeth.

Quinn stood his ground.

'Listen, *Private*,' he growled. 'I'm a sergeant in this army and I do nothing on your say-so. Now, get out of my way, you pile of puke.'

That wasn't entirely correct because the Army's top echelon had made it quite clear that black NCOs wouldn't be ordering white soldiers around anytime soon. Also, in Kincaid's experience, you could bully black men all you wanted and they just submitted as God intended they should. This was intolerable behaviour.

'Why, you stinkin' son-of-a-bitch!' he growled and took a ferocious swing that took Quinn a glancing blow on the jaw as he pushed the girls aside. Quinn easily avoided the next punch and landed a sharp right into Kincaid's gut, knocking the wind out of him. Quinn who'd fought in several bitter campaigns during the War had come a long way from a meek field hand, and had plenty of his own rat-cunning. They traded a couple of blows, drawing some blood, but it looked as if Quinn would soon get the best of it. It seemed that a brawl would develop as a couple of Kincaid's pals moved to his aid, but Hawken put a stop to that. Drawing his Colt Army .44, he cocked the hammer. Even with the din of the fight the white soldiers saw they were looking down the business end of a gun barrel and backed off.

A final left fist to the chin sent Kincaid sprawling to the floor with blood oozing through his teeth and out of one ear. Mumbling oaths, he staggered to his feet, but he wasn't finished. With surprising speed he drew his Army revolver from its holster. Quinn acted instinctively. He launched himself across the bar room and slammed into Kincaid, knocking the pistol aside just as a shot blasted from its muzzle and in the blue haze and black powder stench, silence fell over the sutler's store.

Then the girls screamed as the smoke cleared and everyone stared at Kincaid who writhed on the floor making a gurgling sound rather like water in a drainpipe. He was clutching his gut as a red patch formed through his fingers drenching his uniform tunic and spreading down his breeches.

'Oh, shit,' Hawken murmured through clenched teeth, and that pretty well summed up the mood in the room.

There was no need to call for help, the entire post had heard the shot and about half of them seemed to pile into the bar room within seconds. For a while it was bedlam, men rushed in crushing into each other. Thaddeus Bean tried to calm his hysterical whores while Quinn and Hawken faced off Fort Pierce's men and it looked like the fight would re-erupt at any moment. Hawken still had his revolver drawn and at first everyone thought he'd fired the shot. Moments later Captain Bellamy barged through the door and quickly restored calm, clearing the store in short order.

Kincaid was carried moaning to the infirmary by four infantrymen pushing through Major Schofield, Captain Maloney and Lieutenant McAlister, who were close behind Bellamy.

'Explain,' was all Bellamy said. He addressed Hawken without raising his voice. Hawken shrugged with a baleful, *it-wasn't-me* expression. He rolled his eyes towards Quinn, who had staggered to his feet covered in Kincaid's blood and with a burn across his hand where he'd pushed the pistol's blazing hot barrel away into Kincaid's belly.

'It was self-defence, sir,' Quinn stammered, 'he pulled his gun on me. I knocked it aside.'

Hawken nodded vigorously, but Kincaid's cronies told a different story. They claimed Quinn had taken Kincaid's revolver and gunned him down in cold blood. Thaddeus feigned ignorance, knowing better than to get involved in military matters, and the girls were of no use at all. Reduced to tears, there was no consoling them and no one was able to make any sense of their sobbing babble.

So it stood that one black witness supported Quinn and half a dozen white men did not. Quinn could see things were going very badly indeed.

'We don't have a surgeon at the post, but our medical orderly is studying by mail and has been adequate to date,' Eugene Bellamy said. 'I'm sorry, major, but I'll have to hold your sergeant until this mess is cleared up. Kincaid was a troublemaker and probably deserved what he got I'll warrant, but this'll take some unravelling.'

Ashen faced, George Schofield could only nod as his trusty *B* troop sergeant was escorted to the guard house to join Billy Songbird.

Chapter 2

'Move over, Billy Boy. You've got company,' one of the guards hollered as they shoved Jubal Quinn into the cell. They weren't particularly gentle and Quinn smashed against the wall, collapsing onto the cot. He took a few moments to recover.

Billy didn't mind company as he was a gregarious soul, and although he enjoyed time alone in the mountains, he tended to get lonely in jail. So he helped Quinn up and offered him a mug of water. It wasn't long before Billy was acquainted with the whole, sad story.

'Man, you're in big trouble,' was his summary of the situation, a really unnecessary observation in Quinn's view. Things didn't improve significantly as time went by. Major Schofield interviewed Quinn and Lieutenant McAlister took notes, revealing nothing new.

The following morning there was a great to-do outside the jailhouse and the duty sentry dashed out to see what the matter was. He wasn't gone long and stalked up to the cell bars when he returned.

'You sure are one pitiful nigger now,' he snarled at Quinn. 'Travis Kincaid died in the night. Our sawbones said the ball went clear through his belly being at such close range and took out pretty much everything on its way. Punctured his liver, bowel and spleen. He weren't never going to recover from that, not even with the help of God Almighty. They're gonna hang you for sure now, boy.'

The gravity of events was not lost on Major Schofield either. Officer's call was held in Captain Bellamy's orderly room.

'I'd better return to Leavenworth and get Colonel Grierson in on this,' he explained. 'I don't want things boiling over. Eugene, can you keep a lid on it for a week or two?'

'I'm not worried about the troops here. They're not happy, but they'll do what they're told or I'll strap one or two of 'em to a wagon wheel for a day or so. That'll settle 'em down,' Bellamy replied.

He noted Schofield's scowl. That sort of punishment had been discontinued well before the Civil War.

'Tough maybe, Major, but I've got some hard-arsed *good-ole-boys* at this post. I don't give 'em an inch. I'll not have a mutiny or desertions on my patch.'

'Fair enough, Eugene. You do what you must,' Schofield conceded.

'One problem is the officer commanding Fort Marcy,' Bellamy explained. 'Colonel Charles Fontaine surely despises Nigras and he'll most likely hear this case. It's his jurisdiction fair and square. Perplexing fellow really. He owned slaves on his Texas plantation, but chose to fight for the North to preserve the Union. I doubt if your sergeant will get a sympathetic hearing, especially with half a dozen witnesses swearing it was murder in cold blood.'

'And there are more than a few of the top brass who'd just love to see the black units discredited,' Captain Maloney added.

'In that case it'd be good idea if you stay here with half of *A* Troop, Ezra and I'll take everyone else back to Kansas and return with legal help just as soon as I can.'

'Begging your pardon, Major,' Sam said, 'Jubal Quinn was, *is* my troop sergeant. May I suggest I stay here instead?'

Schofield looked at Maloney who merely shrugged.

'You stay with half of *B* Troop then, Sam,' Schofield said. 'The rest of us had better not dawdle.'

Within the hour *A* Troop and every second man from *B* Troop were packed and away in a clatter of hoof beats and the jingle of bridle chains. Sam was left in charge of twenty troopers and an Apache scout while Corporal Henry Cook was promoted to *B* Troop acting sergeant. Sam went to explain how things were to Quinn.

'You'll just have to sit tight until Colonel Grierson sorts this out,' Sam said. 'Don't worry about the local rednecks, Captain Bellamy and I'll keep an eye on things outside. We don't want a lynching party, do we? But don't worry, trust us.'

Quinn gulped at the thought and, on reflection, Sam realised it wasn't the most comforting of comments. He stuttered over a few more platitudes and left with reassurances he'd no way of knowing he could keep. Billy and Jubal stared at the bars. Quinn simply did not have the right history to make trusting white men a natural inclination.

'Your day just keeps getting better,' Billy observed. 'You know what you need to do?'

'What?' Jubal snapped, because he had no idea what he needed to do.

'You need to get out of here and as far away as possible, as quick as you can.'

'And just how do I manage that? You may not have noticed, but there's a guard at the door and a fort full of soldiers who'll be only too pleased to put a rifle ball into me if I try.'

'Not *you*,' Billy said. '*We*.'

He grinned and winked, he was in the mood for mischief.

'You'd help me?'

'Sure, I'm fed up with being locked up and they don't usually let me out for another couple of weeks to teach me a lesson for being such a big, bad Indian. You *certainly* need to be out of here before then, so it's time for us to go.'

Jubal sighed with his shoulders slumped.

'You keep forgetting the obstacles,' he said, pointing to the guard who was armed and present, even if not very alert.

'We need to talk to my ma — she'll be here with our breakfast directly.'

Indeed Shadow Woman arrived within moments bearing two plates of bacon, pinto beans and corn biscuits and a steaming pot of coffee. It was handy having the provost cells right next to Thaddeus's store. The guard paid her no attention when she entered and put the meals through the bars. She drew up a stool as she often did to keep Billy company and they began talking in whispers. The guard, still indifferent to her presence wandered outside to stretch his legs and visit the latrine. The cell keys remained on a hook along with duplicate keys for the rifle rack, ammunition locker and commissary store.

'Quickly the soap from your wash basin,' Shadow Woman hissed. 'Keep watch, boys.'

Ever the opportunist, she quickly made impressions of all the keys, but she didn't know which was which.

'He's coming back,' Jubal warned.

She replaced the keys and scrambled back to the cell bars just as the sentry entered the room.

With breakfast done, Shadow Woman gathered the plates and spoons and left saying she'd be back at sundown with their supper. She had a busy day ahead. First stop after washing the plates was the blacksmith. He said making keys wasn't his speciality and referred her to the gunsmith who had a workshop adjoining the forge. There was a certain risk attached to this as the gunsmith might recognise the keys for what they were. But as it turned out he wasn't particularly interested in their origin although Shadow Woman said they were for Thaddeus's storeroom, grog cabinet and safe.

If he had doubts he showed no signs. He was a bespectacled, rather studious and preoccupied man who loved the intricate mechanism of firearms, but was appalled at the thought of their destructive power. Surrounded as he was by Colt, Remington, English Tranter and French Le Mat handguns, Springfield, Spencer, Sharps and Ben Henry rifles from the Oliver Winchester New Haven Arms Company, he harboured no warlike intent.

At the time he was intrigued by Major Schofield's plan to canvas Smith and Wesson with a design for a breech opening revolver that would make reloading much quicker. The armourer was studying some rough sketches Schofield had shown him in case he had any suggestions. He was deeply disappointed that the major was gone, because he would have enjoyed discussing the idea with him.

The problem was that Shadow Woman in her haste, had made impressions of only one side of the keys and they weren't very good impressions at that.

'Oh my, but these will never do,' the armourer declared primly, 'I'll need the actual keys to make *proper* moulds. I'm sorry, ma'am, but I couldn't guarantee keys made from these and I always guarantee my work. Lives depend on it you know.'

So there was the rub, it would be suspicious to say she couldn't get the keys. The sutler's store was only a few yards across the parade ground and Shadow Woman, unable to think up any excuse on the spur of the moment, left saying she would have to come back later. The armourer said it didn't matter, it wasn't a long job and he could do it anytime. He went back to studying Major Schofield's diagrams.

Shadow Woman returned to work at the sutler's store. She was patient. Life with the Comanches had taught her that. It was around noon when two troopers came in for tobacco and their news wasn't what she wanted to hear. They were strangers belonging to a column from Marcy that had crossed Major Schofield's path and heard about the Pierce incident. Their commander, Major Horace Devlin decided he would ride to Pierce and escort Jubal Quinn back to Marcy for trial. They were leaving first thing in the morning.

It was time for a change of plan.

If Quinn didn't escape that night, he wouldn't escape at all. Over the years a lot of folk pondered on why Shadow Woman acted as she did. Her son was safe enough and would be free reasonably soon, and although distressing, periods in the guardhouse were not new to him. Of course she fretted that his bar room scuffles could escalate into something worse. The soldiers may tolerate a misbehaved boy, but as he grew into manhood they might not be so lenient and he could be seriously hurt one day. It was a good time for him to be rid of Fort Pierce. In any event Shadow Woman was ready for an adventure, and maybe payback for the troops who had used her so indifferently over the years. Living with Thaddeus was no particular hardship. He'd never beaten her or any other woman for that matter, but gave little thought for her feelings. She usually went along with Billy's vagaries anyway. The Indians around the fort didn't bother to speculate, ultimately events went as the Great Spirit intended and his motives were simply impossible to understand. Some folk thought she just felt sorry for Sergeant Quinn.

In the end her plan was simple and she used other skills learnt from the Comanches. It involved petty theft from Thaddeus's till and storeroom, some serious horse-trading in the village outside the fort and a small arms deal with a shady drummer from Mexico who regularly stopped by on his travels.

As with good music, timing was vital.

Shadow Woman visited the guardhouse as usual at supper and told Billy and Quinn to be ready and alert just after midnight. The graveyard shift sentry would have settled in and the post would be pretty well asleep. She returned right on time.

The sentry was at his desk, chair tipped back and feet up, reading a three-week-old newspaper. He was unaware of Shadow Woman's presence when she crept up behind him and drew a knife from the sash around her waist. Grabbing his beard, she wrenched his head backwards and slashed the blade from ear to ear. His windpipe severed, the guard died in a gurgling spray of jugular crimson that soaked his whiskers and gushed onto his chest as he slumped forward onto the desk. Blood pooled in pulsating spurts for a few seconds and then just oozed across the table surface dripping to the floor.

The Comanches were really good at that sort of thing and did it all the time. Shadow Woman had learnt well from them. She'd skinned enough buffalo in her time and this wasn't much different as long as the knife was sharp.

She grabbed the keys from the hook and with a little bit of fumbling found the right one for the cell door. Billy and Quinn were out instantly.

'You killed him!' Quinn hissed.

'They're going to kill you,' Shadow Woman reminded him. 'What's one white man less anyway? It's not like there's a shortage of them.' She raised her skirt and produced a Remington .44 and a .36 Navy Colt revolver strapped to her thighs by two colourful garters that the Mexican girls so admired.

The boys pushed the pistols into their waistbands and filched a few boxes of ammunition from the guardhouse supply. They also took two Henry repeating rifles from a wall rack, an obvious choice because of their firepower and .44 calibre bullets.

There was nothing to be done about the mess and the guard's body, so they headed for the door. Appalled as he was by the murder, Quinn realised that it had come to *me-or-them*. He was being swept along by irreparable events. If this sort of thing was going to continue, and he had a nagging feeling it might, ambivalence was going to have to become a normal state of mind.

Shadow Woman dimmed the oil lamp and they crept through the door. She and Billy wore moccasins and padded silently along the veranda and Quinn soon realised if he tiptoed, his boots made very little noise. There was no one about but a few prowling sentries. The fugitives would have to be careful about them. They climbed a wooden stepladder to the guardhouse roof that also acted as a firing platform should the fort be attacked. Most of the post buildings were situated that way and encircled the central parade ground so the walls could be manned in all directions. Shadow Woman knew just where to go, she led them straight to a spot along the roof where she'd planned their escape point.

Then she stopped dead in her tracks, Billy and Quinn nearly stumbling over her in their haste. A sentry stood just yards ahead. He had unslung his Spencer rifle and was peering over the parapet. Something had grabbed his attention.

Quinn was fine in an open battle, but this kind of work needed a little getting used to, although Billy took to it naturally. Without hesitation he clubbed the guard on the back of the head with his rifle butt. The poor fellow collapsed, groaning on the adobe roof while Shadow Woman gave him a hefty kick in the groin that hurt so much he couldn't make another sound. For good measure she gave him another thwack with a huge Dragoon Colt she'd stolen from the guardhouse and that should shut anyone up for ages. Shadow Woman tossed the Spencer over the parapet. Rifling through the guard's ammunition pouch, she retrieved as many cartridges as she could stuff into her skirt pocket. You never knew when extra persuasion might come in handy.

They clambered down the wall suffering no more than a few cuts and bruises. Three saddled horses were tethered where they dropped to the ground. Shadow Woman handed a golden Spanish doubloon and several silver escudos to a Mexican boy she had arranged the deal with, telling him to hightail it home and keep his mouth shut. This was smart negotiating. Shadow Woman didn't want to squander her stash of Yankee dollars and Mexico's cash base was in such a shambles that any precious metal was legal tender along the border. Well, maybe not legal, but that wasn't an overused term in Mexico at the time.

Shadow Woman had provided water, about a week's supply of food, a couple of handy knives and some extra powder, percussion caps and .36 calibre lead bullets for the Navy Colt. They quickly mounted and the boys lit out at full speed in the opposite direction to where the Tenth Cavalry troopers were camped along the trail. Shortly they realised that Shadow Woman wasn't with them and they reined up and trotted back a couple of hundred yards. She had retrieved the Spencer rifle and was riding along at a walking pace behind them.

'Whatever are you doing, Ma?' Billy challenged. 'Come on, there ain't any time to lose. Who knows when they'll discover that dead guard, or the fellow we clobbered?'

'I'm not going with you, Billy,' she said.

'But, Ma, they'll know you helped us and they'll hang you. We *all* have to get away from here.'

'Listen, Billy. You and Jubal get clear to the north then circle around and head for the border. They won't chase you into Mexico. I know the Yankee soldiers are real touchy about that right now, what with the revolution and all going on down there.'

'What about you, Ma?' Billy wailed.

'I have a plan. Now get going while you still can. Don't worry, look after yourselves, I'll be fine. I love you Billy, always remember that. Good luck to you too, Jubal. Now skedaddle!'

Billy leant across his saddle and kissed his mother before he and Jubal Quinn galloped away leaving Shadow Woman in a swirl of trail dust.

She nudged her horse forward at a leisurely canter. She soon saw where the boys had left the trail on their way to Mexico. Knowing the pursuit would be focused on them, she had it in mind to return to the Hopi clans of the northwest. They were more peaceful than most people and that shaman wasn't much older than she was, perhaps he'd like her to be his woman for a while. If not, there were plenty of other eligible men-folk in the pueblos and they were an eye-pleasing lot. She still had her looks and with all that practice, certainly knew how to make men happy.

Towards dawn she turned off the trail across rocky country to the Arizona Territory. Even the White Mountain Apaches, who were always tracking for the Army would have trouble following her especially after she made diversions up and down several creeks. Shadow Woman simply vanished without trace and the white soldiers never bothered her again.

Chapter 13

The bludgeoned sentry was discovered just after reveille, and Fort Pierce was in uproar. The poor fellow was only semi-conscious and in a ton of pain. He bore a melon-sized lump on the back of his head while his testicles were just as swollen and turning purple. No one was able to get any sense out of him as he was carted off to the sick bay. His coherence didn't improve after the medical corporal managed to get a decent dose of laudanum down his throat, but it seemed to make him more comfortable.

'I'm sorry, sir, but I can't allow you to talk to him yet,' the medico told Captain Bellamy, 'He's in a poor way and I've had one man die on me already, I don't intend to have another.'

'Well, you are surely admonished, Eugene,' Major Devlin observed. He took a dim view of enlisted men giving orders to officers, although Bellamy didn't see it as insubordination, just a soldier taking his job seriously.

'Be sure and let me know the minute he's able to give us some information,' he said.

'Yes, sir, I'll do that,' the medico replied and resumed attending to his patient.

Sam McAlister turned up about then, the activity in the fort had gained his attention from the Tenth's bivouac area. As soon as he heard about the sentry he made the connection.

'Holy shit,' he said under his breath and dashed towards the guardhouse. He barged through the door to the appalling sight of an empty cell and a dead guard, stiffening with rigor mortis, slouched over his desk. Blood that stained the floor had turned from deep burgundy to dark brown as it seeped into the boards.

Captain Bellamy was furious. His normal composed, efficient manner vanished when he inspected the guardhouse.

'It's that goddamned nigra again!' he roared. 'He's killed two of my soldiers in a day-and-half. I'll hang the rascal myself if I can lay my hands on him.'

'Hang on, Eugene,' Sam said. 'That Indian boy was in the cell as well, and there's no sign of him either. We don't know who was responsible for this murder.'

'Damnit, Billy Songbird's been in the stockade more times than I can remember, and never given any trouble. He practically lives here sometimes. Seems to me your boy arrives on my post and I have two bodies to account for in no time. It don't take a Pinkerton detective to find a common link here.'

Of course there was going to be trouble. Tensions between the Galvanised Yankees and the Buffalo Soldiers were already simmering and this incident would probably blow the lid off. Bellamy was no fool and well aware of how delicate the situation could become. For once he was glad of Major Devlin's presence although he thought the major to be a bit pompous and prone to filibustering. And Major Devlin didn't really want any part of what he considered a contentious issue that could only get worse. He was more politician than soldier with his sights set on the governorship of Texas, and getting mixed up with black folk at all was not the way to go. Texans hadn't taken kindly to the emancipation of their slaves.

'Listen, Lieutenant,' Bellamy said through clenched teeth. 'I want your dammed, black contraband as far away from my post as soon as possible. And that's an order, *Lieutenant*!'

The disappearance of their cordial *'Sam-Eugene'* relationship was not lost on McAlister, but two could play at that game.

'Believe me, *Captain,* there's nothing I'd like better. I'm going after those two and find out the truth.'

'Beware, mister,' Major Devlin warned, 'they'll be in Mexico by now. The Government's policy is quite clear at the moment. The French are backing Maximillian's government and it's only just hanging on against Juarez's rebellion down there. Washington does not have the will or the resources to get involved in any sort of conflict, especially with a European power. Don't go starting an incident that might upset the French or diplomatically embarrass us. Our Civil War was bad enough, no one wants another.'

What the hell do you think we have out here on the frontier? Sam thought, but kept it to himself.

'Do not go into Mexico, is that understood, Lieutenant?' Devlin knew the value of getting confirmation in front of witnesses in case someone got hot-headed later on.

'Yessir,' Sam replied. 'Now if you'll excuse me. *I* have a job to do.'

He saluted and, spinning on heel, dashed from the guardhouse.

'Sergeant Cook!' he bellowed. 'Sound *Boots and Saddles.* I want the whole camp packed up and ready to ride pronto.'

The company bugler had gone with Major Schofield, so there was no one to sound the call, but Henry Cook knew what the lieutenant meant.

B Troop didn't need telling twice. They had no wish to stay at Fort Pierce and they looked sharp with boots polished, uniforms laundered and forage caps all tilted at the same angle. Their hardware sparkled and they were a fine sight as they formed up by twos. The regimental pennant was unfurled as they rode at a trot past the fort gate along the trail Jubal and Billy had taken. Whatever else Eugene Bellamy thought, he knew damn fine soldiering when he saw it. His infantry companies looked downright shoddy by comparison.

Well, that will change, he thought as he returned Sam McAlister's stiff salute when he rode by. Nothing like a bit of inter-unit rivalry to smarten things up, he'd be kicking a few Georgian butts over the next few weeks. Some spit and polish and extra drilling should take their minds off recent events.

B Troop had only one remaining White Mountain Apache scout, Petorio Blanco. The others had left with Major Schofield, but one should be enough. The White Mountain Apaches didn't really care for the other Apache clans and had been scrapping with them ever since anyone could remember. They were quite happy to work for the Army although they were as much mediators as trackers. In fact Petorio had defused many encounters with Apaches that could have resulted in bloodshed. And the pay made things a lot easier for their families back at the Fort Apache reservation.

Petorio didn't take long to pick up the trail and easily found where Jubal and Billy had cut from the main northern pathway. He mentioned the other set of fresh horse tracks he'd detected, but Sam decided not to split his force. It was unlikely they would be able to track anyone without Petorio's help, so he chose to follow Jubal and Billy's trail and the chase was on.

The two reluctant fugitives had ridden all night and stopped briefly by a small creek for some food and to water their horses. It was little more than a trickle, but Billy said they'd better drink whenever they could, because further opportunities might become scarce. Another problem they faced was the night-time cold. Day temperatures were quite pleasant early in the year, but nights were wretched and Jubal had been shivering for hours.

'I'm gonna need a jacket or I might as well go back to Fort Pierce and let 'em hang me, because I'll die just the same with one more night in the open,' he said.

'We're close to the border now,' Billy encouraged. 'We'll be able to shelter at night and do some trading when we know no one's following us. In the meantime we'd better get rid of those yellow stripes on your sleeves. They sure stand out where they're not wanted.'

So it had come right down to it for Jubal. He'd worked damned hard to make sergeant and was proud of his military service. He'd fought many campaigns during the Civil War and had survived the Fort Pillow massacre when so many others had perished. But that was all over now, there was no going back.

'Might as well, I surely won't be wearing them again.'

'That's a pretty accurate assessment, I'll allow,' Billy agreed, 'but you've got to stay optimistic. You've got to move on.'

They'd been riding through country scattered with Arizona Pines and arroyos, some of which were dry and some, like the one they now followed, held water. They tethered their horses and Billy removed the chevrons from Jubal's uniform shirt, which was covered in dust and didn't stand out as Army blue so much anymore.

An arrow makes a quiet swooshing sound from the moment it is released, and Apache arrows were distinctive because of the ragged, barbed tips especially made to cause a nasty, flesh-ripping wound that was exacerbated if the dart was extracted. Billy heard it and dived head first at Jubal sending both of them tumbling behind some riverbed rocks. Not much cover, but all there was. Several more arrows came whistling by, clattering all around them, some impaling broken tree stumps with sharp thuds.

'You hit?' Billy asked, pulling the .36 Navy revolver from his belt.

'Nope, the arrow just dug into my boot heel. No damage done thanks to you. Much obliged.'

They both sneaked a glance to the ridgeline. There were several Apaches moving along the top trying to spread out and start an enfilading crossfire. Billy carefully aimed and fired, spraying up dust at the leading Apache's feet and stopping him in his tracks. The other Indians ducked for cover and that was where Billy proved either really cool or very reckless in a fight, depending on how you looked at it.

He was on his feet in a second, yelling for Jubal to follow. He scrambled up the arroyo bank with Jubal close on his heels while the Apaches' heads were still down. He leapt over the ridgeline and fired at the leading Indian, hitting him in the leg. Jubal loosed several rapid shots from his .44 revolver, without hitting anyone, but causing enough mayhem to send the Apaches scattering for cover.

The downed Indian had lost his short bow and was grabbing for an ancient Patterson Colt belt revolver tucked into his waist band. Billy was on top of him and pointing his cocked pistol right between the Apache's eyes, shook his head slowly, the meaning of which was unmistakable. A couple of arrows flashed by and Jubal hauled the wounded Indian to his feet, using him as a shield. The arrows stopped.

The Apache showed no sign of pain even though his wound was bleeding and it must have hurt like blazes when he put any weight on the leg. He was a tall man, pretty much Jubal's height, and that was unusual for Apaches, who tended to be short and stocky when they got enough to eat.

Billy started yelling at the Apaches in a mixture of Chiricahua dialect and Spanish. Although he couldn't understand a word, Jubal realised that Billy was telling everyone to calm down or their captive would be sorry. Indeed the wounded Apache added to the cacophony, understandably pretty nervous with a gun barrel inches from his head. As quickly as the fight had erupted, it subsided. The Apaches approached with arrows nervously nocked to their bowstrings. A couple of old percussion pistols and what looked like a Hawken flintlock rifle were also evident. Ammunition must have been scarce because they hadn't used those weapons yet.

Billy headed back to the creek bed, motioning Jubal to follow with the gunshot Apache. They sat him down and bathed the wound, discovering that the bullet had passed clean through his leg. Billy gathered what looked like lichen that grew on the lower tree branches close to the water. He slapped it onto the wound which he bandaged with his neckerchief. He explained the fungi helped wounds to heal and stopped them festering, it was a handy and powerful medicine.

'You know, I think we might be in a position to trade now,' Billy announced cheerfully. 'They've cooled down some, so *don't* shoot anyone.'

Jubal had to admit Billy was confident enough. He knew his way around this country and had probably dealt with wandering Apaches before. The conversation sounded a bit abrupt and not particularly friendly, but no one appeared to be trigger-happy any more. After a bit the wounded Apache took off the jacket he was wearing. It sported a hole in the chest surrounded by what looked suspiciously like dried blood and power burns. He tossed it to Billy who handed it to Jubal.

'Try it for size,' Billy suggested.

'Where'd he get it?' Jubal asked screwing up his nose. It was a bit rank, but beggars couldn't be choosers and it fitted well enough.

'Don't ask,' Billy replied. 'Sure it's feral, but we can clean it up later and it'll do the job.'

Billy fished out five .44 lead balls and percussion caps and handed them over. He also poured about half a flask of black powder into and old leather horn the Indians carried. Jubal was horrified at not only depleting their own ammunition store, but also giving them to people who they'd been fighting only moments earlier. Billy was learning to read his expressions pretty well by now.

'Look, I bartered him down from ten rounds, be thankful for that.'

Billy was suspicious that the Apache leader was going to get another jacket the same way he got the first, but kept the notion to himself. This was no time for Jubal to start taking the moral high ground. The concept of stealing didn't really bother Apaches, especially when it came to horses as they felt it beneath their dignity to do the hard work of breaking and training them, so simply taking them from someone who had, seemed eminently logical to them. Items of apparel were evidently considered in the same way.

'But, they wanted to kill us, and them bullets probably won't fit that old relic handgun of his,' Jubal protested.

'That's a good thing ain't it? And anyway the chief here says he's sorry about attacking us, which is a pretty good sign. Apaches *never* apologise.'

'Yeah, sorry he got shot in the leg more like,' Jubal was still cynical.

There was a lot more talk and hand gestures with some of the other warriors joining in. Billy discovered the Apaches would take their wounded comrade down to Janos in Mexico where they knew a surgeon who had fixed up Mangas Colorado a few years ago when soldiers had shot him. Billy agreed that was a good idea.

'This fellow is close kin to Cochise, his name is Snake,' Billy informed Jubal, 'that's why he's so tall. It runs in the family. They surely despise white men for finally murdering old Mangas and trying to parcel the rest of 'em off to Bosque Redondo. Cochise and the Chiricahua have been avoiding whites ever since, but have a red-hot go at any they do meet.'

'Do *I* look white? They didn't have to shoot first and ask questions afterwards,' Jubal said.

'It's pretty much their style. They find it works better that way. Snake said you confused them a bit as they don't get to see many black men and thought you were all slaves anyway. But, the uniform sort of stirred them up.'

'Why on earth would anyone want to call himself "Snake"?'

'Stands to reason, folks are frightened of rattlers, water moccasins and such, so he figures they'll be scared of him too. Warriors are supposed to frighten people. It's their job as they see it. And here's some interesting news,' Billy added. 'It seems your colleagues are on our trail. A patrol left the fort a short while ago.'

'How the hell do they know that? Pierce's miles away.'

'Smoke signals. They ain't that reliable and can only relay very basic messages, but *"cavalry on the way"* is one of them. Why d'you think these guys are so hard to find when they get advanced warning all the time?'

About then the Apaches decided to leave. They helped Snake limp to his horse, hoisted him unceremoniously onto its back and cantered away.

'I guess it's time we were off too. We don't want anyone catching up before we hit the border.' Jubal said. 'How in blazes do we know when we're in Mexico anyway?'

'I come down here a lot. I know,' Billy replied confidently. 'It's easier to tell over in Texas, you just cross the Rio Grande and there you are, but after a while you get to know the local landmarks around here.'

'I hope the Tenth know the landmarks as well,' Jubal mumbled as they rode off at a fast trot.

Finally Billy announced that they had indeed crossed into Mexico and, although it didn't look any different, Jubal felt he was able to relax just a little. They rode out of a narrow coulee into an open valley scattered with Arizona Pines, Rio Grande Cottonwoods and, even some Dogwoods with colourful bracts just coming to bloom that the Spaniards may have planted long ago. There were plenty of neglected pastures and cornfields gone to seed. Some abandoned, tumble-down adobe shacks and a ruined stone church stood close by where it looked as if a village had once thrived. Revolutionary turmoil must have driven the farmers away, which was a common enough occurrence anywhere in Mexico.

'Might rest up for a spell,' Billy suggested, but Jubal didn't reply, something ahead absorbed him totally.

A line of horsemen, perhaps a dozen strong materialised like spectres, slowly spreading out between the trees and buildings. They were a motley group, consisting of young men and a few teenage boys. They were about as ragged and unkept as could be imagined. Some wore tattered butternut Confederate uniforms, but for the most part they were dressed in frayed over-alls or hand-me-down looking dungarees, homespun shirts and trail dusters. But they were all armed, some with as many as six or seven pistols either tucked into their belts and pockets or held in high waisted holsters. Some sported scraggy chin hair, but others were simply too young to shave. There were also a couple of wild looking Comanche boys riding with the bunch.

An older man, who was maybe forty, appeared to be their leader. His face bore two savage scars down each cheek that even his side-whiskers and moustache couldn't conceal. He wore a ragged, black frockcoat and battered stovepipe hat with several feathers sticking from the hatband. At least a dozen appallingly smelly scalps dangled from his saddle horn, but he didn't seem to mind. He was also aiming a brace of Adams pistols at Billy and Jubal.

'You know those desperados Major Schofield was chasing down from Kansas?' Jubal said to Billy, who nodded slowly. 'Well, we just found them.'

'That's not good, is it?' Billy said.

'Nope, it's about as bad as it gets,' Jubal replied.

Chapter 4

'My, my, my, won't you just look what's turned up?' the stovepipe-hatted villain growled in a voice that rasped like a wheelless cart being dragged across gravel. 'Dammed if it ain't a stray nigger buck and a scrawny breed whelp. Maybe I'll just bulk 'em up a little with a meal of lead.'

'Yeah, meal of lead,' the rider beside him babbled, drooling and gurgling as he spoke. 'Yeah, that's a goodun, Claude that surely is a goodun.'

The rest of the band sniggered malevolently giving Billy and Jubal a reasonably accurate assessment of their mental capacity right off. The group had evolved from severely limited breeding stock and possessed genetic deficiencies by the score.

'Idiot!' the stovepipe-hat snapped, cuffing the jabbering fool roundly across the back of his head. Everyone else shut up.

They were the dregs of the Kansas hell raisers who rampaged through three states before, during and after the Civil War. No more than vicious, teenage gangs they had murdered, tortured, robbed and raped their way all over Kansas, Missouri and Kentucky in the name of the Confederacy. Some were with 'Little Archie' Clement and William Quantrill and others rode alongside 'Bloody Bill' Anderson's guerrillas. A few had derived a modicum of respectability by serving with Nathan Bedford Forrest, John Mosby and even General Jeb Stuart, but they were all no better than cutthroats and desperate villains to a man. Most had a passing acquaintance with the James and Younger gangs and all spoke of the

Lawrence massacre in 1863 with pride and affection. After the war their leader, 'Gentleman' Claude Valentine had gathered them from every wild bunch in the South, to continue their terrorism much as before.

Major Schofield and his troopers had culled their ranks considerably in a number of spiteful, running battles during their pursuit, and it irked them to have been so misused by black men. That didn't improve Jubal's position one bit.

'Before I plug you,' Claude Valentine said, ever a man to get straight to the point, 'I'd like to know what a dumb-arsed nigger in Yankee Cavalry breeches would be doing south of the border.'

Obviously a half-breed Indian kid was of no consequence, but this particular half-breed kid was quick on his feet.

'Well, that's a fine howdy-do,' Billy said with indignation. 'Why, here we come riding all this way to join the most notorious band of desperados in the South West, and it looks like we'll get shot to pieces for our trouble.'

Claude Valentine was taken aback. He'd expected the usual begging and whining folks tended to go on with when he threatened to shoot them. He uncocked his pistols returning them to their holsters. He pulled out a clay pipe and tobacco makings and prepared a smoke. He found a Lucifer and slashed it across the idiot's rough-stubble cheek. It flared, leaving a livid scold as he yelped in pain.

'How is that so?' he quizzed, leaning forward menacingly on his saddle horn.

'Why sir,' Billy said, 'most folk know of your marauding ways. When we heard all about you at Fort Pierce, my partner here was so fired up to join you and leave the army that he killed two men who stood in his way. Plugged 'em right between the eyes from a hundred yards with one shot. Damned if he ain't the plum best nigger shot you'll ever see. Handgun or rifle, it's all the same to him.'

Jubal was getting a little agitated as this yarn stretched out, but Billy was in full flight. If you're going to lie, it's best to stick to the truth whenever you can...Sort of.

'Yessir, we also heard you met some hard times and an extra couple of gun-hands might sure be advantageous to you. We're desperate men and we know the army is still out looking for you.'

'How'd you know that?" Valentine said.

'We've got powerful Apache friends, and they passed the news. Why me and Snake, who's kin to Cochise himself, are blood brothers. That's a most sacred bond and he wouldn't be happy if something happened to me. We only just left him and his clan who're probably still close by.'

'These boys,' Valentine indicated the Comanche, 'were out scouting earlier. They heard shots before they picked up your trail. That don't sound so downright friendly to me.'

'They were just letting off steam and celebrating because they were so pleased to see me.'

'Ammunition's precious.'

'We gave 'em a bit. Got enough left over to be useful if you get into a fight with soldiers.'

Jubal had to admire Billy's interpretation of the truth and how he'd nicely massaged the evidence to fit his story.

'What if we just took it?' Valentine drawled.

'Can't see the point,' it was Jubal who spoke, coolly low and slow. 'Sure you'd kill us in the end, maybe. But I'd get two or three of you first and probably wing a couple more. Billy here's no slouch with a handgun himself. He'd get one or two at least. Ain't no point in having a mess of guns and no one to shoot 'em. Seems to me two extra men'd be a lot handier than half-a-dozen less.'

'My, ain't you the wise-arsed nigger then?' Claude sneered. He was curious about these two, but he riled easily.

'Looking at your boys, that mightn't be a bad thing either. Any of 'em read and write?'

'Don't need no book learnin' to shoot a gun,' Claude's moron interjected and got another cuff across the face for his trouble. It seemed that when the boss was in conversation, you didn't interrupt, or maybe Claude just enjoyed hitting him.

Claude did recognise the deficiencies in his gang and conceded that Jubal's argument bore merit. They were not in the best shape and would have to replenish both their food and cash reserves shortly, which of course, they had no intention of doing by legal means. Claude saw that a couple of level heads would be helpful, especially for what he had in mind. He was planning to rob a bank.

'Okay, boys,' Claude declared, 'come on into camp and I'll introduce you around. Niggers and Injuns count differently down here anyway,' he added to justify his ambivalence.

Lieutenant Sam McAlister was faced with similar mixed feelings. Petorio Blanco had long since informed him they were in Mexico, but he pressed on. The troopers followed stoically. They really weren't sure of the politics, and sensed everything wasn't quite right with their young commander. They liked him and thought he was sound for a shave-tail and, orders were orders, even if doubt existed as to their legitimacy.

'How far away are they?' Sam asked as Petorio examined the site where Jubal and Billy had fought Snake's Apaches.

'Less than half a day it looks to me,' Petorio stated. 'There was some sort of fracas here. Lots of Chiricahua tracks and then our two high-tailed it yonder. The Apaches took off the other way.'

'Seems like we'll have to keep our eyes peeled in both directions,' Sam said, admiring how Petorio knew one Apache clan from another just by their tracks. But finding an arrow that was too badly damaged to be worth retrieving had identified its owner. Petorio thought it odd that a band of Apaches weren't able to finish off a couple of wayfarers, but he'd heard Billy was a quick thinker and fast talker when it came to getting out of scrapes. That was just as well because he was always getting into them.

'What're you planning to do, Sam?' Petorio asked, tossing the ruined arrow aside.

The men had forced marched since before dawn, thirty minutes in the saddle, twenty minutes on foot leading their mounts and ten minutes rest. Food and water on the move. They could go all day and cover a lot of territory at that pace, but by evening they were ready to bivouac. Sam had already decided to push on. Who was to say where the border truly ran anyway? Whatever Major Devlin thought, he knew the American Government was keen to see French influence out of Mexico and leave Juarez's insurgents to it, so where was the harm in sniffing around just south of the border.

'We make camp here,' he announced. '*Boots and Saddles* at three tomorrow morning.'

Claude's renegades had made camp utilising the wrecked village buildings, and were settled in. There were several tired looking Mexican and Indian women who kept themselves busy and as far out-of-the-way as possible. Everyone was pretty wary at first, but they began to relax in short order, even to the point of some guarded introductions. Claude seemed happy to let matters take their natural course and see how the newcomers settled in.

The gang members had dubbed themselves with colourful sobriquets that included Buckaroo Bob Scorsby, The Gleeson Kid, Bad Roy Patch, Whiskey Van Harper, and The Kentucky Slasher who the boys just called 'Kaintuck' as the area was known in Daniel Boone's time. Bayou Cottonmouth Jacques was from New Orleans. Growling Bear and Panther were the two Comanche boys who had been exiled from their warlike bands for being so disagreeable, but Claude seemed to be able to keep them under control.

Claude's slobbering henchman was Black Swamp Slim, a product of his daddy's lust for his older sister when she turned thirteen. Slim's incestuous birth left him hair-lipped, with one leg several inches shorter than the other and a rambunctious disposition. He was also impotent, taking it out violently on any woman who crossed his path. When it came to raping, the other gang-members insisted he wait till last as he was likely to murder any poor girl they captured in his frustration, and where was the fun in that. Claude had stunned him many times with the butt of his pistols to stop such excesses, probably scrambling his already turbid brain further, but you can't sell or ransom dead females.

There were a few other surly brutes who considered an introduction to a black unacceptable, and kept to their sullen selves. Jubal didn't help matters by his own truculence. He of course knew the identities of most of the desperadoes from wanted posters and their running battles of the past. Fortunately the gang members didn't link him with Major Schofield's column, as all black men looked much the same to them. His deserter's status may not have been enough to protect him, had they made the connection with the military unit that had been harassing them.

Billy insisted their best chance of survival was to ingratiate themselves within the gang and see what opportunities cropped up. And his chance to do just that occurred around the evening campfire.

The girls produced a reasonable supper despite the conditions and the bandits mellowed considerably with full stomachs. They filled their pipes and settled around the fire. To Billy's surprise they produced some musical instruments and began to play in a fairly tight manner. Cottonmouth Jacques got going on a Cajun squeezebox accordion. Whiskey Van Harper was a more than halfway decent banjo picker whilst the Gleeson Kid and Buckaroo Bob managed the Jaw Harp and one of those new Austrian harmonicas that had become popular during the Civil War. Roy

Patch and Kaintuck formed the rhythm section by playing a set of bones each. Most surprisingly of all, Black Swamp Slim started sawing on a fiddle, and was making a pretty slick job of it too, although he slobbered a bit when he played. Even one of the girl's called Margarita could play a few chords on a battered guitar and sang pretty sweetly.

The trouble was that none of the boys could sing worth a lick, and Billy saw his chance. He'd learnt all the songs at Fort Pierce and joined right in. Immediately his fine tenor voice rang out above the rest and even attracted Claude's attention, temporarily distracting him from lifting one of the Mexican girl's skirts as he pinned her against an adobe wall. He conceded that the boys' music kept the gang together as much as anything else.

They played the Civil War favourites: *The Bonny Blue Flag, When Johnny Comes Marching Home, Kingdom Coming, Lorena,* many music hall hits and of course, *Dixie.* Billy sang them all and amused the crowd greatly by singing the choruses in three different languages and the gang knew dozens of ribald verses. The evening progressed cordially to the point that Jubal added harmony with a tolerable bass-baritone. Luckily the outlaws had long run out of whiskey and mescal. Liquored up, these gatherings usually ended up in a free-for-all, sometimes resulting in serious knife wounds.

'You sing real nice,' Billy commented to Jubal.

'"Jubal, father of all such as make harps and organs,"' Jubal recited. 'Comes from Genesis. My mama was powerful fond of singing. I guess she liked the idea of naming me after Jubal, although I don't play nothin'.'

'I'll teach you one day, if you like,' Billy offered.

'Yeah, I think that'd be nice. Thanks, Billy.'

Eventually they got tired and one-by-one they curled up in their bedrolls or gathered up one of the girls depending on their inclination. Billy much admired Van Harper's banjo picking and borrowed the instrument to play a little.

'You play mighty fine,' Billy said, continuing his expansive mood. Flattery always went a long way towards relaxing folk in his opinion, and didn't cost anything.

'Sure can,' Whiskey Van Harper agreed with pride. 'Learnt direct from Sam Sweeney when we was ridin' for General Stuart in Virginia. Why, Sam could make the banjer sing just by looking at it. Some folk claim he's the best banjer player ever and I've a mind they'd be right. I sure picked up some fine licks from him. Damned shame when the pox killed him.'

They chatted on for a while. It turned out that Buckaroo Bob owned several harmonicas. He called them harps because harmonica was just too dammed hard to say all the time.

'Got one harp off a dead Yankee at Fort Pillow back in '64,' he explained. 'Got this'n off a store in Lawrence, Kansas, why I had to shoot the owner and two clerks just to get it. That was truly an inconvenience.'

He went on to show Billy the letters marked on the tops of each harmonica.

'Seems this'n with G is easy to play along with the banjer. This'n with the C is okay with most everything and this here with the A is just fine with the guitar.'

Billy tried to explain the rudiments of musical keys and scales that Virginia Pritchard had taught him, but he didn't believe he was very successful.

'You were at Fort Pillow?' Jubal said quietly.

'Sure enough was,' Bob replied. 'Killed me a parcel of niggers that day. Didn't waste no powder and ball on 'em, just stuck 'em with bayonets. Seemed the right thing to do. Gen'ral Forrest asked 'em to surrender, but they didn't, so we stormed right up and killed 'em all. Wouldn't have made no difference if they'd surrendered I don't suppose. Reckon Gen'ral Forrest would've ordered us to kill 'em anyway. Buyin' and sellin' slaves before the war sure made him rich. Damned Yankees stopped that and he powerfully hated uppity niggers for taking up arms against the South. Mister Valentine was there too, he was my company captain.'

It was all Jubal could do to stay calm. Memories flooded back as a gunner in the 2nd US Coloured Light Artillery desperately trying to depress their cannons over Fort Pillow's earthworks to bring the barrels filled with canister to bear on the oncoming Rebels. But the elevation was too great and the shots simply fired over the enemy's heads as they clambered up the barbican wall.

The black troops were outnumbered four-to-one and didn't stand a chance. The screaming grey-coated horde swarmed over Fort Pillow's defences, driving the Negro gunners in retreat to the Mississippi bank. There was supposed to be a gunboat protecting them, but it was gone. His comrades were butchered on each side, even when they threw down their weapons and begged for mercy. Jubal dived into the river with bullets spraying all around him, but he got to the other side some four miles downstream.

He suffered a nasty bayonet wound, but was one of the few who escaped.

'You wasn't never a slave, was you Jubal?' Bob asked.

'Nope, don't reckon I ever was,' Jubal lied, noting the *now-you're-learning* look from Billy, and in spirit it was true. But, it was all he could do to manage his fury.

Buckaroo Bob nodded, indicating that Jubal was acceptable having never been enslaved. Right then Bob's life was probably in as much peril as it had ever been. Billy sensed Jubal's anguish, he didn't know about Fort Pillow, but he just knew Jubal was involved. He eyed Jubal and shook his head slowly, putting his finger to his lips. Jubal knew he was right and held his tongue, but promised himself he would remember Buckaroo Bob Scoresby's boastful claims.

Claude Valentine, psychotic killer that he was, watched the evening proceedings with interest. He was pleased at the way things turned out. Two more gunmen were more than useful, and if one was a goddamned nigger, well so what? He knew who to give all the dirty jobs to and wouldn't have to grieve excessively if the son-of-bitch got himself killed. So with as much contentment as he was capable of feeling, Claude grabbed one of the girls and turned in for the night.

The sun cracked through the hilltops, casting purple shadows over the adobes when Panther scuttled back into camp from his morning ablutions. He was stirred up with bad news. Sam McAlister's cavalry patrol was moving out of the coulee and heading straight for them. He shook Claude Valentine awake and got a clout for his trouble, but Panther pointed out the danger before being beaten again. Claude sprang to his feet, hitching up his breeches and strapping on his pistols. He raced through the camp kicking everyone into action. The receiving end of his boot was really painful.

There was no time to mount and run, but the gang had laid plenty of ambushes before, so a few sharp orders were all that was necessary. The boys knew what to do. They were experts at this sort of thing. They grabbed all the weapons and ammunition within reach and ducked behind walls and the derelict adobe structures. Guns were soon pointing from cracks in the masonry and through broken windows. A couple of the gang raced up the chapel bell-tower to get a better vantage point.

The column was still a fair way off, but they could easily be seen in the cold, clear morning. Steam was snorting from the horses' muzzles and the riders were hunched in their ponchos. The rising sun was directly behind the defenders and pretty much in the cavalry's faces. Their forage cap peaks were pulled down, hindering forward vision.

Jubal knew exactly what would happen. The patrol was riding slowly in a column-of-two straight into the village square, allowing the outlaws to mercilessly pour lead into them. There could only be one result – slaughter!

'It'll be murder,' he hissed in Billy's ear as they crouched behind an abandoned, overturned wagon.

'That's surely my assessment of it,' Billy shrugged. 'Seems to me Mister Valentine's boys have the advantage.'

'We can't let this happen.'

'Can't see how we can stop it and what do you care anyway? They're just here to haul your arse back to Pierce then up to Fort Marcy for hangin'.'

'What about a trial? I'd get a fair trial.'

'Yeah, right, black boy. What planet are you living on anyway?'

Deserter and fugitive he may be, but he couldn't stand back and see his former comrades helplessly gunned down. Billy might see this as just a way of resolving some of their problems, but Jubal had other ideas.

I gotta warn 'em, he thought. *I can't tell Billy, he'll only try to stop me.*

And right about then a whole series of misunderstandings unfolded.

Chapter 5

Jubal darted back to where the remuda was corralled. He leapt bareback astride the nearest horse and pulled its halter free. It danced for a second as he dragged its head around and dug his heels into its flanks. The horse jumped with Jubal hanging onto the bridle for all he was worth. Bareback riding takes some getting used to and Jubal had never enjoyed it during training when he first joined the cavalry. The horse's spine was rock hard on Jubal's most tender spots as he jolted along at a fast canter.

He sped past the hidden outlaws straight towards the approaching column. Claude immediately realised what Jubal was about and aimed his pistols at his back. He fired a few shots, but hitting a man jostling and swerving on the back of a galloping horse was chancy at best and the bullets whistled past on either side. A couple of the other outlaws loosed off a few rounds, but they went wide as well and Claude called a cease-fire. He cursed vilely as the aspect of surprise was now compromised.

Sam McAlister heard the shots just before he spotted Jubal heading their way, but at that stage didn't recognise him. He also misunderstood where the shots were from and their intended target. He thought the patrol was being attacked by the advancing horseman even though he was still well beyond accurate pistol range.

The cheeky bugger, Sam thought. *Well, if it's a fight he wants, he'll get one and be damned sorry about it.*

'Column will form in line on the centre!' he bellowed. 'Draw side arms!'

In a fluid movement the two lines of cavalrymen trotted their horses to the left and right and formed a line with Sam and Sergeant Henry Cook in the centre, their revolvers at the ready.

'Column will advance at the trot!' Sam called. 'Advance!'

And the twenty riders moved forward to battle.

Not that they expected much trouble, in their minds they were only going to round up a single miscreant, but things didn't turn out that way.

Jubal saw the cavalry's actions and knew he had to stop them as far from the village as he could. They would soon be within decent range of the gang. He nearly fell of his horse as he drew his pistol, managed to cock it and fire into the air. Meanwhile Claude grabbed a Spencer repeating rifle and fired after Jubal. One shot grazed his mount's flank. It reared tossing Jubal off its back. Luckily he held onto the reins and after being dragged for a few paces the horse pulled up, whining from the pain in its rump. Jubal was losing control, but he holstered his gun and hung onto the reins with both hands.

One of Claude's shots sailed past Jubal and struck Sergeant Cook, grazing his shoulder. He yelped and flinched, but stayed in the saddle. Sam was right beside his sergeant and saw him hit although, luckily not badly.

So the rascal wants to shoot, well we can shoot back, Sam thought.

'At the gallop, Charge!' he roared, wishing that Major Schofield hadn't taken his bugler back to Kansas. But, the column heard well enough and they leapt into full gallop. Sam levelled his Army Colt and fired at Jubal, but it wasn't much use while bouncing on top of a galloping horse. A few of the troopers followed suit, with the same lack of success.

This dramatically changed Jubal's point of view. The sight of a score of cavalrymen thundering towards him was pretty daunting. Just the noise of the hoof-beats and the rattling of hardware was frightening enough, but a couple of bullets spraying up dirt at his feet and whistling past his ears convinced him it was time to head in the other direction. Scrotum pain was incidental now as he leapt back onto his horse that became cantankerous after such abuse by rider and stray gunshots alike. It bucked and pranced from side to side, but finally loped back towards the village, Jubal managing to coax it into a canter. Of course this meant the galloping cavalry were gaining rapidly, and soon they were close enough for Sam to recognise he was chasing Jubal Quinn and he was madder than sin about it.

Don't go barging in when you don't know what to expect. Reconnoitre the enemy position and know his strengths and weaknesses. Make a battle plan. All that good tactical and strategic information Sam's academy instructors had instilled into him. Most of them were Mexican and Civil War veterans who knew what they were talking about from bitter experience. But, now his blood was up, did Sam take a blind bit of notice? None at all.

However the oncoming cavalry had an effect on Claude's bunch as well. They were excellent bullies, rapists and cold-blooded killers of defenceless innocents, but a head-on fight with professionals was not to their taste. Claude knew the day was won if they held their nerve and destroyed the charging column with a solid volley when they were almost on top of them. But this was more than he could expect and despite his yelling and cursing the outlaws started peppering away even before the troopers were within effective range.

Ineffective, maybe, but it did confuse the cavalry. Suddenly black powder smoke was puffing up from everywhere in front of them. A couple of horses were nicked and one trooper's forage cap was blown away. In any event the patrol, stampeding at full gallop, was committed to the charge. Nothing short of a cliff-face would stop them now.

Tantalisingly close to cover, Jubal's horse was shot from under him, but who could tell which side had discharged the bullets. It stumbled forward pitching Jubal headfirst into a cloud of dust and grit. He tumbled several times bruising and scratching just about every part of his body, hurting himself to an extent that he lost his senses for a second or two. He was lucky enough to gather his wits when he did because the charge was almost upon him, if they didn't shoot him to death, he'd be trampled under a battery of horseshoe iron. He was up and running like the devil was after him and managed to duck behind a cotton wood tree. A trooper fired as he galloped past, nicking Jubal's ear that bled in streams.

Normally the troopers would have reined to a halt and come back to arrest him, but they were at the threshold of the village and knew there was trouble ahead. Shooting their pistols until the chambers emptied, some galloped through the plaza, some around the wrecked buildings and the other riders went completely outside the village boundaries. In the confusion of smoke and gunfire, screaming and yelling it was impossible for straight shooting.

Although one of Claude's outlaws in his excitement exposed himself too far in the church tower and received a .44 slug in the neck. Blood gushed in a fountain as he pitched forward and landed with a splat onto the stone pavers at the church door.

Claude Valentine was firing with a fury, but soon his Adams pistols were empty. He re-holstered them and drew his Colt .22 pocket revolver, a great weapon in a bar room brawl, but pretty ineffective in an open-air fight. A hail of bullets sprayed up shrapnel as they smashed into the wall protecting Billy. In a lull that lasted maybe a second he glanced over the wall to see two cavalrymen thundering straight for him. He ducked just in time as the horses hurdled over the wall. One of the troopers, his pistol empty, drew a sabre, slashing it over Billy's head, removing his hat, but leaving his scalp minus only a few hairs. Billy fired several shots after them, but didn't think any struck home.

No one knew where Jubal was in the tumult, but Billy was sure he was out in front of the village, maybe dead for all he knew. He jumped from cover and got buffeted aside by the last of the troopers as he flashed past. Billy somersaulted and scrambled to his feet then dashed to find Jubal. Why did he care? Well, they were partners now, weren't they? And that's what partners did.

He crashed into a few of the outlaws on his way, but they paid no attention. Mostly they were trying to fire some parting shots after the cavalry.

The troopers were through the village, gone as quickly as they appeared. Sam needed to regroup and reorganise. Oh, why hadn't Major Schofield left him the wretched bugler? He'd be damn useful now. But Sam's men were well trained. Individually they knew there was no point in just galloping off to the horizon. With orders soldiering was easy...you just did what you were told. Instinctively they knew they must return to their officer and receive new orders. And that's just what they did.

Some sullen, spasmodic shots spattered from the village, so they cantered out of range and reformed. Sam's first job was to assess their condition and situation.

'Report please, Sergeant Cook,' he was panting and spoke in brisk bursts.

'All accounted for, sir. A couple of light injuries but they're clean wounds and no imbedded shot. All men are fighting fit.'

That was a relief. An imbedded round if not treated quickly usually meant death or amputation, although quick treatment didn't always guarantee a different outcome.

'Got nicked yourself, I see, Sergeant.'

'Yessir, but I'll bind it with my neckerchief, and I'll be just fine, same as the others.'

'Damned if we ain't run into that blasted gang from Kansas again,' Sam declared. 'I'd recognise Claude Valentine and his cronies anywhere.'

'Seems so, Lieutenant,' Cook agreed. 'Looks like Sergeant Quinn's fallen in with bad company.'

Sam allowed time for the men to tend their wounds. He posted sentries to observe the village activity and assigned four men to tether and water the horses that were panting, snorting, wheezing and probably happy for the rest.

'Okay, Sergeant Cook. We got a bloody nose, but came off lucky, I guess. Now let's think of a way to flush those jackals out of there.'

'Could just sit 'em out, sir. Cover the road in and out. Maybe they ain't the patient kind.'

'Maybe so, and maybe not. They're possibly as well supplied as we are. I think we had better get this done right now. How do you assess their strength?'

Now he was starting to think like a soldier.

'About the same as us I reckon from the shooting.'

'Seems like that to me, so attacking a defended position on equal terms of strength isn't a sound proposal.'

'No sir, I do believe not,' Sergeant Cook nodded. He'd been with the 54th Massachusetts when they stormed Fort Wagner and hadn't liked the experience one little bit.

'What we need is a good, old fashioned diversion,' Sam announced, and they made some quick plans.

Inside the village was bedlam. A couple of men were groaning from wounds, mostly trifling, but the Kentucky Slasher had taken a bullet squarely in his leg. He was wailing maddeningly. The bullet had bounced off his shinbone and formed a lump where it now lodged just below the skin.

'Bandage it up,' Claude ordered Cottonmouth Jacques. 'And for God's sake shut up, Kaintuck!'

He was sorely puzzled by the day's events, but had no time to dwell. Firstly he re-organised his men. The soldiers were mounted and ready on good quality horses, but they'd had a busy, tiring morning so maybe a run for it would work. He also knew the condition of his own mounts was variable as they'd been living on what they could graze for weeks now. Some had toughened up like Indian ponies, but others were in decline. His men were confused, not that that took too much doing, but he'd better rally them sharpish before the cavalry came back.

Billy raced clear of the smoke that hung around the village and found Jubal propped up against a tree, battered and bleeding, but alive. Billy slumped beside him. Funny how hot it was now and the shade was welcome.

'You're crazy!' he raged. 'You damn well started a war.'

'Would've started anyhow,' Jubal retorted.

'Yeah, but at least we looked like being on the winning side. I'm pretty damn sure that's all changed. What's the next part of your brilliant plan?'

'We need to get to the horses and skedaddle. I'd rather take my chances with the Apaches. But I don't rightly see how we do that.'

'C'mon,' Billy replied, 'don't be so negative. It's really depressing when you do that, you know.'

It looked as if Claude's reorganisation of his defences was under way. He'd moved the Comancheros around to cover all the approaches to the village. He certainly had enough water and supplies to outlast the troopers, so he seemed to be sitting tight. Unless they found a cannon there was little the soldiers could do to prise him out.

Billy and Jubal's position was vulnerable and needed reconsidering, especially when a pair of black troopers suddenly rode up and blasted off a few shots that ricocheted inches from them. Without any further thought they raced across the open space to the village cover, scaled one of the adobe walls and panting, hunkered down behind it. The troopers showed no interest in trying to catch them, but appeared to be preoccupied with something else.

Shortly Claude spotted them, and he wanted some answers. He'd reloaded his Adams pistols and marched straight towards Jubal waving the weapons in his direction.

But he didn't get a chance to do anything.

'Claude!' Black Swamp Slim yelled. 'I think you wanna come see this.'

Claude heaved a *what-now?* sigh and turned back to Slim's position in the defences.

The troopers moved around the village in pairs until they had surrounded it as best they could considering their numbers. They dragged bundles of burning brush behind them, their yellow bandanas covering their faces. In no time smoke swirled everywhere in choking clouds. There was ample dry kindling around and it hadn't taken long to set up the fires. The surrounding Spinifex and parched cornfields caught alight, dramatically intensifying the smoke. Visibility soon dropped to a few yards and everyone's eyes were watering as they coughed and retched miserably.

Claude was only too aware of the cavalry's next move. They'd come boiling through the smoke, blazing away at anything that moved. It was time to shift camp.

'Saddle up!' he roared, and the gang didn't need coaxing.

They were all mounted, even the Kentucky Slasher, when Sam's men hit the village on foot. Two of the Comancheros were blasted from their saddles, but the troopers didn't have it all their own way. Claude fired at close range knocking one of them tumbling to the ground. Billy and Jubal were racing for the horses when they came face to face with Henry Cook. Jubal and Henry's eyes met for a second.

Damned if he ain't wearing my stripes, Jubal thought as Billy raised his pistol, but Jubal knocked it aside and they both dived for cover in the smoke. Cook aimed, but hesitated and the chance was gone.

In the clatter of gunfire two more troopers were hit. Sam used his sabre and delivered a couple of nasty cuts, but none proved fatal. Billy and Jubal darted across their protecting wall and grabbed the bridles of two spare, saddled mounts. They kicked the horses into action and took off at a full gallop firing a few discouraging shots behind them. Luckily for them, Sam needed all his men for the assault and no one was left to stop a breakout. Unluckily for them, they had no idea which direction to take and found themselves swept up in the outlaws' rushed escape, and just flew along with the mob.

Sam's smoke screen was a two-edge sword. It protected his men at first, but in the end caused more confusion than it was worth. By the time he reassembled his troops and got them remounted to gallop after the bandits he knew it was already futile. They were way ahead and the troopers' horses were just about spent. After only a token pursuit, he raised his arm and halted the column. Sure, they'd bagged a few bad guys, whether Jubal Quinn was one of them he didn't know, but he'd his own casualties to consider. So they trotted back through the clearing smoke to the shattered village to sort out the mess.

In a couple of hours he'd pretty well summed up the situation, and it didn't look very good. On the plus side he didn't actually have any dead troopers although two bore serious wounds and nearly half his men were suffering from lesser injuries. He identified two dead bandits and another who wasn't going to last long, as Claude's gang members, but Jubal Quinn had slipped through the noose. He also had to deal with a bunch of excitable women whom the outlaws had abandoned, although they didn't turn out to be much of a problem.

They were unconcerned about the gang's departure and even kicked the wounded outlaw several times to add to his misery. Sam put a stop to it, but was sympathetic when he heard their story in broken English from one of the girls. They'd been kidnapped from several villages, and were uncertain of their reception if they returned in light of the treatment meted out by the outlaws. But they were stoic individuals, having formed a close bond in captivity. They planned to take the spare horses, supplies, guns and ammunition and make their way to El Paso where there was plenty of work. They'd start a new life there.

Sam could only wish them luck. His men helped them pack up and shortly they left without looking back.

'What're you figuring on doing now, Lieutenant?' Sergeant Cook asked. He filled his dudeen with tobacco and took a few draws. Normally he'd asked permission to light up, but they'd just fought a sharp fight and needed a smoke.

'You'll have to take the men back to Kansas, Henry, and that's a fact. I'm writing my report now. I've cited all the men for their courage and recommended that you be confirmed as *B* troop's sergeant. You're to take this report to Major Schofield or Colonel Grierson and no one else. Not Captain Bellamy or Major Devlin. Do you understand?'

'Well, Yessir and thank you, but why can't you make the report yourself?'

'Because I'm going after Jubal Quinn. I'll catch that son-of-a-bitch if it's the last thing I do.'

As soon as Claude Valentine realised the cavalry had given up the chase he brought the gang to a stop. The Kentucky Slasher was in bad shape and moaned continuously. There were a couple of other men with sabre cuts that appeared survivable. But Claude wasn't interested in his gang's discomfort. He trotted along the line of riders until he came abreast with Jubal. Claude drew one of his pistols and held it against Jubal's skull.

'And now, perhaps you'd be good enough to tell me what in the name of hell-fire that was all about?' he snarled as he cocked the piece.

Chapter 6

Not again, Billy thought. *Partnering Jubal sure was interesting, but also damned hazardous.*

For once the gang was silent except the Kentucky Slasher, who'd fallen off his horse and was moaning and writhing around. No one took any notice of him.

'Well?' Claude hissed.

'Now hold up there, Mister Valentine,' Billy said. 'I opine you're making a serious error of judgement.'

'Seems I've done that already. This damned nigger's caused me infuriating inconvenience I could've done without this morning, and he'll die sharpish for it.'

'I'm truly perplexed you take that attitude, what with you being a military man and all.'

'How's that so? I know what I seen. And I seen this goddamned nigger disrupt a perfectly situated bushwhacking.'

'Well sir, I can hardly believe I heard you say that. Ain't you ever heard of a decoy? That's surely what Jubal had in mind. You think them Yankee cavalry would just come a-chargin' right in, do you? No, sir, they would not. They'd spread out slow and check on their target first. No way that Indian scout they got with them wouldn't have known we were there. Jubal here got 'em all stirred up and reckless. Would have worked real fine too if your boys hadn't started poppin' off shots ahead of time. No sir, it ain't Jubal you should be mean with, it's your fellers.'

Claude had his doubts.

'That right, nigger?' he addressed Jubal. 'You tryin' to decoy them Yankees?'

'Yes sir, Mister Valentine. That's about the way of it. Seemed a good idea at the time. Didn't have no chance to discuss it. Just jumped right on a horse to get the job done. Yessir.'

Jubal was getting the hang of Billy's survival techniques by now.

'Besides, it seems to me we've got bigger problems than mulling over what has been or might have been. Kaintuck don't look too flash to me. Don't reckon your boys are much in the doctoring line. Billy and I might be able to help. There ain't much time to spare. The cavalry'll be on our tail before long. We either fix him here or he'll slow us down too much.'

Claude lowered his pistol from Jubal's head. He turned in the saddle and eyed the Kentucky Slasher who was still moaning miserably in the dust. He stared for a while considering his position then fired the gun, blowing a neat hole in Kaintuck's forehead and a very messy exit-wound at the back of his skull. The Slasher bucked at the bullet's impact, then slumped still and silent.

'Ain't gonna slow us down now,' Claude said softly. 'Fact is his noise was starting to vex me. I do so deplore a fellow who whines, it just ain't manly.'

That was easy for Claude to say, he wasn't the one suffering with lead perforation, but he seemed more relaxed now he'd killed someone and he forgot about the issues with Jubal. Panther and Growling Bear were sent back to see what the soldiers were up to. The remaining nine gang members cantered off to the northwest, putting as much distance between them and the military as possible. The Comanche could easily follow their trail and catch up later.

Meanwhile Sam McAlister was kicking himself for being all sorts of a goose by charging into enemy territory so rashly. And, staring at the aftermath of their short battle didn't improve his mood. His troopers had bandaged themselves up as best they could and apart from grazes and bruising, were back in marching order. His two critically hurt men were a different matter. Both had nasty chest injuries and still carried the bullets inside their wounds. They were bearing up stoically enough, but both were in pain and suffered from blood-loss.

The wrecked wagon that had protected Jubal and Billy was resurrected and the troopers jury-rigged a couple of stretchers to lie on its tray. Hopefully this would be more comfortable than building a travois that'd bounce and scrape over every bump along the trail. Henry Cook didn't think the wagon would last long, and salvaged several long poles from the buildings in case they needed to improvise Indian-style later on.

Petorio Blanco finished applying poultices to the wounds and squatted beside Sam.

'Why, I'm as big a darned fool as that Bill Fetterman who got himself and his company killed up on the Bozeman Trail last Christmas,' he fretted.

'Heard about that,' Petorio said in his usual languid way. 'Can't say as I've ever met any Sioux or Cheyenne, but I believe they're troublesome to deal with. Don't see why you're beating yourself up about it so much though. These fellers are soldiers, it's what they do and it's what they expect. No one's blaming you for the way things came out. You did as well as anyone. Those fellers are patched up tolerable. Young sawbones at Pierce'll probably fix 'em up if anyone can, so long as they get a move on.'

For such a hard-arsed Apache, Petorio was quite insightful at times. His no-nonsense support worked on Sam, who realised that wallowing in self-pity served no purpose and it was time to snap out of it and get on with his job.

'Yes, Henry Cook's just about ready to leave. I'll go and see them off,' Sam replied vaguely.

'What about you, Sam? Henry says you've got other plans.'

'I'm not going back to Pierce. Or Kansas for that matter, not for a while anyway.'

'You'll have to sooner or later. Major Schofield'll want to hear about this from you.'

'I reckon so, but I'm heading after Sergeant Quinn. If I don't track him down this will all be for nothing,' Sam said, gesturing to the battlefield.

'How're you gonna do that, you can't track worth a nickel? You'll have to find water out there too.'

'Maybe so, but I haven't got a choice. It'll be bad enough even if I do bring Quinn back. Anyway, I've got this to help me.'

Sam produced a small refracting telescope from a leather pouch strapped to his belt. It was only about eight inches long, but extended into three sections. *J W Morgan, Optician, Manchester* was inscribed on the brass barrel. Sam handed it to Petorio who peered down the eyepiece and sighted around. He stopped just once at a single spot, concentrated for a moment, and then swept around to view the full panorama.

'You can see for miles. I reckon it'll be mighty useful,' Sam said.

'Hmmm,' Petorio didn't seem overly impressed. 'I'm not sure I can't see better without it.'

'Takes a bit of getting used to.'

'You don't say? You want me to come with you? You'll be hopeless on your own.'

'Thanks for the vote of confidence, but you're right and I'd much appreciate it. Don't know whether the Army'll feel they have to pay you though, this being a renegade operation by all appearances.'

'They're always late with my pay anyway. Besides it'll be a miserable trip back with the troopers. I'll tag along with you. I can always take off if I get fed up. We'll need to carry all the water and provisions we can. Apart from your telescope, what's your fire-power like?'

'Just my Army revolver and Spencer rifle. I've got three spare cylinders and a mess of caps and lead shot for the handgun and three boxes of rifle cartridges, a pretty sharp Bowie knife, and my sabre of course.'

Sabres had fallen from favour amongst cavalrymen during the Civil War with many units preferring to dismount and use short-barrelled repeating carbines when it came to a serious fight. But, fencing and swordsmanship in general were skills that Sam was really good at, so he still carried a sabre when other officers had abandoned theirs as unnecessary and cumbersome. His troopers were all armed with sabres and Sam conducted regular sword-drills.

'Should be enough. I'm going to get some extra ammo from those wounded fellows. Reminds me of an old Apache warrior called Nana who's always causing trouble for the Army in these parts. I recollect him telling me once how he got caught out in a fight with a bunch of Mexicans. His braves had plenty of guns, but they ran out of bullets. He got away that time, but always said it was better to have fewer guns and more ammunition. I've always borne that in mind.'

'We'd better get to it then. You ready to mount up?'

'Might be best to hold up for a bit, Sam. We'll hide with our horses in the church.'

Sam stared at him blankly.

'You'll see,' Petorio said enigmatically, so after giving Henry Cook his final instructions, Sam did as he suggested.

From their hiding place above the village, Growling Bear and Panther saw the Buffalo Soldiers leaving. Being young and petulant they galloped back to Claude Valentine with the news. What they didn't wait to see were two riders who left the village and followed them several minutes later. Petorio Blanco had been around long enough not to miss a couple of Comanche kids skulking about on the high ground. He didn't admit it, but even he may have missed them if it hadn't been for Sam's fancy English telescope.

'Comanche are surely boisterous fighters,' he conceded, 'but they can't beat Apaches when it comes to being sneaky and keeping out of sight. They just don't have the patience.'

They rode for a while on the trail of the Comanche boys. Petorio knew they'd never catch up that day judging by the pace he estimated the outlaws were moving. They passed Kaintuck's body and didn't really know what to make of it, so they kept going.

'They can't keep that speed up forever,' Petorio explained, 'but one thing bothers me.'

'And that would be?' Sam asked.

'What actually do you plan on doing when we finally catch up with them?'

'You know Petorio, I haven't the faintest idea.'

'Figured it was something along those lines. At least I know where we stand,' the Apache scout said brightly. He seemed to be enjoying himself.

Claude called a halt just after dark and they built a fire. He felt confident enough to be able to beat off any roaming Indians and thought it unlikely the Mexican authorities would be prowling around. Juarista rebels had pretty much bottled them up in Mexico City by then and it seemed the rebellion was reaching a climax. It didn't look too good for President Maximillian. Of course, that meant lawlessness abounded in Sonora and Claude's Comancheros fitted right in.

But it was a sullen camp and the bandits were ill at ease after the Kentucky Slasher's murder. It wasn't so much that they cared about him, but were wondering who might be next if they crossed Claude Valentine. Possibly Kaintuck hadn't even been that badly hurt, but Claude was in no mood to loiter. This concern tended to divert attention away from Jubal. Fortunately the outlaws' attention span was generally short and the morning events quickly faded from their confused minds.

But their biggest cause for depression was the loss of most of their musical instruments. Although they could be replaced it would take time and opportunity. They were unaware that the Buffalo Soldiers had salvaged the stash, having several competent players themselves. Colonel Grierson, who'd been a music teacher before his military career, actively encouraged his officers and men to play instruments and liked nothing better than to join in if any of them formed a band. He was a gifted flautist, guitar player and pianist, and an excellent timekeeper with the bass and snare drum. He hoped to form a brigade orchestra one day.

Panther and Growling Bear arrived on horses that were just about spent, but their news that the cavalry had given up the chase was well received. Now there was time to recuperate.

Claude often sat apart from the others at camp, and tonight was just such a case. Whether lost in solitary morbidity or dreaming up more mischief was uncertain.

'It don't seem wise to cross Mister Valentine when he's in a cantankerous mood,' Billy observed.

'He sure was a rager during the War,' the Gleeson Kid said. 'I never seen a man so desperate to kill Yankees, or anyone else for that matter.'

Billy couldn't see how the kid differed in that respect, but held his tongue.

'He don't let folk get close for sure. Makes you wonder why he allows Slim to be so familiar, even if he does thump him about once in a while.'

'Slim's kin, you see,' Cottonmouth Jacques explained. 'Monsieur Valentine took a shine to Slim's Mama, Cordelia-Pearl way back before the War. She was a mighty fetching woman by all accounts and Monsieur Valentine couldn't abide the rough way her Daddy treated her. There was trouble over it and Slim's Papa ended up dead. So Monsieur Valentine took Cordelia-Pearl for his wife. Slim was only a baby then and I don't reckon Monsieur Valentine knew how he'd turn out, but he's kinda stuck with him.'

'He weren't so all-fired mean back then,' Bad Roy Patch offered. 'We was neighbours in Kansas when I was a kid. He was just a farmer like everyone else. Then, about ten years back, murderin' Jayhawkers raided his place one night, cuttin' him up bad. They raped Cordelia-Pearl and shot her dead, then strung Mister Valentine up to a tree before skedaddling. Slim might be simple and he was only maybe ten, but he managed to cut Mister Valentine down before he strangled. Ain't been nothin' but vengeance on his mind since then. Slim weren't never the same afterwards either.'

All this might help to understand Claude Valentine's attitude, but didn't make him any the less dangerous. Jubal suggested it was a pity Kaintuck wasn't kin, but perhaps Claude didn't like him anyway. The boys dismissed it, saying that Kaintuck just got shot at a bad time.

At that moment Claude dragged himself to his feet and approached the others.

'We're out of supplies,' he announced. 'We need more funds. It's time to put you two newcomers to work. We're heading north tomorrow.'

Obviously he felt with the cavalry off his tail, it was safe to leave Sonora and cross back into the Arizona Territory. There were many good reasons for heading north. Arizona was booming. The bonanzas of California may have expired, but gold, silver and copper were being discovered daily by Arizona prospectors. There were funds aplenty to be had north of the border, and nowhere was richer than Tucson.

Nuggets and ore poured into Tucson's assay offices for valuation and were then taken under armed guard across Sentinel Plain to Yuma. There it was shipped down the Colorado River to the Pacific Ocean via the Gulf of California and on to San Francisco. With the promise of rich pickings, Arizona had become the Southwest's El Dorado.

They rode out before dawn the next day, weaving their way through giant Saguaro cacti, mindfully avoiding their spines as they trekked over rugged terrain. There'd been a few spring storms lately and flash flooding left a number of water holes that made travelling easier. They crossed into the Arizona Territory somewhere near to the Mexican town of Nogales.

Panther and Growling Bear rode on ahead as usual to keep an eye out for army patrols, stray Indians, conscientious lawman or any other well-armed threats that might cross their path. Jubal was ready to quit the outlaws, but Billy advised against it for the time being. Even if they got away the Comanche boys would easily track them down. With Claude in his present mood it was better not to antagonise him and just go with the flow until a good chance to take off occurred.

Around noon they heard several rifle shots and a few moments later Panther came galloping back. There was a mining camp over the next ridge and Growling Bear had just shot a lone prospector.

They kicked their horses into action and soon found the Comanche boy crouched behind a rock. He pointed to a figure lying by a ram-shackled hut that had been built close to a small adit carved into the rock face behind it. No one else appeared to be around, but the bandits weren't taking any chances and stayed behind cover. This was just the sort of situation where Claude could put his two new recruits to use.

'Go and check it out,' he ordered Jubal and Billy.

'Ride or walk?' Billy asked.

'Ride,' Jubal replied without hesitation.

The choice was whether to dismount and creep forward behind cover or ride in and be ready for a quick getaway if there was trouble. They'd be an easier target on horseback, but Jubal reckoned if any shooting started, Claude was just as likely to hightail it to safety and take their horses with him, leaving them stranded on foot. So they rode in with rifles drawn and cocked.

The miner was lying still as they approached. Jubal dismounted to see if he was dead while Billy kept a lookout from the saddle. One bullet had grazed the miner's skull and another had penetrated his shoulder, but although he was groggy and in pain he was alive. As Jubal started rifling through his pockets the miner stirred.

'Sssh,' Jubal whispered. 'There's a parcel of rogues just yonder who'll kill you for sure if they think they ain't done it already. You lie still and play dead until we're gone. It's your only chance. Trust me, these men are dedicated murderers.'

The miner seemed to understand and didn't have much choice anyway.

Jubal found a gold-plated fob watch and chain along with five, silver dollars on the prospector. Knowing it would be best to bring something back to Claude, he took the watch and left the cash, figuring the miner didn't look too prosperous and he'd probably need it.

'He ain't dead,' Jubal said to Billy. 'I'm gonna drag him off to the side. Try to keep the boys away so they won't notice. Take this watch it might distract them. They'll surely trash the shack anyway.'

Billy did what he was told and showed the watch to Claude who opened it and found it in good working order. There was an inscription inside the case that read *Zebulon, Rendezvous 1837*. Of course Claude hadn't the faintest notion what it meant, but the watch pleased him and he pocketed it.

The boys did indeed ransack the mine-shack taking pretty much everything in it, although that only amounted to some bacon, flour, a frypan and several sticks of blasting powder wrapped together with fuse-wire. They really enjoyed making a noise and generally creating mayhem, upending the rough furniture and tossing it through the door and windows. They discovered three jeroboams of whiskey and that cheered them up considerably. After a lot of whooping and hollering Claude allowed them a couple of swigs each and then ordered them to put the rest in their saddlebags. There was still plenty of travelling time left and he didn't want the outlaws comatose right now. About then he remembered Jubal who came clattering through the door.

'Looks like you've made yourselves right at home,' he observed. 'Ain't no one else out there. The mine's empty. I don't reckon that feller was doin' too well.'

'Reckon not,' Claude agreed. 'Nice watch though. C'mon let's get going. There's nothing worth bothering with here.'

They left at the gallop. The prospector, who'd passed out in the shade where Jubal had left him, stirred about half an hour later and staggered back to his shack. He knew what to expect inside, but was puzzled that an outlaw should leave him with five silver dollars and his pistol still tucked into the waistband of his pants.

It was nearly sundown when Sam and Petorio approach the mine. There was no reason for them to be particularly cautious and they were surprised by the bellicose reception.

'Just hold it right there you murderin' scum,' a voice roared from the shack. 'I got a bead on you and I'll plug you no doubt about it.'

'Whoa there,' Sam said. 'Petorio here might be an Apache, but he ain't a hostile savage.'

Petorio rolled his eyes and glared at Sam, suggesting he could be as hostile and savage as anyone if he put his mind to it.

'I'm Lieutenant Sam McAlister from the Tenth Cavalry and Petorio is an Army scout,' Sam announced. 'We're on the trail of a desperado gang who've been shooting up folks from here to Kansas.'

The cabin door squeaked open and the prospector edged out. He looked unsteady on his feet, but still pointed a Dragoon Colt shakily ahead.

'Well, in that case, you're too damned late,' he growled and collapsed, pitching forward into the dust by his cabin door.

Chapter 7

Sam and Petorio Blanco hauled the prospector into his shack. They retrieved his cot and laid him down, covering him with their saddle blankets. They dug the bullet out, cleaned up his wound and Petorio applied an antiseptic poultice. A good night's sleep and some breakfast made the world of difference, but it took another day before the prospector was back on his feet. Sam fretted about the time they were losing, but Petorio assured him that with the mayhem the gang left behind, they'd be easy enough to follow.

And, finally the old war-horse recovered.

'The name's Zeb Turner,' he announced over a steaming mug of coffee. 'I'm rightly obliged to you two fellers for stopping by. That was mighty neighbourly of you.'

'Yeah, we're mighty neighbourly folks,' Petorio grinned.

'You going after them scoundrels?' Zeb asked.

'Yes, that black rogue's an Army deserter and I aim to take him back to Kansas for justice. He's riding with a well know band of desperados from the Mid-West,' Sam declared.

'I'd be pleased to join you, if you've no objection.'

'None at all,' Sam said, 'but we'll be riding at a pace to catch up. You might find it hard being all shot up.'

'What, this? Ain't nothin' but a scratch,' Zeb dismissed Sam's concern, with considerable bravado considering his state just a few hours ago. 'Why, back when I was trappin' in the Montana Territory, mmh, must be thirty years past, I outrun a bunch of Blackfoot and Crow bucks through six feet of snow with two arrows stuck in my back. And I've a real hankering to get my watch back. That villainous darkie should have taken the five silver dollars instead.'

Sam and Petorio stared at one another, not knowing what that was all about. Sam shrugged. Thirty years ago Turner was probably more resilient, but he looked still looked pretty tough.

'You'll need something to ride,' he said.

'Got my mule, Jesse, long-tethered where there's grazing, shade and water away a-piece. She's ornery, but reliable when approached right. A mountain cat had a go at her and got busted in the ribs for its trouble, so I don't worry about her out there alone.'

'Okay, you'd better bring her in and gather any stuff that's left,' Sam said.

'Them outlaws didn't get much, but that's all there was. Took this claim over from some other darned fool. There's plenty of ore around the Arizona Territory, but it sure ain't here. Hope I've still got a saddle and my Sharps rifle though. They're in back of the cave, maybe them owl hoots didn't bother checkin' there.'

'Now's good,' Sam insisted, noting Zeb's tendency to ramble at any opportunity.

The saddle and rifle hadn't been stolen thanks to Jubal. Jesse did indeed prove contrary, so Sam and Petorio kept their distance until she became accustomed to them. After that they still kept their distance.

'She won't bite,' Zeb chuckled slyly, but they didn't believe him. Although once they settled into a routine along the trail, Jesse behaved benignly enough.

Within a day Claude's gang was close to Tucson and camped beyond the urban precincts by the Santa Cruz River which flowed continually in those days. They spent a cheerful night on the trail cooking up Zeb's victuals and polishing off his whiskey. The boys were all rolling drunk although Claude, who downed his share, seemed unaffected by liquor. Jubal thought this was an ideal opportunity to take off, but unfortunately Billy, who wasn't stable with drink at the best of times, joined the revelry and was soon rendered incapable and unconscious. Jubal hid his disappointment well and even finished off the last few drops himself. It was damned cold at night in the high country and whiskey helped the boys sleep.

They were in a pitiful state the next morning so Claude left them curled up in their saddle blankets and took Jubal into town to reconnoitre. What they found surprised them.

Tucson had been around for ages since the Spaniards built a fort there, but right now it was booming. Shanties had sprung up randomly as if the entire territory's spare lumber and jetsam had dropped from the sky to lie where it fell. There were some stone and adobe buildings of substance along the main boulevard and around the original Spanish Presidio, but a shambles of huts and tents radiated from there.

The town contained a boisterous cocktail of humanity. Miners from California, fortune hunters from the furthest corners of the earth, Chinese coolies, Arabs from North Africa, Irish adventurers who'd tried their luck on the Palmer River and Ballarat gold diggings of Australia. Army and Navy deserters added to the mix. They worked hard and played harder and generally didn't live very long. Gun and knife fights were the techniques of choice for resolving differences quickly, if not necessarily fairly.

In this tumult dozens of men were hanging bunting across the boulevard, and some of the local working girls attached ribbons and rosettes to boardwalk pillars.

Jubal stopped and asked one of the girls what all the commotion was about.

'Why, ain't you heard, mister?' she looked wide-eyed and truly amazed.

'We're from out of town,' he said.

'Tucson has just been named Territory Capital and Governor Richard McCormick himself arrived earlier today with the whole administration from Prescott. We're preparing a big parade for tomorrow morning. There'll be carousin' tonight, I'll warrant, and us sparkin' gals'll be busy true enough.'

She was enthusiastic about the prospect, business was business. Jubal eyed Claude, who merely shrugged. Whether he considered this an opportunity or a complication remained unclear.

They spotted three banks along with a Butterfield and Wells Fargo Office. All would be plump with cash used to buy the ore at favourable bankers' rates. The gold and silver boom had drawn the usual financial leeches to the scene. There was money to be made, not by back-busting labour at the claims but in processing the precious metals and logistic support for the miners. Saloon owners from California to the Mississippi set up shop to facilitate all the booze, girls and gambling the miners desired. Produce and mercantile providers charged sky-high prices, amassing fortunes the prospectors could only dream of.

'I'd rather live here for a day than a week,' Jubal observed, scanning the price list outside a large tent that served as a general store.

'I dunno, it looks like my kind of town,' Claude replied. 'But, don't worry, we'll soon have plenty of cash to spend, and we won't be staying long anyway.'

They cased the banks that all seemed much the same. Well heeled with cash they might be, but that meant well guarded too. The banks chose Pinkerton private detectives or Wells Fargo security agents for the job. These tough mercenaries were quite happy to shoot first and debate matters later. Ultimately it came down to geography. They would hit the Tucson Municipal Bank at the south end of town during the celebration parade. It was a natural diversion. After a few enquiries they discovered the festivity would begin at ten in the morning.

Claude felt the prices in Tucson were immorally high, although his moral concept was inscrutable at best. He skilfully pocketed a brace of apples and heisted some dried beef and flour from kegs in front of a general store before they rode back to camp.

'You think this is wise, Mister Valentine?' Jubal asked. 'Hell, I saw a company of soldiers and how many lawmen will the Governor have hanging around him?'

'That's the point, don't you see?' Claude said, tossing him one of the apples. 'They'll be so busy toadying up to the Governor, they'll be distracted considerably. And them soldiers are all infantry and artillery as far as I could divine. On foot they won't be catching up with anyone fast.'

Claude was impulsive at times, but observed details well, which had made him a reasonably successful, intuitive leader. He would have liked a longer stay to complete his reconnaissance, but he knew the gang would be recovering and were just as likely to ride into town and ruin the whole project. Anyway if you over-planned things they might lose their momentum. And Claude was a momentum kind of fellow. Hell, if it all went awry, that's what six-shooters were for.

As it turned out the boys were still in pretty poor shape and not really fit for anything much when Claude and Jubal returned. So they rested up, ate the stolen provisions and turned in early. Billy was a bit sheepish about having drunk too much, but Jubal was tolerant about it.

The next morning they broke camp and left for Tucson. Using Zeb's watch Claude timed their departure to arrive at ten. He figured it was best not to loiter in town by getting there too early. Even amid Tucson's hubbub a gang of armed riders would draw attention. But there was one element that Claude hadn't counted on. It became plain that although Zeb's watched worked well, and Claude wound it twice a day, the old prospector had no accurate reference for judging when to set the time. It was half an hour slow, and when the boys rode along the boulevard, the parade had already begun.

And what a grand affair it was. The boulevard was lined with spectators while others crowded onto balconies or pushed for space at second-storey windows. Just about everyone had a flag to wave and plenty of shots were being discharged randomly skywards. Miners and cowboys never seemed to miss a chance to shoot lead somewhere. With cool bravado the outlaws rode past an artillery detachment that was preparing a battery of two twelve-pound field howitzers for a salute as the governor approached. This was no risk as the gunners were only loading powder cartridges without round shot. The projectiles were stored in caissons neatly parked close by and it would take time to load them. In any event the soldiers were too busy to pay Claude's riders any attention.

A brass band from Prescott led the procession, followed by a wagon decorated with coloured ribbons. The wagon carried a bevy of Tucson Belles dressed in bright satin. They held flower baskets and tossed petals into the crowd. Next, riding erect on a tall, black gelding was Governor Richard C. McCormick, a handsome but stern looking man with a neatly clipped moustache. Beside him riding side-saddle on a spirited, palomino stallion was his striking, young wife Margaret, dressed in a fetching deep plum riding habit and top hat tied with a silk bow. Some said she was expecting a baby in the fall, and she certainly displayed sensuous, womanly curves to enhance the rumour. The *Arizona Miner* dubbed beautiful and vivacious Margaret Hunt McCormick, *the First Lady of Arizona*. Even if her husband did own the newspaper, she was still fully worthy of the title.

'Would you not be happier riding in the wagon, my dear?' the concerned governor asked in light of her condition.

'Why no, Richard, darling,' she replied gaily. 'I am but a few months gone and by no means in confinement yet. What kind of wife would you have people think me? Should I not ride proudly beside my noble and esteemed husband?'

He loved her beyond endurance and could never refuse her. Nothing pleased him more than having her proudly by his side.

Several more decorated wagons followed with miners and saloon girls waving to everyone. A troop of baton-twirling marching girls in tights followed. They were a brand new fad that had sprung up across the country and were especially popular with the miners who cheered and whistled as they passed. An infantry company marched with their Springfield rifles sloped across their shoulders, all spit and polish. They were volunteers from Fort Whipple, who were only too happy to get into town and away from outpost drudgery. Jugglers, acrobats and stilt walkers were scattered throughout the parade. Some lasso-spinning cowboys rode on prancing quarter horses. A crowd of hangers-on followed, just happy to march along with everyone else. They were all having a great time.

'Looks like our *window-of-opportunity* just narrowed a mite, is all,' Claude observed calmly.

The gang tethered their mounts to a hitching rail outside the Tucson Municipal Bank, leaving Buckaroo Bob to guard them. Fortunately there were few spectators at this end of the boulevard. Most of the crowd were watching the beginning of the parade, and then fell in pell-mell behind as it passed. Facing the bank, the outlaws pulled bandanas over their faces.

Finding the bank locked, Claude shot the bolt to pieces and kicked in the door. With all the background gunfire, no one took any notice. Only two men were inside. One was a clerk. The other an armed Pinkerton agent sporting a dapper bowler hat they seemed to favour. Dandy or not, he was armed with a sawn-off scatter-gun and two Remington revolvers.

He raised the shotgun, but not quickly enough. The outlaws' element of surprise and their willingness to kill proved fatal. Half a dozen pistols opened up and blasted his chest to shreds. He clattered over a chair and pitched onto the floorboards writhing and coughing blood. He wouldn't last long. Panther leapt onto him and sliced his scalp from his skull. The guard could only groan miserably as he slumped back to the floor. The Comanche boys were delighted to find the Remington revolver cylinders were converted to accommodate new rim-fire metal cartridges, and the guard had a bandolier full of spare bullets. This was a rare find and the Indians eagerly helped themselves to the weapons and ammunition.

The terrified clerk raised his arms and urinated at the same time. Jubal was surprised this didn't generate any derision from the gang-members, but they'd probably seen people piss themselves in fear so often it was unremarkable.

The Gleeson Kid and Cottonmouth Jacques launched themselves over the counter and quickly emptied a couple of cash drawers. They stuffed the notes into their pockets and a gunnysack. Claude casually walked around the counter and grabbing the teller by his collar, stuck a pistol barrel into the poor wretch's sweating face.

'I'll say this once,' Claude snarled. 'Open that big safe back yonder or I'll blow your head to smithereens.'

'I don't have the k-k-k-key. Only the m-m-m-manger has w-w-one. He's at the p-p-parade,' the clerk could barely be heard, his lips were trembling and drool sluiced from the corner of his mouth.

Claude cocked the revolver's hammer.

He arched his eyebrows and inclined his head slightly.

'I don't have the key. I swear!'

Claude blew his brains out and let the body slump to the floor.

'Then you're of no further use to me,' Claude addressed the teller's corpse as he stepped over it.

'Well now what, Claude?' Black Swamp Slim demanded. 'We got no key.'

'Shut up, Slim,' Claude replied. 'This is what these are for.'

He pulled one of Zeb Turner's black powder sticks from his frockcoat pocket. The safe was an old, imposing English unit built by a Wolverhampton firm. Whether Claude knew anything about explosives or safes was problematic, but he seemed confident enough. He simply cut off a short length of fuse, stuck it into the blasting stick and jammed it into the lock. He struck a match on the floor and lit the fuse.

It spluttered into life.

He dived behind the counter with the rest of the gang just as the charge exploded.

Some miners were using Alfred Nobel's newly patented blasting powder called *dynamite*. Fortunately for the gang, Zeb Turner couldn't afford it, although the results of the less powerful black-powder explosion were spectacular enough. With a thunderous roar, the safe door ripped from its hinges and slammed into the counter, crushing it to splinters. The outlaws were hurled across the bank. Most of the windows were blown into thousands of glass shards that shot into the street as brutal missiles. Some onlookers were badly cut and, totally bewildered, simply stood stock-still in shock as debris clattered around them. The hapless clerk, unprotected by the counter was blown to pulp, but he was of course beyond caring.

'Claude's barking mad,' Jubal hissed. His face was no longer black after being coated in grey dust.

'Nothing much gets past you eh, Jubal? But he sure has a way of moving things along,' Billy conceded.

'Ain't he feared of dying, damnit?'

'Seems not, all that hate sure has to boil out somewhere.'

Although neither man had yet fired a shot, they were now implicated in a very serious crime indeed.

Dust and black powder smoke filled the bank, leaving the outlaws coughing and heaving as they staggered to their feet. Singed papers and bank notes floated about the room like a swarm of butterflies. There were cuts and bruises aplenty, but that was nothing new. With their heads spinning they ransacked the safe and found several thousand dollars that had not been destroyed in the blast. They pocketed as much as they could, and then dashed outside just as the parade reached the bank.

Darned fool gunners, Richard McCormick thought, *they've started firing too damned early.*

In front of him a cloud of black-powder smoke swirled across the boulevard. A masked cowboy was desperately trying to hold a horse remuda together and several bystanders were either sprawled on the street or crouching on the boardwalk nursing cuts and pulling glass splinters from their wounds.

Suddenly a bunch of men burst from the Tucson Municipal Bank firing revolvers indiscriminately into the street. The horses pulling the front wagon reared and bolted when their driver slumped forward with a bullet in his chest. Two of the girls tumbled overboard and crashed into the dust in a swirling rustle of silk and satin petticoats. The wagon surged forward until the horses swerved, tipping it over and pitching the wounded driver and remaining women onto the street. The band scattered dropping their instruments as they went. Several bullets tore through the bass drum's pigskin pad. More bullets whistled past the governor's head and one grazed Margaret's palomino. It reared, bucked and bolted. Although a noted and expert horsewoman, she was taken by surprise and thrown to the ground. Landing awkwardly with a dull thud, she lay still.

The parade was reduced to chaos. Horses bucked and pranced on the sidewalk, battering down veranda posts and stumbling on the wooden planks, their hooves stomping them to chips. The crowd ran amok colliding into each other and trampling folk underfoot. A stilt walker crashed down and broke a leg before a wagon wheel rolled over him crushing the other one.

The lieutenant commanding the infantry was a veteran who'd defended Little Round Top and fought at Cedar Creek. He'd reached brevet major by War's end and kept his head amid Tucson's frenzy. He rallied his men and led them forward, but it proved difficult in the pandemonium.

The bandits wrestled with their mounts and vaulted into the saddles as the terrified horses galloped away. His own horse gone, Whiskey Van Harper shot a cowboy down and leapt onto his mount then thundered away as the infantrymen reached the front of the parade and formed a line. It took a few seconds to load their single shot Springfield rifles.

'Present!' the lieutenant bellowed.

'Fire!'

Forty rifles bullets blazed after the outlaws and Van Harper tumbled from the saddle. He was dead before hitting the dust. Although no one knew it, the West had just lost one of the finest banjo pickers of the day.

The artillery sergeant, another Gettysburg veteran who'd commanded a battery on Cemetery Hill, was pretty quick-witted too in the confusion raging around him. Before the smoke from the infantry's volley had cleared his men were ramming explosive shells into their howitzers. The field guns boomed and the missiles howled through the air after the escapees. Two crumping explosions blasted either side of the trail, but the outlaws galloped on through with grit and stones peppering them from above. The artillerymen knew their business and roared off another salvo, but the gang was out of view and the shells exploded harmlessly in their wake.

There was almost a vacuum of stunned silence on Tuscan's boulevard, punctuated by some woeful groaning from injured victims and the hysterical sobbing of the girls from the front wagon. Some of them were badly hurt.

Richard McCormick jumped from his horse. His wife was limp in his arms. Her pulse was feeble. At first he thought she might just have been knocked unconscious, but suddenly blood stained through her petticoats as she began to miscarry her baby.

And then Margaret McCormick stopped breathing.

Chapter 8

As Petorio predicted he was having little difficulty trailing the outlaw gang. The posse even used the same campsite for the night, but were unaware of the events that had befallen Tucson. They piled up a big fire, cooked some supper and passed around the last of Sam's booze supply. On inspection, Zeb's wound was healing nicely. Clean dressings and Petorio's efficacious poultices were doing the job. Sam and Petorio weren't smokers, but Zeb lit up.

'At least that blasted nigger didn't steal my baccy,' Zeb said. 'He don't seem to have the makings of a successful bandit to me.'

'I believe that's not quite what he had in mind when he took off from Fort Pierce,' Sam replied.

'Damned sure he didn't,' Petorio agreed, 'only a total fool would get mixed up with that bunch. You were lucky they only stole your watch, Zeb.'

'I'll allow your darkie saw to that, but I still want it back.'

'What's so special about a watch? It hardly seems to matter much out here when you can tell time close enough by the sun. And there's plenty of that in Arizona.'

'Well sir, I'll tell you what's so special about that watch. You ever heard of the last Mountain Man's Great Rendezvous of eighteen and thirty-seven?'

'Bit before our time,' Petorio and Sam shrugged in agreement.

'Then you sure missed something. I was born in eighteen and ten as close as I can cipher. I come out West from Independence in eighteen and twenty-eight. Trapped beaver all through the Rockies for the American Fur Company. Had me both Arikara and Nez Percés wives on occasion. My, they were sweet things, but apt to wander. Can't blame 'em really, I wasn't much for stayin' home, myself. They'd take up with another feller, and I didn't have the time or skill to wrestle for 'em back. Tried marriage to a white woman once, but she proved tiresome and none too sweet at nights. She thought canoodling was a chore, and I'd say I was mighty fond of canoodling. Still am for that matter, although the occasions don't come around so regularl these days. She'd go on to distraction about sinnin', *the Curse of Eve* and such, so I left her with a missionary at Fort Laramie in the Wyoming Territory.'

'Wrestle?' Sam arched his eyebrows.

'It's the way of some tribes, 'specially in the north. You want a feller's wife, you wrestle for her. Sometimes her husband'll pay a bribe if he reckons he'll lose. Sometimes that's okay, but other times he just has to fight it out. Never was much on wrestling myself and I sure never wrestled no grizzly like Joe Meek claims. Only a darned fool'd take on a bear.'

Sam wasn't sure how to react to this information, although he'd climbed down from the moral high ground considerably since coming out West.

'Don't make us much different from other animals,' Petorio observed. 'Mostly they fight for females or territory or because they're just plain cussed. You ever see stags in the rutting season, Sam? I reckon they're plain disgustin'!'

'Reckon I have, and I reckon I know what you mean. But, to be honest I just haven't had the time to dally with womenfolk myself. Too busy studying engineering at the Military Academy.'

'What're you doing out here, if you're an engineer?'

'I guess I wasn't the sharpest at school and with the military reducing after the War, there simply weren't enough vacancies. The fancy, connected boys didn't want anything to do with Black Regiments, but for me it was the Tenth or nothing. And, I can't say I'm sorry about that. Anyhow, I opine *'Fighting Phil'* Sheridan and George Custer didn't do much engineering either, although I recall Robert Lee was a keen builder in his day. And most folk reckon George McClellan should have stuck to engineering for all the good he ever did as a field general. Come to think about it, what's an Apache doing with the Buffalo Soldiers up in Kansas anyway?'

'S'pose you wouldn't have heard, you'd only just settled in at Leavenworth before we lit out after them bandits with Major Schofield. Colonel Grierson thinks the Department of the Interior's going to send the Ninth and Tenth to the Southwest Territories sometime soon, so he hired a few of us to see how we'd get along with his troops. We trained with the cavalry school at Fort Riley as well.'

'So far, so good,' Sam concluded.

'Anyhow, as I was a-tellin' it,' Zeb rambled on. Like most mountain men, he liked to hold court without interruptions. 'Us trappers rendezvoused most every year if we could make it. Everyone came to Yellowstone from all around. The beaver was just about hunted out though, and damned if folks back east and in Europe just stopped wearin' beaver hats. Just like that. What d'you reckon made 'em do that?'

'It's called fashion, Zeb,' Sam explained. 'Well-heeled folks are crazy for it. One day it's this, the next something else altogether. They just all go along with it.'

'You don't say? I truly wonder what'd make some folk so simple-minded.'

Petorio shrugged, he rather liked dressing up in his best at times. He owned a silk top hat with painted eagle's feathers tucked into the band and a fine, red velvet waistcoat for such occasions.

'We all knew it was the last rendezvous,' Zeb continued, 'Jim Bridger, Kit Carson, Joseph Walker and Indians like Shoshone chief Red Elk were there, along with dozens of Frenchies from Canada. Must have been two thousand Injuns and hundreds of trappers. I bought my second wife there. Prettiest little thing you ever did see. I was mighty fond of her until she ran off with a Paiute boy.

'We surely had a wild old time, drinking, and frolickin' and sparkin' and Joe Meek brought a parcel of watches as gifts for the Chiefs. I took a likin' to one and he gave it to me out of friendship. I had the engraving done by a feller in San Francisco and kept it ever since.'

Zeb was busy after his beaver trapping days. He'd guided oxen yoked prairie schooners along the Oregon Trail, hauled freight to Santa Fe, crewed barges down the Columbia River, scouted and hunted buffalo for the Army with Jim Bridger through the Platte River country and driven Butterfield stagecoaches on the southern Oxbow Trail from Tipton, Missouri to San Francisco. He'd nearly frozen to death surveying the 38th parallel with John Fremont and even been sketched by Alfred Miller and George Catlin. In eighteen fifty he tried his luck prospecting around Sutter's Fort with middling success, and that's what he'd been doing on and off ever since. Through all his adventures, he'd managed to keep the watch safe and working.

'Seems you ain't missed much in your time,' Petorio said, by no means sceptically.

'No man could help it. The West was opening up like an explosion,' Zeb said. 'Anyone who was there just got blasted along with events. It'll all be gone before we know it. Why I hear the Central and Union Pacific Companies are planning a railroad line to span clear across the country. There're plenty of Indian tribes who ain't too pleased about it.'

'Since when do white folks care what Indians think?' Petorio sneered.

'Can't say as they ever have,' Zeb admitted, 'but Injuns don't mind scrappin' amongst themselves either.'

'Trouble is there are just so many of you,' Petorio said and then turned in for the night.

'Hope I ain't upset him,' Zeb said to Sam.

'Don't worry, if you have. He'll either get over it or scalp you,' Sam replied and pulled his bedroll over his shoulders. 'Night, Zeb.'

They rode into Tucson the following morning and immediately saw all was not well in the Territory's new capital. It wasn't so much evidence of the previous day's events, but an air of gloom that hung over the town. A carpentry crew was reboarding the bank and signs

113

of fire remained. That was nothing unusual, hastily built structures often burnt down in frontier towns. Sometimes even entire towns.

As they passed the town marshal's office they reined up. An open coffin roughly made of unfinished wood was propped up against the hitching rail out front. Sam and Petorio had no trouble identifying the body of Whiskey Van Harper. A sign hung around his neck with a message scrawled in red majuscule. Some of the paint trickled macabrely down from the lettering. The meaning was clear.

'MURDERER!

HE GOT HIS JUST DESERTS'

A small crowd hovered around and an enterprising photographer was doing a roaring trade taking images of folk posing beside the coffin. He sold new, popular four-and-a-quarter by six-and-a-half inch cabinet cards for five dollars each.

'Well, well, well,' Sam said. 'This is interesting. Maybe we ought to have a chat with the local law.'

Marshal John Wilson Reynolds was perched on a chair with his boots resting on a battered desktop. He was reading a day-old copy of the *Arizona Miner* while papers and wanted fliers were strewn everywhere including a pile on the floor beside him.

The marshal was having a bad week and was not in a particularly sociable mood when confronted by a trio of smelly, trail-dust covered strangers. Tucson was just fine until this week. He'd been in control in his characteristically *laissez faire* manner. He happily accepted weekly *'licence'* fees to allow pimps, saloon and gambling joint managers to police their own establishments and only bother him if vigilante justice was about to erupt into total chaos. He was by no means cowardly and had waded in with six-guns blazing often enough to prove it. But, his system of unofficial deputies, who were nothing more than bar room bouncers and bare-knuckle brawlers generally worked well, especially as somebody else was paying them. If occasionally a miscreant was quietly carted up to Boot Hill after a little overly exerted force had been administered, well this was the Wild West after all, and no place for sissies.

Now Mister *Fancy-Pants*, Governor Richard McCormick comes flouncing into town with a troop of infantry, two police constables and a pansy, county sheriff all trying to undermine his authority. And what did they have to show for it, four dead folk including the governor's coquettish wife? Sure, they'd taken her body to Prescott, but they'd be back. Worst of all, they were Yankees and Reynolds, who'd fought with Colonel John Baylor's Texas cavalry during the War, purely despised Yankees.

And here was a Yankee lieutenant staring him down in his own office.

'Who the blazes are you?' Reynolds demanded.

'Lieutenant Sam McAlister of the Tenth Cavalry. This is Petorio Blanco, my scout and Zeb Turner, who's assisting us.'

'And I should be impressed by that exactly how?'

'I'd like to know about that dead fellow you've got outside.'

Reynolds tossed the newspaper to Sam.

'Front page'll tell you all you want to know,' Reynolds said.

It did.

**Cold-Blooded Slaughter in the Streets of Tucson
First Lady Brutally Slain.**

Yesterday in broad daylight a gang of desperate cutthroats blasted the Tucson Municipal Bank to shreds. The desperadoes viciously gunned down Broderick Watkins, the duty teller, Pinkerton agent, Frederick Chambers and local teamster, Ortan Villiers. Tragically Mrs Margaret McCormick, who was violently thrown from her horse, did not recover from her injuries. The First Lady of Arizona will return to Prescott with her distraught and inconsolable husband tomorrow. It is believed she will be laid to rest in the Territorial Mansion Gardens there.

The perpetrators of this heinous crime are a dozen, ruthless, unknown outlaws who are understood to have escaped to Mexico. Our valiant soldiery heroically brought down one of the foul gang.

There was more about how a great day was ruined and Arizona was turning to anarchy and no one was safe in their beds at night (or day for that matter). All of which was perfectly true, but it had always been the case and one little bank job really hadn't changed anything.

'One good thing that's come out of all this,' Petorio observed, as he read over Sam's shoulder, 'Our little dust up with those fellers doesn't seem nearly as bad after all.'

Sam glared at him.

'So you don't know anything about the gang?' he asked the marshal.

'Can't say as I do. They were masked and from the sketchy witness accounts I have, no one knows them from hereabouts.'

'I might just be able to help you there,' Sam said a little smugly, especially as John Reynolds's antagonism seemed to thaw marginally. *Maybe we Yankees are good for something after all,* Sam thought, recognising a secessionist redneck when he saw one.

'Is that so? Perhaps you'd be kind enough to enlighten me?'

'Before I do, if this happened yesterday, how come you don't have a posse out after them?'

'A posse? And just where do you suppose I'd get the manpower? The governor has taken his lawmen and troopers back to Prescott, leaving me with a town full of miners and exploiting opportunists. They're either making fortunes or dreaming of doing so. Why would they risk their lives when there is gold and silver to be found just about anywhere in the territory?'

Reynolds didn't add that it was precisely how he liked the status quo to remain.

'Surely there's a reward?' Zeb asked. He disagreed about gold and silver being found just about anywhere, and wasn't averse to supplementing his income.

'Damn right there is, Old Timer. The besotted governor has put up the cash from his own pocket as well as the territory coffers.'

Reynolds picked a sheet of paper and passed it to Zeb. It was quite clear.

Wanted Dead or Alive
$500 Reward
For the apprehension of each member of the outlaw gang that robbed the Tucson Municipal Bank

A very brief description of the desperados followed, but it could have applied to most of Arizona's male population, and indeed some of the females.

'Don't this make it a lot more interestin', Sam?' Petorio said.

'Not interesting enough for the worthy citizens of Tucson,' John Reynolds added.

'Maybe so, but I reckon there's about a dozen of them rascals left. That's two thousand bucks for each of us if we get 'em all,' Petorio was positively purring at the thought.

'I'm sure US Army officers can't accept rewards,' Sam said primly.

'Speak for yourself, soldier boy. I quit.' Petorio said cheerfully. 'What about you, Zeb?'

'I just want my watch back, but I sure ain't refusing any reward.'

'You ain't caught 'em yet, and it may have escaped your attention that there're a dozen of them and only three of you. Besides they'll be in Sonora by now. I for one wouldn't be keen to cross the border. It's dangerous and out of my jurisdiction.'

'Not you maybe,' Sam said, 'but we've been there before and we'll go back. Also they don't know we're after 'em so we'll have an element of surprise, don't you think?'

'You go and surprise them all you like,' Reynolds invited with largess. 'Bring any of them back and the reward's yours. But how do I know you won't just bushwhack some strangers, and claim they're the gang?'

'That fellow out there is Whiskey Van Harper, known associate of Gentleman Claude Valentine and a gang of outlaws wanted for murder, rape, robbery and just about anything else in Kentucky, Missouri and Kansas. We've chased them all the way here. Contact Major George Schofield at Fort Leavenworth and he'll send someone directly to identify any miscreants we bring in.'

'Then fill your boots, gentlemen,' Marshal Reynolds said. 'Go catch the bad guys. I eagerly await your return.'

After a bath, a shave and a few grocery purchases, they rode south to do exactly that.

Jubal Quinn was an unhappy man. He could see no redeeming qualities in his behaviour over the past week. Unfortunately for him, as a man of conscience, he felt he was declining into the depths of barbarism and depravity. The Civil War had been brutal enough, but at least he was fighting for a just cause then. Now he was simply a bloodthirsty hooligan in the eyes of the world, and he didn't like the feeling at all. Even the thought of some extra cash didn't cheer him up.

That night around the campfire, Claude divvied the loot smartly enough. He was scrupulously fair. It was as if he was indifferent to wealth. As a result Billy and Jubal found themselves each $436 richer.

'Don't seem much for two men's lives,' Jubal sulked. It was just as well he was unaware of Ortan Villiers and Margaret McCormick, not to mention two, if not fatally, still badly shot up cowboys plus numerous broken bones and trauma left in their wake. Billy, on the other hand, was as sanguine as ever and little troubled by conscience. He was pragmatic about what was done and concentrated on the future.

'I'm going for a leak,' Jubal whispered. 'Come with me.'

'You don't need my help to piss,' Billy said. 'Hell, only gals do that.'

'I gotta talk to you,' Jubal hissed. 'I don't want anyone overhearing. *OKAY?*'

They got up without raising any suspicion and went off a pace, but not out of view.

'Act naturally,' Jubal said.

'How can I? I can't just conjure up a piss when I don't need to. Anyway I can't go if folks are looking,' Billy added coyly.

'Turn your back to the camp and listen,' Jubal said, unbuttoning his pants, because he really needed to go. 'I'm leaving tomorrow night, you coming?'

Billy seemed hesitant.

'I ain't taking no more of this bullshit, Billy. And you might be a bit feisty at times, but you ain't no cold-blooded killer, hell I know that. We've got to get away or we'll be dead quick smart. You've gotta see that, Billy.'

'Reckon you're right, these boys ain't much fun without their music anyway.'

So the decision was made and Jubal felt better. His bladder certainly did.

They rode deeper into Mexico the next day. Sonora wasn't all desert, rock and giant cacti. There were a number of small, fertile valleys with good water supplies. They passed several villages that prospered moderately, but showed no signs of excessive wealth. With money now in their pockets, other than extorting some gourds of mescal, the outlaws left these communities alone. But towards dusk while riding along a ridgeline they spotted a hacienda in the valley below them. An adobe wall surrounded it and beyond that were rich fields growing corn and vegetables. They could see a fruit orchard alive with spring blossoms, an orange grove and olive trees. Pens held pigs and goats, while chickens scratched around the courtyard. The main dwelling and outbuildings were decorated with brilliant flowerbeds and grape vines grew along the verandas.

A few Andalusia and Moorish cattle grazed nearby, but there was no sign of a main herd. They spied several women going about their chores and children at play, but there was no indication that any vaqueros were at the rancho. This was no hardscrabble farm, but a very prosperous settlement situated in a fertile valley. It looked like the main manpower force was away on a roundup. None of this was lost on Claude.

'Well now, lookee there,' he said. 'I do believe I'm feeling sociable, so we might just go a-calling tomorrow morning.'

Claude was in no hurry. He considered dawn an excellent time for attacking folk and taking them by surprise. If Jubal's mind had not been made up before, it was now. He had to warn the hacienda of their danger.

They camped and after supper settled into another night of bacchanalia.

The drunker they are the better, Jubal thought, although he eyed Billy nervously. Billy however, seemed content to drink coffee and sing a few campfire songs. It had a settling effect on the gang and, in time the outlaws drifted off to a befuddled sleep.

It was well past midnight when Jubal nudged Billy awake. It took a moment for the Kiowa boy to come to his senses and remember what he'd promised Jubal. Once that was established he was eager to get going. They'd laid their bedrolls and saddles close to the remuda and quietly gathered their stuff. Every movement seemed to crunch, clang, jingle or clatter, but a strong, rustling breeze helped to conceal any noise they made.

Their mounts were separated by several horses when they saddled up and stowed their weapons and gear. The horses jostled a bit at being disturbed, but were familiar enough with Jubal and Billy not to fuss greatly. Billy placed his foot in the stirrup and was about to hoist himself into the saddle when he heard a pistol being cocked.

'Going somewhere, Billy?' a cold voice hissed.

It was Buckaroo Bob Scoresby who'd been on night watch. He was by far the best horseman in the gang and spent more time than anyone guarding and tending the animals. Billy and Jubal had seen him on the other side of the camp, but he must have heard them and come to investigate.

'Couldn't sleep, so I thought I'd go and check out that hacienda for Mister Valentine before it gets light and folk're about.' Billy whispered. 'Ssssh, we don't want to wake the others.'

Buckaroo Bob cast his eyes in the direction of the sleeping outlaws with their associated snoring and flatulence. No one stirred.

'Not much chance of that, but I don't actually believe you…'

He said no more. His voice faded to a gasping rasp as Jubal grabbed him around the neck and plunged his knife through Bob's kidneys into his bowel.

'Hurts like hell, don't it Bob?' Jubal sneered as he twisted the blade out and stabbed again through Bob's rib cage, damaging his spleen and lungs causing terminal bleeding.

Bob sagged to the ground wheezing, writhing and unable to get to his feet. Blood was oozing steadily from his wounds. He tried to speak, but the pain was too great and blood choked his gullet. Jubal crouched beside him and whispered into his ear.

'I done punctured your gut, Bob. Your shit'll poison your blood. You're a goner no doubt about it, but it'll take a while, as I'm sure you know. I could've just knocked you cold, but *I* was at Fort Pillow and *I* remember what you damn, murdering Reb bastards did there.'

'Impressive,' Billy said, 'remind me not to cross you when your temper's up. But, it's time to go now, I think.'

In fact it was not blood-poisoning but blood-loss that finished Buckaroo Bob. As shock set in, he started shivering and convulsing. His body temperature dropped suddenly to a point where it could no longer sustain life. Bob slipped into a coma and died within minutes.

Billy raided Bob's pockets for cash and took his harmonicas as well. Then he and Jubal leapt into their saddles. Billy untied the remuda and then it was time to make some noise. They fired a couple of shots and whooped the horses into a stampede. The outlaws sprang to their feet. Groggy with sleep it took a few seconds for them to regain their bearings, but of course it was too late. A fusillade of bullets hurtled into the night, but the escapees and horses were thundering away out of effective range.

There was no way that Billy and Jubal could drive the frantic animals for long and they soon scattered leaving the two fugitives galloping down the valley towards the hacienda. They couldn't be sure above the clamour, but they thought they heard Claude cursing them to eternal damnation in the blackest, deep, fiery pits of hell.

Chapter 9

Billy and Jubal galloped full tilt to the hacienda. But approaching the main gates they heard a musket crack and the ball whined overhead. They reined up savagely. Their horses reared and bucked so violently they were both nearly throw to the ground. Another musket ball blasted into the dirt just in front of them, it ricocheted against a rock, and luckily bounced harmlessly away.

'Whoa there!' Jubal yelled. 'We don't mean you any harm!'

'Goddamnit!' Billy said. 'Can't people stop shooting at us for just one minute?'

'We don't want trouble,' Jubal addressed the shadowy figures along the wall. 'We're here to warn you you're in great danger. Bandits are coming.'

There was a lot of muttering from within. A couple of sombrero-covered heads bobbed back and forth.

'You stay put, hombres,' one of the defenders called. His voice was heavily accented, uncertain and sounded very young. 'You wait there.'

Billy and Jubal did as they were told, albeit impatiently. Their horses seemed to sense their frustration and pranced around, cutting up the dust with their hooves. After several minutes they heard a female voice call from the wall.

'What do you want?' she said in a soft voice with a Spanish accent that pronounced *you* as *dew*.

'No messing about, straight to the point with this gal,' Billy observed. 'And good mornin' to you too, ma'am,' he added. 'I think you'd better listen to what we have to say, because you're in big trouble.'

'Listen, ma'am,' Jubal said, knowing it fell to him to be the serious negotiator. 'You need to know that a bunch of cutthroats'll be here directly and they're madder and meaner than hell, I assure you. There's no doubt they'll ransack this place and kill everyone they find.'

That sort of information was bound to be an attention grabber and a long, considered pause followed.

'How do we know you're not tricking us?' the woman asked at last. 'You could be part of the gang.'

'In truth, ma'am, we were, but no longer and we got away from them. We know what they're capable of. You've just gotta believe us. We don't mean you no harm, but this gang does.'

There was another pause and some discussion from the walls. Finally a decision was made.

'We're going to open the gate, but we have rifles aimed at you, so no tricks.'

'No, ma'am, no tricks.'

Jubal and Billy raised their arms and nudged their horses forward, guiding them with their knees. The residents of the hacienda lit torches and soon the courtyard was bright enough to see reasonably well.

Three young women stood before them, each armed with a single-shot percussion pistol. They were flanked by a middle-aged man and woman, both pointing Baker muzzle-loading rifles at them. Ancestral hardware maybe, but Jubal's professional eye judged the weapons to be in good working order. The two wall guards were just boys of eleven or twelve. The remaining women and children drifted into the courtyard to see what the excitement was about. They totalled around twenty, ranging from a baby to the older couple.

'Is this everyone?' Jubal asked in dismay.

'What's it to you?' the central girl said. She looked about eighteen while the other two were a similar age with a likeness that suggested they were sisters.

'Don't you have menfolk?' Billy asked. 'With guns.'

'Only Papa and these boys,' the girl replied.

'Well, you're going to need some,' Billy said, dismounting. The reception party raised and cocked their guns.

'For heaven's sake, put those pieces down,' Billy said. 'If we'd wanted to shoot you, you'd all be dead by now, and you're sure making me edgy.'

'Please,' Jubal said, ever the mediator.

They slowly lowered their weapons while Jubal dismounted too.

'We've got to talk,' he said. 'Who's in charge?'

The three girls looked at each other for a moment and finally the central one assumed the responsibility. She'd done all the talking so far.

'I am Pepita,' she said.

'I'm Billy Songbird and this is my partner Jubal Quinn. We sure ain't no angels, but we mean you no harm either.'

'You'd better explain the set-up here, if we're going to help you,' Jubal suggested. 'I don't know how long it'll take the outlaws to arrive, but I doubt we have more than an hour or so. We scattered their horses, but they'll round them up soon enough, and they'll come straight here.'

Pepita might have appeared to be the girl-in-charge, although she was nothing of the sort, but her English was the best.

They had stumbled upon the property of Don Margil Junipero Daniel O'Conor. He was a recently widowed Hidalgo and rancher of note in Sonora. The sisters were his daughters, Alameda and Teresita. They were a pair of Spanish beauties, but with remarkable green eyes and long, velvet, auburn hair, although it was a little tussled since they'd just been roused from their beds.

Their spokeswoman, Pepita, an enchanting beauty herself, was however the daughter of the older couple Javiero and Benigna who managed the domestic affairs of the hacienda. She was a tiny spitfire with brown, almost black eyes and truly bronze, satin-smooth skin that was evidence of her Aztec heritage. Her brother Segundo, Don Margil and the remaining twelve vaqueros were driving a herd north to fulfil a lucrative contract supplying beef to feed the loggers at a new timber camp called Flagstaff in the Arizona Territory. All the hacienda servants were Mestizos, with varying multi-racial cocktails of Spanish, Papago, Kickapoo and Yaqui bloodlines.

'O'Conor?" Jubal queried.

'Si, Señor,' Alameda said with a prim curtsy. Her English seemed good enough to Jubal. 'We are of the line of the great conquistador, Hugo O'Conor.'

Apparently old Hugo who'd been an Irish mercenary, had done well in the Spanish Army and was even given the title *'Don'* when it meant something in Mexico. He was a big shot around Sonora and Arizona about a hundred years ago and begat scions randomly throughout the area. This was just one such branch of his family, hence the girls' emerald eyes and red-tinted hair.

'This doesn't really matter,' Billy insisted. 'What the hell are you doing here unprotected? What if the Apaches attack?'

'We do not fear the Apaches,' Benigna said confidently.

Jubal and Billy exchanged glances. Of course everyone was afraid of Apaches. It was pure lunacy not to be.

'Whatever,' Billy said. 'But Apaches ain't the problem right now, and the outlaws on their way here are just as fearsome. No doubt about that. What have you got in the way of weapons?'

It was pretty much what they saw. Three single shot pistols and the Baker rifles plus farm tools, axes and machetes. Billy and Jubal looked doubtfully at each other.

'These are fine weapons!' Pepita declared, sensing their disapproval. 'Papa and Don Margil carried these guns through Texas with Generalissimo Santa Anna. They fought at the Alamo,'

'I'm sure that's true, darlin', but I'd keep that piece of information to yourself if you go north of the border,' Billy advised.

'How long have the menfolk been gone?' Jubal asked.

'A week.'

Bugger!

A herd moved slowly, but it would still take two or three days to catch up with them and bring news of the danger.

'There's no way we can defend this place against determined outlaws,' Billy concluded. 'You've got to make a run for it and hide, but I dunno where.'

'There are many coulees and small ravines just to the west. You could hide an army there,' Pepita ventured.

A lot of indecision followed. Javiero and Benigna chose the servant's option and awaited instructions. Despite their Irish genealogy, Alameda and Teresita took the haughty, pure-Spanish attitude that no upstart Indian or Negro would order them around. But, they were unable to come up with any alternatives. The other women and children simply looked puzzled and couldn't understand the gist of the conversation anyway. Pepita cast her eyes about and seeing no leadership coming from any direction, took it upon herself to act.

She quickly instructed everyone to get all the warm clothing, food and water they could carry and gather at the rear gate of the hacienda. It opened into a corral. They all scurried away, even Alameda and Teresita, realising that although it was beneath their dignity to do anything physical, it was still chilly and they liked their comfort. It seemed interminable, but finally they were all assembled by the gate.

'Put the children on horses,' Jubal said. 'There won't be enough for everyone, but the kids will be the slowest. The fittest will have to go on foot.'

They turned to go through the gate when a dozen shots rang out. Shards of adobe sprayed the group as bullets ricocheted off the walls. Everyone ducked. The women screamed and children wailed and sobbed. Billy swore.

'That was quick,' he said with even a hint of admiration.

'Get everyone into the corral!' Jubal yelled, 'we'll cover you.'

'We?' Billy looked at him.

'You and me, Billy. C'mon,'

They leapt onto the hacienda wall and crouch-ran along the top. There were no ramparts, just a couple of stools at its base for lookouts to stand on. They couldn't make out anyone in the darkness, but saw plenty of muzzle flashes. Bullets zinged past and often smacked into the wall beneath their feet. There were several shadows darting below and Billy shot off a couple of rounds. All that did was draw returning fire, but the shadows retreated. Billy and Jubal dived forward and lay still on the wall. Then the shooting stopped.

A glimmer of indigo pierced the black, eastern sky. Just a smudge, but dawn was breaking.

'They're saving ammo,' Jubal whispered. 'There aren't enough of 'em to surround the place, so they'll wait until first light, and then attack with the sun at their backs. We won't see a dammed thing and be sitting ducks.'

'We'll never hold 'em off anyway,' Billy said. 'But right now they can't see us too well, even if we can't see them either.'

'Yeah, we'd better get going while we still have night cover. We don't have long.'

They scrambled back along the wall and dropped into the courtyard. They led their horses into the corral and broke down the fence rails.

'Ride double. Ride triple if necessary,' Jubal yelled. 'Get everyone mounted. We've only got minutes before they're through the gate.'

Then he heard a violent argument between Pepita and Don Margil's daughters. They were both mounted on fine Arab thoroughbreds and were not going to ride double with anyone. The

Don's daughters didn't embrace the sharing concept well. They sat haughtily on side-saddles. Pepita was pleading with them, but the girls remained aloof and unmoved.

'What?' Jubal growled.

'It seems our pure blood-line Spaniards don't want to muck in with the Indian riff-raff,' Billy observed.

'Yeah, like we have time for this. Billy, take Alameda,' Jubal said as he rode next to Teresita and hauled her from her saddle and dumped her behind him. She squealed and thumped his back, but he ignored her. Billy yanked Alameda from her horse in the same manner. She raised her fist but he glared at her in a way that deterred aggression. Pepita saw the way of things and quickly got everyone mounted on the vacated animals.

Several shots rang overhead.

Suddenly there was an explosion and the front gate shattered in a million splinters as another of Zeb's blasting sticks was put to use. Wood chips clattered everywhere and the children were nearly knocked from the horses. Choking smoke swirled through the courtyard and was still drifting thickly when Claude Valentine, with both pistols raised, strode through the portal, kicking ruined timber fragments out of his path. The others followed and soon all the outlaws were inside the walls of Hacienda O'Conor.

'I guess Claude couldn't wait for sunup,' Billy said.

Then old Javiero jumped from the horse he shared with Benigna. He carried the two Baker rifles and trotted back through the corral to the rear gate.

'No, Papa!' Pepita screamed. She leapt from the saddle and raced after him

By the time Jubal realised the danger, Javiero was propped beside the rear gate and blasted a shot into the courtyard.

'Reload for me,' he said to Pepita, handing her a powder horn and pouch of lead balls and wadding. She was pretty sharp at it too.

But two muskets were pretty well ineffective against the gang's firepower. They soon saw where the shot came from and blazed away as they advanced. Javiero got off one more shot before he was hit in the shoulder and was pitched backwards by the bullet's force. Bayou Jacques and Bad Roy Patch stormed through the gate. They shot Javiero to pieces and grabbed Pepita.

Jubal was too late. He fired until his revolver was empty. The outlaws dived back behind the wall, dragging Pepita screaming and kicking with them. A hail of bullets flew from the rear gate. Teresita screamed in Jubal's ear. There was nothing he could do, it was run or die.

His horse reared, nearly throwing Teresita, but she hung on, gouging her fingernails deeply into Jubal's ribs as they galloped away after the others.

Claude had been furious, but calmed down once he was in action. He liked to concentrate on what needed to be done rather than why it was being done. The gang could have climbed Hacienda O'Conor's walls without much difficulty, but a stick of blasting powder rammed under the gate was much more effective and scared the pants off of everybody inside. He puffed on the cigar he'd used to light the fuse, it wasn't bad and worth savouring. The shooting had stopped and Roy and Jacques were dragging a screaming hellcat across the courtyard. She was kicking, clawing and cursing them for the miserable, cowardly, carrion they were.

Claude heaved back his hand and slapped her viciously across the face, momentarily sending her head spinning and blurring her vision.

'Shut up!' he yelled. 'How can I think straight with your carry-on?'

Explosions and gunfire didn't seem to trouble his thinking, but screaming females got on his nerves. Screaming anyone for that matter, as he had demonstrated by silencing the Kentucky Slasher. He initially thought he'd shoot her there and then, but figured she'd probably amuse the boys later if they could hold her still long enough. That sort of thing calmed them down and stopped them grumbling.

'Tie her up,' he ordered Roy and Jacques.

This proved difficult because she struggled and kicked, but they eventually got it done. Thus subdued, Pepita slumped to the ground, sobbing for her father who lay dead beside the rear gate.

'Panther, Growling Bear,' Claude summoned. 'Get after them, and let me know where they go. They won't get away, they'll be travelling too slow. We'll track 'em down directly.'

The Comanche boys nodded and ran back to where they'd tethered the horses. They leapt into the saddles with a couple of whoops and galloped away just as the first crimson rays of sunrise beamed over the horizon and shone into the distant, purple hills.

'Okay boys, let's see what we can find that's useful around here,' Claude said.

They tore into the place. Finding plenty of food, they stashed corncobs and beans into their gunnysacks. Meat on the trail was less of a problem because game was abundant. The hacienda was well appointed with velvet drapes and Italian lace window shades. The furniture was handsomely crafted from oriental hardwoods and Spanish leather. Fine woven carpets from the Levant covered the floors. The disturbed beds were made up with starched, Irish linen. Bronze, copper and silver figurines decorated the tabletops and a library of ornately bound books filled shelves that lined several walls. This was wealth indeed, but Claude had no use for any of it. You can't tote furniture on horseback.

They raided the grain silo, fed their mounts and took what they could carry. The gang drew water from the well for the horses and replenished their canteens. They killed some chickens and hung them from their saddle pommels. Now they were well stocked for a long chase.

'I think it's time to be going,' Claude announced after they'd scrounged all they could.

They tied Pepita to Buckaroo Bob's horse and mounted up. In single file, The Gleeson Kid, Bad Roy Patch, Bayou Cottonmouth Jacques, and Black Swamp Slim, leading Pepita rode through Hacienda O'Conor's courtyard out of the rear gate into the corral and to the open country beyond. Tears rushed down Pepita's cheeks as she passed her father's body, but she was helplessly bound to the saddle.

Claude mounted up and took another cigar from his frockcoat pocket. He drew in the smoke with satisfaction then lit the fuse of Zeb Turner's last black-powder stick and tossed it fizzing and spluttering through the door of the main hacienda building. He nudged his horse into a canter and cleared the rear gate as the stick exploded.

The pigs squealed and charged through their pen while the remaining chickens squawked in panic and launched themselves everywhere in a haze of feathers. The window shutters crashed into splinters and gouts of flame shot from the chimney, blasting debris sky-high. Some masonry crumbled, but the stout walls held, although a boisterous fire started almost immediately. Fire licked up the fine drapes and spread to the imported furniture. Soon the beds and books were alight and some of the ornaments turned molten in the blaze. In moments just about everything of value in Hacienda O'Conor was either totally reduced to ash or burnt beyond redemption.

Like all days, Claude pondered as his horse jogged along behind the other gang-members, *there are low points and high ones.*

'What in blue blazes was that?' Sam demanded.

He'd just mounted up with Petorio and Zeb. They'd trailed the outlaws from dawn to dusk. Sam would have had them ride through the night, but Petorio reminded him that he might miss the trail in darkness and they'd lose valuable time backtracking. Also they needed to be rested and in good shape if they got into a fight, and that was very much an option.

'Sounds like blasting powder to me,' Zeb said. 'Any mines around here?'

'Who knows?' Petorio replied. 'But it's just over this ridgeline, so we'd better take a look.'

From the hilltop they saw smoke and flame billowing from the ruins of Hacienda O'Conor. In the far distance they spotted half a dozen riders just about to disappear from view. Sam put the J W Morgan telescope to his eye and ranged through the giant cacti.

'Six of 'em, and no prizes for guessing who,' Sam surmised.

By the time they reached the hacienda the roof beams were alight. The dry timber flared and soon collapsed, bringing tiles and shingles crashing into the flames. Sparks shot hundreds of feet skywards and smoke billowed in an ominous black cloud.

'Better than Fourth of July eh, Sam?' Petorio commented.

'Not for the folks who lived here, but they must have gotten away. I only see one body.'

The storehouses and servants' buildings were still intact, and it looked as if the flames wouldn't spread further. There was nothing they could about the fire, so like the outlaws, they helped themselves to some vegetables, oranges and grain before watering their horses. They'd all been on the trail long enough to know you ate fruit and greens whenever you could to avoid mouth ulcers and constipation.

'What about him?' Zeb asked, pointing to Javiero's body.

'I reckon the folks'll be back before the buzzards and jackals. We don't have time to stop and dig holes in the ground,' Sam said with unusual callousness, but he could see he was closing in on the outlaws and was hungry for this to be over without distractions.

They rode after the gang.

Jubal and Billy lead their forlorn group into the hills. Benigna was inconsolable and wept for her lost family. As much as the others tried to comfort her, it was to no avail and her sobbing continued. They rode into a labyrinth of half-dry arroyos, gullies and twisted chasms etched into the rock by a millennia of flash flooding and seeping moisture freezing within the surface and cracking away small stone chips. Scrub and cacti grew profusely and the party moved carefully to avoid thorns.

'Plenty of hiding places,' Billy observed. 'Pity we don't have more guns, we'd hold them off forever.'

'I don't think Claude is interested in these people anymore,' Jubal said. 'The poor wretches just got between him and us.'

'He'd have trashed the hacienda and probably murdered everyone anyway,' Billy justified. 'No doubt about that. It's his nature to be wanton.'

'Maybe so, but it's us he's after. So I reckon it's time we took off and left these folks to hide.'

'We may not be able to do that,' Billy said quietly.

"What do you mean?'

'Take a look.'

A group of figures stood across the base of the coulee, blocking their path. They'd emerged like phantoms from crevices in the rock wall. More figures were silhouetted against the skyline, crouching in rows along the either side of the ravine.

There were at least forty of them, and they were Apaches.

Chapter 10

'Reckon we can make a run for it?' Billy asked.

'No chance,' Jubal replied.

Some Apaches from the ridgelines scrambled down the sides of the ravine, scattering rocks and dust before them. In moments they had encircled the hacienda refugees. Only a few were armed with muskets and pistols, but others carried lances, bows, hatchets, machetes and even a couple of Spanish cutlasses.

More figures crept from hiding places until Billy and Jubal were hopelessly outnumbered. But, they noticed not all the Apaches were warriors. Women and children appeared, and then Billy recognised Snake. It seemed the surgeon down in Janos had known his business and Snake walked almost normally. A neat bandage bound the wound where Billy had shot him and there were no signs of weeping or infection. Only this time he had more than just a few warriors with him, it looked like his entire clan surrounded them.

To Jubal and Billy's surprise Benigna dismounted and walked slowly towards Snake, speaking rapidly in Spanish. There was no doubt by her tone and frequent sobs, that she was relating the night's events. Snake's stern expression actually softened as he listened while several of the Apache women gathered around and embraced Benigna who dissolved into tears once more.

'Well, what do you make of that, Jubal?' Billy said.

'We are not all barbarians, Señor Billy,' Alameda announced sharply, 'and neither are the Apache. We have lived in this valley for many years and we are, as you say, *in harmony*. Everyone shares the land here. We do not interfere with their ways and make sure the Jesuits don't bother them either. They take only what beef they need, and we have quite enough to spare.'

'Sort of protection payments,' Jubal said cynically.

'Indeed not, Señor Jubal,' Teresita explained pertly. 'Papa and Chief Cochise are friends and allies. We are a team and protect *each other* from bandits or soldiers. Some of our vaqueros have married Apache girls. Sometimes they live at Hacienda O'Conor and sometimes they live with the tribe, depending on what work needs doing or the mood that takes them.'

'You'd better explain how things are to Snake,' Jubal said. 'Those rascals'll be down the arroyo before we know it. He's got the numbers all right, but no firepower at all. He shouldn't risk his people on our account.'

'He already knows. Benigna is just filling in the details,' Teresita said.

'I think you should all go with Snake then,' Jubal suggested. 'It's us they want. We'll lead them away and you can go back to the hacienda once it's safe.'

'We must go to Papa and tell him what's happened,' Alameda insisted. 'Segundo will need to know about Javiero and Pepita. Please, you must come with us. You have so many guns and we need your protection.'

'Are you crazy, woman?' Billy said. 'The bad guys are after *us*, not you. Coming with us will make you targets as well.'

To this Alameda and Teresita showed surprising grit as well as their characteristic stubbornness. They felt they must reach their father, and were resolved to use any means to do so. Somehow they thought if he returned, everything would be put to rights. Certainly strong men were needed to rebuild Hacienda O'Conor, but what Don Margil could do in the short term was uncertain. Perhaps the girls thought he'd chase down the bandits and exact retribution. Not a bad idea in fact.

'Teresita and I have good horses. We will outride any banditos. Your horses are in good shape as well and anyway if they get too close, you can shoot them dead.'

Or they can shoot us dead, Jubal thought, but kept it to himself.

'Billy's right, y'know,' he said. 'We'll lead 'em off, while everyone else hides, and then you can head back to the hacienda.'

'And where do you plan to lead them off to, Señor Jubal?' Alameda challenged.

'I can't say as I've worked out the final details, as it's just come up, but I reckon we'll find a way out of this arroyo and head west.'

'Then you might just as well let the bandits shoot you now,' Alameda said triumphantly. 'There is nothing but Sonora desert to the west. You'd die of heat or thirst and save those bad men the trouble.'

'We know the country well,' Teresita added. 'We are a team, no? Alameda and I will guide you, and you will defend our honour.'

'I'm not sure we'd be classed as honourable men,' Jubal said.

'You may be more so than you think,' Teresita insisted. 'We must leave the coulees to the south and go east into high country. There is a trail beside the road to Nogales. It is rough, but cooler and there is water. No one will see us up there.'

Jubal looked at Billy who shrugged.

'What?' Jubal snapped.

'I know she's kind of bossy, but we've got to go somewhere. If nobody has any other suggestions, we might as well head back north.'

'I expect we're wanted men in the Arizona Territory,' Jubal reminded him.

'Hell, no one knows we were in on that bank job. Who recognised us? Anyway we can give Tucson a wide berth and head on up to California. Why, I've heard it's a grand place.'

Jubal thought for a moment, but eventually agreed, hoping the girls wouldn't slow their escape. Alameda and Teresita jumped from behind Jubal and Billy and skipped over to their thoroughbreds. They shooed the previous riders down and removed the second side-saddle pommel from their sockets. Both girls leapt astride their horses and were ready to go. Light and well mounted, it didn't look as if they'd slow anyone down. Jubal and Billy would probably be hard pressed to keep up.

Snake was becoming agitated, so Teresita and Alameda explained the plan to him. There was a fair bit of nodding and gesturing, and he seemed to approve. He wasn't concerned about his ability to hide everyone from the outlaws, the Apaches were well practised. He even solemnly held his hand out so that Billy and Jubal could shake it, and then waved them on their way. There was no more time for goodbyes.

It was none too soon. Just as the dust settled in the wake of the disappearing riders, lookouts along the ridge waved frantically. No one needed instructions. These were formula concealment and ambush tactics. The women and children melted into crevasses along the ravine slopes while the warriors climbed to the ridgeline.

Some of them propped themselves beside rocks of any size, others loaded what guns they had and the remainder prepared for some archery. Snake's Apaches had no intention of just hiding. They were ready for a fight.

Panther and Growling Bear were waiting for the outlaws at the beginning of the coulee. The gang entered. The Comanche lads concentrated on the trail, while the others scanned the skyline. They were not being particularly cautious, but neither were they careless. The Apaches were so adept at concealment that it was doubtful if the gang would have spotted them anyway.

Unfortunately Benigna wasn't an Apache and she thought her daughter was dead. It would have been worse if Pepita was riding at the front of the gang, but she trailed behind, led by Black Swamp Slim. But a mother's love is unavoidably effusive, and Benigna was overjoyed to see her daughter still alive. She raised her head and cried before Snake wrapped his hand across her mouth and dragged her back under cover.

It was just the hint of movement and no more than a squeak, but that was enough to alert the outlaws. The Comanche boys' heads were up and Claude drew his revolvers. They reined to a halt just as the Apaches heaved boulders over the ridgeline. They clattered down gathering debris into a small avalanche along the way. The outlaws' horses reared as rocks crashed onto the trail in front of them. Claude blasted off several shots, but couldn't find any decent targets in the swirling dust. The others blazed away without doing any damage, but it prevented the Apaches shooting back accurately.

A suddenly hail of arrows and lances hissed downwards and spattered into the ground with sharp thuds. Wisely Claude decided to disengage the fight from a poor position against unknown odds. The gang turned and galloped back along the trail followed by more arrows and the occasional musket ball.

Snake dashed onto the trail, but saw that there was no more to be done. He gave Benigna a withering look that normally would have been accompanied by a sound thrashing for spoiling the ambush. But even he couldn't punish a woman who'd just lost her husband, and whose daughter's future was tenuous. Like most Apaches, he wasn't a gushy kind of fellow. Even so, he put his hand on her shoulder and his eyes softened as the anger faded and Benigna was comforted by such rare intimacy.

Sam, Petorio and Zeb were just entering the ravine when they heard gunfire. That stopped them. Petorio sensed rather than heard the riders approaching. Zeb was about a second behind.

'Quick!' he urged rather unnecessarily.

The three spurred their horses off the trail behind a large grove of Sonora cactus, just as Claude burst from the coulee. The gang were hard on his heels. They hauled on the reins and stopped in a jittering group, their horses panting and scraping the earth.

'Anyone hurt?' Claude asked, hoping not to be inconvenienced by injuries.

Slim pulled an arrow from in his saddle leather and tossed it aside, but that was all.

'Goddamnit, Claude,' he yelled, 'we lost the bastards. I was so hankerin' to blast the shit outta the breed and that darkie.'

'Calm down, Slim, you'll still get the chance,' Claude said. 'They can't stay in there forever. They've got to come out somewhere and I'm betting it sure ain't the way they went in.'

Once more Panther and Growling Bear were despatched to circle eastwards and track down Billy and Jubal. Claude had confidence in the Comanche boys. With their customary yelp they kicked their pinto mustangs into a gallop. They loved nothing better than thundering around the countryside and it was what they did best.

'The rest of us will hole up in the hacienda and wait for news. If they *are* damn fool enough to come back this way, they'll have to ride right past us and we'll get 'em for sure.'

After the outlaws were safely out of sight, Sam, Petorio and Zeb came out of hiding and rode after them. Petorio peered nervously down the arroyo for signs of whoever had driven the villains out, but saw nothing.

'Well, well, what'd you make of that?' Sam asked, rhetorically as it turned out. 'Seems to me that friends Songbird and Quinn have had a falling out with their benefactors.'

'Looks like they're on the run from two posses now,' Zeb agreed.

'It appears so, but does it look to you like those rascals have thinned out some?' Petorio said. 'Damned if we couldn't have taken 'em by surprise when they came riding by. Pity.'

'We haven't finished yet, not by a country mile.'

However, no one had noticed that Pepita was with the outlaws.

'Reckon we'll let 'em do the work for us. We'll follow on and find a spot to hide up and keep an eye on things through my 'scope.' Sam decided. 'When the Indian kids get back, we'll just tag along. The way I see it they're most likely to kill each other and save us a peck of trouble.'

They followed the outlaws' trail, going cautiously as they knew there was no hurry.

While Sam and his companions were leaving the coulee, Claude rode through the rear gate of Hacienda O'Conor. The main building was still well alight although there was little smoke now and most of the flames had subsided into glowing, scarlet coals.

Javiero's body lay where it had fallen. Sam's prediction proved wrong and scavengers were already showing an interest. Flies swarmed in a growling, frenetic horde, while several turkey buzzards pecked at Javiero's tongue and eyes. A jackal prowled around the body, snarling at the birds. He darted in and started gnawing at Javiero's fingers. Smaller black vultures soared overhead awaiting their turn, gliding in lazy orbits propped up by the morning's developing thermals.

Pepita's scream was beyond anguish, a piercing wail of pure, irreparable misery. Somehow she found the strength to wrench her arms free from the saddle horn with such desperation that the rawhide ties cut deeply into her wrists drawing blood. With difficulty she gathered stones and hurled them at the scavengers. The vultures flapped languidly up and the jackal skulked off a short way. Fumbling, she managed to cradle her dead father on her lap.

Between sobs she shrieked abuse at Claude, cursing him to hell and back. Her tirade used every foul profanity she knew, and having lived close to cowboys all her life, she knew plenty.

Being cursed didn't really bother Claude. He was realistic enough to be pretty much resigned to a fate of hellfire anyway. Once again it was the volume that bothered him. He hauled Pepita to her feet, pulling her face within inches of his.

'My my, but I do like it when gals talk dirty,' he snarled, 'and ain't you just the little outhouse mouth when your fire's lit?'

'You have no respect,' she whispered. 'My father was a gentle, good man. You are just evil. There is no shame in you. I despise the very air you breathe and that I must share this place with you.'

'Test my patience further and you won't have to. I'll see to that.'

Undeterred Pepita lashed out with her feet, but Claude easily held her at arm's length and her kicking was useless.

'Alright, alright, if it'll just shut you up,' Claude said. 'Take her, Slim and tie her to something she won't get away from. Kid, you and Cottonmouth come here.'

The Gleeson Kid and Cottonmouth Jacques ambled over and Claude ordered them to lift Javiero's body. He was light and they had no trouble carrying him to the main house. Claude simply flicked his fingers in the direction of the fire and they pitched Javiero through the shattered doorway. There was a thump and sparks flew about for a moment before settling. The body sizzled and crackled as flames erupted from it.

Pepita screamed again and clawed and spat at Slim who would have lost control had not Bad Roy helped him subdue her. Claude strode towards her with a look of pure malevolence.

'Listen, my little virago' he snarled, 'if you want to behave like a slut, my boys'll be only too happy to oblige you. One more peep out of you and I'll gag your mouth. You hear me, girl?'

Pepita was all played out in any event. She nodded weakly and slumped next to a hitching post while Slim and Roy secured her. She had only sobs left.

'We're right sorry about this, missy,' Slim said with a leer as he tugged the rope as hard as he could, causing Pepita to gasp from her already aching lungs.

'Hope that ain't too tight.'

Slim didn't mean a word of it of course. Luckily Roy ensured she could still breath, he was interested in keeping her alive. Pretty girls didn't come along every day, and he planned to take advantage of this one.

They settled down to breakfast, scraped some coals from the fire and cooked a couple of chickens. They fed Pepita, gave her some water and released her long enough for her to relieve herself, then retied her. There was still no fight left in her and she gave no trouble. Despite his threat, Claude cuffed the outlaws if they showed too much lascivious interest in Pepita. He wanted them ready to ride at a moment's notice and lechery would just have to wait.

'This is really boring,' Petorio complained.

Sam, Petorio and Zeb had approached Hacienda O'Conor as far as they dared. There was ample cover and they found a spot to wait. Sam focused his telescope and although he couldn't see everything, he could make out who came and went. That was what counted for now. It was probably a good thing he was unaware of Pepita, as he was just idealistic enough to charge to the rescue, a tactic that would certainly result in indiscriminate bloodshed.

'You told me Apaches don't get bored,' Sam reminded him.

'No, I said we were patient and good at hiding. That's not the same thing.'

'You call this boring?' Zeb challenged. 'Why, I recollect when I was trapping way up in the Oregon Territory. Now that was the fairest country you'd ever see. No wonder the Limeys and us squabbled so hard over it. Must have been back in eighteen and thirty or some such. Met a big old grizzly on the trail and was he mean. Mostly they'll ramble off if you don't hassle 'em, but this'n chased me right up an Aspen. Luckily he was too big to get up after me, but he sure tried to shake me out. Then damned if he didn't just sit himself down and wait. Every time I reckoned he'd lost interest I'd shimmy on down that tree and he'd chase me right back up again. Why, I was there for a week or more. Now that was boring.'

'You survived, I see,' Petorio said, noting that grizzlies weren't the only things prone to rambling.

'Well as luck would have it, along sashays a pretty little gal of a bear. Why she wiggles her saucy rump right at him and off he goes for a spot of canoodling. I'll allow that the thought of canoodling sort of takes a man's mind off most everything else.'

'No argument there,' Petorio said, although Sam felt he was unqualified to comment, so he merely stated that he wouldn't be bored if a grizzly was trying to eat him and Zeb must have been hungry after a week up a tree.

'I do admit I bolted my next meal some. Had stomach cramps and gas for days.'

Not wanting to hear further about Zeb's gastric phenomena, Sam unpacked beef jerky and fruit for lunch. Zeb fed some of the grain from the hacienda to Jesse and the horses to supplement their range feeding.

Nothing was happening at Hacienda O'Conor and Petorio was still bored.

Alameda and Teresita led Jubal and Billy clear of the arroyo's twisted labyrinth and soon they were climbing into high country where pines began to appear. Altitude and tree-shade cooled the air, although they were only just in the foothills of the majestic Western Sierra Madre soaring in the southern distance. They spied the main trail north through the pines and far beyond it a faint, brown smudge of smoke from the hacienda. Whatever emotions that evoked in Teresita and Alameda, they remained silent, although Billy thought he detected a few tears as they left Hacienda O'Conor behind.

Billy led the way, with the girls behind and Jubal acting as rearguard. His neck and back were starting to ache after continually twisting in the saddle, but he didn't trust Billy's concentration to be up to the task. There was no doubt that the ride would have been delightful under other circumstances, but there was no time for sightseeing.

Just after noon Panther and Growling Bear found them. They'd cut the trail with little difficulty and came cantering up the mountain track. Jubal's vigilance was rewarded as he spotted them some way off.

'Trouble, Billy,' Jubal called. 'Those blasted Comanches again. You go on ahead with Alameda and Teresita.'

Billy kneed his horse into a fast trot and the girls followed.

Seeing their quarry speed up, the Comanche boys kicked their mustangs into a gallop and fired off a few shots. The new Remington revolvers had a surprisingly good range as the metal cartridges were superior to percussion cap-and-ball, and bullets thwacked into the pine trunks either side of the trail.

Jubal turned his mount and drew the Henry rifle he'd stolen from Fort Pierce. He homed in on Panther and squeezed the trigger, but his horse was nervous and fidgeted as he fired. The bullet whipped Panther's hat off and seared his scalp. The Comanche yelped, but remained in the saddle. Jubal fired again, but the shot was hurried and futile. However, it was enough to deter the chase. The Comanches turned off the trail and were immediately hidden and soon out of range.

Jubal knew there was nothing to be pleased about. As always Panther and Growling Bear were the scouting team and they'd race back to Claude with the news. In Jubal's view, all they could do was to keep going and get as much distance between themselves and the outlaws as possible.

He urged his horse onwards.

The Comanches' arrival at the hacienda didn't go unnoticed. Sam saw them through his telescope when they clattered down the hillside. A lot of activity followed. The outlaws bustled about and mounted up. They untied Pepita and flung her into the saddle and re-secured her. She was quiet now, seemingly resigned to her tragedy. It was only then that Sam discovered her.

'They've a woman riding with them,' he declared.

'Comforts along the trail?' Petorio suggested.

'Don't think they'd have time to pick up any chippies on the way. I'd say she's a hostage,' Zeb added.

'We'll see,' Sam said. 'C'mon let's get going.'

Some folk claimed the Comanche could go for a week without sleep, but right now Panther and Growling Bear were pretty worn out, while their mustangs for all their prairie hardiness, were spent. They needed rest before they collapsed. An hour or two and some watering and grazing would restore them. The boys decided to have a meal, rest up and follow on. It would give them a chance to check Panther's head wound, which appeared trivial although it wept slightly. The five remaining outlaws could easily deal with Billy and

Jubal, and the Indian boys would catch up by nightfall or the next morning. As the others rode away the Comanches saw to their horses then raided the storehouse for food. They were unaware of Sam, Petorio and Zeb when they rode past outside the walls, who in turn failed to notice the Indian boys had stayed behind.

It wasn't until they'd climbed a little way into the hill country that Petorio, who'd had a prickling feeling, looked back and saw the mustangs.

'We've left a couple behind,' he observed.

'Maybe so, but it's too late now,' Sam said. 'It's probably just as well, catching them would've surely meant gunfire, and that would only have brought the others back. We'll just have to leave the small fry. We've got bigger fish to catch.'

Panther and Growling Bear tethered their horses by a water trough inside the main gateway then tucked into some oranges and tossed a bunch of corncobs and potatoes into the fire. They found several bottles of claret that the others missed. Once they'd pushed the corks through the bottlenecks, they settled back to enjoy the wine.

Soon they grew drowsy and dozed off where they were slouched on the ground.

A lance whistled through the air and thudded into the dirt only inches from their toes. They were instantly awake. Their eyes jerked up to see Snake walking through the hacienda gate holding his ancient Paterson Colt.

Chapter 11

Panther and Growling Bear were in deep trouble and, wine befuddled or not, they knew it. The sight of an approaching Apache, archenemy of the Comanche tribes, sobered them up. They bolted towards Snake, who stood between them and their horses. They were quick, but Snake was quicker. He shot Panther in the foot, shattering most of his toes to pulp.

Growling Bear darted past Snake only to be belted in the face by a war club from another Apache warrior guarding the gate. Growling Bear's front teeth sprayed into bloody shards and he sunk to the ground. He staggered to his feet and received another tough blow and more broken teeth for his trouble. Other Apaches appeared in the Hacienda O'Conor courtyard. They dragged Growling Bear across the dust and dumped him beside Panther. The Apaches hoisted the two Comanche boys to their feet and hauled them towards the smouldering ruins.

They flung them into the fire.

Each time Panther and Growing Bear leapt from the flames, the Apaches grabbed them and threw them back. This went on for some time until the boys were severely singed. Their shirts and breeches were blackened and charred as skin flaked from every part of their bodies in agonising hunks. Snake nodded to his warriors. They lassoed the boys who could no longer stand, then tied them to the stake that had held Pepita earlier. There was no shade and the afternoon sun baked down on the Comanches' burnt flesh.

Shortly afterwards Benigna arrived with the women and children. She recognised Panther and Growling Bear even though she'd only glimpsed them from the arroyo, but she knew who they were all right. She spat on both boys then herded the hacienda pigs and set them to work. They snorted and snuffled around the Comanches before gnawing into them.

Panther and Growling Bear bucked and kicked for a short while, but soon their energy was spent. To their credit they remained silent throughout their torture and the Apaches conceded that plenty of good medicine was derived from their stoicism. In their view, a brave who died well was considered to transfer much of that courage to those who witnessed or administered his death.

Benigna rifled through the Comanche's saddlebags and found the stolen money. Snake saw no use for it. Even if he wanted to buy something, folk would assume he'd stolen the cash, which was indirectly true. But to Benigna it was a windfall that would provide much needed hardware to rebuild the hacienda. Snake was far more interested in the boys' arsenal and the remains of their wine and mescal.

Towards evening the Comanches were almost done for, their hands and feet had been chewed away and the pigs were starting on their bellies. They'd lost so much blood they were blue and their brains had ceased to function. Their skin hung in raw, dehydrated strips. It was around then that a pair of wandering, evangelical priests stopped by. They'd travelled past Hacienda O'Conor often and were appalled at the destruction they saw, but they were more offended by the sight of two tortured Indians gasping their last breath and piously admonished Benigna.

'"*Vengeance is mine sayest the Lord*,"' one of the devout worthies quoted.

'Then I must be doing His work for Him!' Benigna retorted. She'd lost a husband and a daughter to the Comanches and was in no mood for a sermon or sanctimonious hypocrisy.

The priests eyed Snake and his warriors uncertainly then continued their journey, feeling it was safer to camp along the trail than spend a night amongst rambunctious savages. This was of course, harshly pompous. The Apaches learnt most of their cruelty from the conquistadors who'd embraced human distress during the Inquisition, which had only been laid to rest a mere fifty years earlier. The Indians certainly never shied from homicide if the need arose, but they had neither the time nor inclination to linger over a killing and despatched their victims with alacrity. It was the Spaniards who taught them how to prolong the process, although in truth the Apaches took to it like naturals.

The priests' decision was undoubtedly wise, because Snake was now the proud owner of two new Remington revolvers and a bandolier almost full of brass cartridges. Shooting a couple of meddling friars would be fun, and a good chance to try the weapons out. In the end he decided itinerant clergy weren't worth the bullets and let them go.

Benigna was soon far too busy organising everyone into cleanup and repair duties to worry about a brace of priests who would just be two extra mouths to feed. Her grief was profound, but there was work to be done and someone had to get on with it, and that someone was Benigna. But, at least the pigs had been fed.

Along the high trail it was no contest. Jubal, Billy and the girls were riding exhausted mounts. Even so, there was a mild rebellion from the Spanish-Irish beauties when Jubal insisted they walk at times to relieve the horses.

'Señor Jubal, you jest, no?' Teresita said incredulously. 'You do not expect my sister and me to walk along this rocky trail?'

'Yes, ma'am, I do,' Jubal said, the all-assertive sergeant once again. 'The trail ain't that rough. Your Pa drove a herd of longhorns along here after all. And if we don't save the horses, they'll drop on us and then we'll be walking all the way.'

'I will not walk,' she declared, apparently yet unaware of how much danger they were in.

'You get down or I'll drag you down,' Jubal growled.

He'd have done it too, but Teresita whipped her thoroughbred into a canter as he marched towards her. Jubal grabbed Alameda's bridle before she could follow her sister while Billy chased after Teresita. His nimble range pony picked its way better than the thoroughbred and he soon overtook her. He snatched her reins and pulled the horse up nearly unseating Teresita. She was furious and laid into him with her riding crop.

'Goddamnit, woman,' Billy yelled, 'you'd be the most foolish and spoilt wild cat I've ever met.'

There was nothing else for it, he slapped her sharply across her cheek and that was a watershed in their relationship. Not only had an Indian defied her, but actually struck her. She was dumbfounded, and that suited Billy fine.

'Now perhaps you'll see some sense,' he said softly. 'I'm truly sorry I thumped you. It ain't my style to hit on women-folk, but it ain't my style to stand a horsewhippin' either. Please understand this ain't no joy ride. We have desperate villains on our trail. We *must* rest the horses.'

Teresita stared at him as her dazzling emerald eyes welled with tears. She lifted her chin defiantly and just as Billy thought there would be more trouble, she nodded slowly and dismounted. Whether she actually saw the sense of Billy's insistence or was simply stunned by the fact that a man she considered the *hired help* had dared to strike her was unclear. But, at least she was doing what she was told even if she smouldered inwardly.

They waited for Jubal and Alameda to catch up. It was evident that Teresita had been crying, but they made no comment. What was there to say? They trudged on in sullen silence for a time and then remounted. They made good progress, but it was only a matter of time before the outlaws caught up, and that happened about an hour before dusk.

In time honoured fashion the gang announced their presence with gunfire and bullets zinged through the pines, thumping into tree trunks and spraying up dirt as shots ricocheted along the trail. Seeing their quarry the outlaws spurred their horses into a gallop. Jubal, Billy and the girls did the same. They had reached the highest point along the trail and the path levelled out and widened as the thunder of hooves echoed through the hills.

The gap closed by the minute. Jubal drew his revolver and fired a couple of shots behind him. There was no hope of hitting anyone from a lurching saddle, and it certainly didn't deter the pursuit. The horses would not be able to keep up the pace for long.

'We have to find a place to make a stand,' Jubal yelled. 'Seems like only half-a-dozen or so of 'em. It's our only chance.'

'I'm looking,' Billy called back. 'Believe me, *I'm looking*!'

Good defensive locations were hard to come by. The country had plateaued and although there were pines either side of the trail, no decent rock formations to hole up in appeared.

And then they overtook a group of soldiers who were marching ahead of them. There were thirteen in all, twelve bearded infantrymen marching two abreast with a corporal at the head of the column. Their blue uniform jackets, red pantaloons and white forage caps were caked with dust and sweat. State-of-the-art Chassepot breech-loading rifles, with fixed 13-inch bayonets were slung over their shoulders. The sound of gun fire and galloping horses startled them momentarily, but they were disciplined.

On the corporal's command they halted, turned about forming two ranks across the trail. As the front rank knelt and aimed their weapons Jubal tugged on the reins and his horse swerved to the side and dashed past the troops. Billy lurched to the other side of the trail while the two thoroughbreds hurdled right over the soldiers. The rear rank ducked to avoid being struck by hooves. Luckily the animals missed the bayonets that could have raked their bellies. The girls landed safely and the four fugitives galloped away.

'Who the blazes were they?' Billy yelled.

'Search me, and right now I don't care,' Jubal called back.

Claude's renegades were firing spasmodically as they chased Jubal and Billy, barrelling pell-mell towards the double rank of soldiers, who assumed they were under attack from bandits, which was more or less the case.

'*Linge d'devant, presentez votre arme!*' the corporal roared.

The front rank raised their rifles to their shoulders.

'*Epauler-joue!*'

Each soldier sighted a target

'*Decharger!*'

Six rifles cracked in unison and from the swirling blue smoke, six .43 inch round-headed bullets, far more devastating than minié balls, blasted into the charging riders. The Gleeson Kid was ripped from his saddle and tumbled into the dirt, bleeding from two wounds in his shoulder and chest. A passing round seared Pepita's horse. It reared. She screamed and was tossed to the ground. With her hands bound she fell badly and cracked her skull. All her senses blurred. For an instant agony blazed through her brain and then she lost consciousness. Her horse bolted for the trees, although with a painful graze it didn't go far.

'*Linge a revers, presentez votre arme!*' the corporal bellowed once more.

Six rifles bristled from the second rank of troops.

'*Decharger!*'

Another crackle of musketry ripped through the gang. Bad Roy Patch was hit, his kneecap shattered, almost severing his calf and foot. He lost balance and tumbled from the saddle, crashing savagely onto the leg. It tore away as he rolled in the dirt with arterial blood gushing from the stump. A .43 bullet took away most of Cottonmouth Jacques' shoulder bones and he too pitched from his mount.

Claude was dismayed. This was precision stuff, unlike the frantic rabble he usually faced. The rear rank advanced through their kneeling comrades while they reloaded. After discharging their volley they automatically knelt and reloaded while the others rose, advanced and presented their rifles again. In this manner an almost continual stream of lead tore into the outlaws.

But Claude and Slim managed to dash past that line of death and galloped full tilt along the trail. Only the corporal had time to spin around. He aimed his Lemat pistol, selected the lower shotgun barrel and pulled the trigger. A withering blast of shot flayed Slim's back, ripping his jacket open and shredding cloth and flesh in its path. At first Slim felt as if he'd just be clouted with a club, but for some reason he felt little true pain.

Seeing that a third volley was unnecessary, the corporal ordered a cease-fire. The troops advanced, and they were in no mood for clemency. Three bayonets skewered Bad Roy, which judging by his injuries was more merciful than anything else. The Gleeson Kid staggered to his feet, a revolver in each hand. He blasted a few shots away at what should have been easy targets, but he was light-headed from his wounds and his hands unsteady. The troops reached him unscathed and drove their bayonets straight through him, red icicles of steel jutted from his spine. With a last groan he slid backwards and slipped from the bayonets' grip.

Six soldiers loomed over Cottonmouth Jacques, poised to impale him in the same way. He was groggy and bewildered with shock, but was able to gather his wits enough to see the way things were.

'*Non! Non! Je suis Francais,*' he gasped.

With bayonets poised the soldiers hesitated just long enough for their blood to cool. After all this wounded man was no longer a threat, and killing him unnecessary. The corporal hoisted Jacques to his feet, and that was painful in itself. He wanted to know who the hell they were and Jacques enlightened him. It was all a terrible mistake, he assured them. They weren't attacking the soldiers, but chasing four riders with whom they had unfinished business.

The corporal surveyed the carnage and merely shrugged, as if this sort of slaughter happened all the time. Jacques's shoulder was in poor shape, but they bound it up as best they could. Then at least, the blood stopped flowing.

The infantrymen scavenged whatever they thought would be useful. Water, food, weapons, ammunition and the Yankee dollars all received attention. The dead men's worn boots and tattered clothing were deemed unworthy, and they showed no interest in the horses at all. They also found Pepita, who recovered slightly and managed to sit up, although she felt as if her head had been stoved in by a hammer. The soldiers showed a great deal of interest in her. With her hands still bound and head spinning she was unable to put up much resistance. A burly trooper heaved her over his shoulder and marched away.

Jacques was in too bad a condition to walk, so the soldiers helped him onto one of the horses and led it along the trail. Light as she was, the burly trooper soon tired of carrying Pepita, especially as her senses returned and she began to struggle. So he hoisted her up behind Jacques and made sure she stayed there, prodding her with his bayonet if she showed any inclination to escape.

With some daylight left, the soldiers reformed and marched away to find a suitable campsite.

'Sounds like our lads are at it again,' Petorio observed on hearing the popping of gunfire. 'Dammed if they don't attract trouble like troopers to a whore-house.'

'Maybe they caught up with Jubal and Billy,' Zeb suggested.

'I don't think so,' Sam said. 'That's volley fire if ever I heard it. They've run into something new altogether. C'mon, let's go and see what they've done this time.'

They cantered along the trail until they reached the battle scene. The bodies of the Kid and Bad Roy lay where they had fallen. Three horses grazed idly together amongst the pines. The column of soldiers was just disappearing as they marched determinedly away. Sam and Petorio caught a glimpse of their uniforms and exchanged questioning looks.

'What d'you reckon, Sam? You're the expert.' Petorio asked.

'Damned if I know, Mexican Fedarales maybe. They look a bit like Zouaves to me. Some of the volunteer, New England regiments wore outfits like that at the beginning of the Civil War, but the Army has standardised uniforms now. And what the hell would anyone other than Mexicans be doing here anyway?'

'We'd better take care then,' Zeb said. 'They seem able to carry out some damage when they've a mind to.'

Simply bypassing the troop was not an option. They had no idea whether any of the outlaws had escaped or been taken prisoner, and they needed that information. And then there was the girl. Sam had only seen through his telescope, but she was beguiling. He was convinced more than ever that she was no bandit's slattern, but a captive. She had just seemed so sad and vulnerable, so in need of protection. He'd thought of her all day, without being able to understand why.

'They've taken the girl with them, you know,' Petorio observed, reading Sam's thoughts. He was getting good at that.

'A damsel in distress or otherwise really shouldn't be our top priority right now,' Sam said absently, although he didn't mean it. But, he was still a lieutenant in the US cavalry and should not be distracted from his duty for any reason.

They tied the dead outlaws over their horses, and led the three spare mounts as they followed the mysterious soldiers into the twilight.

Their camp wasn't hard to find. The troopers had built a robust fire and began cooking a deer they'd brought down after a short hunt. Sam, Petorio and Zeb tethered the horses at a distance. They dropped the dead men onto the ground to unburden the animals. The horses would deter any coyotes and there were no signs of bears or wolves, so they'd be safe for a while. Petorio said he didn't want to lose his bounty just because local scavengers felt peckish.

They waited for moonlight, then with revolvers drawn, crept towards the camp. Petorio motioned them to stop. He'd spotted two sentries in the shadows, although they didn't appear particularly alert or sober. There was a lot of noise coming from the camp as the soldiers succumbed to the effects of mescal.

'Can you take care of the sentries?' Sam whispered to Petorio, who nodded enthusiastically.

'Don't kill anyone, just knock 'em out and tie 'em up,' Sam said. 'Zeb go with him, make sure he doesn't get too excited. Then spread out around the camp, I'll need cover. Give me one of your best whippoorwill calls when you're both in position.'

'You're going into the camp?' Zeb asked.

'Dunno, but I want to be prepared. I don't want to think they captured an innocent woman from the hacienda and we did nothing about it.

'You're just a saint among men, Sam,' Petorio grinned. 'Come on then Zeb, if you want to see a big, bad Apache in action.'

'I've snuck up on plenty of Indians in my time, chief, but show me what you've got.'

'Look and learn,' Petorio said and they silently melted into the night.

Petorio was as good as his word and subdued the first sentry with his pistol butt. He dropped into Zeb's arms. The mountain man dragged him to the stoutest tree and tied him securely. Petorio indicated for Zeb to stay put while he dealt with the remaining sentry. In this way they were equally positioned around the camp. Shortly Petorio located the other sentry and crept behind him. He stunned the second man and bound his hands and feet. He'd just finished and about to give the *all ready* signal when a shot echoed from the camp.

<h1 style="text-align:center">Chapter 12</h1>

'Sam, I declare you must be the most vexing man I know. You're the one who said, *wait for the signal,* damnit,' Petorio muttered and dashed for the camp only yards away.

Sam was no Petorio or Zeb when it came to sneaking around in the dark, but he crept close enough to be hidden in the shadows just beyond the firelight. He'd brought his sabre and it was the devil's own job to keep the damn thing from jangling as he moved, but it might be handy in a close fight. Mescal seemed to affect the soldiers at once, as if they were unused to strong liquor and they were quickly into the mood. Shouting and joking, they sank further into their cups, but Sam could follow little of it. They certainly weren't speaking much Spanish. He was no linguist, but he recognised snippets of French and English and what he took for German. It was all very confusing.

There was, however an orderliness about the camp if not among the troops. Two neat rows of bedding lay either side of the fire, their rifles were stacked trellis-style in three sets, evenly spaced around the camp. It appeared they'd eaten and cleaned up before the boozing began and their minds turned carnal. The diligent layout was what he'd expect of his own Tenth Cavalry troopers, although he'd never tolerate drinking on patrol.

Sam recognised Cottonmouth Jacques who looked seriously knocked about, but he was talking to some of the soldiers and sharing a drink. He saw the girl as well, and despite her tousled state, thought she was the prettiest thing he'd ever seen. It soon became clear that the soldiers thought so too. They dragged her kicking and scratching into the centre of the camp. The corporal ripped the camisole from her shoulders and dropped his breeches. There was no doubt as to his intent, or indeed that of the others. But rank had its privileges, even a lowly corporal got first go, although she would fight him all the way.

Sam was having none of it. There would be no rape tonight if he had anything to do with matters, and especially not against this girl, for whom he'd developed a perplexing fondness. Maybe it was just that she was so damned pretty.

He strode into the camp, sabre in one hand, pistol in the other. With no plan formed in his mind, he blasted a shot into the air.

'Now hold on right there!' he bellowed, holding the gun and sword at arm's length. 'Everyone freeze. There are guns trained on you right now, and if I don't kill the first man that moves, then goddamnit, my companions will.'

Exactly what he expected was unclear. He certainly looked fearsome enough and got their notice, but the response was surprising. The entire group snapped to attention including the corporal who added a salute. And it was no sullen acknowledgement, but a snappy *longest-way-up-shortest-way-down* effort that would have been acceptable at West Point. Of course the fact that his breeches were around his ankles detracted from the *spit-and-polish* effect somewhat. It was the drilled reaction of disciplined, enlisted troops in the presence of a commissioned officer.

About then Pepita realised no one was holding her, and did she make the most of it. Leaping to her feet, she laid into the corporal with punches, kicks and a barrage of abuse. It seemed to her things had changed little from the morning. She'd simply exchanged one bunch of violators for another. After landing a few really solid blows to the corporal's shins, she started on the others until Petorio stepped from the shadows and grabbed her firmly, but with commendable gentleness under the circumstances.

'Hush, Señorita,' he purred. 'Be still, please. No one is going to hurt you now. I promise.'

'He's right ma'am.' Sam said, rather formally all things considered. 'We've been trailing you and those bandits with a mind to liberate you. Trust me, it's the truth.'

That wasn't essentially correct when it came right down to it. The rescue idea was a late development, but Pepita didn't know that. She simmered down when she realised there was no immediate danger and really no choice. There was no chance of overpowering Petorio.

'You still back there, Zeb?' Sam called. He wanted the soldiers to know that even in all the commotion, he still had reinforcements, although the troops showed no indication for hostility.

'I got 'em covered just fine, Sam,' Zeb called. 'Let 'em know there's a Sharps buffalo gun here that'll blow 'em clean apart with a single shot. That'd be a mightily discomfortin' experience in my view.'

There was no argument from the soldiers.

'Just who are you men, anyway?' Sam demanded.

'Legionnaires, sor,' the corporal said with a thick, Hibernian drawl.

'French Foreign Legionnaires?'

'Exactly, sor, that's what we are.'

'You don't sound French as far as I can tell.'

'Well, no sor me darlin', that's the whole point, to be sure. We're *foreign* legionnaires. We're Jocks, Fritzes, Dutchies, English, Dons and Dagoes here, so we are,' the corporal said, turning to his men and giving them an *officers-can-be-so-thick-at-times* look. 'The Frenchies formed the Legion these thirty years past, to do the dirty business in their colonies, so they did sor.'

'Mexico ain't a French colony, damnit. What the hell are you doing here?' Sam asked.

'Now I'd say, sor, that's a long story.'

'I'm sure it is, but would you mind pulling your trousers up before we get to it, and leave the Lemat on the ground for the moment, please. I think it'd be a good idea if you put the hooch away and make some coffee instead. Then you can tell me all about it.'

Sam had a way of being civil, yet with a tone of authority that left you in no doubt that he meant business. So everyone calmed down and the legionnaires exchanged their lustful looks for rather sheepish ones. Pepita remained in a justifiable huff, but accepted a cup of coffee from Petorio. Cottonmouth Jacques simply looked puzzled.

'The Legion was sent here when Ferdinand Maximilian came to rule Mexico, so it was sor. We come a-marchin' in with fifes and drums a-playin'. Sure 'twas a grand sight, by all that's holy,' the corporal, whose name was Liam O'Brien, explained. 'It was an Emperor thing to be sure, concocted by France, Belgium, Austria and the treacherous English. They put a piss-farting Archduke on the throne in Mexico, so they did, hoping for a share of the action if it all worked out. Trouble is it didn't work out, no sor, not at all. The Juarista's up and rebelled as sweet as you please and we've been scrappin' with the devils ever since.

'We were a light company with two full platoons only months ago, so we were, with a captain to lead us, a lieutenant, two sergeants and nearly sixty men. By the Blessed Virgin, they were our glory days. But, they're mostly gone now, 'tis the brutal truth and shame of it. Fought like the furies north of Mexico City, so we did, then cut off from our battalion by all the saints, we were. There was no way back, rebels surrounded the city as thick as flies on a turd, and that's the truth of it. There was no breaking through, no sor, we could not. So we started north, sure there was no other way, by the Holy Mother and all the Saints, fighting like the devil for every step, we were. Some of these fellas scrapped in Italy and North Africa, and even a couple served in the Crimea, but the rebels fight like the very banshee, so they do, sor.

'Malaria, cholera, bandits, rebels, Indians, starvation and thirst, by all that is holy, they leaned us out, sor. Some died of sheer exhaustion or just lost hope and sure they were darlin' men all. What you see, sor is all that's left.'

'I understand why you'd be trigger-happy,' Sam observed sympathetically

O'Brien nodded. Considering his endless entreaties to holy deities, his conduct didn't reflect any particular piety.

'What exactly do you plan to do?' Petorio asked.

'Get to the border as quick as we can. 'Tis safe there at least, then we'll decide,' Liam said vaguely.

'You may not find it all that safe in the Arizona Territory,' Sam warned, 'but you're not far away. Another day and you'll reach Nogales just south of the border. There's even a road from there to Tucson.'

'Ain't that just the very devil of it now, but we'll only know by looking,' Liam said. He seemed to think that Arizonan danger was in some way inferior to Mexican danger.

'You might even find some more accommodating girls in Nogales,' Petorio added dryly.

'We've got money enough, to be sure' Liam said cheerfully. 'Considering those fellas weren't dandy dressers, by the holy Saint Patrick, they carried cash aplenty.'

Sam was going to say something about stolen loot, but decided it was better to let matters stand. He was all for bedding down for the night, but Pepita looked uneasily at the legionnaires. Petorio, sensing her wariness, suggested they return to the horses and camp there.

'No offence,' he said, 'but I think this young lady would be more comfortable elsewhere.'

'None taken, sor me darlin', none at all to be sure,' Liam said with a shrug. He even apologised to Pepita albeit grudgingly, explaining that the Legion ranks were mainly composed of felons on the run from most European police forces. Or, in his case, fleeing a lynching-party of outraged Sligo fathers for lustfully devaluing their daughters. So how did she expect them to behave? She gave him a searing look and didn't seem in a forgiving mood. Liam agreed with Petorio that it would be wiser to find more obliging girls in Nogales. Not that he minded fiery women, but conceded Pepita was probably beyond his capabilities. Sam was unsure who was now in more danger, Pepita or the legionnaires.

'I'll have to take him with me,' Sam said, indicating Cottonmouth Jacques. 'He's wanted in Tucson for murder and armed robbery, not to mention a host of crimes in three American States.'

Liam O'Brien shrugged once more. It was a matter of indifference to him.

'How come you didn't just kill him like the others?' Petorio asked.

'Said he was French,' Liam explained. 'To be sure, should've made no difference, but our officers were all French. It is the common language for the Legion of course. We all had to learn it. Sure it's not so hard if you use it all the time, though my grammar ain't the best. Come right to it, neither's my English and, to my shame I have none of the Erse at all. We just responded out of habit, that's the truth of it.'

He gave another shrug. Perhaps he wasn't French, but he'd picked up many of their languid ways. Sam couldn't find too much fault with his English either. He spoke with a mellifluous lilt and pronounced words like *devil*: *divil*, and *th's* as *t's*.

'I'll need the horse too,' Sam cautiously insisted, thinking there might be some objection. But, O'Brien said the legionnaires were proudly infantrymen who, formed in a solid square, could see off a cavalry charge every time. He considered horses nothing more than trouble. They needed constant care and were generally only useful as food. Sam was welcome to it.

Zeb stepped into the camp and hauled Jacques to his feet, slapping him around the head when he complained. He hadn't forgotten Jacques was a member of the gang that shot him, stole his watch and left him for dead. He wasn't particularly compassionately disposed towards Jacques.

'You've got a couple of fellers nursing sore heads out there,' he told Liam. 'They'll appreciate some of that mescal.'

So they took Pepita and Jacques back to the horses. Once more they hoisted the bodies across their saddles and travelled a little further by moonlight. In a while Sam judged them sufficiently removed from the legionnaires for Pepita's comfort, and they set up camp. They soon had a snug fire going and ate a little of their rations. Pepita was starving and relaxed noticeably after a meal.

Claude Valentine and Black Swamp Slim rode into the night. Claude knew his gang was in tatters. If the others had escaped the mysterious Zouaves, they'd have caught up by now. It wasn't as if they were setting a blistering pace, in fact Slim's tardiness was puzzling. Finally Claude reined to a halt while Slim caught up. Slim seemed vague, even for him. His eyes were glazed and his head hung slackly to one side.

'Should be safe enough to rest a spell,' Claude observed as he dismounted.

Slim didn't respond. As his horse stopped he slumped forward in the saddle.

'You okay?' Claude asked, showing concern when he chose to.

'Dunno,' Slim mumbled. 'I feel real peculiar, Claude. I reckon I got shot in the arse. It don't hurt much though.'

Claude reached up and dragged him from the saddle. Slim collapse to the ground, his legs simply crumpled like rubber. Claude turned him over and saw the damage. Slim's back was raked by shotgun pellets that had driven into his spine, severing sinew and nerve-endings as they'd torn their way through. The Lemat pistol had been devastating at short range. Slim's backbone was shattered, paralysing his legs and pelvis. There was no way he'd get back on his horse. Claude had seen many such wounds during the Civil War resulting in a unanimously dire prognosis.

'I can't get up,' Slim moaned pathetically. 'My back's all shot up.'

'It's a fact, Slim you're all blasted to hell and then some. But we'll just stop and rest here a spell while you recover yourself.'

Claude hoisted Slim into a sitting position.

'I'll just hang onto you until you get some feeling back, then we'll be on our way,' Claude said. 'Ain't no rush, them soldiers aren't on our trail.'

'You reckon I'll be okay, Claude?' Slim stammered.

'You'll be fine. You have my word on it, Slim. Have I ever lied to you?'

Slim's mind was never the sharpest, but by then it was pretty dull even by his standards. Had he been his usual self he'd have remembered that Claude lied to him all the time, but right now it was comforting just to have company.

'We've had some high old times eh, Slim?' Claude crooned. 'A ton of raids and stiff fights. Some good nights.'

He talked on in this way for some time, then drew his Adams pistol and blew the top of Slim's head off. He laid Slim gently by the side of the trail and covered him with a blanket.

'Someone will be along by and by to bury you good and proper for sure, Slim,' he said. 'I apologise, but I just don't have the time. I've got me a nigger and a breed kid to deal with. So long, son, I'm truly sorry you're dead, but I guess nothing lasts forever, and in our line of work it's most likely sooner than later.'

Damned fool that Slim was he'd saved Claude's life more than once. Above all, he'd been loyal, which was a rare quality indeed, and one of the few things Claude Valentine truly admired. He mounted up and rode away with genuine regret.

Cottonmouth Jacques sulkily filled them in on the details of events along the trail. Pepita added the bits he missed, and enjoyed jabbing his wrecked shoulder from time to time until Sam told her to stop. Strangely, she didn't seem to mind doing obeying him. When Jacques explained it looked as if Jubal and Billy had two women riding with them, Pepita quickly deduced that Teresita and Alameda must have gone along to catch up with Don Margil and the herd and give them news about the hacienda.

'They want their papa to make everything right for them again, as he always does,' she said. 'Since their mother died, he indulges them so. They both need a really good spanking. They're silly and playful, but we grew up together and I love them anyway. Maybe it's a duty, but I don't mind.'

Pepita explained that the Flagstaff lumber camp was north of Tucson somewhere, but she wasn't sure how far. If that was where Teresita and Alameda were heading, the question remained whether Jubal and Billy would stay with them all the way. It was unlikely Sam's posse could overtake them with Jacques in tow, and the corpses draped over their horses. Sam decided the best plan was to take the outlaws, dead and alive, back to Tucson. There was a reward to collect after all, and the bodies weren't getting any sweeter. They'd get some directions to Flagstaff and pick up Jubal and Billy's trail. No one had a better idea or wondered where Claude and Black Swamp Slim were. Well, no one except Pepita and Zeb maybe, and they kept their thoughts to themselves.

'Sure looks like the end of the line for you, Cajun boy,' Zeb said with relish. 'I don't reckon you'll get back to Kansas. They'll hang you in Tucson for sure. Of course that wound could just fester you to death first. You might take some comfort in that. I opine hangin'd be a right disagreeable experience.'

Pepita stuck close to Sam, as he was the only person she trusted right now, which was fair enough after what she'd been through. Zeb and Petorio were kindly, but Sam was the one who'd strode right up and saved her, and that wasn't to be dismissed lightly. Possibly it was his lack of guile, and the innocence in his eyes that she found engaging, or that she'd just liked him from the moment she first saw him.

'Y'know,' Zeb said, 'Cain't never understand rape myself. It just don't stand to reason.'

Petorio raised his eyebrows. Obviously he hadn't given the matter any thought.

'How's that so?' he asked, although he actually didn't care overmuch, but by now he'd learnt to humour Zeb.

'Well seems to me if women ain't in the mood then they ain't exactly, what I'd call juicy, if'n you know what I mean. Woman's just got to be in a juicy frame of mind to make canoodlin' worth a damn. And I surely don't see a woman about to be raped being disposed to juiciness. I'd say that'd be a right unsatisfactory experience.'

'I see your point,' Petorio agreed, but added nothing to the philosophy.

'I don't think we should talk that way in front of Pepita,' Sam protested, without knowing why and sounding a bit priggish.

Pepita smiled and inched closer to Sam, reassured that after a day of abuse, someone was prepared to embrace nobility and be her champion. Unlike the inhibited Spaniards, whose friars found fault and damnation in all of life's facets, Benigna had told her daughter much of lovemaking's wonders. She stressed that women needed to be proactive in these matters if they were to derive their full benefit. Fathers were less inclined to explain matters to their sons than mothers to their daughters. So men, she explained, were pitifully ignorant and prone to lustfulness unless given some guidance. Pepita was well aware of the risks of unwanted pregnancies and disease, but also that a time would come when she was ready to embrace such joys. But it was up to her, and she alone would know when that time was right and with whom she would share it.

And then, Señor Zeb Turner, she told herself with a coy smile, *though it's none of your concern, I shall be as juicy as any woman and it will not be an unsatisfactory experience.*

Pepita was exhausted and soon became drowsy. Sam wrapped his saddle blanket around her and she nestled against him. He gently placed his arm around her. She didn't find that disagreeable and even snuggled closer as she drifted off to sleep.

'Considering her dealings with men so far,' Petorio commented, 'she doesn't seem to mind you.'

'I don't think she sees me as a threat,' Sam replied.

'Now would you take that as a compliment, or not?'

'I'll take it as one,' Sam said with a smug grin.

No one had anything to say to Cottonmouth Jacques, so he dozed as well. Petorio took the first watch, and then Sam while Zeb covered the dawn shift. They awoke later than normal, expecting coffee. It was the last sentry's job to get a brew going and rouse the others, but that was not the case. Petorio nudged Sam.

'Zeb's gone,' he said. 'Took Jesse during his watch. I'd say an hour ago, maybe more.'

Chapter 13

'Now where the hell do you suppose he's gotten to?' Sam demanded. It was one of those pointless questions folk ask when it's perfectly obvious no one knows the answer or they would have said so. But Sam asked anyway. Petorio shrugged while Pepita stretched and rubbed her eyes. She'd slept really well after two harrowing days and Zeb Turner's whereabouts did not concern her.

'I'm sure he has his reasons.' Petorio said. 'He's a loner and liable to just up and wander without much communication. His trail leads our way, so I expect we'll catch up. Maybe he's just hunting up some lunch with that cannon of his.'

So they loaded up and headed off. In a while, heralded by buzzards and black vultures orbiting overhead, they came upon Slim's body. It was stiff and his face was pretty messy, but Sam recognised him right off. He'd been chasing the outlaws long enough to be intimately acquainted with them.

'Well, well, Black Swamp Slim as I live and breathe,' Sam gloated. 'Damned if these rascals ain't dropping faster than we can count. Claude Valentine must be getting downright lonely.'

'Zeb stopped and looked him over,' Petorio reported after scratching around in the dust. 'Slim's horse is just yonder, you want to bring him along, Sam.'

'Might as well. Hardly seems like it now, but he's worth five hundred dollars. No point in wasting it.'

So they hauled Slim across his saddle, secured him well and rode on.

Jubal and Billy had at last found a defendable spot for the night. Their horses were spent and they had to rest. It was a large rock, maybe the size of a small cabin that gave them a good lookout and plenty of cover as well as decent water flowing from a clear spring close by. Alameda and Teresita insisted they light a fire and frankly, Jubal and Billy were just too damned tired to argue. They had an excellent position and no one was likely to sneak up on them unnoticed, and the night was chilly.

The girls proved next to useless when it came to camping out, needing most things done for them and being overly coy about their toilet, but eventually they settled down. They too were exhausted, and after something to eat they were asleep in no time, snugly wrapped in their saddle blankets. Jubal took the first watch, changing with Billy a few hours before daybreak. The best vantage point was about half way up the front of the boulder, so the guard was posted there, while the others were hidden behind.

Billy hunkered down as comfortably as he could. Now he was a fairly alert sort of fellow when the mood took him, but being changeable by nature, he didn't make the best lookout. The fact that he experimented with Buckaroo Bob's harmonicas didn't improve his vigilance. Jubal was going to tell him to stop, but it sounded kind of sweet and he was soon asleep himself. By dawn Billy too, was dozing fitfully. There was a slight crunch as a boot heel scraped the rock. Billy heard it and jerked awake, but was a split second too late. Claude Valentine smashed his pistol barrel viciously across the side of Billy's head. He felt an instant of bone-jarring pain before being enveloped by a mind-numbing void.

Alameda and Teresita awoke early and giggled off to the spring to bathe. They squealed and splashed each other. The water was freezing, but they were enjoying themselves. Jubal grinned to see some gaiety for once. He took a bag of oats and hand-fed the horses. There was range grazing enough, but the thoroughbreds were used to a supplemented diet.

He heard the click of a pistol hammer being cocked. Spinning around, he was once again staring down the barrel of Claude Valentine's gun. Claude's glare was terrible. His face was livid and the scars on his cheeks seemed to swell awesomely.

'Goddamnit, I should have blown you to hell for the contraband piece of shit you are,' Claude hissed. 'I was a fool to have ever trusted a damned nigger. Most likely you ain't even a decent field hand, you son-of-a-bitch.'

'Where's Billy?' Jubal stammered with a chill streaking through his body.

'Back on the rock, he won't wake up for a time, and I'll finish him off before he does. After you, of course,' Claude said. He hadn't plugged Billy straight away, as the shot would've warned Jubal. 'Over all, I can't say as I mind killing folk, but your dyin' will give me particular pleasure.'

His eyes were piercing, they seemed to lance through Jubal's skull, and Claude relished the fear he saw there. Jubal knew there was no talking his way out of this one. He was riveted to the ground, almost hypnotised by Claude's gaze, so close, intense and filled with sheer hatred. Claude just stared, then almost imperceptibly the lustre faded from his eyes and his pupils glazed over.

He stood rigid for a moment then flopped to his knees, almost hovering midway. Finally he pitched forward and smashed face first into the dirt. A throwing knife was buried up to the hilt in his right shoulder blade. Jubal's gaze followed Claude as he fell, but as he raised his eyes he realised he'd simply exchanged one gun barrel for another. This time it was a Sharps buffalo rifle.

'Where the hell did you come from?' Jubal was incredulous. 'I really didn't think you'd pull through.'

'Nearly didn't,' Zeb Turner said, 'but I'm tough and I got some help along the way.'

Keeping his eyes on Jubal he inched towards Claude. He bent forward and pulled the knife from Claude's scapular, causing him to groan and spasm. Zeb wiped the blade across Claude's back and replaced it in its sheath.

'He'll live, I guess,' Zeb diagnosed with indifference. 'Turn him over, there's a good fellow.'

Jubal obeyed and heaved Claude onto his back resulting in more wincing and moaning.

'Now, I'll have my watch and chain, if it ain't too much of an imposition.'

Jubal removed the watch from Claude's waistcoat fob pocket and slowly passed it to Zeb.

'Much obliged, I'm sure,' Zeb said with a grin. 'It's what I came for. I know you meant well, but you'd have been better taking my cash money. This watch is a precious memento given to me by Joe Meek, probably the most notable mountain man of all.'

'Like I said at the time, I needed something to decoy the bandits away from you.'

'Yessir, I kind of ciphered as much, and for that I'm going to give you a piece of information that may interest you. It should make us even.'

'What sort of information?'

'Well, friend, them desperados ain't the only ones chasin' you.' Zeb announced. 'You got a cavalry lieutenant and an Apache scout hot on your trail, and they mean to take you back to Fort Pierce for trial on the charges of murder and desertion. Now to my way of reckoning there can only be one outcome for a darkie like you.'

'That's my opinion too,' Jubal said. 'But, I didn't kill no one. No sir.'

'I'm afraid most folk seem to think otherwise.'

'I take it Lieutenant McAlister and Petorio are the ones following me?'

'They surely are, and that Indian can track a man over granite after a rain storm, so you're going to have the devil's own job shaking him off.'

'I know. He's the best I've seen.'

'So, here's how I reckon we play this. I'm going to squat right down here with this rascal and wait for them to catch up. You can do pretty much as you please, but my suggestion is you high-tail it out of here as smart as you can. Seems to me that squares us up real neat. Now I warn you, I've warmed to them two fellers, they're tolerable company along the trail, so I'll probably just trek along with them for a bit. If it comes to a disagreement between them and you, I won't have no second thoughts in sidin' with them. I'll plug you as soon as look at you.'

'Fair enough,' Jubal conceded. 'I'd better see how Billy is. I don't reckon we have much time to spare.'

'Seems so,' Zeb agreed.

Alameda and Teresita showed up then, still glistening a little from the creek. They squealed in unison when they saw Claude and then Zeb menacing the camp with a buffalo gun. Jubal looked nervously at Zeb.

'I know they ain't hostages,' he said enigmatically without mentioning Pepita. He wasn't going to let Jubal know they had a good idea where the fugitives were heading. He thought he'd done enough for them already.

'No time for explanations,' Jubal addressed the girls. 'Pack up, we're out of here right now, and by God, I mean *right now!*'

Jubal's tone galvanised the girls into action. Billy was coming round. He was dizzy and his jaw had swollen to twice its size, turned livid purple and throbbed like blazes, but Jubal got him saddled up. He swayed a bit, but managed to stay on horseback.

'So long,' Jubal said to Zeb, 'and thanks.'

'You're welcome, but you won't likely find me so accommodatin' next time.'

'By the way, that watch was half-an-hour slow. You'd better check with Claude, 'cos I don't think he reset it.'

'I'll surely do that, but that ain't the issue where this timepiece's concerned, it's the sentiment.'

As the four riders disappeared, Zeb hauled Claude over to the boulder and propped him up against the rock face. Sitting seemed to reduce Claude's blood flow, although it pained him greatly.

'Didn't think you were the sentimental type,' Claude sneered.

Zeb hit him hard then stoked up the remains of Jubal's campfire, made some coffee and waited for Sam and Petorio.

Sure enough they turned up in a couple of hours. Claude was looking pretty green, even after Zeb had settled down and given him half a canteen of water. Pepita didn't care about his condition. She leapt from her horse and drew a knife she carried tucked into her skirt. She'd have slit Claude's throat, but Sam tackled her at the last moment, pulling her away from Claude and wresting the knife from her grip.

'Let go!' she screamed. 'He killed my Papa, he deserves to die.'

'And so he will,' Sam said. 'He'll hang at Fort Leavenworth. Can't we at least take a couple of these bandits back alive?'

She fought a little more, but in the end she lost the inclination. She collapsed, sobbing against Sam's chest as he embraced her awkwardly. Her hatred had flared and withered, and for the moment she was a spent force. She sat by the fire and Zeb handed her his freshly replenished coffee mug, while Petorio and Sam eyed him curiously.

'What?' Zeb asked with a shrug.

'You wanna tell us about it?' Petorio said.

'Caught up with Claude all right, but tothers gave me the slip.'

Petorio sniffed around for a while, examining all the marks on the ground.

'Looks to me like they lit out a few hours ago, still headin' north. There're four of 'em for sure, it's an easy trail to follow.'

So they resumed the trek, shortly approaching Nogales, and the moment Sam was dreading.

'We'll leave you in town,' he said with regret to Pepita. 'I'm sure there'll be folk who'll take you back home safely.'

She pondered on that for a while and then shook her head.

'No, Señor McAlister, if you do not mind, I will come with you,' she said. 'I will see this scum behind bars in Tucson at least. I think I must find Alameda and Teresita too. They will need someone to look after them, they are not very practical.'

Sam thought that in Jubal and Billy's company they might have to learn some practicality, but kept it to himself.

'But what about your mother, she'll want to know you're safe?'

'I must go with you,' she insisted, with a pleading look that he found irresistible.

Petorio and Zeb exchanged glances, shrugged and said nothing.

So they stopped at a general store in Nogales, where Don Margil often bought supplies. Pepita knew the owner and his family well. She wrote a letter to Benigna explaining she was in safe hands and would return with Alameda and Teresita. The storeowner promised to deliver the letter when he planned to travel south later in the week. Pepita took the opportunity to buy a wide-brimmed hat and some spare clothing that she was going to put on Don Margil's account, but cashed up Sam gallantly footed the bill for her. An extra blouse and cotton skirt would be useful along the trail.

They hadn't reached Tucson by day's end so they camped by the roadside a little before sunset. Petorio caught some rabbits and started a cooking pot with ample peppers, beans and wild herbs.

Sam blamed himself for what happened next, but it probably was unavoidable. You see, Bayou Jacques had been so pitiful all day that everyone rather forgot about him, being far more wary of Claude, who was recovering well from his knife wound. Jacques appeared benign by comparison and no one noticed as he quietly worked the rope that bound his wrists. It must have pained him considerably as he had to wriggle his injured shoulder a fair bit.

Eventually he was free and didn't waste time. Pepita was the nearest and most vulnerable target. He leapt forward, grabbed her and roughly hauled her to her feet. He drew the knife from her waistband and held it to her throat, drawing a rill of blood that dripped down her neck onto her heaving breasts.

'Nobody moves,' Jacques yelled, and everyone, including Claude obeyed. 'Now, here's 'ow this 'appens. You untie Monsieur Valentine and saddle up *les chaveau*, now! You will do it, or I kill the mademoiselle. You know I will, *oiu*?'

Sam's feet seemed rooted to the spot. There was nothing for it, the bandits would escape. After all his effort, it was a disaster.

'You will throw down your weapons,' Jacques ordered, occasionally lapsing into Louisiana patois in the excitement. '*Vite!*'

And that was his big mistake. Anyone could tell that defenceless, Claude and Jacques would simply gun them all down.

Zeb Turner was in no mood to embrace that concept. Indeed he saw no choice.

In a flash he levelled his Sharps rifle and a shot exploded through the night. The roar was overwhelming and the rush of the bullet's path could be heard for a split second. It burnt a piece of Pepita's hair as it passed and ploughed into Jacques's skull. The gun was designed to kill buffalo at long range, so it didn't leave much of his head on his shoulders. It vaporised to pulp, spraying blood, bone shards and sinew over Pepita.

She screamed and dived away from Jacques's torso. It stayed erect for a few seconds as jets of arterial blood gushed upwards. Then Jacques seemed to ooze like molasses to the ground in a crumpled heap. Claude saw his chance in the confusion and was about to bolt, but Petorio, ever a man to prioritise, anticipated trouble from him. He drew his revolver and belted Claude across on the back of his neck, knocking him down.

Sam rushed to help and comfort Pepita. She wailed into his shoulder staining his shirt with a fair portion of Jacques's remains. He turned to Zeb in a fury.

'What the hell do you think you were doing?' he raged.

'Getting us out of big trouble,' Zeb replied defiantly.

'You could have killed Pepita, goddamnit!'

'Listen Sam,' Zeb said, lowering his voice. 'She'll be fine after she's cleaned up. You know they'd have killed us as soon as we put our guns down. I'm sorry, but I didn't see any other way, and it got the job done, didn't it?'

'Hell, I thought it was a pretty damned good shot,' Petorio agreed. 'Nice one, old man.'

They were fond of Pepita, but obviously hadn't developed the same attachment Sam had. Amazingly she was the one to defuse things.

'I seem to be staining your shirts a lot lately. I wonder if we can still claim the reward without his head,' she mumbled into Sam's shoulder, even managing a smile and there were no more tears.

'Yep, and we still have one almost whole villain left,' Petorio said, checking Claude's bonds and securing him to a nearby tree. 'I don't think I killed him when I belted him.'

'He'll have to piss in his pants if he wants to go on my watch,' Zeb said, ''cos I ain't untyin' him for nothing.'

Sam took Pepita down to a creek that ran beside the road and on into the Santa Cruz River. They found a quiet pool surrounded by soft grass that grew after the spring storms. He brought their saddle blankets, his spare shirt and Pepita's new clothes.

To his surprise Pepita was not at all reserved in front of him. She undressed as if it was the most natural thing in the world and waded naked into the water carrying her blood-splattered clothing. She gave a little squeal as she sank to her shoulders, rinsing her blouse and herself, then she bobbed under the surface to clean her face and hair. When she re-emerged she faced Sam and waded back to knee-deep water.

'Do you like what you see, Señor Sam?' she asked, smiling flirtatiously.

'I don't recall seeing anything that pleased me more,' he admitted.

'I think you need to bathe as well, Señor Sam,' she said with what he discerned to be a brazen wink.

Sam was flabbergasted. Not that he was unaware of female bodies, but he realised then that he hadn't given the matter nearly as much attention as he should. She looked purely beautiful in his eyes. Naïve he might have been, but he wasn't a complete idiot either. He pulled off his boots, unbuckled his gun-belt and stripped down to his underwear, then splashed into the creek. It certainly was bracing, but he hardly noticed. He gathered Pepita in his arms and kissed her with a passion he hadn't realised he was capable of. For once no instruction manual was necessary.

'Señor Sam,' she whispered. 'It is time for me to give freely to one man what so many men have tried to take by force.'

Sam hesitated. This was a big leap for him.

'*It is time*, Sam,' she insisted huskily. Pepita was a headstrong woman when it came right down to it, and she'd made up her mind, so that was pretty much that.

They might have been a bit hesitant and awkward at first, but being young and enthusiastic they took to lovemaking straight away and got the hang of it in no time. Sam couldn't believe how anything could just feel so downright nice. A strict Presbyterian upbringing might have been a drawback with all the inhibitions those good, God-bothering folk imposed, but he overcame that disadvantage commendably. So the next couple of hours passed with more pleasure than Sam thought possible. Pepita reflecting on her mother's admonition not to place too high an expectation on love's first encounter, found to the contrary, she wasn't disappointed at all.

Was her passion driven by the danger and excitement of the previous days? She didn't rightly know, and cared even less. Certainly the fact that life expectancy in Northern Sonora was proving tenuous, may have helped in a *grab-it-while-you-can* sort of way. When it came right down to it, she was just really enjoying herself. By midnight they were both feeling pretty good and smug about how things had worked out..

'So, do you find me juicy enough, Sam?' she asked mischievously.

'I guess so,' he stammered, which seemed a pitifully inadequate response, but Pepita understood his sincerity and that was worth an entire volume of florid prose.

Exhausted and hungry they returned to the camp where Petorio had kept some rabbit stew for them, occasionally stirring the pot and adding water so it didn't dry out.

'Now there's an interestin' development,' he said to Zeb who was curled up and trying to sleep.

'Yep,' Zeb murmured. 'Looks like Sam has got himself a girl. To my way of thinking, soon as she'd set her mind on it, the boy didn't have a chance. I wonder if they remembered to get their laundry done.'

Petorio doled out some supper and a cup each of good bourbon he'd saved. Zeb woke up enough to join in, and they celebrated with a toast. Petorio and Zeb agreed to share the night watch, believing Sam probably wouldn't be able to stay awake anyway. So he and Pepita bedded down together, relaxed in the notion that they wouldn't have to sleep alone again.

Next morning Sam awoke feeling he was pretty much king of the world with Pepita beside him as they rode into Tucson.

'At least we'll sleep in a bed tonight,' Sam declared with relish. Pepita smiled shyly, and seemed just as pleased at the thought. Zeb and Petorio were less enthusiastic and Claude wasn't consulted at all. In his experience, Petorio found hotel beds to be more often than not lumpy, of a dubious sanitary standard and accompanied by fleas. Zeb harboured similar misgivings, but Sam was all fired up and there was no discouraging him.

Riding through Tucson's main boulevard attracted attention, as it must when you lead four horses with bodies in varying stages of decay and mutilation strapped over the saddles. A blizzard of flies swarming over the corpses didn't help their anonymity. Quite a crowd fell in behind them as they reined to a halt outside Marshal John Reynolds' office. They didn't have to enter because Reynolds was on the street immediately. If there was one thing he couldn't abide, it was folk grossing up his main boulevard with festering humanity.

'What in blue blazes have you got there?' he bellowed, clattering down the boardwalk steps.

'Why, outlaws, Marshal,' Sam replied cheerfully. 'We done bagged the lot of 'em, except a couple of Comanche boys and Buckaroo Bob Scoresby who's dead. I don't rightly know where the Indians are, but they're out in Apache country, so I ain't bettin' on their chances.'

'How the hell would you know, they're all shot to pieces?'

'We did identify 'em before they got shot,' Sam insisted.

'And you expect me to believe you?'

'Yessir, I'm a US Cavalry officer. I'm sworn to tell the truth,' Sam was rather enjoying Reynolds's bewilderment, and was having fun messing with him. In fact since he and Pepita had become lovers, he was in a pretty good mood just about all the time.

'We've come to collect the reward,' Zeb reminded everyone.

'Well, that's just fine,' Marshal Reynolds said, 'but how am I supposed to verify these are in fact the desperados who robbed our bank?'

'Why, sir, you have my word,' Sam insisted.

'That may not satisfy Governor McCormick, who just happens to have returned from Prescott.'

'Then you'll have to notify Fort Leavenworth. They'll send Major Schofield to sort matters out.'

'In the meantime I'd better lock up this one live fellow, while you take the others over to Waylon Doolan's cold storage up the street. We can't have them getting any riper.'

'Cold storage?' Sam quizzed.

'Yessir,' Reynolds said. 'Old Waylon carts ice down from the mountains by the wagonload all winter. Dug hisself a great hole in the ground and built an adobe block house around it. Why, he keeps ice all summer and sells it for twenty dollars a bucket come July. Now ain't that enterprise for you?'

They rode over to Waylon's place and after, some discussion about the condition of the *meat,* as he called the bodies, they piled them in a corner of one of his ice pits.

'You think the marshal'll renege on the reward money?' Petorio asked.

'Dunno,' Sam replied, 'it may not be up to him. Depends on what the governor says, I guess.'

They checked into a hotel in the Presidio where Pepita enjoyed a hot bath and insisted Sam join her. He certainly found that to be a novel and pleasant experience. She had a habit of coming up with good ideas he would never have thought of. Afterwards Sam wrote a detailed report to Major Schofield and mailed it at the Butterfield Stage agency. After siesta Pepita showed him the Old Spanish town. They ate an early supper, drank a little wine and danced a piece in the cantinas. They talked and talked, happy to discover so much about each other. Sam couldn't remember when he'd had a better time until Petorio and Zeb found them.

'You sure chose a good time to lose focus, Sam,' Zeb admonished. 'We've got trouble and it'll be headin' for the jail any time now.'

Sam gave him a questioning look.

'We were having a beer at one of the saloons on the boulevard,' Petorio said, 'when a couple of Governor McCormick's pistol-hands came in buyin' drinks all round and agitatin' the crowd. Seems he's still pretty steamed up about his missus getting killed and wants the justice process sped up some.'

'Maybe it's best in the long run,' Zeb suggested.

Sam glared at him. He was having none of it. That wasn't his style. They'd brought in a prisoner and he'd receive a fair trial no matter how villainous he was.

'We'd better get over there in case the marshal needs help,' Sam said.

They left Pepita safely at the hotel and the posse of three headed for the jail where a noisy crowd was rapidly building. Marshal John Reynolds stood at the jailhouse door, his legs braced with a shotgun at the ready. Sam, Zeb and Petorio stomped along the boardwalk and stood beside him.

'Looks like a difference of opinion, Marshal,' Sam observed.

'Seems so, don't it? Appears that Governor McCormick's lackeys have been stirrin' up these local boozers and they want Claude Valentine swinging from a tree directly. I could only drum up one deputy who's guardin' him inside with a scatter-gun.''

'You care?' Petorio asked dryly.

'Yessir, I care,' Reynolds snapped. 'Some folk around here don't necessarily admire my ways, but I won't have mob rule without my say so. That fellow back in the cell rode with Jeb Stuart and Nathan Forrest during the War, and that damn well counts for something in my book.'

It seemed that rebel cavalry still bonded even two years after Appomattox. But the crowd was getting ugly and there sure were a lot of them. Liquored up with Richard McCormick's free booze, they didn't need much encouragement. A sly looking fellow at the head of the pack had even brought a rope and was tying a noose, encouraged by his cronies. A lot of backslapping and mutual confidence-building swelled through the mob.

Then a shot cracked into the night air and Pepita marched through the swirling sea of drunkards, brandishing Claude's confiscated Adams pistols. The startled crowd parted as she strode onto the boardwalk beside Sam.

'Of all people, I want this man dead,' she yelled. 'He killed my father and tried to ravish me, but this is not the way!'

The trouble was that one gunshot and the sight of a tiny woman, albeit armed to the teeth, only distracted the crowd momentarily. Soon they were bellowing for rough justice once more, and her voice was lost beneath the din.

'What the hell are you doing here?' Sam hissed, glaring at Pepita. 'Can't you see it's dangerous?'

'Why, I've come to your aid, my darling,' she replied, giving him her sweetest smile, and wondering what he thought had been safe about the past few days.

At that second, with a single roar the mob surged forward, but this time a volley of musketry halted the charge as bullets ripped up the dirt at their feet. The vigilantes shuddered to a halt, with those behind pushing over some of their comrades in front. They fell silent. The French Foreign Legionnaire troop had formed in two ranks across the boulevard. Liam O'Brien stood at their side with his Lemat pistol raised.

'You will disperse!' he roared, all authority although no jurisdiction, but he was used to this sort of thing. Controlling unruly mobs in Mexico and North Africa had been a daily part of the job, just in a different language.

The mob recognised that facing down a small group who could be easily overwhelmed before they got off a shot was one thing, but taking on a dozen trained soldiers was quite another. The crisis was defused and the crowd quickly sobered up. They skulked away grumbling among themselves. The Legionnaires sloped their rifles over their shoulders and marched past the marshal's office.

'Thought we'd take up your suggestion about Tucson, sor,' Liam called as they went by. 'It seems like a nice, lively town, don't you know?'

'Thanks for your help,' Sam said.

'A pleasure for sure, sor me darlin'. Evenin', miss,' he added, cheerfully waving to Pepita. 'Pleased to see you in such fine health, now that I am.'

Despite their past differences she smiled back as the Legionnaires disappeared along the boulevard. Although she could never condone being taken by force she was in a more forgiving mood.

'You might want to deputise that lot,' Sam said to Reynolds.

'I could do just that,' Reynolds conceded, 'but first I'm going to tour the saloons and crack a few heads together so it'll discourage another attack on the jail.'

'You think Governor McCormick will drop the idea?'

'It's unlikely, Lieutenant. He's mightily cut up about his missus, and the town ain't too keen on the fact that there have been three other murders with no one swinging for 'em.'

'I think I might pay the governor a visit and talk things over,' Sam said. 'I'll wager Claude Valentine deserves the rope, but there *must* be a trial.'

'Justice *seen* to be done, eh?' Reynolds commented cynically.

'It's better than a lynch mob. Let 'em lose on one suspect, and they may get the taste and choose someone less deserving next time.'

'You do what you think you must, Lieutenant, but I'm going to discourage them in the old fashioned way.'

With that Marshal John Wilson Reynolds, rifle in hand, strode down the boulevard to dispense his own brand of crowd control.

Governor Richard McCormick had established himself in one of the best hotels close to the Spanish Presidio. He was enjoying supper surrounded by his tame deputy sheriffs, secretaries, advisers, administrative assistants, general toadies and a resident journalist who wrote only what he was told to. The governor knew the wisdom of distancing himself from the lynch mob. His hirelings may have stirred up the crowd, but he of course, claimed to know nothing about it.

Sam, Pepita, Zeb and Petorio had no difficulty seeing him. It was almost as if he expected them. The deputy sheriffs didn't bar their entry to the dining room, but escorted them straight to the governor's table.

'Well, howdy,' Richard McCormick greeted effusively. He rose and shook each of them by the hand with a decent, firm grip, gallantly kissing Pepita's in the process. They politely introduced themselves.

'Why, it's an honour to meet you fine heroes. I must congratulate you on bringing those vile perpetrators to justice. Come join me. I have some claret you might like to taste. Bring some chairs for our friends,' he added to a couple of secretaries who hopped to it, and soon four chairs scraped across the floor.

A waiter clinked glasses onto the table and poured the drinks. The wine wasn't bad either.

'We've come to tell you there's been trouble at the jail,' Sam came directly to the point.

'Thought I heard something,' McCormick said, 'but it's hard to tell, the jail's a way off. Nothing Marshal Reynolds can't handle I hope. Does he need help from my deputy sheriffs?'

You had to give Richard McCormick his due, he knew how to play the political game. And, he wasn't the head of the territory's largest newspaper for nothing either.

'No, sir,' Sam said, 'the marshal has everything under control.'

'Good, good,' the governor beamed, although there was just possibly a trace of irritation in his tone. 'Reynolds is a very capable fellow.'

'I was wondering if you might be able to prevent further disturbances.' Sam challenged.

'It's the marshal's problem, although I'll loan him any assistance I can,' McCormick indicated his deputy sheriffs who were certainly armed for the task with two Remington six-shooters and a Spencer repeating rifle each, as well as ammunition bandoliers strapped over their shoulders.

'I want Claude Valentine alive when I take him back to Kansas for trial,' Sam insisted.

'Why would you do that? We can just as easily try him for murder and armed robbery right here in Tucson.'

'He's wanted for prior felonies back east.'

Governor McCormick's mood changed. He didn't raise his voice, but his tone was unmistakable.

'Well, that ain't going to happen, Lieutenant, make up your mind to it. He killed four people on the streets of Tucson including my wife! He ain't going anywhere. This is an Arizona matter and it'll get dealt with in this territory.'

'Does it matter?' Pepita asked. She viewed a trip to Kansas as a very distant event, and how many lawyers would intervene before Claude got there? Here in Tucson the affair would be quickly resolved.

'It matters to me,' Sam said stubbornly.

'What about Jubal Quinn and Billy Songbird?' Petorio reminded him. 'They're the ones we started out chasin'. Claude and his rogues are just extra, we still ain't caught who we're really after yet.'

While the debate ensued, Richard McCormick beckoned one of his secretaries and whispered in his ear. The earnest young man in a serge suit and choking white collar scuttled back with an iron strong box and placed it on the table in front of the governor. McCormick took a key from his waistcoat pocket, opened the box and withdrew three wads of bank notes. He tossed them onto the table in front of Sam.

'There you go,' he said, all smiles again. 'There's a thousand bucks in each of those piles, reward money for bringing in the villains. One for each of you, five hundred dollars per bandit and a little bonus thrown in.'

He obviously didn't think Pepita had anything to do with apprehending criminals, and although that was mostly true, Sam thought he could have given her more credit.

'There's a moral principle involved,' Sam stammered lamely.

'Hell, what's a moral principle, but just a point of view?' McCormick argued. 'Why there're Mormons up in Utah who hold high moral principles that most normal folk dispute, what with all their wives and such. No, sir, there ain't no moral issue here, just pragmatism. You take the money and I'll take the jurisdiction.'

'Claude'll get what's coming to him either way,' Petorio said. 'It could be weeks before Major Schofield gets down here. Hey, we deserve the reward. It wasn't as if it was a Sunday picnic down in Sonora.'

'Wisely spoken, my aboriginal friend,' McCormick oozed. 'That's sound thinking if ever I came across it.'

Pepita looked at Sam with her pleading, irresistible eyes. Petorio's expression was clear, *get the money while it's on the table and head off after Jubal and Billy in quick time.* Zeb's thoughts were impossible to read. He'd reclaimed his watch after all.

'Why not put it a vote?' McCormick purred. He was a pretty shrewd poker player. In his view Sam and Petorio were known cards, and he reckoned he'd figured Zeb out. Ultimately Pepita proved the wild card. She considered she was just as entitled to vote as anyone, it was her father Claude had killed after all. She sided with Petorio and that was enough to tip the balance. Zeb went along with them.

'Okay.' Sam conceded. 'But, Claude must go to trial. I absolutely insist on it, or no deal.'

'Oh, he will,' McCormick assured him. 'I personally guarantee it. You have my *absolute* word in front of all these witnesses that it will be so.'

There certainly were plenty of witnesses, although the chance of them contradicting anything Richard McCormick said was unlikely. In any event they took the money, shook hands once again and left. Sam, still harbouring doubts about whether he could accept rewards, simply gave his share to Pepita. They had no reason to return to the jail so they went back to their hotel in the Presidio, decided to turn in early and resume their chase at first light. Now that an early night had its new attractions, Sam's misgivings soon faded.

Chapter 15

Teresita and Alameda were complaining to the point where it was driving Jubal and Billy to distraction. They rode along a trail to the east of Tucson, but the girls wanted to stop in town. This made little sense, as there were plenty of signs indicating Don Margil's herd was only a short way ahead. Cattle tracks were plain to see, indicating where they had grazed during rests and night stops.

'Oh, *Joooble*,' Teresita mewed, pouting in a way she knew her father could never refuse. 'Can't we please stay in Tucson tonight? The Presidio is so gay. There's music and dancing, and the food is magnificent. Papa takes us there whenever he goes to town on business. Oh, we must stay there tonight.'

'You seem to forget that we're wanted men in Tucson, Miss Teresita,' Jubal reminded her. He was obviously not as easily swayed as Don Margil. 'And, from what that minin' fella said, I figure Lieutenant McAlister has given the local law a good description of us. It would be plumb foolishness to go anywhere near town.'

'But we have been riding for so long. You wouldn't want my bottom to get blisters, would you, Jubal?' she said, eying him flirtatiously.

'I ain't riskin' my neck just so you and Alameda can go cavortin'. Now hush up, girl, we'll keep goin' for another hour or two.'

'A piece of cavortin' sounds fine to me,' Billy said, seriously muddying the waters.

'You got a death wish, or what?' Jubal challenged. 'Besides, your head's still all swollen and black where Claude thumped you. I don't think any gals'll be dancin' with you for a while yet.'

'I would dance with you all night, Billy,' Teresita said. She pronounced his name *Beeley*, which he found charming in its way. 'You are so brave to be wounded and not complain at all.'

'Got the sense knocked out of your head more like,' Jubal said. 'Don't forget we've got an Apache tracker on our tail who can't be far behind.'

The girls were deploying a classic *divide-and-conquer* strategy, but Jubal was made of sterner stuff and led them north. As a concession to the girls' saddle-sore behinds they went at an easy pace and camped earlier than usual. Jubal and Billy normally took turns in hunting game, but as Billy's jaw was so badly bruised, Jubal took on the chore full time until he got better. There was normally a fair amount of game around: jackrabbits, pronghorns and even raccoons if you were in the mood. Sometimes they'd fish in the bigger creeks and waterholes. Jubal left large prey alone as they simply didn't have the horsepower to cart extra rations around, but by-and-large, they didn't often go hungry.

Jubal bagged a couple of decent sized hares and a huge rattler that tasted a bit gamey, but wasn't bad once you got your head around the fact you were eating a snake. Billy had shown him how to boil up the meat first, and then stew it with beans and chillies in the Texas style. Jubal was content with his haul. It was after dark when he returned to the camp. With moonlight enough to guide him, he spied the fire from a distance. But, although it blazed heartily, the camp was empty. Billy and the girls were gone, and so were their horses.

The little buggers, Jubal thought, shaking his head wearily. *They just couldn't leave it alone, could they?*

He doused the fire and headed back to Tucson, cursing the fact that he wasn't even going to get any supper. The easiest thing to do was to just camp out and head north in the morning, leaving them all to their fate. But, of course he wasn't going to do that. Although Billy was insufferably fickle, he had winning ways and Jubal liked him. As for the girls, well he'd said he'd take them to their father, and that's just what he intended to do. It had been *their* idea after all.

It was past midnight when he rode into Tucson. Mostly the town was quiet except for some mumbled carousing from a couple of saloons and beer tents along the main boulevard. The Presidio was another matter. Singing and guitar music drifted from several cantinas where tequila and mescal flowed without reservation.

He found Billy and the girls in about the third or fourth bar room he visited. Teresita and Alameda were dancing wildly with some Mexican vaqueros while Billy, despite his swollen jaw was belting out songs for all he was worth. The fact that his belly was full of mescal probably deadened the pain. He was also getting quite good at accompanying the guitarist with Buckaroo Bob's harmonicas.

Luckily they'd arrived in Tucson while Sam and his companions were visiting Governor McCormick otherwise they'd have surely bumped into one another.

It was a testament to Jubal's forbearance that he let them revel on for an hour or so. Truth to tell, after his long ride he was enjoying the music, a beer and a tasty plate of tortillas and chilli beef. The rattler could wait for tomorrow's stew pot. The cantina was full of laughter and fun. Cigar smoke drifted to the ceiling and the efficient barman ensured that booze flowed freely. A few card games were in progress and bar girls toured the crowd, cheerfully touting for business.

But, eventually Jubal decided they'd delayed long enough and it was time to go. The girls were reluctant, although Billy was really beyond putting up much resistance. But, a couple of the Mexican charros, who'd succumbed to Teresita and Alameda's teasing ways, had different ideas.

'Donna dew theenk dew can tak' these señoritas outa here,' one drunkard slurred through a shaggy, mescal drenched moustache. 'We ain'ta gonna let dew, no, no, Señor Blackie.'

He took a swing at Jubal, who easily dodged aside and cracked the cowboy's jaw open with a solid punch that stung his fist like crazy. Another vaquero charged at him, but he was full of mescal and Jubal had time to draw his pistol and clubbed him down. Two more piled into Jubal, knocking him to the floor. His pistol skidded away and clanked against a spittoon. They hammered punches into any part of Jubal they could hit although alcohol blurred their aim more often than not.

Billy sobered up in a flash and entered the fray. He dived for Jubal's revolver. Retrieving the gun, he laid into Jubal's attackers. A couple of good stiff clouts across their ears did for them and they tumbled off Jubal. There were four more Mexican cowboys who decided to join the melee. Jubal leapt to his feet and met one of them head on. He adopted a pugilist stance and drove home several quick, mean jabs, knocking the man senseless. Billy was less stylish, but equally effective. He stuffed Jubal's pistol into his belt, and grabbed the nearest chair. He swung it with all his strength, smashing it across a vaquero's face, spraying splinters, teeth and blood everywhere. Teresita grabbed a tequila bottle from the bar and crashed it over the nearest cowboy's skull dropping him to the floor while Alameda helped despatch the last fellow with the spittoon. She squealed in horror as some of its tobacco stained, bile-ridden contents oozed out and down her arm. In a reflex she grabbed the bartender's apron and wiped the goo off. The bartender, ever a man to provide service in his establishment, produced a water pitcher for her.

The fight was over. Alameda calmed down after dousing her arm and washing it clean. Jubal left two twenty-dollar bills on the bar to cover the damage and disruption, and the four of them stepped over the groaning, wrecked vaqueros. Feeling pretty satisfied about *a job well done*, they strode out of the cantina, mounted up and rode towards the boulevard.

As they approached the main street they heard a terrible commotion. Several armed men marched up the boulevard towards them. They carried torches and Jubal saw lawman's badges glinting on their chests. He signalled the others to stop and they took cover in a side alley, noisily kicking over some debris in the process, but the procession of lawmen was making so much fuss that the fugitives went unnoticed.

They saw Claude Valentine being dragged along the street. He was kicking and fighting and cursing until one of the deputy sheriffs tied a bandana over his mouth, pulling it harshly through his teeth and holding his tongue down firmly. Claude was thrown to the ground beneath a large tree that stood in a grove at the edge of town. The lawmen threw a noose around his neck and tossed the rope over a strong branch. They ungagged Claude and without any further ceremony, hauled him into the air. He bucked and kicked for quite some time before his body finally went limp and he was still. The lawmen secured the rope end to the tree trunk and simply walked away.

The four riders waited a short while before cautiously moving onto the street and checked to see that the deputy sheriffs had indeed gone. They rode beneath Claude's dangling body, staring in horror. His face was livid purple, and his blackened tongue lolled from between clenched, bloodstained teeth.

'Ain't a pretty sight, even in the dark, is it?' a cold voice spoke from the shadows. They heard the familiar click-clack of a rifle being cocked and a bullet injected into the breech.

Jubal, Billy and the girls spun around as one. A single lawman stood in the street, aiming his rifle at Jubal's chest. Jubal gasped an exasperated sign. *Goddamnit people just keep doing this to me*, he thought.

'Now you don't know who I am,' the town marshal said, 'but I've got a pretty damned good notion who you might be. My name is John Reynolds, and I'm supposed to be the law in this town although that authority seems to have been usurped lately. I've got enough trouble on my plate right now, without you adding to it. So if you don't want to wind up looking like this fellow here,' he waved the rifle at Claude, 'you'd better get going as fast as you can.'

Jubal thought he was getting a lot of that sort of advice lately, with a couple of let-offs thrown in. He needed no more encouragement. With a nod to Reynolds, he spurred his horse into a canter and led the others out of town.

Possibly I'm letting two bank robbers go, Marshal Reynolds thought, *but possibly not. Anyway if Richard McCormick wants to take the law into his own hands, he can do his own bandit chasing.*

Petorio brought the horses to the hotel at dawn, as the Presidio barely stirred. A few market stalls were opening, but generally folk stayed up late and slept late in the Spanish style. The rest of Tucson was quiet. Blue smoke drifted into the calm, chilly sky from miners' tents, a few horses snorted in corrals and desert birds began their morning chorus.

Sam found it difficult to rise early from a cosy bed beside Pepita. He loved her closeness, exploring and continually discovering new ecstasies. He was intoxicated by her scent and the overpowering redolence of their lovemaking. He delighted in the soft caress of her fingers and stroking the smoothness of her arms and legs. He didn't regret having waited to experience such pleasure, believing it could only be possible with Pepita, which was a bit naïve, but he was still young and romantically idealistic.

Reluctantly they climbed from under the bedcovers and washed up. They joined Petorio and Zeb for a breakfast of eggs, tortillas, oranges and coffee then mounted up.

'Good thing we turned in early last night,' Petorio announced. 'Accordin' to the livery stable hand there was a fair old ruckus in one of the cantinas down the street. A couple of local cowboys got worked over pretty good. Said there was a big black fella involved.'

Sam and Zeb exchanged glances then dismissed the thought.

They rode from the Presidio and turned north into the main boulevard and on to the edge of town where huge Jacaranda trees grew, transported from central Mexico and planted by the original settlers. They were in full bloom with great lilac-blue pools scattered around each trunk. The rising sun's rays pieced through the branches silhouetting Claude Valentine's body dangling beneath one of the sturdier boughs. It swayed just slightly as a zephyr rustled through the leaves. Blossoms drifted down, covering Claude's head and shoulders.

John Reynolds sat propped against one of the tree trunks with his rifle across his thighs. He'd been up all night and looked tired, drawn and in a sour frame of mind.

'So you reckon thirty pieces of silver were worth it?' he sneered.

'Goddamnit! Goddamnit!' Sam roared. 'That bastard McCormick double-crossed us. He promised Claude would get a fair trial.'

'He didn't actually say anything about the trial being fair,' Petorio observed.

Sam glared at him.

'But, he did promise a trial, I'll grant you,' Petorio added hastily.

'Oh, he got a trial all right,' Reynolds said.

'But, there was no time,' Pepita said.

'Time enough, as it turned out,' Reynolds said. 'Just before midnight McCormick's deputy sheriffs bustled into the jail, guns out and took over the place. They charged Valentine there and then with murder, robbery, rape and God knows what else. The governor dug up some pettifogging charlatan to conduct a defence just to make it all legal and proper.'

Reynolds than recounted what could only be described as a judicial travesty or good, old-fashioned western law-enforcement, depending on your point of view. Claude Valentine may have been guilty to the core, but there was little evidence to prove he'd committed the particular crime for which he stood trial. No witnesses had actually seen him rob the Tucson Municipal Bank, and no one claimed they saw him murder any of the victims.

Claude said nothing in his defence, just cursed the court for the stinking, abolitionist sons-of-bitches they were. The money found on him was ambiguous, and the bank manager acknowledged that there was no way of identifying one bank note from another. Although Sam had shown Reynolds the money he found, he'd not actually surrendered any of it to the marshal. This reluctance was understandable as Reynolds was unable to guarantee where the cash would wind up.

While Claude's gang of ragamuffin trail tramps was suspiciously solvent, it was by no means proof of a crime. Whiskey Van Harper had definitely been at the scene and was identified as one of Claude's gang members. Claude's connection was still circumstantial and the court didn't bother to call Sam for corroboration. Whiskey Van Harper's involvement was probably the most damning piece of information although no proof existed that Claude was actually riding with him at the time, but it was close enough. Vengeance, rather than proof was the issue in this case. In any event men had been convicted on far less evidence in the past, which could have been seen as a legal precedent.

In the absence of a jury, Richard McCormick, acting with governor's prerogative found Claude guilty and glibly sentenced him to death. So, once more Claude was led to the gallows, but this time he knew what to expect. He knew it wasn't going to be pleasant and he didn't go quietly. In case they interfered, Marshal Reynolds and his deputy were relieved of his side arms. The weapons were only returned once Claude was hauled cursing and struggling from the ground and his legs had ceased twitching. Claude's face, now drained of oxygen, looked a very similar colour to the jacaranda blooms. For a moment Pepita's eyes were drawn irresistibly to Claude's savaged face, and then she turned away with a gasp. Justice may have been served, but there was no satisfaction for her in the end.

'I'm just glad it's all over,' she whispered.

'What do you plan to do now?' Sam asked Reynolds.

'Cut him down and bury him, I guess,' the marshal replied. 'I knew you'd be comin' by this way, just wanted you to see how things panned out. I'm not here to give you trouble. Like you said, Confederate Cavalry or not, he probably had it comin'.'

'I'm sorry it ended this way,' Sam said.

'So am I. I don't care for things getting out of my control in my town. There's no more room for me here with Governor McCormick and his deputy sheriffs. I'm heading out just as soon as I've finished at the undertaker. There's a mining camp just started south east of here that some wag has named Tombstone. I think I might try my luck there.'

He unclipped his marshal's badge and tossed it into the dirt.

'This should cover the cost,' Zeb said, handing Reynolds a hundred dollars in bills.

The marshal didn't refuse.

'Thanks,' he acknowledged, 'looks like there'll be enough left over for a drink.'

'Reckon so, adios.'

'Adios. Things didn't go all your way though,' Reynolds added. 'I heard there was a fight in the Presidio last night. Heard a big, buck nigger was involved.'

'Heard that too, it don't necessarily signify,' Sam replied.

'Maybe not,' Reynolds said with just a hint of smugness, 'but I heard he had a half-breed kid and a couple o' feisty Mex gals with him. Now, that might signify.'

Could they have been so close, and simply missed their mark? Sam couldn't believe it, and Reynolds's attitude told him all he needed to know.

'I'm guessing you had 'em and you let 'em get away,' he challenged.

'Let's just say they're kinda slippery customers.'

And for the second time that day the marshal watched a quartet of riders hasten northwards in a swirling dust cloud and clatter of hoof beats.

Chapter 16

'I'll bet that son-of-a-bitch Reynolds told 'em we were after 'em,' Sam seethed as they rode through the morning. He was so hopping mad he could hardly contain his rage. Zeb wisely decided not to mention the fact that Jubal Quinn already knew a posse was on his tail.

'Don't sweat it,' Petorio advised. 'Things could be a whole lot worse. They ain't that far ahead and look the trail's easy to follow. You could do this on your own.'

Sam couldn't see what was so easy about following such a well-used trail, but Petorio knew his business. Soon he found the spot where Jubal, Billy and the girls cut away from the main road to Prescott and rejoined the eastern cattle trail.

'They've been ridin' all night so they'd have to go slow and careful. They'll need to rest their horses too,' Petorio said. 'I reckon we'll catch up before nightfall.'

Actually Jubal and the others were making good time. Teresita and Alameda were finally used to dismounting and walking the horses part of the way. They'd stopped complaining and seemed to be enjoying the exercise. They had been smart enough to pull on decent riding boots before leaving Hacienda O'Conor and now they threw their jackets over their saddles as the day warmed up. They were comfortable in cool blouses and riding skirts. They both flirted outrageously with Billy, saying how much they admired his singing and harmonica playing. The fact that he was a good-looking boy didn't hurt either, not to mention last night's bar room bonding.

'Don't let 'em turn your head,' Jubal admonished. 'Once you get *woman distracted* and the blood rushes from your brain to the front of your pants, there ain't no sense nor concentration to be had from a man. You remember that, Billy.'

'Why Jubal, I do believe you're plumb jealous because them gals have taken such a fancy to me.'

'No doubt that's probably true,' Jubal admitted, 'but we're gonna need your full attention if Lieutenant McAlister shows up.'

'I'll be good,' Billy promised, but he didn't mean it for a second.

They spied a distant cavalry patrol and met another ranging out of Fort Whipple after Apache raiding parties. It was an anxious moment, but the veteran lieutenant in charge was unaware of their notoriety and told them he'd seen a cattle herd not far ahead. He said they'd catch up in no time and bid them good day, wondering about their hasty departure.

The day was becoming humid and unsettled. A cold air mass was pushing down from Alaska and colliding with warm, sultry, south-easterly winds from the Gulf of Mexico. By midafternoon huge thunderheads surged up from the west generating green-grey hail clouds and spectacular lightning bolts with the distant rumble of thunder. Jubal hoped they'd find either a cabin or a cave for shelter, or they were likely to be in for a wet night.

The lieutenant's advice proved correct and they soon spotted the cloud of dust churned up by the long horns. Don Margil had found good grazing and stopped for a couple of days to fatten up the herd before driving them on the last leg of their journey. Teresita and Alameda squealed with delight and galloped ahead to meet their father. When Jubal and Billy caught up they'd finished hugging him and barraged him in babbling Spanish about their adventures.

Don Margil was a man of correct appearance, even on a cattle drive. His hair was pulled neatly into a queue and his goatee meticulously trimmed. His vaqueros were much more what you'd expect, covered with trail grime wearing wide brimmed sombreros and leather chaps. There was some concern from the cowboys until the girls reassured them everyone had been saved except Pepita and Javiero, and after that it wasn't hard to identify Pepita's brother, Segundo. In a wailing tirade he vented his grief and frustration. Jubal couldn't understand a word, but he got the gist of it.

Segundo and some of the other vaqueros were all for galloping back to Sonora immediately, but Don Margil was more level headed. What damage there was had already occurred and nothing could be done about it. It was better to deliver the herd and then return together to rebuild Hacienda O'Conor. More importantly they would have funds from the sale to finance the job. Of course this was easy for Don Margil to say because his precious daughters were safe and accounted for, although he grieved for the loss of his dear friend, Javiero. They'd been through so many narrow escapes in their long lives and were no strangers to sudden and violent death, but Don Margil profoundly regretted not being with Javiero at his end.

Segundo was by far the most vocal of the vaqueros and in open rebellion. The others were prepared to go along with their boss, but sorrow and uncertainty overcame Segundo. He rode to the supply wagon, gathered some water and travelling rations and would have galloped south without pausing for goodbyes, but after a heated discussion his comrades persuaded him against the idea and he calmed down.

Don Margil extended a hand to Jubal and Billy.

'I must thank you for rescuing my beautiful girls from bandits, pirates, drunkards, hostile Indians, mountain lions and poisonous snakes,' he greeted with a smile.

'Seems they have their own way of relatin' events,' Jubal observed, 'but I'm pleased to make your acquaintance, sir.'

'The story may have been embellished, but I've learnt to edit out the truth over the years. Even so, I'm in your debt. They are so charming and pretty, no? I would be in despair if anything should befall them.'

'No argument there, Señor,' Billy agreed.

They talked back and forth for a while as Don Margil was filled in on the details. Jubal and Billy went to great lengths to stress they were innocent bystanders in the whole affair and stood no chance if they were captured. Although they needn't have worried Don Margil was not overmuch in love with Yankee soldiers. As an eighteen-year-old lieutenant he'd marched with Santa Anna's army into Texas in 1836, and although ultimately victorious, saw hundreds of comrades slaughtered when they stormed the Alamo defences. He'd borne the humiliating rout by Sam Houston's rag-tag Texican Army at San Jacinto, and fought bitterly against Zachary

Taylor and Winfred Scott's columns at the blood-baths of Buena Vista and the Chapulepec Palace outside Mexico City eleven years later. He was heartily sick of being bullied by gringo troops. No, sir, his sympathies were positively un-American.

He was bitter about the Yankees taking over California and all the South West. His sister Frescura still lived on a rancho in Marin County on the northern shore of San Francisco Bay that had once been part of Mexico. She was of a more adaptable nature. As a no-nonsense businesswoman she'd maintained her large holdings despite political turmoil and macho pressure. Having never married, and with no allegiance to anyone but herself, she'd beguiled a series of influential lovers, which was a shrewd tactic.

Don Margil was fond of his sister and visited her whenever he could. Much as he loved his daughters, he knew they would be a distracting liability when there was hard work to be done and decided to send Teresita and Alameda to stay with Frescura until he'd rebuilt Hacienda O'Conor. They loved their aunt and enjoyed sojourns in California, although they'd only been girls on their last visit.

He'd also decided on just the two minders he'd need to escort them on the journey.

He discussed the matter with Jubal and Billy as they drove the herd northwards at a leisurely pace. He appeared unconcerned when Jubal pointed out they were likely being hunted by three very capable and determined trackers.

'You have adequately avoided capture so far,' Don Margil observed.

'More like narrow squeaks,' Billy admitted, even he acknowledged they'd been lucky.

'You look well armed, and my girls assure me you can shoot straight.'

'If you mean huntin' down supper, well yes,' Jubal said, 'but they ain't seen us do too much shooting at *people* yet.'

Not wanting to be choked by trail dust, Teresita and Alameda rode ahead of the herd and Jubal and Billy followed with their father to catch up. He told his daughters of his plan, and they seemed excited at the prospect, although Jubal and Billy hadn't actually agreed to do anything yet. Jubal knew Billy would go along with whatever the girls wanted, so he resigned himself to a trip to California. Billy had mentioned something about it earlier, and in many ways he couldn't think of a better plan. In fact he warmed to the idea, determining they could keep heading north into the wild Canadian North West Territories. Control of Canada had finally been vested from the Hudson Bay Company, and just been declared a Dominion of the British Empire. Violating Mexican sovereignty was one thing, but Lieutenant McAlister would be less inclined to conduct unauthorised forays into the domain of Europe's most powerful nation.

Don Margil clinched the deal by digging a small pouch from his saddlebags and handing it to Jubal, it contained gold dust assayed at over four hundred dollars. Jubal considered the pouch uncertainly until Billy reached across and pocketed the money. In his eyes a covenant had been reached, and ultimately Jubal agreed, if a little reluctantly. Don Margil was quite good at judging the price of a man.

Matters came to a head anyway when one of the drag vaqueros galloped up and reported four riders were trailing the herd, and it looked to his sharp eyes as if one of them was wearing a US Cavalry uniform.

Four riders? Jubal wondered. *Someone has joined the posse.*

'Don't worry,' Don Margil assured Jubal and Billy. 'They won't attack us, we outnumber them more than three-to-one.'

'Maybe not,' Jubal replied, 'but they might just get help from one of them cavalry patrols that are prowling round here.'

'You two vamoose with the señoritas, you'll have a good head start,' Don Margil said. '*Mis muchachos* and I will discourage them.'

'I'd rather there wasn't any shooting,' Jubal added piously.

'Do not worry, amigo,' Don Margil gave a cheerful wave. 'We won't start anything, but we certainly know how to finish things.'

He galloped away and gathered his men.

'We've almost caught up,' Petorio announced, with an *I-told-you-so* sort of tone. He was secretly relieved because the trail they were following was now so imbedded with cattle tracks that even he was having trouble making out what was what. He paid special attention to see if Jubal and Billy left the trail, but Pepita insisted they would go to Don Margil and there was nothing to worry about. This was confirmed when they ran into the cavalry patrol who reported meeting the fugitives. Sam was surprised to discover the troops at Fort Whipple knew nothing of the Fort Pierce breakout, and had no warning about a dangerous deserter. Then again Major Schofield and Captain Bellamy were sure Jubal and Billy had absconded to Mexico, and didn't really expect them to come back, so what was the point in raising a nationwide hue-and-cry?

Sam wanted the cavalry to join them in the hunt, but their lieutenant said his orders were to round up a couple of small, wandering Apache and Navaho gangs who'd decided to go raiding and needed pulling into line. Also they were a detachment from the 8th Cavalry Regiment, manned mostly by unsuccessful ex-miners who soon tired of frontier soldiering. They had a huge desertion problem of their own, so the lieutenant wasn't particularly interested in one, black miscreant from the 10th.

The herd stopped its ambling trek as Sam's posse approached. All the cowboys formed a line across the trail. They were armed with an assortment of hardware, including vintage Dragoon Colts, but all in good condition and ready for business. It was destined to be a tense confrontation except when Segundo spotted Pepita. With an overjoyed yelp he galloped towards her. At first Petorio thought they were under attack and drew his pistol, but fortunately Sam realised the approaching rider wasn't brandishing any weapons and gently placed his hand over the barrel of Petorio's gun, pushing it down.

Sam was pretty relieved that he had done so when Pepita and Segundo embraced in a gush of tears and caresses. His relationship with Pepita would have soured immeasurably if they'd gunned down her brother at the moment of their reunion. But emotions aside, Don Margil's crew still blocked the trail, and showed no signs of relenting. Leaving Pepita and Segundo to their chatter, Sam, Zeb and Petorio slowly rode forward.

'I think you must go no further, Señor,' Don Margil said.

'Well, I don't rightly see how that is you decision to make, *Señor*,' Sam replied. 'In case you haven't noticed, I'm a US cavalry officer on official business. And this is US territory as I recall.'

That probably wasn't the most tactful way of putting it, especially as Don Margil still fumed over the loss of the South Western Territories after the American invasion in 1847. But Sam didn't know that and he wasn't in the mood to be frustrated further in his chase after Jubal Quinn.

Don Margil appreciated his own dilemma. It was unwise to mess with the gringo authorities, especially as so much money was involved in his cattle deal, but then his daughters were precious, and he'd given his word to their two companions. But, even then events were being taken out of everyone's hands.

Although Arizona was generally considered a dry Territory, massive thunderstorms were by no means uncommon, especially in spring and summer, and a great line of them was now approaching. They rumbled and swirled miles into the sky spraying out rain, hail and lightning. Several bolts cracked nearby. The cattle became restless and started calling and shuffling about. The vaqueros knew they'd have to go and tend them.

At that moment a dark, gyrating black shadow stabbed down from the base of the mightiest billowing cloud mass, gathering intensity as it dropped to earth. It formed an immense funnel that quickly spread. When it reached the ground everyone could see rocks, scrub and even small trees ripped up and hurtled into the air in every direction. The roaring of frenetic wind grew from an ominous growl to a reverberating howl.

'I'll be damned, a twister,' Sam murmured.

Although tornadoes occurred, they were uncommon in the southwest. Having never seen one, Pepita was amazed and curious. The spectacle mesmerised her. Sam and Petorio had witnessed a couple in Kansas, and Zeb remembered plenty during his travels through Colorado, Wyoming and Montana. They knew how dangerous a twister funnel could be.

But, the threat didn't come from the twister that rambled aimlessly around the hills, it came from the cattle. The tornado touch-down scattered debris into the herd, causing some minor injuries, but galvanising the cattle into action. They turned away from the maelstrom and thundered back along the trail in a stampede at full speed.

In the face of five hundred bellowing, panic-stricken longhorns there was no time for further conversation. The vaqueros were, of course seasoned experts and merely bolted aside to let the animals pass. Sam, Zeb and Petorio, acting more on instinct, ripped at the reins, turned their mounts around and galloped along the trail ahead of the herd. Segundo and Pepita were swept along with them. Rainsqualls lashed at their faces, stinging their eyes and making it almost impossible to see ahead.

No one knew how long the herd would run, but Jesse and the horses were keeping ahead. They'd probably outpace the herd, but in the blinding rain Pepita's horse tripped and stumbled, tossing her to the ground. Hearing her piercing scream above the roar of stampeding hooves and thunderclaps, Sam hauled on the reins and dragged his animal to a halt. Turning, he galloped back to Pepita who sat dazed on the trail. She was stunned and for a moment unaware of the herd that charged towards her. Sam leapt from the saddle and pulled her to her feet.

'Quickly!' he bellowed. 'Get on my horse.'

He literally threw her into the saddle and slapped the horse's rump, sending it galloping to safety. Then he turned and stared certain death in the face. The longhorns were closing in at terrifying speed. He was a moment from being trampled to pulp. He drew his Army revolver and calmly aimed at the surging, bovine tidal wave. He blasted several shots and a leading steer stumbled forward, tripping others behind.

Suddenly two horses bolted past. Their riders, Petorio and Segundo blazed away with their pistols until the chambers were empty. Sam was aware of Zeb, mounted on Jesse who stood rigidly defiant in front of the stampede. He blasted several heavy calibre shots in quick succession into the beasts from his Sharps buffalo rifle. Half a dozen animals pitched into the dirt right at Sam's feet. Most of the others reared to a halt, milling in confusion and bellowing while a few trotted past on either side. Sam stood limply, his arm hung to his side loosely holding his spent revolver, as he stared at the pile of carcasses before him. Segundo used the last of his ammunition to despatch a couple of grievously suffering steers.

Pepita, regaining her senses, rushed to Sam. She leapt from the saddle and just about knocked him over as she clung to him, kissing his cheeks, his nose, his mouth, in fact any part of him she could reach. The raindrops mixed with her tears. She was a very emotional girl.

'Seems like there were some developments along the trail,' Segundo observed.

'Guess you could say that,' Zeb replied cautiously. 'Now you ain't gonna give us all that *brotherly-honour-and-defendin'-my-sister's-good-name* palaver, are you? 'Cos if you are, Petorio and I might have somethin' to say about that. Sam is a sound boy and Pepita could do a whole lot worse.'

'She certainly seems fond of him,' Segundo replied.

'Yep, he surely makes the lass happy.'

'Then I am happy. Remember, Señor we are Mestizos, and more in harmony with life than Spaniards who think so much of honour that it obsesses them and addles their senses.'

The storm was moving away in a meandering path of mild destruction. As twisters go, Sam had certainly seen worse at Fort Leavenworth, and while thunder and lightning still rumbled and flashed it looked like the tornado was playing itself out. The stampede was halted and the cattle just milled about. Don Margil and his vaqueros rode out of the rain. Their revolvers were drawn, and they were still fully loaded.

'Thank you for stopping the herd,' Don Margil said. 'It was truly a great service. My men would have taken days to gather the scattered beasts. And, now señors, I fear you must be our guests until we reach the Flagstaff lumber camp.'

'Where are Quinn and Billy Songbird, goddamnit? Sam snarled.

'They have escaped into the storm and will be well away by now.'

'You can't abduct an Army officer,' Sam raged.

'I think this says I can,' Don Margil replied, casually indicating his pistol.

'He's gotcha there, Sam,' Petorio remarked with his usual aridity.

He had a point, the rainstorm may have dampened the percussion pistols' powder, but you'd have to be six kinds of a fool to put that theory to the test. Sam, Zeb and Petorio had no choice but to surrender their weapons and come quietly.

Chapter 17

'Look on the bright side,' Zeb said, rather too cheerfully in Sam's opinion, 'at least we'll get a beefsteak for supper. I do prefer mine cooked rare.'

'I can't believe Don Margil would dare kidnap a United States officer,' Sam stormed. 'Doesn't he realise how serious this is? And how does he expect to get away with it when I make my report? He could be hanged.'

The vaqueros rounded up the herd and butchered one of the fallen steers. They built a massive fire to dry their clothes and cook a meal. Indeed the beefsteaks were huge and satisfying, although Sam's appetite was a bit jaded. Pepita made a great fuss of him for risking his life to save her and that put him in a slightly better frame of mind, although it irked him that she also spent a lot of time with Segundo. Sure, he was her brother, but he was also one of Sam's captors.

Don Margil was content to have sacrificed only a few animals. If the stampede had continued and the herd scattered further, his losses could have been much greater. His joviality didn't help Sam's mood much either.

'We could make a run for it,' Petorio suggested. 'I doubt if they'd really shoot us.'

Sam eyed the armed guards who constantly hovered close by and wasn't so sure. Anyway, without their weapons and ammunition they'd have a poor chance of apprehending Jubal and

Billy. Around the campfire Don Margil explained how things stood as he saw it.

'I think we'll be well back into Mexico before anyone knows about this,' he said confidently. 'This herd will last the loggers all year, and I'm sure everything will have blown over before I have to negotiate another contract.'

'You might find the Army has a long memory,' Sam snarled.

'Possibly, but of course your credibility may be brought into question. It seems to me that you have conducted an unauthorised raid into Sonora. Now my government could construe that as an invasion, and may want an explanation that you Yankees mightn't be prepared to give.'

'I don't think you have much of a government left these days,' Sam argued. 'Is Maximillian even still alive?'

'Who knows, but Benito Juarez will succeed eventually, of that I am sure. It will be government for the people at last. We are very adaptable when it comes to recovering from turmoil, Lieutenant McAlister, and I am not without influence. You never know they might even let Generalissimo Santa Anna back from Jamaica to lead the Army.'

They talked on and Don Margil acknowledged his gratitude to Sam's posse for helping destroy the gang who'd killed Javiero and burnt Hacienda O'Conor to the ground. Sam still sulked, and even Pepita's efforts failed to cheer him up until he finally nodded off to sleep.

In time they drove the herd into Flagstaff. It wasn't particularly developed, consisting of scattered tents and a couple of cabins, but the logging company knew the railroad would reach them soon and then a town would blossom. Most notable was a tall pole made from a local ponderosa pine trunk, maybe one hundred feet high from which the *Stars-and-Stripes* proudly waved.

'An army feller came by way back before the War to survey a road from the New Mexico Territory to California,' one of the loggers explained. 'Raised the flag on one of them tall trees, and it's sort of tradition now.'

The loggers were prepared, having felled enough timber and built a corral for the cattle. Don Margil quickly found the lumber boss and transacted their business. He paid his men off directly and they all headed back to Sonora without delay. Segundo tried to persuade Pepita to return with them, but her heart was set on accompanying Sam wherever he might go.

'Give Mama my love,' she said. 'Tell her I'm fine. Tell her I'm in love, even if it's with a Yankee soldier. I know she will be happy for me, I hope you are too.'

'I am and I have long since realised, that once you've set on an idea, there's no one who'll change your mind.'

He kissed her and rode off with the others.

Don Margil told Sam he'd left their weapons at the logging boss's cabin, and bid them good day. All their hardware was accounted for although the guns were still empty and would take time to reload, when chasing Don Margil and his cowboys would be beyond worth. Still smarting from his humiliation, Sam stalked off to the camp's beer tent and ordered a drink.

'Now, that's mighty unlike our boy,' Zeb observed. 'I'd credited him with more grit. It ain't like a little setback to vex him into his cups.'

'What do we do?' Petorio wondered. 'Wait for him or join him?'

Pepita looked at them both and shrugged, they had hit a dead-end. But moments later Sam appeared from the tent with a pitcher of beer and four mugs. He poured everyone a drink and grinned.

'You know,' he said, sounding like his old cheerful self once more, 'if you want to find out stuff, you just have to ask the right people.'

'Find out what stuff?' Petorio asked.

'The barman told me that a big Negro fellow and an Indian kid with two little stunners in tow, passed through Flagstaff yesterday and headed North West. I guess they didn't have much choice other than to come this way, so looks like we're on their trail again. Drink up, we need to get going. I'm sure you'll easily pick up their tracks in no time, Petorio.'

'Segundo confirmed they'd agreed to take Teresita and Alameda to their Aunt Frescura's estate in California,' Pepita added to prove Sam wasn't the only one capable of sleuthing.

Jubal, Billy and the girls had ridden through the storm with lightning bolts crashing all around and rain slashing bitterly at their faces. Teresita and Alameda squealed, but otherwise bore the discomfort well and they soon cleared the weather as it rushed by. They pressed on until evening and then as the vaqueros had, lit a fire to dry out for the night. The following morning dawned fine and clear, so they hit the trail early. They passed through Flagstaff only stopping briefly to ask about any trails leading north. Jubal and Billy noticed the way the loggers were eyeing the Mexican girls, and thought it best not to dawdle. They knew all too well that a brace of pretty nubiles in a camp full of lusty loggers was only going to cause strife and Teresita and Alameda had a knack of attracting trouble. The last thing they needed was another bar room brawl.

There were no major tracks or roads north of Flagstaff. No white settlers really had much need to go there, so Jubal and Billy had various choices. They took the easiest way that led onto high, cool, well-timbered plateau country and followed trails used by Pima and Navaho Indians over the years. It was slow going and they rode for several days. Water wasn't an issue as Billy always found enough from any number of creeks that were supplied by spring rainstorms. Then they arrived at what appeared to be a real problem.

The ground simply disappeared.

They rode through Ponderosa timber, chaparral and pinyon-juniper to find themselves staring into an enormous void. A chasm dropped for over a mile and was miles across. The view was so unbelievably vast.

'I'll be damned, now ain't that awesome?' Billy pondered. 'I've surely heard about it, but I never thought it really existed and was just folk romancing.'

'What do you mean?' Jubal asked.

'I opine it's what white folk call the Grand Canyon, and ain't they just spot on about that, though?'

'I'd rightly say so, it don't seem possible such a sight could be all in one look. Damn, it's a big hole in the ground!'

Staring at the majesty before them was all well and good, but Jubal soon brought them all back to earth.

'Of course you know we have to cross that don't you, Billy?' he said

'Does look a mite steep and I don't see any trails leading to the bottom,' Billy conceded, although Teresita and Alameda were unconcerned and suggested they simply ride along the canyon rim and go around it. It had to end somewhere.

'That could take weeks,' Jubal said. 'There's no real trail, and we'd have to pick our way carefully, maybe even back-track some.'

'I'd say *damned carefully*,' Billy joined in. 'It's a mighty long drop to the bottom.'

At that moment shadows emerged from the trees and blocked their path. They were Hopi warriors armed with bows and arrows, lances, hatchets, an eighteenth century English Collier fowling piece and a daunting Harper's Ferry blunderbuss. Although they looked martially businesslike, they made no threatening moves.

'I think you will need my help again,' a voice came from behind the warriors and Shadow Woman stepped through their line.

'Ma!' Billy yelled, jumping from his horse and hugging her with delight, almost squeezing the breath out of her.

'What are you doing here?' he asked after he put her down. 'How did you ever find us?'

'Finding you was easy,' Shadow Woman smiled. 'You've been clumping around in this woodland for days, going around in circles some of the time from what I hear. These are my Hopi friends. We've been camping along the canyon floor and hunting up here.'

It turned out that Shadow Woman had arrived at the Hopi shaman's pueblo just when he and his neighbours decided to take a trip to the Canyon. They liked visiting there because of its beauty and spiritual significance, food was easy to come by and white men hadn't found their way down there yet. They were on a summer roaming vacation.

The Hopi people weren't particularly warlike unless driven to it, as in the case of the Navahos who'd bullied them for ages. They had no qualms about helping Kit Carson round the Navaho up, but they appeared at ease with the Hualapai and Havasupai tribes who lived in and around the canyon.

They asked Shadow Woman to accompany them because they always enjoyed hearing about her adventures at Fort Pierce and with the Comanches. When one of the hunting parties spied Jubal and Billy, they rightly determined who they were and sent word to Shadow Woman. It took her a full day to climb the canyon wall, and even so, they'd have to go right back down again in the morning.

'You know you've got four riders after you,' Shadow Woman advised, 'and they're catching up fast.'

Jubal was amazed at the speed news got around via the *moccasin telegraph*, but Billy took it in his stride. They introduced Teresita and Alameda and explained the task of escorting the girls to California. Billy was able to communicate quite well with the Hopi people in a mixture of sign language and a Shoshone dialect that was similar in many ways to the Comanche his mother had taught him. His good ear for sounds helped greatly and he was able to translate for Jubal and the girls, along with the English and Spanish that some of the Indians knew.

'There are several trails to the canyon floor,' Shadow Woman explained, 'but they are treacherous, slow and well hidden. If we go down there and cover our tracks I doubt even a White Mountain Apache scout will be able to follow us.'

It took all the following day to negotiate a rocky, narrow and very suspect path to the bottom. Teresita and Alameda's thoroughbreds proved cantankerous, but the Hopi had a way with animals and eventually got them safely to the canyon floor. The Hopi warriors covered their path well, and created some misleading trails just for good measure. Shadow Woman was right, even Petorio Blanco missed where they had gone. And the Hopi had a few extra tricks up their sleeves to put the pursuers off the scent.

'Hell's bells!' Sam cried as they approached the canyon rim just after sunrise. 'It surely wouldn't do to stumble into that for lack of attention. Ain't that just majestic, Pepita?'

She nodded and thought it was a really romantic setting. Petorio and Zeb had both visited the canyon before and although they were equally impressed by its beauty, they also knew what a navigational obstacle it was going to be.

About an hour after he lost the trail, Petorio realised he wasn't going to pick it up again.

'They've gone down to the canyon floor,' he surmised at last. 'Damned if I can tell where or how. I dunno about going down there and that's a fact. Seems like a whole bunch of ways to get killed. You ever been to the bottom, Zeb?'

'Nope, can't say as I have, mostly skirted the rim on tother side, huntin' and trappin' and the like.'

'How the hell did Quinn and Billy manage it then?' Sam asked.

'Got some local help, I'd expect. There's a few folk live hereabouts,' Petorio advised.

'Perhaps we can find someone to guide us.'

'Maybe, but I've got a feelin' they plumb don't want to be found. I sense there are people around, but they're staying hidden.'

'How long will it take to go around, Zeb?'

'Days perhaps, I really don't know.'

Just then they heard the 'whoosh, whoosh, whoosh,' as a tomahawk somersaulted through the air and struck a ponderosa pine only a few feet ahead. And suddenly there was the thwack of arrows thumping into tree trunks and into the dirt ahead. Sam drew his revolver and fired several times, but could see no definite target. Some shadows darted between the trees, but even Petorio couldn't take an accurate shot. Suddenly a thundering roar erupted from the blunderbuss and shards of stone and iron ripped through the branches, shredding leaves into confetti. The noise of the blast and the zinging pellets had the intended result.

'Welcoming committee, I'd say,' Zeb called. 'I don't think they mean to kill us, or we'd be dead already. I'd say this is a right discouragin' experience to scare us off.'

'Works for me,' Petorio said. 'Discretion, don't you think?'

Discretion it was, and they galloped back through the trees along the canyon edge, firing a few parting shots as they went.

Shortly the woodland thinned making their escape easier and soon they came to a large open area where the rock was just too solid for anything other than stunted scrub to grow. In the middle of the clearing was a huge red-white-and-blue marquee. Several wagons were parked in neat lines with teams of mules and horses tethered here and there. The wagons were laden with all sorts of equipment including a large wicker basket, crates, a sturdy metal tank and a great number of sand bags. A Union Jack and Old Glory flew from two posts at either end of the marquee.

There was a bustle of activity and enterprise about the camp. A small party of men were milling around an enormous silk sheet that must have been well over fifty feet long. It lay on the ground and was weighted down by a few handy rocks and some wooden chests and a couple of ammunition boxes. Even so the sheet billowed in the wind occasionally and men rushed to secure the flapping material that looked in danger of becoming damaged or sailing away and disappearing into the canyon. They seemed not to have heard the gunfire, but then they had problems of their own.

'I say, you sir,' called one of the men. 'Yes you, soldier chappy. Jump down and hang onto that end, do lend a hand there's a good fellow. You others, make yourselves useful. Look lively now. We don't want the bally thing ripping to shreds.'

They left the horses with Pepita and did what they were told. Eventually the men found enough weights of various descriptions to secure the silk sheet.

'By Jove, jolly good show everyone, bravo!' the man who appeared to be leading this party called with some relief. 'Thank you, gentleman,' this to Sam, Zeb and Petorio. 'Please, do join me, Frederick is just putting on some tea and I have a rather superb fruit cake.'

He was a dapper, handsome fellow in his mid thirties, dressed in tartan plus-fours and a matching waistcoat. His cravat was held in place by a generous diamond tiepin. A short swarthy man looking much more at home wearing a broad-brimmed Stetson and western gear accompanied him.

'May I introduce myself,' he said profusely with an elegant, English accent. 'I am Lord Byron Phillip Darrel Duppa.'

'But you can call him Darrel,' the other man said in a southern states drawl.

'And this is my dear friend and colleague, Jack Swilling,' Lord Duppa continued, taking Pepita's hand and kissing it formally. 'Charmed, young lady, absolutely charmed,' he gushed.

Sam introduced everyone. Frederick, who was Lord Duppa's butler and addressed him as *m'lud,* was dressed in a black tail suit and white bow tie. He was unphased by the extra guests and found folding chairs and stools for everyone. He poured the tea and cut the cake. Sam thought coffee tasted better and added a fair bit of sugar to his, but he enjoyed the cake.

'I'm sorry there is no milk,' Duppa said. 'I believe the local Indians keep goats and sheep that the Spaniards brought here, but they've proved devilishly elusive chaps. I think our balloon has frightened them.'

'Balloon?' Zeb queried.

'Oh yes,' Duppa beamed. 'Ain't she a beauty? Cost an absolute fortune, but then money's no object, what?'

It was great when you got a generous allowance from your folks back in England, and Duppa's was significant. With six thousand British pounds per annum to play with, supplemented by what he'd made prospecting around Prescott over the past four years, his funds were virtually limitless. Along with swashbuckling, ex-Confederate cavalryman, Jack Swilling, he'd procured acreage along the Gila River close to Pima Indian Country and planned to farm there shortly, but right now he was having fun.

'To aeronautics, gentlemen,' Lord Duppa announced, raising his teacup in a toast. 'It is the future, and we must all play our part in it. Can you believe in a mere thirty three years it will be the twentieth century?'

'Don't know as I'll see that,' Zeb said with a touch of sadness, 'but I'd like to just for the pure statistics of living through two centuries.'

'Well, sir,' Duppa went on, 'eat healthily, drink red wine and keep clear of spirit liquor, and you have every chance.'

'Keeping clear of the spirits is goin' to be the problem.'

'I saw a balloon when I studied at the Point,' Sam said. 'They'd used some in the War. A colonel was telling us how good they were for reconnaissance.'

'Until someone takes a pot-shot at you,' Zeb said. 'Then you're plumb out of alternatives.'

'Ah, not so, my pioneering friend,' Duppa explained. 'This ain't any ordinary hot-air variety. Why, sir, this balloon is inflated with pure hydrogen. It has four compartments, so if one is holed, then tothers'll still do the job.'

Lord Duppa explained how he'd brought a hydrogen production machine on one of the wagons. By passing an electric current through water, the hydrogen separated and was piped into the balloon's gas chambers. His crew was busily hand cranking an electrical generator with cables attached to a sealed water tank. It was a long and tedious process as the tank needed periodical replenishment and the cranking team had to be replaced when they grew tired.

'It should be fully inflated by morning,' Lord Duppa said confidently.

'And then what?' Petorio asked cautiously. He could see no sense in this venture at all. The view from the canyon rim looked fine to him.

'Why, sir,' Duppa looked genuinely puzzled, 'this land is a scientific delight. I have visited the fossil-bone sights in the Wyoming Territory and there's a great crater not far from here in Arizona that I believe was caused by a fireball from outer space. I'll wager the rock layers down the canyon face hold the secrets of evolution over millennia. Have you not read Darwin's *Origin of Species* published a few years back? Why 'tis pure enlightenment.'

At this stage most of them reckoned Lord Duppa was barking mad except Sam who had some knowledge of astronomy and physics, although his strict, fundamental and arbitrary Christian upbringing made the concept of evolution somewhat problematic.

'I plan to soar over the abyss,' Duppa continued grandly, 'and descend to observe the archaeological mysteries of its depths. Then rise again like a phoenix. *Phoenix,*' he repeated in the sidetracked manner he favoured at times. 'Why I do believe that is what I shall name our dirigible.'

'*Your* dirigible, my lord,' Jack Swilling hastened to point out. 'You ain't got no one half crazy enough to go up with you yet and I don't see no volunteers close by.'

And then Sam had an idea.

'Why, if you would permit it, we'd be honoured to accompany you on your venture,' he said formally, and Duppa was overjoyed.

'Just hold on,' Petorio said, 'there ain't no *we* about it.'

Sam looked hurt, but Petorio and Zeb were adamant. Nothing would induce them into Lord Duppa's flying machine. As Petorio said, they got all the view they needed from the top of the canyon wall.

'First off, how do you steer the damned thing?' Zeb asked.

'The greatest of all natural energy sources,' Duppa declared, waving to the skies. 'The wind carries us, sir.'

'The wind blows in all different directions as I divine, how does it know where you want to go?'

'Ah, I see you have a solid brain on your shoulders, sir. Yes indeed, we had to calculate that. We despatched a party with another hydrogen producing device and ballast to the north rim some weeks back. They arrived a few days ago, and we have communicated by heliograph using another of nature's resources, don't you know?

'You see the wind tends to blow one way for some days and then changes. My observations suggest it is better to traverse the chasm in the early hours of the morning before heat stirs up air currents and turbulence. The time is now right for our departure. We will cruise across and land with the help of our north-side crew then await a wind change and sail back. My good friend Jack here, will be in charge of this camp to await our return, while I shall oversee tother side.'

Sam, Zeb and Petorio debated long and hard, but there was no budging the Apache or the Mountain Man.

'Look,' Petorio said at last, 'we know what will happen to Jubal Quinn back in New Mexico. They'll hang him for sure. Hell, you didn't like what happened to Claude Valentine and he was evil as sin. We don't even know that Jubal murdered anyone for sure, and he *did* save everyone at Hacienda O'Conor. Let it go Sam, you've done enough. Why you're probably AWOL yourself, as I don't recall any orders from Major Schofield about this. Let's head back and give someone else the grief.'

Sam considered that for a while. It made sense. They may not have apprehended Jubal and Billy, but they'd managed to see Claude's outlaw gang into oblivion, even if they hadn't actually done all the work themselves. But, it went deeper than that.

'I just can't,' he said at last. 'I set out to do a job, and I ain't quittin' till it's done.'

'Or till you're dead,' Zeb said. 'Goddamnit Sam, I declare you're more stubborn than Jesse.'

In the end they decided that Sam would ride in the balloon with Lord Duppa while Zeb and Petorio patrolled the south rim in case Jubal and Billy should backtrack. When they landed Duppa explained that they could signal to each other by heliograph and decide what to do then, although Zeb and Petorio suggested that they wouldn't be hanging around forever.

Pepita was silent throughout the discussion, but finally she spoke.

'I will go with you, Sam,' she said nervously.

'Capital, just capital!' Duppa cheered, clapping his hands before anyone could object. 'We'll bring champagne!'

<h1 style="text-align:center">Chapter 18</h1>

They weren't quite sure what to expect, but in the morning they awoke to an immense surprise. The balloon was simply gargantuan. The vast bladder hovered way above them, swaying gently from its tethers. The team had secured at least twenty ropes to trees, rocks, wagons and any other anchoring points they could find. The basket suspended below the balloon appeared tiny until you got close and then it seemed as if it would hold five or six people with ease.

Frederick placed a ladder against the basket and was loading a handsome hamper packed with choice consumables. He didn't forget two magnums of champagne. Otherwise and by necessity they travelled light. Sam brought only his rifle, side arms and telescope strapped to his belt. Pepita insisted on taking a change of clothes as they planned to be on the northern rim for a few days. Lord Duppa assured them that the party across the canyon was well supplied and would provide all they needed.

'Splendid weather, what?' Duppa beamed. 'An absolutely super morning for our jaunt skywards, don't you think?'

Sam didn't know what constituted perfect aviation conditions, so he just nodded. Pepita looked doubtful, but Duppa's enthusiasm was infectious.

Sam hoped m'lud had all the angles covered. He used the peer's heliograph to signal the party across the canyon to apprehend anyone answering Jubal and Billy's description who might climb up on the northern side. The team across the ravine acknowledged and would keep an eye out. He knew he could rely on Petorio and Zeb for a while anyway.

So they clambered aboard assisted by the ever-serene Frederick, who showed no uneasiness about the flight.

'I was with the 17th Lancers at Balaclava in '54, you see sir,' he explained in answer to Sam's puzzlement. 'After the Charge I doubt if anything could dismay me ever again.'

And if you think m'lud Duppa is a trifle eccentric, you should have seen Lords Lucan, Cardigan and Raglan in full swing, he thought, but of course knew it was not his place to venture such opinions.

Apart from Frederick's provisions, the basket was stashed with small sand bags. Above their heads was a relief valve operated by a cord to release hydrogen should they wish to descend.

'It takes a bit of planning, don't you know?' Duppa said. 'First we soar into the middle of the canyon, then release enough gas to descend and see what's down there. Finally we'll drop a couple of ballast bags over the side and gently float up tother side.'

Without further comment he put his plan into action. Sam admired the way he'd co-ordinated his crew. With the help of Zeb and Petorio, they released the mooring lines simultaneously. Frederick pulled up the dangling ropes and stowed them efficiently in hessian containers hooked to the balloon gondola.

As they lifted gently skywards, Sam gasped and Pepita gave a squeal that amused Duppa profoundly. Any misgivings vanished quickly as they admired the spectacle, and it was quite a different experience to sitting on the canyon edge whatever Petorio might think. It was eerily quiet and they could actually hear the rushing

Colorado River as it swept along way below them. Pepita was so excited she started bobbing about with delight.

'Do be still, miss, if you would be so kind,' Frederick admonished in his quiet manner. 'We don't want to upset the basket, now do we?'

She pouted, but he smiled in a fatherly sort of way to let her know he wasn't angry. Lord Duppa didn't even notice. He was just as enchanted as Pepita. Indeed it appeared that Frederick was the only one actually controlling the aircraft.

'Has Lord Duppa ever flown a balloon before,' Sam quietly asked Frederick.

'Actually sir, I do believe this is an inaugural flight for us all. M'lud and I have read extensively on the subject, so there's nothing to worry about.'

'That is indeed comforting,' Sam replied a little sadly.

'Dashed exhilaratin', what?' Duppa chortled. 'Trail blazing the skies, damnit, we could cross the Atlantic if the wind's right and we brought enough bubbly.'

They all took turns casting around with Sam's telescope and the mood was becoming quite festive. Frederick popped a champagne bottle and the cork sailed off into the abyss. He filled glasses for everyone. Pepita had never tasted champagne before and giggled as the fizz tickled her nose and she really liked the taste.

Lord Duppa and Frederick's research seemed to be paying off and they managed the craft competently. However, archaeologist and naturalist though he was, Duppa had overlooked the canyon's bellicose fauna, who had just noticed an intruder in their territory.

Two giant Californian condors were perched on the canyon rim after gorging on a pronghorn carcass. Normally they'd have stayed put all day to let breakfast digest, but the balloon required investigation. Four bald eagles were spiralling in an early thermal current with the same idea. A leviathan had violated their airspace and they didn't plan to tolerate it.

The immensity of the intruder didn't bother these predators. The condors lurched into the air and idly soared in ascending spirals to get above the balloon while the eagles swarmed up from below. The eagles broke into pairs and flashed past the basket, confused at first by the balloon's huge shape, but they sized it up quickly enough. It was soon clear they planned to rip the canopy with their talons, although they were tentative at first.

Waving and yelling didn't deter the raptors, as they plunged dangerously around the balloon. And then the condors arrived. They may have lumbered into the sky, but once airborne they glided effortlessly on their ten-foot wingspans. The condors swooped past and everyone in the basket heard the rip as one slashed into the balloon's covering. A steady hiss followed as hydrogen seeped away.

'I think it's only a small tear, m'lud,' Frederick commented, 'and it may be better that we descend away from these birds in any event.'

'Indeed so,' Duppa agreed airily. 'My word those fellows are fine specimens, don't you think?'

It didn't take long for the balloon to ease gently earthwards. There was no real cause for alarm until the condors turned for another attack. They lunged so close to the basket that Sam could make out their crimson skulls and piercing eyes. Without thinking he drew his revolver and fired several shots at the birds.

'Noooo!' Duppa and Pepita screamed in unison.

'The canopy, sir,' Frederick remarked urbanely, 'best not to risk shots going through it, causing a fire risk. I believe that was m'lud's concern.'

Duppa merely nodded. He was once again distracted, revelling in the adventure.

'The condors!' Pepita wailed. Her concern was for the condors, not the balloon. 'They're sacred to the Indians. We believe destroying the condors threatens all the tribes. Everyone knows that, you idiot!'

Sam gave her a *first-I've-heard-about-it* shrug, but the damage was done. One of the massive birds was tumbling into the canyon depths as its mate dived after it, peeling pitifully.

'Oh, this is a terrible thing to happen,' Pepita whispered.

Sam failed to see why she was so appalled. The gunshots had scared the eagles away and driven off the condors. The *Phoenix* was drifting gently downwards, which was Duppa's original plan, and wasn't the balloon capable of flying safely with one bladder punctured anyway? Duppa explained his northern team had the resources to repair the balloon when they landed. So, to him it was a sound result, although they didn't get as much time to survey the canyon walls as they'd hoped. They kept a sharp lookout for any of the birds that might return.

There were figures moving around beside the Colorado River. Sam peered through his telescope and, as they drew closer he recognised Billy Songbird and Jubal Quinn. Grimly he reloaded his Army revolver. He meant business.

Jubal, Billy and the girls had a pleasant night on the banks of the Colorado River. The Hopi had decided to settle for a while, erected hogans and established a comfortable camp site. They'd barbequed some venison and fish over a roaring fire accompanied with baked tomatoes, corn and potatoes. Their hosts made a very tasty drink from cacao seeds called *xocolat* they'd discovered way down in Central America. The girls found they preferred to mix it with goat's milk for sweetening. It was a rare treat because the Hopi had to travel a long way to gather the seeds, but they considered this a special occasion.

Friendly strangers didn't happen by every day. Shadow Woman amused them all with her anecdotes and the Indians enjoyed hearing about Jubal and Billy's adventures in Mexico. They'd wound up having quite a party, and would have slept in, if they hadn't been awoken by the sound of gunfire.

Now the balloon hovered high above them, but they were able to make out the attacking condors and saw puffs of blue gun-smoke from the airship basket. Jubal knew about balloons, but the Indians looked up in awe. He explained that it was, however daunting, nothing more than another white man's machine, although as it slowly descended, it looked like it might very well land right on top of them. And the Hopi knew that most white man's machines only brought trouble and suffering. There was no hiding Jubal's surprise when the balloon was low enough for him to see a figure in cavalry blue leaning over the basket's side.

'You stand fast, Sergeant Quinn!' Sam bellowed, a little pompously in everyone's opinion. 'You're under arrest. I intend to take you back to Fort Leavenworth to answer the charges.'

No way! Billy thought, and Jubal was having none of it either. He knew it was time to cut and run.

'I can't do that, Lieutenant,' Jubal yelled. 'That feller back at Pierce pulled a gun on me. It was self-defence. I ain't hangin' for what ain't my fault.'

'Maybe so, Jubal, but there's the small matter of a dead soldier back at Fort Pierce's guardhouse.'

'That was an accident, sir,' Jubal called knowing how unconvincing it sounded, but what else could he say.

'It won't wash, Jubal. In my opinion it's a poor kind of *accident* that leaves a man with his throat cut clean across.'

Jubal realised he couldn't just turn around and point at Shadow Woman, who was quietly negotiating with the Hopi shaman while Jubal and Sam were arguing.

'You'll need to borrow one of those?' she said, indicating several fishing canoes and pirogues drawn up on the bank. 'It's an impressive machine they've got up there, but I don't think they'll be able to chase you down the river in it. Get going, boys, the current'll take you faster than that contraption.'

Once again Billy kissed his mother goodbye, then grabbed Teresita and Alameda, just about dragging them to one of the dugout pirogues. But the girls had other ideas. To them getting into a canoe on the rapid, murky Colorado River was as daunting as riding in a balloon, and they didn't plan to board without a fight.

'We don't want to go in that *tiny* boat.' Alameda wailed.

'It ain't that small,' Jubal growled, 'and if we don't hightail it right now they'll capture us.'

'You don't even know if they can land here,' Teresita said, 'and we are having such fun.'

'They can land alright,' Jubal countered, although he'd only seen tethered observation balloons on a couple of occasions during the War and they were simply winched back to earth when the crews needed rotating.

'You go on then,' Alameda challenged. 'We are enjoying ourselves so much. Let's stay for a week.'

They had told their father about the Hacienda O'Conor disaster, and saw no need to hurry to San Francisco. Distractions along the way were quite acceptable in the girls' view.

'We gave our word to your Pa to take you to California, and that's damn well what we plan to do,' Jubal said.

'What about our beautiful horses?' Alameda wailed.

'Your Daddy'll buy you new ones, no doubt.'

'We'll take care of them,' Shadow Woman added. 'You can come back for them whenever you want.'

'You can't make us go!' Teresita retorted.

Billy held her tightly by the arms and glared into her green eyes.

'Miss Teresita,' he said in a low, slow voice. 'You know I don't hold with hitting on womenfolk. But, you also know I'll do it if need be, and that's gettin' a real close option now. You got two choices, either you get in the boat or you get put. One thing is for sure, *you'll end up in the pirogue!'*

She stared at him for a second and she knew he meant what he said. So with as much dignity as she could muster, she took Alameda's hand and with Billy's help, they both clambered on board. The narrow craft rocked alarmingly, but after some squealing and fidgeting they settled onto the floor of the boat.

Jubal gathered their weapons, ammunition and saddlebags and tossed them into the pirogue.

'Stop right there,' Sam roared, but of course got no response.

Right, if that's how you want it, he thought grabbing his Spencer rifle and loosing off a couple of shots at the canoe. He saw the water spraying up where the bullets hit. Jubal and Billy blazed away with their revolvers, their bullets zinging through the balloon's rigging.

'Damn them,' Sam couldn't hide his outrage.

'If you shoot at people, old chap, you've got to expect them to shoot back, don't you think?' Lord Duppa observed with his customary blandness.

And right then they got into trouble. The Hopi warriors unleashed the secret weapon they'd lunked down the treacherous path from above the previous evening. It was the treasured Harper's Ferry Blunderbuss they'd traded from the Shoshone, who'd appropriated it from Meriwether Lewis and William Clark more than half a century ago. The warriors balanced the barrel on a stout ponderosa pine support. A fierce jet of lethal, rock and metal shrapnel belched from the flared gun barrel into the *Phoenix's* rigging.

The balloon was drifting just above a line of coyote willow, arrow weed and cat claw acacia trees that hugged the Colorado banks. The Hopi's light artillery sliced through several of the basket restraining lines, pitching it forward so it hung precariously on its side. Unfortunately to aggravate matters, ballooning was an inexact science and it was just at that moment that they bucked in a small pocket of turbulence and the basket snagged on the upper branches of the trees, tipping it even further. Sam, Duppa and Frederick grabbed the rigging and hung on, but Pepita wasn't so lucky.

Along with the picnic hamper and a couple of bottles of fine French champagne, she was pitched from the basket. Sam lunged and grabbed her hand as she disappeared over the basket edge. He caught her just in time as she dangled in mid air. The basket tilted a little more and Sam felt himself slipping towards its rim. Frederick saw the danger and grasped Sam's ankle while hanging onto one of the *Phoenix's* rigging lines. Calmly he gathered more rope and wrapped it around Sam's foot, securing him to the aircraft. He then inched towards Pepita, hoping to haul her back on board. Sam couldn't hold on much longer, he could feel her hand slipping away. Sweat glistening down his arm didn't help.

Suddenly the pile of sandbags pitched forwards and tumbled out of the basket. It swayed wildly, further skewing the gondola. With the weight of ballast gone, the balloon surged free of the trees and soared into the air. But the final lurch forced Pepita's hand from Sam's grip, and she dropped from sight with a piercing wail as she fell. With the weight adjustment the basket righted itself and Sam clambered to the edge. Peering over he saw Pepita's body dwindle to a tiny speck as it splashed into the grey-brown Colorado River and was engulfed by its icy, rushing water.

The sand bags, imported from France with the balloon, were weighted in the new metric system that had only been an approved legal measuring alternative in America for a year. Each was marked at ten kilograms and nearly twenty had spilled overboard along with Pepita who, tiny though she was, still weighted the equivalent of almost five extra bags. With the ballast gone the effect was dramatic and instantaneous. The *Phoenix* reared from the tree line, tearing free and scattering shattered branches onto the riverbank. It hurtled upwards alongside the canyon's northern wall.

At first Lord Duppa thought they'd be dashed onto the rock face, but the balloon surged clear and continued aloft. There wasn't a lot they could do to control the vessel, they simply had to follow its path.

But their problems weren't over.

Sam simply clung to the basket, secured by Frederick's quick thinking, but he hung dangerously close to the edge and his weight was tipping the basket once again. Duppa's trusty assistant crept forward and ever so slowly, gripped Sam's belt and gently drew him back. The redistribution of load helped to right the gondola slightly, and the imminent danger passed, although Sam had yet to come to his senses. His true love had been snatched from him and he was numb with grief and disbelief.

To make matters worse Sam's shots hadn't killed the condor, but merely dazed it as the bullets sped past. It recovered desperately close to the canyon floor, but managed to soar away with its partner to a perch high on the cliff face. With acute eyesight they observed events, and seeing the *Phoenix* glide upwards once again, they were out for revenge. They'd worked out that raking the balloon with their claws caused it considerable discomfort, so they planned to do the same again, and this time, although they weren't to know it, there was no one in a position to shoot back.

It was all the gondola occupants could do to hang on as the condors swooped in for the attack, and emboldened by the condors, the eagles decided to join in. Just as the balloon emerged over the north wall the birds attacked, slicing into the canopy. Hydrogen escaped in great bursts as the *Phoenix* gyrated wildly when another gas chamber ruptured. Losing its means of floatation the balloon dropped suddenly and thumped onto the rim of the canyon.

'Jump!' Duppa yelled as he pitched himself to the ground.

Frederick followed as the basket slithered down the canyon side, becoming snagged in the rocky outcrops and tree stumps that clung there. They slowed the balloon, but didn't stop it entirely. The rope that Frederick had used to secure Sam was now his death-sentence as he was caught and would be dragged to the Colorado River a mile below. Frederick grabbed Sam's arms and hung on grimly.

'Hold him!' Duppa yelled.

He scrambled to the canyon edge and clinging onto whatever he could, he inched towards the basket. The balloon canopy still held an enormous amount of gas, but it was sagging by the second and as it did, the basket oozed downwards. Duppa drew his knife and slashed at the ropes holding Sam until they fell away. Duppa grabbed a handy branch and dragged himself clear as the basket finally broke from its perch and plummeted to the canyon floor.

Sam was left dangling and Frederick would never have been able to drag him to safety had not Duppa helped from below. They hauled Sam over the lip just as the *Phoenix's* steel fittings scraped against some hard rock strata. The sparks were enough to ignite the hydrogen mixed with air and the balloon erupted into a massive, raging fireball.

Sam, Frederick and Lord Duppa lay panting on the rocky ledge as the flames roared past them, blazing ferociously for only seconds before extinguishing without a trace of smoke. The *Phoenix* and its gondola were destroyed, and only the smallest fragments clattered down into the Colorado River. Luckily for the condors and eagles, they swerved clear and survive the blast, but they took off in a hurry, deciding they'd had enough excitement for the day. The condors returned to their perch, nursing their frayed nerves and the eagles drifted away on a thermal looking for lunch and soon forgot about their adventure. They'd seen lightning strikes and range fires before, and were unable to differentiate between them and a hydrogen explosion.

Duppa was the first to recover. To his relief Frederick and Sam suffered no serious damage.

'Somehow I don't see that phoenix ever rising from the ashes again,' he announced wearily, but knew there would be no consoling the desolate cavalry lieutenant.

Chapter 19

'It was my fault,' Sam groaned. 'I'm sorry. I'm so sorry.'

Lord Duppa and Frederick could do nothing to calm him.

'If I hadn't been so damned trigger-happy, Pepita would still be alive and your balloon wouldn't have been destroyed.'

'Don't worry about the bally old balloon, dear boy,' Duppa said. 'It can be replaced eventually.'

He was a *stiff-upper-lip* kind of guy, and soothing words weren't his natural strength. Having never lost a loved one, how was he ever to know how that felt?

'The loss of the young lady is indeed a tragedy, sir,' Frederick, who was better at that sort of thing, said. 'It was hardly your fault though. No one could have guessed the Indians possessed such a formidable weapon, and the vultures weren't particularly helpful, I must say.'

'Yes, dashed effective, what?' Duppa chortled, his attention once more jumping from one topic to another with ease.

Frederick gave him a rather pained, but resigned look. Duppa's charm was his unbounded enthusiasm, but Frederick had been genuinely fond of Pepita although disaster and strife were never far away in this rugged and remote country. Death was commonplace and dwelling on tragedy wasn't a luxury you could afford if you expected to survive out here.

There wasn't much time to mope anyway, as shortly the north face team arrived. They were a tough bunch of adventurers known for their resourcefulness and range skills. But, even they were amazed at the balloon's destruction.

'Spectacular, my lord,' their leader commented wryly, 'although not quite the smooth landing you'd planned.'

They peered over the precipice at the ruined *Phoenix*. Not that there was much to see. Sam's telescope had miraculously escaped and he looked through it. It wasn't the balloon's smouldering debris that caught his attention, but the pirogue that was still in view, cruising smoothly with the Colorado River current.

'They ain't gonna to get away with it,' he muttered. 'Lord Duppa, I need a favour, if you please.'

'Anything, old chap,' Duppa replied, pleased that Sam had bucked up.

'I only have my revolver and 'scope left. I'll need a good, saddled horse, a rifle, ammo, some food and water.'

'Our team is well stocked, that's no problem, but do you really mean to go after them?'

'You're damn right, I do.'

Duppa's team proved an invaluable source of information, and explained the trail geography as it was the way they'd come. It turned out that the best ford was at Fort Mohave on the Arizona, California border. Prairie schooners and ox-drawn freight wagons used the river crossing all the time The Havaspupai Indians who lived at the western extreme of the canyon had proved helpful in guiding the party along the canyon rim. If Sam could beat Jubal and Billy to Fort Mohave it was the best chance he had of stopping them, especially with the help of the military contingent there.

'You plan to catch up with them?' Duppa asked. 'It seems to me that the river current is carrying them mighty well.'

'May I venture to suggest that it may not all be plain sailing?' Frederick remarked. 'It is very likely they'll encounter rapids somewhere, and that'll slow them down. To portage that vessel over trouble spots will prove difficult. I only glimpsed mind you, but it looked rather heavy to me.'

'I'd like to borrow one of your signalling mirrors too,' Sam added. 'They were insistent we all learn that new International Morse Code when I was at the Point.'

On the canyon's southern rim, Petorio, Zeb and Jack Swilling heard the gunshots, but were unable to make anything of it, or connect the soaring condors with events. They were dismayed to see the flash as the *Phoenix* exploded. They had no idea what to do and there was absolutely nothing they could do. So it was a great relief when they saw the heliograph flashing and Jack Swilling started recording the message in a notebook.

'Lord Duppa, Frederick and your soldier buddy are safe,' he said, 'but, I'm afraid the girl is lost. She fell from the balloon.'

Petorio and Zeb stared blankly at one another. Much as they loved Pepita, they realised there would be no living with Sam now. However, the problem was moot. Sam was stuck on the north side of the canyon, and there would be no replacement balloon in the foreseeable future.

Meanwhile Jack Swilling was scribbling in his ledger as the heliograph flickered for some time. Finally it stopped and Jack flashed an acknowledgement that he'd understood and copied the message down.

'Sam has some instructions for you,' he announced. 'Your bad guys are on a raft and headin' down the Colorado. He wants you to take your stuff and the spare horses and travel west to Fort Mohave. Says he'll meet you there.'

Petorio and Zeb again exchanged glances.

'Thought you were goin' home?' Zeb quizzed.

'Reckon I was, but things change, don't they?'

'Seems so. I've a feelin' the boy needs us more than ever now.'

'Here take this,' Jack said, handing them his heliograph and the note pad. 'We've got plenty of spares and you'll probably want to stay in touch. I remember generals holdin' great store by communicatin' in my solderin' days. I've written the codes down for you. See, the dots and dashes mean letters and numbers. It's a pain in the arse to start with, but you'll get the hang of it with practice.

So they packed up, bid Jack Swilling farewell and headed west.

Pepita's biggest regret as she plunged earthwards was her last words to Sam. She'd called him an idiot. How was he to know about condors? There weren't any back east. On hitting the water she wasn't sure whether the impact or the cold shocked her more. In the end she decided it was the needling bitterness of billions of gallons of melted ice. Washed down from the Rocky Mountain snowfields, the Colorado River wouldn't warm up until it flowed into the Gulf of California. Crashing into the river may have been numbing, but she was still alive to feel the icy water.

She had no way of knowing how far she sank, but her billowing skirt that may have cushioned her fall was now filled with air and she surged back to the surface. She burst clear of the water, gasping for breath in spasmodic gulps. Pepita was barely an adequate swimmer, as there wasn't a great deal of opportunity to practise in Sonora, but she was able to stay afloat, at least temporarily. Then the skirt that was her initial salvation became a lethal, waterlogged liability. The air pockets dissolved and the sodden material started to drag her down.

She fought for as long as she could, but her efforts exhausted her and she succumbed to the black water's urging and began to drown. She managed to fight back to the surface a couple of times, but finally with no strength left, she slid to her doom.

Jubal pushed the pirogue from the riverbank, jumped in and grabbed a paddle. It was a solid wood dugout, harder and heavier to manage than he'd thought. He blazed a few random shots at the balloon, not knowing whether they hit or flew wide. Soon he was too busy controlling the boat. He tossed a spare paddle to Billy and, after a faulty start, they co-ordinated control of the pirogue as it moved into the midstream current. They were all aware of the blast from the blunderbuss, but Jubal and Billy had no time to look up.

Then Teresita and Alameda screamed.

Someone dropped from the balloon and sailed to earth for what seemed such a long time before splashing into the Colorado River. She was unmistakably a woman, but they failed to recognise her and thought she'd been killed on impact. When they saw her emerge and struggle for life they acted remarkably. Although Billy was no river man, Jubal had fished in pirogues on the Mississippi which flowed beside one of the plantations where he'd been enslaved. He was at least a little water-savvy.

'Grab her,' Jubal roared. 'I'll handle the boat.'

Paddling like fury he drew the pirogue close to the struggling woman and Billy reached under her arms just as she was about to disappear. Now, hanging onto dead weight dragged down by sodden clothing was not easy. A rocking canoe didn't help either, but then Teresita and Alameda launched into action. There was a time when they'd have simply stood aside and waited for someone else to do the work, but now they carefully manoeuvred themselves to the gunwales and grabbed Pepita by her legs and waist.

The pirogue tipped alarmingly with the weight on one side and Jubal leant out as far as he could to act as a counter balance. With one final effort they hauled her on board and she landed unceremoniously in the pirogue bilge, retching up water.

'Pepita!' the girls chorused.

The fourth rider, Billy surmised.

They hauled her into a sitting position, although she still spluttered water and couldn't speak for a moment. Teresita and

Alameda hugged her tightly which didn't help her breathing, but was a great comfort anyway.

And then they looked up and saw the balloon burst into flames.

'Sam!' Pepita screamed. 'Oh no! Please. No!'

She watched in anguish as the fireball rolled down the canyon wall and evaporated into a yellow glow before disappearing.

There was a lot of confusion and mixed emotions on the boat at that stage. Pepita was inconsolable, although the others didn't yet know why. Billy was relieved because their hunter was suddenly out of the picture. For Jubal, who'd been harbouring guilt all along, it just added to his burden. Teresita and Alameda were simply overjoyed to see Pepita. They prioritised in their own fashion and blazing wreckage came a poor second to being re-united with their friend who they thought was dead. They didn't understand Pepita's sobbing, but then they hadn't just fallen from the balloon and that was bound to upset anyone.

Jubal and Billy didn't have any more time to reflect. They used their hats to bale water until they were satisfied that the boat would stay afloat. Still the pirogue was heavily loaded and they needed to concentrate on navigating along the Colorado River. It wasn't so much hard paddling as the current bore them nicely, but the craft tended to skew to one side or another so they needed paddle-power to keep on a steady course. In time they became quite proficient and began enjoying the view.

Pepita didn't actually recover, but managed to sob out her story, while Teresita and Alameda filled her in on their adventures. Being used to non-Spanish speaking people, they now spoke in

English so Jubal followed the story, although it didn't really tell him anything he hadn't deduced.

Now jumping into a canoe and heading west might seem like a good idea when you're in the need of a quick getaway, but it wasn't the most thought out plan. Food wasn't a problem, as there was plenty of game living along the Colorado bank. Both Billy and Pepita knew how to gather herbs and native vegetables that were good to eat. There was no shortage of water, although it was muddy in midstream, but cleared towards shore where the current slowed and sediment settled. They could always strain it anyway.

But, of course they had no idea where the river would take them. Jubal figured that sooner or later they would come to a ford or settlement and negotiate transport to California. They were still cashed up with the money from the bank hold-up and Don Margil's gold dust. Their first day went smoothly enough, and they camped on the riverbank that night. By then they had the whole story from Pepita.

'I loved him so much,' she wailed at the end, but finally fatigue overtook her and she fell asleep.

Teresita and Alameda made a great fuss of her and shared their blankets ensuring she was comfortable. She slept in her underwear and they hung her skirt and blouse beside the fire to dry. Pepita was just too exhausted and grief-stricken to be modest about it.

'I wonder what she'll do now,' Billy pondered.

'Go back home to Hacienda O'Conor, I guess,' Jubal replied.

'No, no, we will not permit it,' Alameda said. 'She will come with us to Aunt Frescura's ranchero. We cannot let her go on alone after this. *We* will take care of her.'

Well, well, there's some hope for our gals yet, Jubal thought with a smile, although the last thing he and Billy needed was another woman along. But, she was feisty, resilient and determined so they could do a lot worse.

The following morning they carefully repacked the pirogue to balance the load. They helped the girls on board and shoved off. At first they travelled smoothly, and even took time to enjoy the majesty of the canyon, although Pepita saw it only as a monstrous juggernaut that had taken her darling from her. And it had more peril in store for them all.

They swept around a curve in the river and although the canyon walls didn't narrow perceptively, great rocks, sediment and debris had piled up on either side of the river. Whether spring floods, an earth tremor, landslides or a gradual build up had caused the constriction no one knew, it may indeed have been all of those forces, but a blockage there was. As a result the water surged forward alarmingly and the pirogue was sucked along with it.

Initially it seemed as if they were simply making better time. The current was smooth and the pirogue stayed nicely in the centre of the river. But the riverbed dropped sharply and water tumbled away in a series of savage white water cataracts. They spilled through the abyss, as there was nothing they could do but hang on. The rapids pitched them violently and even spun the pirogue around so they headed stern first until another swirling current righted them. Icy water drenched them to the skin and pooled dangerously at the bottom of the boat. They crashed into rocks around which the maelstrom swirled.

'Glad we didn't choose one of them birch bark canoes, it'd be smashed to pieces by now,' Billy yelled above the roaring water, and remarkably cheerfully in Jubal's view.

They surged out of the rapids into still water and all sighed, but the pirogue was swept away again before Jubal and Billy could dig at the water with their paddles. They missed the opportunity to reach shore and plunged into white water once more to be so badly battered by the torrents that Pepita nearly lost her grip, but Jubal hung onto her, saving her from pitching overboard.

Drenched again, she thought absently, but regained her hold on the pirogue bulwarks.

They burst clear of the rapids once more and the river calmed, but only for a moment. They looked ahead and saw flat water, but it seemed to be shrouded in mist. And then they heard a sinister rumble and knew they were in trouble. They were heading for a serious waterfall. It was a twenty-foot sheer drop and the pirogue was pulled relentlessly towards it. There was no respite, in seconds their boat shot over the edge and was flung into midair. It hung there for a second then plunged into the swirly eddies below.

They screamed as they went down. Everyone was tossed from the boat and splashed into the heaving foam. The heavy pirogue then became a lethal weapon. Hitting the riverbed vertically it bounced straight back up and reared almost completely out of the water, crashing down on its back and just missing Teresita and Billy. They grabbed the hull and clung on for all they were worth. Jubal gasped for air as he burst to the surface. Recovering quickly he saw Alameda struggling to stay afloat. He reached her and despite her flaying arms, pulled her to the pirogue. The boat was smooth, but

Jubal ripped off Snake's jacket and flung it over the hull. It was tough enough for the four of them to hang on, balanced on either side by each other's weight.

Desperately they looked about, but there was no sign of Pepita.

They had no idea how long they hung onto the pirogue, it can't have been more than moments or fatigue would have claimed them. As it was, the waters calmed and they urged the boat to the shoreline with agonising slowness. Jubal thought every kick would be his last, but eventually his feet found the bottom and he pushed the vessel to the bank.

They staggered ashore and collapsed on the pebbly riverbank.

After a while Jubal sensed there was someone in front of him. He hauled himself to his knees and stared at a pair of very shabby and dusty boots. Three other equally forlorn pairs of footwear stood behind the first. He raised his eyes and stared into the eyes of a scrawny rascal with a salt-pepper beard that only grew in patches.

'Lookee, lookee,' said the villain, who appeared to be the group leader. 'I think we found ourselves some spendin' money.'

He wasn't talking about Jubal and Billy's cash funds either, in fact the river men didn't even bother to search them carefully enough to discover the money and gold dust that Billy and Jubal had stashed into their boots and down their pants where no one really wanted to go.

As it turned out they'd stumbled into the camp of a bunch of traders who weren't particular about the provenance of their merchandise. They saw four healthy bodies, especially two pretty girls, as a handy investment to trade with itinerant Indians and vagrant Mexicans who roamed around the South West.

No more than river pirates, they'd pitched a couple of tents by the shoreline where some wagons were pulled up with horses and mules grazing close by. Several piles of trade goods were stacked in the wagons and on the ground in anticipation of imminent commerce. They included gunpowder kegs, old flintlock and percussion rifles that didn't work very well, but adequately for the Indian trade. There were whiskey kegs, rum and gin bottles that acted as basic native currency, supplemented by rolls of calico, strings of colourful beads, mirrors, knives, china and metal goods that were all also eminently negotiable tender. Slaves, especially strong and handsome ones would prove an easily movable asset.

A large, flat-bottomed raft was moored to the bank. It was lightly loaded, but looked as if it was the vessel the traders used to take pelts, game and anything else the Indians might supply for on-trading down river. The Indians often bartered gold nuggets or bags of dust they'd found or stolen from miners. Considering they admired brightly coloured artefacts, they weren't particularly interested in gold, but were well aware of the white man's obsession with it.

The four ruffians tied Billy and Jubal to a tree after thumping them savagely into submission, and trussed Teresita and Alameda to another stout trunk. The girls recovered enough to put up a squabbling fight, but after a couple of sharp slaps their resistance evaporated. The pirates were busily stacking their wares, but by the way they leered at the girls, who knew how long they'd keep their minds on their work? Towards late afternoon they appeared satisfied with what they'd done and settled around their campfire. They stoked it up and put on a stewing pot. Then they grabbed a stoneware whiskey jug and passed it around, taking a few solid plugs each.

They paid little attention to their prisoners and failed to notice a tiny movement behind Billy and Jubal.

Billy felt something sharp bite into the rawhide thongs that bound his wrists.

'Sssh!' Pepita whispered, as he started. 'Stay still while I uncut you and Jubal.'

She worked away at their bonds, hunched down to avoid being seen. The straps soon fell clear.

'Don't make a move until I give the signal,' Pepita hissed. 'Then free the girls.'

'What sig…?'

'You'll know.'

And she was gone.

Pepita wasn't actually sure what the signal would be, but she knew she must cause a diversion to allow Jubal and Billy to jump the river pirates. The wagons looked like the best source of materials for the job. She went cautiously so as not to upset the horses. Quietly slipping around the camp, she edged behind the wagons. It didn't take long to find what she sought. In one wagon along with cigar boxes were bags of lucifers.

She took some of the matches. She also found a massive bowie knife that would do nicely. The next wagon contained the whiskey and black powder kegs. She pulled one of the kegs down and flipped its stopper out with the knife. After laying a short powder trail she placed the keg under the first wagon, lit a match and tossed it into the gunpowder that spluttered to life. Then she ran, slashing the tethers that held the remuda, and led the animals away.

The pirates saw her and leapt to their feet. Two of them took after her, while the other two turned to their prisoners. Jubal and Billy charged and slammed into the men. Surprise and desperation were in their favour and with some savage blows, viciously silenced the rogues. Jubal ripped a knife from one of the men and freed Alameda and Teresita.

Pepita was soon overtaken, but just before the villains caught her she released the animals, spun round and lashed out, kicking the first man in the groin with all her might. He went down in silence. Without pausing she ducked under the other man's arms and drove the bowie knife into his gut with all her strength. He grunted and slumped to his knees, grasping his hands around the knife hilt as blood oozed out. Pepita pushed his fists aside and dragged the knife away as a scarlet fountain gushed from the open wound. She was in no mood to be messed about by lowlife river trash.

And then the gunpowder exploded. It ripped through the wagon floor and the river men's trade goods rocketed skywards along with wooden shards torn from the wagon. The blast knocked everyone over and they covered their heads as wreckage clattered around them. The horses and mules bolted for the hills and it was unlikely they'd be recovered any time soon.

Jubal was first to his feet and checked on everyone. They were bruised and dazed, but generally in one piece. Pepita slowly emerged from the smoke haze looking sheepish and a little unsteadily, but otherwise unharmed.

Of course no one was angry with her, but Jubal did point out that the horses would have been a good source of transport. Pepita shrugged, insisting she'd have hung onto them if she hadn't been attacked. Jubal didn't mention it, but thought the river-men weren't in Claude Valentine's league and blowing things up was probably unnecessary.

'That was the signal, then?' Billy asked.

'I got the timing a bit wrong, that's all,' Pepita retorted with a pout.

'Maybe a slight overkill, but we got the job done in the end. Thanks Pepita.'

With squeals of delight, Alameda and Teresita raced forwards and gushed all over her, lavishing hugs and kisses. Pepita had just been lucky, after they'd all tumbled over the falls she'd been swept quickly to the riverbank before she could get into trouble.

'Looks like it's back to the river again then,' Jubal observed, eyeing the barge.

They decided that river travel should be safe enough, after all the pirates had brought their vessel this far and against the current. The river must have slowed down considerably to have made that possible. They recovered weapons and ammunition to replace those lost in the Colorado River. After salvaging food, water, and the undamaged trade-goods, they stowed them aboard the barge before casting off. They neither knew nor cared whether the rive-men were dead or alive, but they'd take advantage of their merchandise and turn a profit if the opportunity arose. Those ruffians only had themselves to blame.

Indeed the river proved benign from then on and they reached the Fort Mohave crossing after a leisurely cruise, much to Pepita's relief. She'd swallowed enough of the Colorado River to last a lifetime, although now Sam was gone, what she planned to do with that lifetime, she really didn't know.

Chapter 20

Fort Mohave was pretty much the end of the line when it came to frontier outposts. It was set a little way from the riverbank beyond the flood line. A trail led down to the river where a ferry stood ready to be drawn back and forth by two teams of mules on either bank. When not in use the ferry was secured to posts driven into the bank.

Levees had been erected, but how successful they were at holding back floodwater was problematic. Mohave resembled Fort Pierce in many ways, especially as a sleepy shantytown had sprung up along the riverbank. It consisted of tents, cabins, a reasonable hotel and saloon and a Wells Fargo agency that controlled any business in the area.

A stern-wheeler riverboat was moored further down-stream in deeper water. Jubal and Billy manoeuvred the barge to the river edge and fastened it to one of the docking posts. The town was quiet, everyone seemed to be around the paddle-streamer and only a couple of idlers eyed them sullenly before shuffling off.

Leaving Billy, Alameda and Teresita to guard the barge, Jubal and Pepita went to the Wells Fargo office to negotiate further travel.

'Well, sir,' the agency clerk said enthusiastically. 'San Francisco, is it? This must be your lucky day. Why, the *Colorado Belle* is anchored just yonder. She'll be steaming up to leave at dawn tomorrow. That's your best plan, I'd say. We operate this concession for the West Coast Steamship Company, you know. Paddle-steamer'll take you down to Yuma where you can connect with one of our fast schooners or steam packets that'll sail round the Baja

Peninsula, stopping at San Diego, Santa Barbara, Monterey and San Francisco.'

'Sounds like a long way around,' Jubal said warily.

'Week or two depending on winds of course, but they're favourable this time of year and it's fair sailing weather.'

'What about the stage?'

'Used to run, but there's been so much bandit trouble around here lately, that we can't get no one to drive the coach. It's a hot, dry, dusty and bumpy ride anyway. A sea voyage is just what you need, yes sir. Salt air is most efficacious according to latest medical assessments.'

Jubal turned to Pepita with a questioning look.

'I've had all the bandits I need right now,' she said. 'We don't want to put Alameda and Teresita at risk either.'

'Okay, we'll take five through tickets to San Francisco, thank you.'

'Yessir, wise choice, if I may say so,' the clerk beamed as he was paid a commission for every fare he sold.

'Boarding at half-four tomorrow morning. Sailing at five, and the captain doesn't wait for stragglers.'

Jubal asked the clerk if he was interested in brokering a deal for the goods on board the barge. The clerk being a man of enterprise closed his office and accompanied them to the river. After inspecting the merchandise he looked very sceptical indeed.

'May I ask where you obtained this shipment?' he whispered.

'Confiscated it from a bunch of pirates up river,' Billy announced proudly. 'I reckon they wanted to sell *us* off to Mexican slavers, but we got the better of them.'

'I think you should know that much of this looks familiar. I've got a feeling the black powder was stolen from the fort itself. I'd be careful if I was you, the soldiers are sure to want it back if they see this load.'

The clerk agreed to take the barge and its cargo off their hands for a hugely discounted price, but then there were risks involved, weren't there? He grabbed some tarpaulins from a wagon behind his office and covered the stores, eyeing the fort nervously. Actually he needn't have worried, as there was only a solitary sentry inside the gates and no one patrolling the walls. Nearly all the fort's troopers were out scouring southern California for the bandits that had terrorised the stage line to a standstill.

They checked into two rooms at the hotel, ate buffalo stew in the bar room and shared a few bottles of beer. Teresita and Alameda occupied themselves teasing a couple of soldiers who'd drifted in after duty. They confirmed that there was only a skeleton crew consisting of a single platoon manning the fort. The off-duty troopers only stayed a short while for lack of funds. No one else was in the bar as the townsfolk were enjoying the salon on board the *Colorado Belle* that actually served wine and had a fine banjo player. It made a nice change from Mohave cactus hooch and the hotel's honky tonk pianist was unreliable, being dead drunk most of the time. Jubal thought it best to steer clear of the paddle-steamer until sailing time to ensure their anonymity. He didn't mind the town being deserted. There would be plenty of time to enjoy the riverboat facilities tomorrow.

Jubal and Pepita turned in early. With a dawn start, they knew they'd have to wake everyone up. Billy and the girls stayed for a nightcap and promised to be good. Jubal was just sleep when he felt someone shaking him to his senses.

'Jubal, wake up!' Pepita hissed.

'What?'

'We've got trouble. I went down to check that Billy and the girls hadn't been tempted to sneak off to the riverboat and draw attention to themselves.'

'I'll kill 'em...'

Pepita was sure Jubal's black face turned red.

'It's okay, they're still here, but those two soldiers are back. They've bailed Billy up at the bar. I think they've found out about the stolen loot.'

Jubal pulled his boots on and stuffed his revolver into his belt. He was about to creep along the passageway, but Pepita grabbed his arm.

'Not that way,' she whispered. 'I've got an idea.'

She explained quickly and they hustled back along the corridor to a stairway that led into an alley behind the hotel. Pepita checked that the coast was clear and they crept down the steps to the front of the saloon. Pepita pulled her blouse and camisole down into a tempting décolletage. *Not too bad either*, she thought as she pushed open the bar room door. *That should keep them interested.*

There were only six people in the bar including the bartender. Billy was staring down the barrel of a Remington Army revolver in the hands of one trooper, while the other soldier held Alameda and Teresita at gunpoint.

'Now, matey,' the first trooper was saying. 'A couple of bar flies came up to the fort sayin' you brought a barge-load of contraband to the ferry crossing. I think we ought to take a look. A lot of stuff's been going missing lately. If we recover some of it, it'll set us up good with our captain when he gets back off patrol.'

Now that was a complication they could well do without and Billy knew it. They'd probably be able to explain the merchandise and get away with it. But, they were still fugitives who had no time to waste and dared not risk identification. He was still wondering what to do about the two armed troopers when Pepita stormed into the bar room.

She marched up to Alameda and Teresita and slapped them both across the cheek. She hoped it wasn't too hard, but needed to look convincing.

'This is my patch, you bitches!' she hissed. 'You want to turn tricks, you go elsewhere.'

She turned and faced the second, rather startled soldier. 'You wanna woman, soldier boy?' she mewed, sidling up to him and stroking his arm. 'These two rabbits are no use. You want a woman who knows how to make a man *very* happy, no?'

Jubal eased through the doorway. He was behind the first trooper in a couple of huge strides and clouted him across the head. He collapsed with a groan and slumped motionless over the table. Billy was on his feet and with the stealth and speed of a cougar. He drew his revolver and smashed it across the other soldier's face. He clubbed him a couple more times until he lay still on the floor. The barman lunged for a shotgun lying on a shelf behind the counter, but Jubal turned his gun on him and shook his head. The bartender wisely took the hint and raised his hands.

'Now we don't hanker to hurt anyone,' Jubal assured him, although how he considered two battered troopers to be unhurt was ambiguous. 'But, we'll do what we have to do there's no doubt about that. I'm afraid we're going to detain you gents for a bit.'

They hauled the stunned troopers behind the bar and forced the bartender to close up early.

'Ain't as if you've got any customers anyway,' Billy observed cheerfully.

They found rope in the hotel storeroom, bound the soldiers and gagged the barkeeper. A nervous night vigil followed. Jubal fretted that the troopers would be missed, but no one came looking for them. They recovered during the night and Pepita gave them some water. Their heads hurt like mad and they started cursing foully, so Pepita gagged them as well.

'You only have yourselves to blame,' she admonished primly. 'That is no language to use in front of a lady.'

'Didn't seem much of a lady last night,' one of the soldiers muttered as she drew a scarf across his mouth.

'That was last night. It's almost dawn now.'

At first light the *Colorado Belle's* calliope hooted a boarding call. They bundled the three captives into the storeroom, locked it securely and pushed a hefty cabinet in front of the door. Then they hurried along the riverbank and boarded the steamer. As the clerk anticipated, the captain didn't delay. As soon as they boarded sweating deck hands hauled up the boarding plank, and cast off. The giant paddle wheel slapped at the river surface and they were on their way.

The bartender and troopers managed to free themselves in about two hours. It was no easy task as they were squeezed shoulder to shoulder with no room to manoeuvre. It took another hour to kick the door open and move the cabinet. The troopers hurried back to the fort and reported their internment. Their sergeant thought they'd been asleep in the barracks and hadn't missed them at all. In the end he decided he had neither resources nor inclination to go chasing downriver, suggesting the troopers probably got no more than they deserved for carousing with loose women and tavern ruffians.

Eventually they recovered the stolen property. The Wells Fargo agent was crestfallen, and had to do some fast-talking to stay out of the fort stockade. Even though he'd paid very little for the cargo, the Army still confiscated the lot. As most of it was originally theirs, they felt justified.

The *Colorado Belle* chugged peacefully towards Yuma. Its crew were sublimely unaware they carried two desperate fugitives from justice and their accomplices. It was by no means the largest of river-steamers like the huge vessels that plied the Mississippi and Missouri, but it sported a comfortable dining and games salon on the upper deck, ten moderately plush and sizeable cabins and a large cargo bay below as well as ample deck space. Billy and Jubal shared one cabin while the girls occupied another. The bridgehouse sat proudly above the salon, where the captain and river-pilot negotiated the Colorado's occasional, treacherous vagaries. Back east, paddle-steamers were probably past their peak with the advancing railroads, but there was still a place for river travel in the Wild West.

The other passengers were mostly miners who'd made enough to head for San Francisco to enjoy their wealth, although usually only temporarily. Teresita and Alameda were at their enchanting best and flirted shamelessly, insisting they only drink the most expensive wines from the *Colorado Belle*'s cellar. Not that it was an extensive cellar by European standards or those of New York and New Orleans.

Billy spent most of the time on deck watching the country pass by. He loved cruising and thought it beat horseback any time. Pepita was mostly quiet and a little melancholy. Teresita and Alameda attempted to cheer her up, but sometimes it was difficult. She smiled for them occasionally because they tried so hard to make her feel better. They even joked about being slapped. Teresita said it had only happened twice in her life and both times in the last couple of weeks. Indeed Hacienda O'Conor seemed so far away and they all felt a little homesick.

'You didn't have to hit so hard,' they chirped, but not unkindly.

'I had to be convincing,' Pepita replied.

'I think you made a very convincing whore, Pepi,' Alameda said. 'But, you are too kind hearted. I think you'd have to be a really hard woman to be a harlot. You know the gringos call them *hookers* in honour of a big Yankee general. I don't think I could salute a *General Strumpet*.'

'I think I'd make a good courtesan,' Teresita announced, quite liking the sound of the word, but not entirely understanding the job description. They giggled as they thought up as many different names for working girls as they could.

Jubal got into a card school with some miners and a shady tinhorn who'd been exiled from the Mississippi circuit and now cruised the Colorado River, fleecing anyone gullible enough to let him. The miners were generally poor players and Jubal easily picked the tinhorn's false moves. He could have cleaned out everyone without cheating, but settled for a few dollars to pay for meals and a drink. He'd judged their mood well, but the tinhorn wasn't satisfied until he'd fleeced every dollar and ounce of gold dust from his victims. The miners left the salon in an ugly mood.

The next morning the tinhorn failed to show up for breakfast and at first everyone thought he'd just slept in. Along about noon a cabin steward rapped on his door and reported to the captain he was missing. There was not much the captain could do other than turn the steamer around and go trolling for gamblers overboard, but he wasn't prepared to do that. He had a schedule to keep and connecting passengers for San Francisco. And who really cared about one seedy river-rat anyway. The miners' spirits improved remarkably and they appeared to have been reimbursed. So they were able to spoil Teresita and Alameda once more.

A week later a bloated body, washed up close to Yuma. It was discovered by a party of lawmen and surveyors who'd been commissioned to study the viability of building a territorial prison in the area. The body had provided three square meals daily for thousands of fish and snapping turtles, but the lawmen were convinced the cause of death was six or seven deep stab wounds, rather than drowning. By then any suspects were long gone.

Jubal, Billy and the girls transferred to a sleek schooner by the name of *Miranda Jane* for the remainder of their journey. None of them had sailed the ocean before and they were excited. Billy thought sailing ships were the most beautiful machines he'd seen, especially this handsome fore-aft rigged three-master. Initially it was a slow, hot tack-and-jibe south past Baja, but when they turned into the Pacific Ocean the cool sea breezes took effect as the ship glided swiftly with a handy following wind. Pepita was the only one to suffer seasickness, it was so unfair and after the first day she just wanted to die. In time she did recover a little, but was burdened with bouts of sickness throughout the voyage. Afternoons and evenings were her best times when she cheered up a little.

The seas off Baja were full of wonders. The girls shrieked with delight at the sight of dolphins that chased and frolicked across the schooner bow. The ship's master allowed them to go forward with the first mate and gaze over the side. The master was beguiled by Alameda and Teresita's seemingly innocent charm and they soon had him eating out of their hands.

Billy loved the sea. Virginia Pritchard had explained the oceans, but this was beyond his dreams. He befriended some of the crewmembers who took him aloft where he spent hours scanning the horizon from the crow's nest. He also entertained them with songs and his harmonica playing and quickly learnt the jigs, shanties and hornpipes the crew's musicians taught him. There was a sharp fiddle player and a squeezebox accordionist on board, so Billy loved nothing more than joining in when they tuned up and started playing. A few rust spots were forming on the harmonicas after their drenching in the Colorado River, but they still sounded just fine.

The sailors spoke a different language and Billy paid close attention to learn as many nautical terms as he could. Soon he was *belaying, avasting, starboard* and *larboarding* with the best of them.

Like Billy, Jubal preferred to stay on deck, but for another reason altogether. He didn't know why, but eerie dreams haunted him at night. He envisaged his ancestors crossing the Atlantic middle-passage crammed together and chained under the decks. Living in their own filth and dying in droves, it was torment beyond endurance. He heard their mournful cries, although when he asked Billy about sounds at night, he answered it was quiet except for creaking planks, whispering rigging and the wash of waves. Possibly it was just Jubal's imagination dredging stories from his childhood on the plantation. Mostly life was hard enough back then without recalling the horrors of the slave-ships, but the old folk told them anyway. They didn't want their children to forget their origins and many claimed they'd return home one day. But, somehow he felt their dread and despair and he found it difficult to sleep below, even though he was provided with a comfortable bunk.

Once they spotted a pod of humpback whales on their way to Alaska for the summer. The girls were delighted when they saw a calf swimming beside its mother accompanied by a group of delinquent dolphins. Billy was simply amazed at the humpback's size.

'No one is going to bother that monster,' he said to no one in particular.

'No one 'ceptin' us maybe,' one of the old salts replied. 'And sharks I s'pose.'

'Have to be a damned big shark.'

'Oh aye, they got some big sharks in the ocean, sonny.'

A couple of days later they saw one. The wind died and the schooner drifted slowly with the current. The captain wasn't dismayed and explained that there were often calm periods, especially in the evening and early morning. Billy and Jubal were idling at the stern when the ship's cook tossed a pail of scraps overboard. A huge, black dorsal fin sliced through the calm, indigo waters and a twenty-five foot monster lunged to the surface, rolled on its side and presented several gaping rows of razor-sharp teeth. It gorged down the cook's discarded meat bones in a single, jaw-snapping gulp.

The old salt leant on the taffrail beside them, sucking on a whalebone pipe engraved with scrimshaw around the bulb.

'That's the one to fear,' he remarked between puffs of blue tobacco smoke. 'It's a great white, or white pointer some folk calls 'em. Snap you right in half in one bite. I seen a man go overboard in calm sea once, slipped clean out of the heads, he did. We threw out a line and when he was hauled in there weren't nothin' left from the waist down, so we chucked the rest back, 'cos there weren't no point in keeping it.'

Billy and Jubal decided that although they liked sailing, you had to be pretty tough to take it on as a vocation.

'Doesn't look so white, why its top half is blacker than me,' Jubal said.

'Aye, you have a point,' the old salt conceded, 'but the *great-black-grey-and-white* don't have quite the same ring, do it?'

San Diego and Santa Barbara were charming towns in the Old Mexican style. The hidalgos were still influential and owned land all along the west coast. It reminded Pepita of home, which made her a little melancholy, but Teresita and Alameda took her shopping in the markets while the ship restocked with water, meat and vegetables. She enjoyed just being a girl again and bought a shawl and a necklace. Alameda declared they looked so beautiful on her, but then she thought sadly that Sam would never see her wearing pretty things again.

The schooner picked its way gingerly through the Monterey kelp-beds where playful sea otters eyed them curiously as they floated on their backs. Torturously hunched cypress pines clung to the rocky coastline, battered into deformity by relentless westerlies. They took the opportunity to take a hot, fresh-water bath and a rewarding seafood feast at a waterfront café. The meals on board were a little monotonous and it was the first time Jubal had tasted lobster. He'd eaten plenty of crawfish gumbo and oyster pie back along the Mississippi, but freshly boiled Pacific Ocean lobster was by far the nicest thing he'd ever tasted.

Then it was all aboard once again for the short voyage to San Francisco.

Chapter 21

The *Colorado Belle* was over four hours downriver when Zeb Turner and Petorio Blanco rode into Fort Mohave. The heliograph hadn't been much use as they took a short cut away from the canyon and they were hopeless at using the code anyway. Sam flashed a last, exasperated message telling them to get going to Fort Mohave as quickly as possible and he'd meet them there.

They were well ahead of Sam so there was no hurry. They found a bathhouse at the back of a Chinese laundry and cleaned up while waiting for their gear to be washed and dried. They took a room at the hotel and went to the bar where they soon discovered that a black man, an Indian and three fine looking gals had caused the bartender considerable abuse the night before.

'*Three* women?' Petorio said.

'Yessir, and right beauties they were,' the barman replied as he poured two beers with whiskey chasers. 'Two looked like sisters maybe, and tother was a feisty little spitfire if ever I saw one. Locked two troopers and me in the storeroom all night. Funny thing is they didn't steal nothin' — even left cash money for their room and board. You fellers want venison stew and taters for supper later on?'

'Yeah, sounds fine to me,' Petorio said absently, but his mind was elsewhere.

'You thinkin' what I'm thinkin'?' Zeb asked.

'Seems like,' Petorio agreed, 'but I reckon it'll be best to keep this to ourselves. We don't know for sure, and we don't want to get Sam's hopes up for nothing.'

'Yep, but we ain't gonna find out until we know where they are headed.'

'Oh, I can help you there, sir,' piped up the eavesdropping Wells Fargo agent who had come in for a snack and was seated on the stool next to them.

'Allow me to introduce myself, gentlemen. The name's Tillman Caswell.'

'Howdy,' Zeb and Petorio said cautiously. Zeb bought another round and included a beer for Tillman who was in a chatty mood.

'…So your friends should be in San Francisco in a fortnight at the latest,' Tillman concluded. He finished his drink and left without bothering to buy a return round, but Zeb didn't push it. Tillman wasn't his first choice in drinking companions.

Sam turned up two days later. He was hot, grime-smeared and smelly. Petorio and Zeb guided him to the bathhouse and arranged for his laundry.

'Funny how a thing like that bothers a feller,' Zeb mused. 'Why I recall up in the Montana Territory when me and Jim Bridge was out dodgin' Blackfeet an' trappin' for six months and, 'ceptin' to drink, didn't touch a drop of water all that time, no sir. It was so darned cold we huddled up closer than canoodlers, but I don't recall us smellin' none.'

'It's relative,' Sam said, as the Chinese attendant poured a pale of steaming water over his head. Petorio handed him a whiskey bottle that they hadn't completely polished off themselves.

Sam had an interesting trip around the canyon's northern face, running into two cavalry patrols that were unsuccessfully chasing bandits. They warned him to be careful, so he'd made cold camps and travelled with his eyes peeled. A few shots came his way and he outran a group of riders. He didn't know whether they were outlaws or not, but in light of the cavalry officer's advice, didn't bother to find out.

'This is hazardous territory in my opinion,' he said and no one disagreed.

Petorio and Zeb faced the dilemma of telling Sam about Jubal and Billy and that they were long gone with no way of catching up. In all honesty they were tired of chasing around the southwest after men with whom they shared some empathy. There was also the matter of Pepita that remained unresolved. In the end they took Sam to the Wells Fargo office so Tillman Creswell could tell him what he knew and Sam would have to make up his own mind, which of course he did.

'Looks like we're headed for San Francisco,' Sam declared.

'Can't see us beatin' them on horseback,' Petorio said.

'And I'm damned if I know how we'll find 'em. Frisco's a big city now,' Zeb added. 'Folks keep addin' to it even though it gets shaken down by 'quakes and goes up in smoke periodically. Mind you I do recall them heydays in the '50s bein' dandy fun. It sure was a wild town in the boom time, but I do believe it's quietened down some now.'

'Railroad, gentlemen,' Tillman declared. He still smarted from the confiscation of his contraband, but ever the entrepreneur, saw an opportunity.

'Don't see no railroad around here,' Sam insisted.

'No sir, but a spur line runs only twenty-five miles away. It ain't a passenger service by a long chalk, but Mr Leland Stanford himself is developing the track. He's personally overseein' the line to cash in on the minin' boom and run the railway from Sacramento clear across California, Arizona and New Mexico to Santa Fe.'

'Impressive, but where's the railway line?' Sam asked.

'North, like I say, only a day's ride is all.'

'But it ain't no passenger train?' Zeb insisted.

'No, sir, but I've a small problem that needs solving and I believe you're three fellers who're up to the job. Help me and I can fix travel warrants for you all the way to Frisco on the freight train.'

'Keep talkin', mister,' Sam said sceptically.

'Well, sir,' Tillman explained, 'the Irish navvies and Chink coolies ain't been paid for a couple of months and they're getting' kinda agitated, especially the Paddies, who're mighty thirsty by now. I've got the payroll in a strong box guarded at the fort. It came up from Yuma on the *Colorado Belle* a couple of days ago. But what with the diggings and all I can't get anyone to take it up to the railhead. Everyone would rather be out prospectin' and the Army can't spare anyone. Now I don't get my bonus until that cashbox is delivered, so if you gents were to escort that shipment for me, I'll authorise your passage on the supply train in return.'

Tillman gave them a shrewd, *well-what-about-it* look.

'I don't suppose highwaymen have anything to do with the reluctance to carry your payroll?' Sam observed.

'Three well-armed and determined fellows like you wouldn't be troubled by road agents. Why they're nothin' but cowardly scum, you'd scare 'em right off.'

'What's to stop us just galloping away with the payroll?'

'Oh, I wouldn't recommend that, sir,' Tillman warned. 'It would be very unwise to make an enemy of the Southern Pacific Railroad.'

'Bandits seem to think otherwise.'

'Unfortunately bandits are reckless by nature and interested only in immediate gratification. They fail to consider the consequences of their actions, which is why so many wind up swinging at the end of a rope. Anyway, if I can't trust a US Army officer, who can I trust?'

Sam nodded, hadn't he said as much to Marshal Reynolds back in Tucson?

In the end they agreed. It wasn't so much chasing Jubal and Billy, but if there was any chance Pepita still lived and they didn't explore it, there'd be no living with Sam. More importantly Zeb and Petorio thought they'd have difficulty living with themselves. Anyway if they didn't go with him, Sam was just pig-headed enough to go alone.

Their transport was a dusty Abbott & Downing Concord coach. It almost broke Zeb's heart to see the once-magnificent vehicle stripped down with the doors, lanterns and boot removed. The faded red paint was peeling away in ragged strips.

'Think she'll last a day?' Sam asked.

'The wheels and bearings look sound,' Zeb reported. 'She'll go like the wind with all the excess weight removed. I jehued for the Butterfield line when these rigs were in their glory-days. I guess the railroad'll finish off the stage before bandits do.'

It didn't take Zeb long to hitch up the team that seemed docile and experienced. Tillman wasn't much help, but Zeb found the horses positioned themselves. He regretted not knowing their names, as a proficient jehu could coax more from a team by calling them individually, but he was confident in his skill at the reins.

They loaded the strong box along with their saddlebags, weapons, ammunition and water canteens, also stashing six full water kegs on the backboard for the horses. The Mohave Desert was no place to run dry. Petorio mentioned the chest didn't weigh much, but Tillman assured him it contained fifty thousand dollars in bank notes. Sam rode beside Zeb as shotgun guard and Petorio led their spare horses as outrider. Jesse was proving cantankerous and Zeb tethered her to the coach so she had no choice but to trot along. They would travel at a slow, steady pace because there were no relief teams along the way.

The day went well and the road was in fairish condition, broad and open although there were potholes to negotiate. Zeb regained his teamster skills after the first few miles. Petorio ranged ahead and on the flanks, but reported no signs of trouble or tracks left by large numbers of riders except once when he identified the trail of a military column. Towards late afternoon he tied the spare animals to the rear of the Concord and rode ahead once more. The trail narrowed and he wanted to check it out. Shortly afterwards he cantered back to the coach, waving madly for Zeb to pull up.

'There're half a dozen scoundrels waitin' just around the next bend. They're hidden behind rocks and scrub, but I picked 'em out and I don't reckon they saw me.'

'Bushwhackers?' Zeb asked.

'Don't reckon it's a welcoming committee.'

'We'd better backtrack,' Sam said dismally. 'We'll have to find another trail.'

'I don't think so,' Petorio replied looking past the stagecoach to where they'd been. He spotted a cloud of dust swirling a mile or two behind them. 'Bunch of riders comin' in a hurry. I reckon they've boxed us in, so we'll have to break through 'em one way or tother. Take your pick, Sam.'

'Half a dozen ahead you reckon?' Sam said and Petorio nodded.

'More than that behind?'

'I'd say so.'

'Nothing else blocking the track ahead?'

'Didn't see anything.'

'Okay, jump on board, Petorio. Cut the spare horses loose. We'll concentrate our firepower.'

Petorio freed the horses and climbed into the coach cabin. Zeb lashed the team into a gallop as they clattered away. Instinctively Jesse and the spare mounts cantered behind the stage. Petorio passed up two boxes of ammunition for Sam's rifle and he wedged them under his seat. Zeb's buffalo gun lay at his feet, but he was unlikely to have a chance to use it, although you never knew and it was best to be prepared. Petorio was ready with a fully loaded Henry rifle and two revolvers with spare loaded cylinders in his pockets.

Big Sol D'Angelo was a bandit boss of middling success. He'd left Sicily for the Californian goldfields in '55, after trouble with neighbouring families over standover territory, a couple of women, matters of honour, feuds and vendettas that just got too complicated. He soon discovered that robbing miners was much more lucrative than actually being one. There were risks from the authorities of course, but you were still in danger of being robbed if you decided to remain strictly honest. As the law in California was at times tenuous, Big Sol was prepared to take his chances.

The trouble was civilization was smothering the West in leaps and bounds and it was becoming harder and harder to make a dishonest dollar. He'd drawn a gang of ne'er-do-wells from every back-alley, gin-joint and waterfront boozer on the West Coast and now they were the principal terrorists around Mohave.

So he was especially irked when a few days ago a large portion of his marine enterprise had been blown up and one of his men killed. The three survivors reported that a band of two score brigands had set upon them and they were lucky to escape with their lives, although no sign of these forty thugs could be found.

Apart from the damage, a large amount of valuable merchandise was stolen. But despite this financial setback, Sol thought his luck was about to change. He posted lookouts along the road, knowing that sooner or later some choice pickings would come along. He figured the railroad payroll had to show up any day soon, and it looked like it was here with only a driver and two guards. It was easy enough for some of his boys to circle ahead of the stage and block the road, while the remainder of the gang trapped them from behind.

The coach thundered into the pass. The six outlaws ahead heard it coming and spread out across the trail. They weren't intent on murder, simply to bail up the coach, grab the cash and go, but they weren't averse to homicide if it came to a shoot-out either. As the coach roared towards them one of the bandits fired a warning shot into the air. Normally that was enough to encourage a driver to stop, but they hadn't counted on the driver being Zeb Turner.

Yelling like crazy, he lashed at the reins, urging the team even faster. The outlaws still thought they might stop and shot at the coach this time. Sam raised his rifle and fired. Even with the two, massive through-bracings that suspended the coach cabin, he stilled bounced around alarmingly, and hitting something was just about impossible. Petorio, hanging grimly to the window frame, blasted several shots, bringing down one of the riders as the stage surged past them. The outlaws spurred their horses into action as the following gang members caught up and hurtled into the chase with Big Sol leading the charge.

There was no way the stage was going to outrun the bandits. The team had been on the go all day and were tiring. The leading outlaws drew alongside the coach and fired their revolvers. Bullets smashed into the woodwork, spraying Petorio with splinters. He pulled a particularly nasty one from his arm, but although it bled it wasn't going to prove fatal. While Petorio was temporarily out of action, one of the outlaws grabbed the railing on the stage roof and swung himself from the saddle right onto the swaying coach.

He clambered over the cabin and made a grab for Sam, trying to force him off his seat, but he had to hang on with one hand to avoid being tossed overboard himself. Sam swung around and took a shot, but the stage jerked over a rut and the bullet flew high over its target. The bandit struggled to draw his revolver and finally aimed at Zeb. Meanwhile another rider drew alongside and hung onto the cabin window, but by then Petorio had recovered. He stuck his pistol into the bandit's face and pulled the trigger, just about taking his head off. The body dropped from the saddle and crashed under the coach's rear wheel. The stage lurched violently just as the first bandit fired. The bullet smashed into the woodwork between Sam and Zeb. The outlaw was tossed forward and Sam grabbed him by the scruff of the neck and using his forward momentum, flung him between the trailing pair of horses. The bandit screamed and tried to hang onto the traces, but his hands slipped as he was dragged beneath the coach. There was another mighty jolt that nearly knocked Zeb from his seat but Sam grabbed his shirt and hauled him back.

The other riders were closing fast and would have overrun the stage, but they were bunched together in the narrow pass. Then the coach burst into open country and some bandits fanned out to the sides while others galloped ahead. A hail of bullets smashed into the stage and then disaster struck.

The ancient coach's rear axle had had enough. Clumping over a rough road at a sensible pace was one thing, but banging over falling bodies and thumping back to the ground with spleen-crushing force was another. The axle snapped, shearing off the rear wheels. They spun away, tumbling into the riders and bringing down a couple of horses. The coach smashed into the rocky trail and somersaulted into the air. The water casks were flung from the stage and those still full exploded as they struck the ground. The traces ripped apart and the team galloped free. Zeb and Sam found themselves airborne and then crashing back to earth with a bone jarring thump. Sam felt as if his ribs had caved in, but drew his revolver and fired into the ranks of the milling bandits.

Zeb lay still.

Petorio tumbled inside the cab and was dazed for a few moments, but quickly recovered. He was one damn tough Apache. He dragged himself from the coach, looking around for someone to shoot at. He sprinted towards Sam who dragged Zeb behind a rocky outcrop. Bullets sprayed up the dirt at his feet and whipped past his ears.

'Goddamnit, Sam,' he yelled, 'we're purely outnumbered.'

The bandits initially hung around the coach. A couple dived inside and retrieved the strong-box while the remainder took pot-shots at Sam, Zeb and Petorio. Ricocheting rock chips spewed everywhere and they kept their heads down.

Then as suddenly as the shooting had started it stopped. The bandits turned and galloped away with the strong box hanging between two riders. At first Sam thought they'd simply got what they wanted and couldn't be bothered finishing off the payroll guards, but then a group of about fifteen well armed men galloped past followed by a troop of cavalry. They disappeared in hot pursuit of the gang ignoring the couple of dismounted bandits who lay unconscious in the dirt.

After the dust settled Sam and Petorio anxiously checked on Zeb. He'd been knocked out, and it looked as if he sprained his ankle, but his breathing was even. Petorio raced back to the coach and returned with a canteen. A few splashes in Zeb's face and a choking gulp of water revived him.

'Hell's bells, my foot hurts,' he complained, while the others smiled with relief.

'I'll see if I can round up the horses and guns,' Petorio said. 'You stay with Zeb. I don't think he'll be walking for a bit.'

Just then a lone rider appeared from the dust haze. He rode slowly, stopping just in front of Sam. He was a striking figure, riding proudly erect and sporting neat whiskers trimmed to a pointed goatee. He was dressed in an immaculate frock coat, freshly pressed pants and polished elastic sided boots.

'Well, you nearly made it, gentlemen,' he said cheerfully as he dismounted. 'The railhead's only a quarter-of-a-mile away. Come on, let's hoist your friend up on my horse and we'll walk back.'

But, it wasn't necessary, Jesse trotted up and nuzzled Zeb, if he was to be carried it would be by her.

'And just who in God's name are you?' Sam demanded a little harshly, but he'd had a bad day.

'Why, I'm Leland Stanford, sir. I own the railroad.'

He sounded genuinely surprised that they didn't recognise him because he owned a great slice of California as well.

'I arranged for the payroll shipment with that scheming rogue, Tillman Caswell. It was just a matter of hiring some tough fellows. Looks like you fitted the bill. We were expecting the stage any day.

My Pinkerton agents and that cavalry detachment have been chafing at the bit to go after those rascals.'

'Sorry we lost your strongbox,' Zeb said sincerely, more that they'd been bested by the outlaws than Stanford's loss.

'That's okay, boys, you did your best.'

'You don't sound very concerned,' Sam said. 'I mean you were taking a terrible risk. Those villains could have hit us anywhere on the trail. It was just lucky you heard the shooting and came to our rescue. If we'd been further from your camp, you'd never have known and the bandits would have gotten away scot-free. Even now you may not catch them.'

'The posse's on fresh horses and the bandits have been riding a-piece. I'd say the chances of apprehending them are good. I also deduced that little ravine was well favoured for an ambuscade.'

'It was still a terrible risk,' Sam insisted.

'Not at all,' Stanford replied. 'There was never a danger of me losing any cash. Do you honestly think any sane man would trust a scoundrel like Tillman Caswell with fifty thousand dollars? Why, that chest is only filled with newspaper. It was just a decoy to flush out the bandits.'

That was when Lieutenant Sam McAlister, a United States cavalry officer, landed a right hook squarely on the jaw of one of the most powerful, rich and influential men in the State of California.

Chapter 22

'Uhm, Sam,' Petorio said through clenched teeth, 'you know you just slugged the guy who owns the railroad we're trying to hitch a ride on, don't you?'

Sam was too mad to care, but simmered down after the punch and boy, did he feel better, even though his knuckles hurt. Leland Stanford lay sprawled on his back in the dust, stunned for the moment. Soon he stirred and dragged himself to a sitting position. He shook the cobwebs out of his brain and ran his hand over his jaw to check all his teeth were still in place. Satisfied, he held out his arm to Sam.

'Fine right hook you've got there, son, now help me up.'

Sam hauled him to his feet.

'Maybe you've got a right to be sore, but I wouldn't make a habit of fisticuffin' me, if I were you.'

'Sorry, sir,' Sam said lamely, 'I got carried away.'

'So it seems, but what for? You were quite prepared to ride shotgun for fifty thousand dollars, but the main job was to shake out the outlaw gang, and that's just what you did. So, how is that any the less important?'

'I suppose I didn't think about it that way, I was just so darned eager to get to Frisco. Mr Creswell wrote us a pass to ride on the railroad.'

'Did he now?' Stanford arched an eyebrow. 'Seems he's overstepping his authority to sell tickets. This ain't an approved passenger line, *yet.*'

Sam looked disappointed.

'But, hell, you fellows have done me a great service. I'm heading back to San Francisco within the hour. We'll leave the Pinkertons and the Army to tidy up here. Those two fellows look out cold and shouldn't give any trouble. Round up your horses, if you can find them. We'll put 'em in the caboose and I'd be proud to have you as guests in my personal carriage. How's that sound to you?'

'We're mighty grateful, sir,' Sam replied, realising that this was a good time for toadying. He introduced Petorio, Zeb and himself, and was about to babble on about what they'd been up to, but Stanford cut him short.

'No time now, son,' he said. 'Tell me all about it on the trip. It'll help pass the time.'

They helped Zeb off Jesse and up the steps into Stanford's luxurious passenger car. It was ornately laid out with comfortable, leather furniture. A mulatto waiter hovered close by.

'Make yourself useful, man,' Stanford ordered, 'a stiff whiskey for Mr Turner here, and then see if you can rustle up the camp surgeon before we get going. Also tell him there are a couple of rough-necks lying out on the desert who'll need his attention.'

Petorio and Sam managed to corral their horses and recover their scattered weapons, including Zeb's buffalo gun. There were stalls in one of the boxcars, so obviously livestock was transported regularly to the work site. They hadn't noticed the activity before, but realised it was a boiling hotpot of physical enterprise accompanied by the rhythmic clinking of stake-driving hammers as they secured rails to the crossties. Accidents were the order of the day, so a resident surgeon was on hand. He was a nervous looking man, but confirmed Zeb suffered from nothing more than a sprain. He applied a firm bandage around Zeb's ankle.

'Just keep this on for a couple of days, sir, and try to stay off that leg for a week and you'll be fine in no time at all.'

Zeb thanked him, rested his foot on an ottoman and went back to enjoying his whiskey, which was not cheap hooch, but twenty-five year-old, single malt scotch. Stanford's valet, whose name was Alex, brought a box of contraband Havana cigars and soon Zeb was puffing away contentedly. His foot had stopped hurting by the time Petorio and Sam joined him. Alex poured them each a glass of scotch. Soon, with great belching gusts of steam from the locomotive, they were under way.

'Punctual fellow, Mr Stanford,' Zeb observed checking his watch that had survived the stagecoach crash.

Stanford joined them later. The train was rattling along with a mildly hypnotic, swaying *click-it-tee-clack* rhythm that soon had Zeb dozing off. Stanford was an effusive host and really seemed happy to have company. He was proud of his achievements so far, but knew greater things were to come.

'Why gentlemen, I am convinced the Central Pacific will have cut straight through the Rockies and joined the Union Pacific on the Great Plains within two years. Then this great nation will be truly united. Immigrants will pour into California and the Southern Pacific Railroad will be ready to carry them from the Mexican border right up to Canada.'

'You'll become a very rich man,' Petorio observed sceptically. Although he'd come to terms with living with white people, he felt there were enough of them in the West already.

'I am already a very rich man, Mister Blanco,' Stanford replied smugly, 'but I intend to be great deal richer.'

So they rode in the lap of luxury to San Francisco where they left their host to his grand vision. In view of Zeb's ankle, they were pleased they'd brought their mounts because the railhead stopped a few miles short of the town wharfs, and it was the hilliest damn place they'd ever seen. Leland Stanford offered them the use of one of his carriages, but they said Jesse and their horses had served them well so far so they preferred to use them.

They rode up and down hills along Montgomery Street to the wharfs. Having been there before Zeb made an excellent guide, pointing out areas to avoid, such as the east side of town now known as the Barbary Coast, where criminals of every degree and persuasion gravitated. In his day, Zeb explained only huge gangs of vigilantes dared enter the Coast or Chinatown to apprehend serious felons. The local constabulary didn't go there at all.

They checked into a hotel on Jefferson Street, and left Zeb in the parlour with a copy of the *San Francisco Gazette* and a cigar. Petorio went in search of a livery stable while Sam headed for the West Coast Steamship Line's office. It was a bustling, wooden-slat and iron building that erupted with people. Although the original gold fields of the forty-nine rushes were long mined out, San Francisco was still the main port of entry for hopefuls seeking new bonanzas all over California, Arizona and notably the Comstock Lode in the Virginia Range of Nevada.

Sam grabbed the attention of a rattled clerk and asked about arriving ships from Yuma. The clerk said eight vessels were due in the next week or so. And no: he didn't know exactly when they were arriving. It depended on the winds and currents, even for steam ships. And no: he didn't have passenger manifests. Apart from a copy carried by the ship's purser and delivered on arrival, they were kept at the port of departure and only couriered to head office if there was a mishap. And no: he didn't know which wharf they moored at, that was up to the harbour master at the time of arrival, and depended on how many ships turned up and departed on any particular day.

Sam thanked him for his helpfulness and decided all he could do was patrol the docks every day and wait for passengers to disembark from every ship that had called at Yuma. He did get the names of the eight West Coast Steamship vessels with Yuma on their schedules, so that narrowed the hunt down considerably. When evening approached he learnt from the stevedores that no new ships were due to dock, as most skippers preferred not to brave the Golden Gate entrance to the bay at night.

So he rode up to the military Presidio to see if he could arrange some extra muscle. After tethering his horse, he marched through the main portal of that magnificent edifice where generals abounded and colonels did the work of errant boys. Two sentries saluted dubiously, and a very sceptical major received him at the front desk. Sam snapped to attention and saluted for the first time in ages.

'Lieutenant,' the major drawled, 'perhaps you'd like to go away and return when you're appropriately dressed. You are aware that this is the headquarters for the US Army's Pacific Division, are you not?'

'Yes, sir,' Sam replied, still at attention. 'With respect sir, I have been on the trail for several months now with just one change of shirt, breeches and underwear.'

'Is that so? On the trail from where?'

'Fort Leavenworth, Kansas, with the Tenth Cavalry. Been hunting down secesh renegades through the southwest.'

'Well, bully for you, Lieutenant. The Tenth you say, ain't that Ben Grierson's nigra outfit?'

'Yessir.'

'Damn fine soldier I must say. Drew half a Reb division away from Vicksburg, tryin' to catch him on that Mississippi raid. Can't see why he's wastin' his time with darkies though. He made brevet general during the War, you know, but commanding nigra troops won't get him promoted again if General Sheridan has anything to say about it. What the hell are you doing way over here all alone anyway? Have your secesh renegades come this far?'

'No sir, we caught 'em all. I'm chasing a deserter. Alleged to have killed a couple of men back at Fort Pierce.'

'And just where in blue blazes is that?'

'New Mexico Territory. Captain Eugene Bellamy commanding.'

'Well, well, I knew Eugene during the War. He was a light colonel then and a brilliant regimental commander. Served with him at Shiloh, Chickamauga and the Wilderness. And now he's holed up in some God-forsaken backwater in the middle of nowhere. Waste of a damned good infantryman if you ask me, but that's the Army nowadays.'

Even though the major was more sympathetic, he said it was unlikely they would spare any troops to patrol the harbour for someone who had *allegedly* deserted, was *possibly* a murderer, and *might* arrive on *some* ship or another at *some* time.

'You have to understand, Lieutenant, we've got brass to spare in Frisco, but all our line troops are spread out thin from Baja to Fort Vancouver. But, you go get yourself to a tailor in town and have him fix you up with a smart, new uniform, then come on back. By then I'll have had time to check with Leavenworth if the damned Indians haven't cut the wires again. We'll have to relay through Sacramento, Salt Lake, and Cheyenne, so it'll take a couple of days. You come back then and I'll see what I can do for you.'

Sam saluted stiffly and stomped away, knowing a brush off when he heard one. It wasn't the Pacific Division's responsibility and they weren't getting involved unless instructed to by the Department of the Interior. He returned his horse to the livery stable and met Zeb and Petorio for supper. After grumbling for a while he decided all they could do was patrol the wharfs and keep a good lookout for all vessels from Yuma that were arriving in the next week.

The following day Zeb's foot was much improved, so he perched on a bench outside a dock tavern about half way along the quayside. He'd made himself a crutch so he could hobble about. Petorio and Sam split up and started to walk the beat along the waterfront. Sam frequently scanned the bay with his telescope that still worked fine although it had suffered minor dents and scratches.

The *Miranda Jane* slipped through the Golden Gate at dawn. The ship's master reefed sails and made for a vacant pier at the eastern edge of the wharfs. Teresita and Alameda were excited to be back, although they'd only been children on previous visits and had spent all their time on Aunt Frescura's property. They'd never been into the city before, so this was a thrilling prospect. The master manoeuvred the *Miranda Jane* with admirable precision. The ship gently nudged the jetty and crewmen heaved mooring ropes across to longshoremen who secured them to massive iron bollards bolted to the wharf. The crew lowered a boarding plank and disembarkation began. Although the skipper was enchanted by Teresita, Alameda and Pepita, he was keen to have his passengers off the ship as quickly as possible, so he could begin unloading cargo. Time was money and pretty girls were just a passing fancy.

Jubal and Billy were only too happy to oblige. Their gear was packed and they hastily led the girls down the gangplank. They really had no idea where to go next. With Billy leading, and more or less herded by the crowd, they veered left along the dockside. Teresita and Alameda followed with Jubal and Pepita just a few yards behind. Once clear of the dockside hubbub, they would seek directions to Aunt Frescura's property. The wharf was a seething mass of humanity, but for an instant the crowd parted and Sam McAlister confronted them.

'You won't escape this time,' Sam yelled. 'I'm taking you both in.'

He reached for his revolver, but then he saw Pepita and froze. Her face turned white and, with just the slightest sigh she collapsed to the ground. Sam had no idea what his emotions were at that moment. Relief, surprise, love, the whole damned gamut most likely, but Billy'd had enough.

'Why won't you just damn well leave us alone?' he roared, drawing a Remington pistol he'd taken from the Colorado River pirates. Sam's distraction gave Billy his chance and he was faster to the draw by a second. He cocked the weapon and fired before Jubal could stop him. The bullet smashed into Sam's chest and, after staggering a few steps forward, he crumpled to the ground.

Pandemonium followed. Stevedores, factors, streets girls, urchins, idlers, coolies and dandies all flew helter-skelter to escape the shooting. Petorio wasn't far off and the uproar caught his attention straight away. He drew his pistol and fired a shot into the air to clear a path through the crowd, but that didn't work very well and just caused more confusion and panic. Several people close to the pier's edge were pitched over and splashed into the sea so other passers-by had to race and grab ropes to haul the drenched victims back.

Petorio saw Jubal and Billy, raised his pistol and aimed, but there were too many innocent folk running pell-mell in front of him. So he lowered the gun and charged on. Billy saw him and grabbing Teresita by the hand, bolted along the wharf. Jubal took hold of Alameda and followed closely.

'What about Pepita?' Alameda wailed.

'She'll be okay,' Jubal assured her. 'She just swooned and there are plenty of folk to look after her. We'll find her later, I promise.'

They dashed away and headed unknowingly for the Barbary Coast. That was dangerous territory, but they were desperate. There were tough customers to be sure in the ramshackled, crime ridden, drunken, filth and disease wracked whore town that stood between the Chinese quarter and the Frisco Bay. But then Jubal and Billy could be tough customers when driven to it, and it was a good place to disappear, especially as the law was reluctant to follow.

Petorio reached Pepita first. She was breathing shallowly. He was unable to determine what was wrong with her. One of the streetwalkers knelt beside her and pulled a phial from her garter. Bearing her legs in public wasn't really an issue for her.

'Take whiff of this, sweetie,' she crooned, holding the phial under Pepita's nose.

'Just smellin' salts, dearie,' she said, noting Petorio's concern as Pepita awoke with a start. 'You go and check on that feller, he don't look too flash. This little poppet'll be fine.'

A couple of burly longshoremen knelt beside Sam and Petorio was worried they might rob him, but it turned out they were just trying to protect him from the stampeding crowd.

'Is he dead?' Petorio asked.

'No, but he's hurt bad,' one man replied.

Petorio examined Sam's wound. The bullet had smashed into his telescope that he'd stuffed down his shirt-front. The brass instrument had absorbed much of the bullet's impact, but pieces of shattered lens and metal shards were lodged in Sam's chest.

'I think he needs to get to the city hospital,' one Docker said.

'Dunno,' the other replied. 'Most folk that go in don't come out.'

And then Pepita was at Sam's side, holding and kissing him and weeping uncontrollably. Petorio eyed the longshoremen with a *they're-in-love* expression, to which the men nodded sympathetically. About then Zeb hobbled up.

'Goddamn, that boy found trouble again,' he said

'What're we going to do?' Petorio asked. 'He's hit bad and we'll have to get that stuff out of his chest. Pepita, you said the girls had a rich aunt around here. If we could get Sam there, maybe we'll be able to find a decent sawbones.'

'Yes, El Rancho O'Conor. It's on the north shore of the Bay,' she replied between sobs.

'Hell,' one of the dockers said, 'everyone knows Rancho O'Conor. Doña Frescura, why she's a fine woman, there's plenty here who can thank her for findin' them work and providin' a square meal when times were hard. There ain't too many who don't owe her one way or another. Harvey here and me own a skiff we use for off-shore fishin'. We'd be pleased to take you across the Golden Gate directly.'

They gently manhandled Sam onto a small handcart and took him along the wharf to Harvey's craft. Petorio helped Pepita and Zeb limped along behind. They all squashed into the boat and Harvey's companion whose name was Floyd, cast off. Police whistles sounded dimly in the background, but they took no notice. The morning breeze was freshening and they made good time. Doña Frescura's house stood on a small hill overlooking the bay. It was a sumptuous, whitewashed, stone building, surrounded by verandas with sweeping lawns and gardens. A pathway led from the front steps right to the beach and before the skiff had crunched to a halt, Floyd leapt ashore and raced for the house.

Doña Frescura appeared with her maid and servants. She was a woman who immediately inspired respect, still a remarkable beauty and someone you knew instinctively not to mess with. Floyd explained what had happened and Doña Frescura dispatched her staff to prepare hot water and bandages. They laid Sam on a huge, soft bed in about the most luxurious room Zeb and Petorio had ever seen.

''Ceptin' a real fancy bawdy house in Denver back in fifty-nine...' Zeb started, but was stopped in mid sentence by Doña Frescura's glare. She was not interest in his previous accommodation arrangements.

She sent one of the staff for a leather case containing tweezers, scissors, a lancet and needles. Shortly her maid appeared with a pot of boiling water and Doña Frescura tossed all the instruments into it.

'Cleanliness seems to be the answer,' she announced. 'It appears to reduce infection. Midwives have been aware of this for ages, yet physicians remain regrettably ignorant of the fact.'

The servants pulled Sam's boots off and ripped open his shirt, exposing the mess. Without hesitation or trepidation, Doña Frescura lifted the tweezers from the boiling water using a pair of tongs. She went to work picking the shrapnel from Sam's chest. He groaned and writhed occasionally and she ordered Petorio and Zeb to hold him still. She worked for hours, never getting tired or impatient. While she worked Petorio and Zeb explained how they'd got there.

'Ah yes, little Pepita,' Doña Frescura said, smiling at Pepita who knelt beside the bed, holding Sam's hand all the time. 'I remember you as Teresita and Alameda's playmate. They were mischievous little rascals then, and nothing seems to have changed. But, you have grown into a beautiful young woman, and I assume you have feelings for this unfortunate young man.'

'I love him, Doña Frescura,' Pepita sobbed. 'Oh, I love him so much.'

Finally she was done. She was confident she'd removed all the metal and glass fragments and even found the lead ball that had penetrated just under Sam's skin. She stitched up the larger wounds and after washing Sam's chest again, bound it with clean, linen bandages. He rested peacefully and all they could do now was wait. Doña Frescura sent Zeb and Petorio to clean up and arranged beds for them in one of the guest rooms. Pepita would not leave Sam's side.

'He must live, Doña Frescura,' Pepita whispered, staring up with pleading eyes. 'It is so important now.'

'He's a very sick man,' Doña Frescura said, 'but I've treated worse in my time. The man you love is important, but what could be more important? It wasn't sea-sickness you suffered from on the boat or mere girlish vapours that cause you to collapse at the wharf, was it child?'

'No,' she replied.

'So you are now Señora McAlister?'

'Oh, I hope so, Doña Frescura,' Pepita sniffed and another tear rolled down her cheek. She leant closer to the bed and whispered into Sam's ear. 'Damn you, Sam McAlister, you will live to give our baby your name!'

Chapter 23

'Sam, I have fallen from the sky, swallowed gallons of water, fought bandits and rapists, been chased through the desert by stampeding cattle to be a mother to this child, so you can damn well hang on to be a father. Do you hear me?' Pepita said a little louder than she'd wanted to.

Sam stirred, opened his eyes for just a moment and grinned.

'I reckon the whole of Central California heard you if that's where we still are. I feel like there's an anvil on my chest.'

She gave him some water, waiting until he fell asleep, kissed his brow and joined the others. She felt that she would like a glass of wine.

Petorio, Zeb and Doña Frescura were seated around the dining table when she entered the room. They saw at once that Sam was going to recover. She embraced and kissed them then sat on a spare chair.

'Thank you for bringing him safe to me,' she said as Doña Frescura poured her a stiff drink.

'Well, he did get shot on the way,' Zeb mentioned, 'and he did try to kill us all on a stagecoach. I reckon he's too damned stubborn to die. Ever!'

'You know he'll go after Jubal and Billy again when he recovers, don't you?' Petorio warned.

'I'll try to stop him.'

'I don't like your chances.'

'He's going to be a father, he should know better.'

'Now ain't that the best news we've heard for ages?' Zeb beamed. 'But, I don't know whether it'll stop Sam. It's his damned sense of duty. He feels he's failed unless he brings Jubal in.'

'I don't want those boys to hang,' Pepita said.

'Billy shot Sam and damn near killed him,' Petorio observed.

'I know he didn't mean to. They could have left me in the Colorado River but they didn't. I've heard their side of all this. That man at Fort Pierce was killed by accident and Jubal didn't kill the guard, Billy's mother did. Jubal will never give her up though.'

'How're we going to stop Sam?'

'It appears that prey and quarry are in too close proximity,' Doña Frescura observed. 'A wolf pack will chase relentlessly when they know there is a chance of a kill, but even they will abandon the hunt if they lose the quarry.'

'Yes, ma'am, I seen 'em do it too,' Zeb said. 'Why, I remember one time when I was ridin' with John Fremont on the Platte River...'

'Later perhaps, Señor Turner you can regale us with your frontier anecdotes, but right now it's down to business. You all seem to agree that you don't want them killed, so we'll have to think of something else, not to mention getting Teresita and Alameda back safely. If they've gone to ground on the Barbary Coast, it won't be long before they get into trouble.'

Doña Frescura rang a small bell on the table to summon her maid.

'Are Floyd and Harvey still here?' she asked.

'Si, señora, they are in the kitchen eating their own weight in food.'

'Good, they'll need their strength. Please ask them to join us when they've finished their meal.'

The maid bobbed pertly and left. When the boys arrived Doña Frescura explained what needed to be done.

'Pepita and Señor Turner will remain here to care for Sam,' she concluded. 'The rest of us should be on our way.'

'No ma'am, Señor Turner is comin' too.'

They all eyed his foot.

'Like I said, Señor Turner is comin' too.'

'And you reckon Sam is stubborn,' Petorio said. 'C'mon then, old timer, there's no show without you.'

Zeb insisted on bringing his Sharps rifle.

'Bit conspicuous,' Petorio commented.

'Bit of a deterrent,' Zeb replied.

'Will you be alright, cariño?' Doña Frescura asked Pepita, who nodded. She had the entire household for backup anyway.

Doña Frescura owned a sailboat, and they took that as well as the skiff. So things weren't nearly as crowded on the way back, which was as well because it was a longer trip into the wind. They arrived at just on dusk. Because of Zeb's immobility and Petorio being unfamiliar with the waterfront, they stayed to guard Doña Frescura and the boat, while Harvey and Floyd set out in search of Jubal, Billy and the girls.

Jubal and Billy found lodging deep in the Barbary Coast district. It was a second storey room with a balcony overlooking a trash-strewn alley that smelt of rotting vegetables, rancid cooking oil, human sweat and excrement. Teresita and Alameda were appalled.

'No, no, Señor Jubal,' they complained, 'this is intolerable. You must take us to Aunt Frescura across the bay immediately.'

'You're damned right,' Jubal agreed. 'Billy you stand guard, while I get some food and organise a boat to ferry us across. Lock the door after I'm gone and don't let anyone in.'

After Jubal left, Billy settled onto the bed that he suspected harboured a vast horde of fleas and other unsavoury matter. Teresita plonked herself beside him and sobbed quietly while Alameda sat sullenly on a chair in the corner.

'We should have stayed with Pepita,' Teresita said.

'She'll be okay,' Billy replied. 'There were plenty of folk to look after her.'

'I wish there were plenty of folk to look after us.'

'I'm sorry how things turned out,' Billy said. 'But, we'll get you to your auntie's place. That's a promise.'

'What will you do then?'

'Keep headin' north, I guess. Jubal has a hankerin' to go to Canada, even if it's cold in winter.'

'I will miss you,' she said. 'I think you are a nice person, if you can only stay out of trouble.'

'Thank you, but staying out of trouble seems to be difficult for me.'

They sat and thought about it for a while and probably dozed off. Alameda brought the chair closer to her sister. Gunfire, screams, foul language and the sounds of fighting echoed from the streets below. They wondered what had become of Jubal and were concerned after darkness fell and he still hadn't returned. But, at last there was a knock on the door.

'Billy, it's me,' he hissed. 'Open up. Don't shoot.'

He'd bought some tasty pies, but thought it best not to enquire too closely about their contents. They were all so hungry they didn't care and washed them down with bottles of black porter that tasted pretty good as well.

'We're in luck,' Jubal announced smugly. 'Just now I ran into two fellers with a boat. They've agreed to take us across the Golden Gate tonight. They said to meet them in the alley in half an hour.'

'Can we trust 'em?' Billy asked.

'Damnit, Billy, we can't trust anyone, but we've got these,' he said patting the revolvers stuck in his belt. 'They've got some hard arses around here for sure, but hell we can be just as hard when pushed to it.'

They met the two men as planned and crept through the streets. There were plenty of seedy characters about, but armed to the teeth as they were, no one was inclined to bother them. The two men who didn't give their names appeared confident at first, but as they approached the wharf they stopped abruptly.

'What's up?' Billy asked.

'We've got company,' one man said, 'and the wrong kind.'

Looking back, Jubal became aware of several shadows darting for cover behind them. They seemed to be small and agile men armed with knives and machetes.

'Tongs!' one of their guides hissed. 'Thugs from one of the Chinee gangs.'

'What're they doing here?'

'Heard about your two lovelies no doubt. Want to take 'em back to Chinatown for whorin'. Chinks'll pay big for white gals. Word gets around fast on the Coast.'

'What'll we do?'

'Run!'

And they set off. If they'd asked Teresita or Alameda to run when they lived at Hacienda O'Conor they wouldn't have had great success, but now the girls sped away like the wind. But the Tongs were fleet and there sure were a lot of them. The wharf was in sight, but there was no hope of reaching it. They could even hear the panting of the runners behind them and their pounding feet on the rough cobblestone street.

The first of the pursuers was upon them. With a piercing scream he raised his machete to take a mighty swing at Jubal's neck, intent on slicing his head clean off. Petorio stepped from the shadows and slammed his bowie knife into the Tong's throat. He dropped in a fountain of blood. Without missing a beat Petorio aimed his handgun and blasted two shots into the Tongs, hitting a target both times. *Not bad for left-handed*, he thought.

Suddenly a monstrous boom echoed down the narrow laneway as one of the Tongs pitched to the ground with a hole blown clean through his chest. Another shot quickly followed and took away one of the Chinaman's arms. After that the Tongs decided to abandon the chase, they'd go looking for trouble elsewhere. They melted into the shadows, leaving their wounded to die on the streets.

'Knew the Sharps would come in handy,' Zeb muttered.

'Yeah, nice and subtle, Zeb,' Petorio said.

Jubal, Billy and the girls came to a panting halt at the wharf. A lone woman stood before them looking serene in an immaculate velvet cloak drawn around her to keep out the evening chill. Teresita and Alameda rushed to her, sobbing with relief and joy. They hugged her as if they would never let go. Jubal and Billy approached looking very confused.

'Doña Frescura, I presume?' Jubal said, and she nodded.

'Don Margil asked us to bring the girls to you,' Jubal explained. 'Hacienda O'Conor was destroyed by bandits and he wants them to stay here until he's made repairs.'

'*Mis muchas gracias, señors*. You have fulfilled your obligation. For that I'm indeed indebted to you, but now I must bid you *adios*.'

It was then that Billy realised there had been a lot of unexplained gunfire, but he'd been in such a hurry he'd failed to determine from where or from whom. What the hell was *she* doing here, anyway?

She knew they were coming!

It was a trap!

As he turned he felt an instant of blinding pain and then oblivion. Armed with batons procured from the San Francisco Police Department, Harvey and Floyd stunned Jubal and Billy. A trap it was indeed, and one so easily sprung. Harvey and Floyd had quickly tracked down Jubal, who was prowling the dockside taverns looking for a ride across the bay. They stitched up a deal and raced back to warn Doña Frescura and the others before returning to lead Jubal and Billy into the net. Petorio and Zeb were hidden nearby to waylay the fugitives and this had placed them handily to deal with the unforseen Tongs.

'Well done, gentlemen,' Doña Frescura addressed Harvey and Floyd, 'I am sure I can leave the arrangements to you.'

'Yes, ma'am, you can rely on us.'

'Please remember, they are not to be robbed or molested, just disposed of.'

Harvey and Floyd nodded. Petorio helped them lift Jubal and Billy onto a handcart and they clattered away along the dockside.

'Señor Turner, Señor Blanco, will you be joining us?' Doña Frescura asked.

'Yes ma'am, we'd be honoured to stay until Sam is better, if that's okay with you.'

'Of course, you are most welcome and I do hope you have a pleasant sojourn at El Rancho O'Conor.'

Doña Frescura handled the yacht back across the Golden Gate in the dead of night with no qualms at all. You had to admit she had class. She'd calmly stood in front of charging Tongs, witnessed murder and bloodshed in the streets of San Francisco and now acted as a gracious hostess. Teresita and Alameda sat either side of their aunt on the transom bench. They clung to her arms, making it no easier to manage the tiller, but she didn't complain. They perked right up when they heard Pepita was safe, but Sam had been such a wretched nuisance they were indifferent to his condition. They were relieved to have finally reach safety, but fretted for Jubal and Billy.

The girls silently wondered what would become of the two fugitives as Doña Frescura steered her sail-boat towards a beacon fire she instructed her household staff to light and guide them back safely through the night.

Jubal awoke and felt as if his head was the size of a giant melon. He groaned and rolled over, dropping onto wooden decking. He'd been asleep in a hammock squeezed next to Billy who stirred and moaned. The floor was heaving and it only took Jubal a second to realise he'd felt that sensation before. They were on board a ship under full sail.

'Billy, wake up,' he whispered.

'What?'

'I think we've been shanghaied,'

'Aye, that's one way of puttin' it,' said a cheerful voice from above. A bearded face appeared in the hatchway. 'Ahoy there shipmates, the name's Cornelius Flanagan, pleased to meet youse. Look lively now, the skipper wants to see youse topside.'

They staggered through a hatchway onto the open deck. The ship was a huge, three masted square-rigged vessel, wide and ungainly, and certainly not built for speed. Standing at the helm on the poop deck stood the ship's master overseeing his crewmen who scrambled to obey his every command. He was short, heavily bearded and all sinew. He did not introduce himself when Jubal and Billy stood before him.

'Mister Flanagan, take the watch, if you please,' the captain said. 'You men, follow me.'

They entered the captain's great cabin, although it wasn't that grand. It spread across the ship's stern with windows that faced aft. A desk stood in the middle of the cabin, with a bunk to one side. There was only one chair behind the desk and Billy would have given anything to sit down, his head was throbbing so much. The skipper pointed to an open ledger on his desk.

'I am Captain Thomas Trevallyn. You have signed the ship's articles and are indentured to me for the duration of the voyage. We will train you in sailing skills and you will man one of the ship's boats. I will put you with Mister Flanagan's crew. There is only one rule on board the *Juliet Brown* and that is, you do what you're told without question. I hope I make myself clear.'

'I don't recall signing no book,' Billy protested.

'Many men say that when they're drunk.'

'We weren't drunk, we were slugged.'

'I only have your word for that.'

'I bet that don't even look like my signature,' Jubal complained. Billy had never had to sign anything, so he didn't know what his signature looked like, but Miss Virginia Pritchard had made him print his name often enough, and the mark on the Captain's register didn't appear anything like that.

'Again, I only have your word for that. In any even the point is moot. Questioning me is tantamount to mutiny, so I suggest you get out of the habit right now. You will rejoin Mister Flanagan on deck and he will show you the ropes. And in future you will address me as *captain* or *sir*. Do I make myself clear?'

'Yessir!' Billy and Jubal said at once. If there was one thing they'd learnt, it was when to toe the line. They'd get used to the *aye-aye* business in time.

Flanagan explained the *Juliet Brown* was one of the last Yankee Whalers. He was a master's mate and would school them in seamanship and manning the oars on one of the whaleboats, of which he was the coxswain. Luckily they were fast learners and got stuck into their training, as they had no alternative. Flanagan informed them that flogging still occurred at sea, although conditions were much improved from the barbarity that prevailed thirty years before when he was pressed into service.

It was surprising how quickly they became accustomed to their duties and the rancid smell of previous whale kills that never left the ship. They sailed with a skeleton crew en route to Vancouver to pick up the remainder of their compliment that included several Inuit harpooners, who were considered the world's best.

'So we hunt the whales around here?' Billy asked one morning. 'We saw some off Baja.'

'Oh nay, matey,' Flanagan said. 'There're too many ships along this coast, why we'd be lucky to bag one or two.'

Indeed they had sighted numerous other vessels during the voyage.

'Where then?'

'Between Esperance Bay and Cape Leeuwin, aye that's the finest whalin' ground in the world. 'Tis the home of the southern right whale, they're easy prey and richest in oil.'

'Where on earth is Cape Leeuwin?'

'Why, tother side of the world in the Southern Ocean. We're bound for the southwest tip o' Australia's Swan River Colony.'

Jubal had no idea where Australia was. He knew immigrants came from there to the American gold fields and ex-convicts from penal settlements in New South Wales made up many of the Barbary Coast miscreants. But, Virginia Pritchard had told Billy precisely where Australia was and he remembered her pointing it out to him on a globe in her schoolroom.

'It'll take months to get there!'

'Aye, we're normally away for two or three years, maybe more.'

Billy and Jubal were appalled, even when Cornelius explained that with a hold full of whale oil they received not only their monthly pay, but also a hefty bonus.

'You'll be rich men when we get back,' he explained. 'Ain't nothin' to spend money on at sea, so keep clear of gamblin', and you'll go ashore with more money than you've ever dreamed of. Captain Trevallyn's a stern, but honest skipper. He always sees his crew paid off fair and square.'

'Shanghaiing folk don't appear too honest to me,' Jubal grumbled.

'Captain Trevallyn tries to avoid pressing men, but he loses so many to the Comstock Lode when we come to the West Coast, he's no other choice or he'll never have enough men to crew the ship. But we have to put into Frisco because that's where the market for whale oil's best. Why, back in the fifties the whole of Frisco Bay was clogged with empty ships when all the jack tars skedaddled to the goldfields. Besides those two fellows who brought you aboard said they was kin and could speak for youse.'

'Did we look like their kin?' Billy demanded.

'Well, it was dark,' Cornelius replied rather unconvincingly.

They hugged the coast on the voyage to Vancouver. At times they saw land smudged across the eastern horizon, tantalisingly close, but much too far to swim. Flanagan added they would be held under guard in port, so they could give up any thoughts of jumping ship when they docked. They spotted few whales, but as they closed on Puget Sound the lookout spied a large pod.

'Whales ho, two points off the starboard bow!' he yelled.

'Boat crews at the ready,' Captain Trevallyn bellowed. 'It's time to see what our new hands are made of.'

Trevallyn knew that men improved with practice and it was a good opportunity to test his crews. He also had two apprentice harpooners on board and this would be sound training. They could see the pod of humpbacks leisurely cruising northwards. The *Juliet Brown* sailed on and hove to a few miles ahead of the pod. A whaleboat was launched from either side. They were sleek, narrow and pointed at prow and stern so they could be steered from either end. A crew consisted of eight oarsmen, a steersman and a harpooner. Sweeps and a mast lay in the bilge of each boat. A sail was also stowed on board, but Captain Trevallyn instructed the boat masters to give the crews rowing experience, and damned hard work it was too. After some time of backbreaking work, Jubal wasn't sure that he didn't prefer picking cotton.

But they got used to it and soon their oar strokes settled into a steady rhythm. It would have been heavy going to chase a whale from behind without using sail, but the whaleboats were coming to the pod head on. And in a moment they were among them, perhaps a dozen gentle leviathans surged around the boats. The harpooners stood poised at the bow. They brushed alongside one monster, who simply nudged Flanagan's boat aside, nearly capsizing it. A fluke reared from the seas and flopped to the surface, spraying salty foam over the rowers. Another whale lifted its huge flipper and slapped the side of the other boat, veering it off course.

Flanagan wrestled with the steering oar to bring the whaleboat close enough for a true shot. Then right in the midst of the pod the harpooner let fly. The savagely barbed spear plunged into a whale's back. The enraged beast gave a mournful cry as the harpoon wedged into its blubber. The harpoon rope with floats attached played out and Flanagan abandoned his steering sweep to clinch the line around a sturdy post bolted to the whaleboat hull. As the rope reached its full extent the vessel swirled around with a jolt and the stricken humpback dragged it backwards through the sea.

The boat rocked violently, terrifying the new crewmen.

'Not to worry, lads,' Flanagan called heartily. 'He'll drag us until he tires, then we'll finish him off.'

But that was not to be. In its panic the harpooned whale turned aside and ploughed across the path of the oncoming pod. The boat hit another whale and was lifted clear of the surface. As they thumped back onto the waves the whale's fluke shot into the air and smashed onto the boat. Three crewmen were killed instantly as the boat was dashed to pieces. The last of the whales crashed into the wreckage and tossed what remained of the hull in all directions. Another crewman was dragged to his death, trapped beneath the belly of one of the whales and drowning in moments. The harpoon ripped from the whale's back and it surged away to rejoin the pod.

Billy was tumbled crazily in the turbulent wake of the whales. With his lungs exploding he gasped for air as he burst to the surface.

'Jubal! Are you okay!' he yelled.

'I'm here,' came the reply and he saw Jubal's head bobbing in the water only yards away. 'And if you call floating in the ocean miles from land okay, well I am.'

Flanagan surfaced close by, although there was no sign of any other crewmen.

'Just hang on,' Flanagan said, 'tother boat'll come and pick us up.'

But it didn't. In all the confusion the whaleboats had become well separated. The other craft had hoisted its sail and was heading after the pod at full speed. They may not even have been aware of what happened to the Flanagan's whaleboat. Trevallyn probably wouldn't risk his ship with an undermanned crew in complex recovery manoeuvres. Finally even Flanagan conceded help was either a long way off or not coming at all.

'We'll have to swim to some wreckage, if we've any hope of staying alive.'

There were several pieces of flotsam drifting around and they headed for the largest. Flanagan was the best swimmer and first to reach part of the whaleboat hull. He dragged himself on and it looked big enough to act as a raft. But, Billy and Jubal were struggling and it seemed they would drown.

And then Billy saw the huge, black form of a dorsal fin and knew he was doomed. Another appeared and in moments twenty black triangles sliced through the water towards them. The great whites had come to feast. Frantically he started for the raft, but even if he reached it, it would be no use. Then he felt a thump in his back and he screamed.

He felt no pain. In fact he was surprised to still be conscious of what he did or did not feel, but he was aware of Flanagan's laughter. *The man's hysterical in the face of death,* he thought.

'They're not sharks,' Flanagan shouted. 'They're Orcas. Killer whales.'

'Yeah great, we've got a choice between sharks and killer whales.'

But the Orcas weren't interested in human food and they weren't known to attack people at all, much preferring whale tongues or seal meat and there was a lot more of that about. They took turns in gently nudging Jubal and Billy to the raft. They even butted other pieces of wreckage towards them. They playfully swirled around the castaways for a while, slowly guiding the wreckage towards shore. But they eventually grew bored. Two young males broached clear of the water, showering the raft with spray as they crashed back to the surface. Then the killer whales remembered they were chasing the humpbacks and sped off in pursuit of a meal.

Jubal, Billy and Cornelius clung to the raft as the icy water lapped over them. Eventually they realised that no one was coming to the rescue and they would die if no other passing ships spotted them. That night Flanagan succumbed to hypothermia and slipped into the sea. By the next morning Jubal and Billy lay semi-conscious on the raft, and would be swept away on the first decent wave that washed over them.

'I think we're done for this time, partner,' Jubal mumbled between mouthfuls of salty water.

'Now there you go being negative again,' Billy whispered. 'Hell, we've been in tougher spots than this.'

But that was the last thing he said.

On the southern tip of Puget Sound a French-Canadian trapper and his family were gathering herbs and fishing by the shoreline. The days were warm now and game plentiful. Living in one of the most engaging parts of the world with two well-favoured, dutiful wives and five children, the trapper was a contented man of a gentle disposition. His family loved to come here and often saw killer whales, seals and otters capering close to shore.

His six-year-old daughter stopped by the water's edge. Two men lay inert on a small beach. The trapper knelt cautiously beside them.

'Are they dead, Papa?' the little girl asked.

Epilogue

'Pepita and I got married right there on Doña Frescura's estate,' Sam said. 'It was a swell do, Zeb Turner stood up for Pepita's Pa and gave her away, right solemn he was about it too. Petorio was best man of course and Teresita and Alameda made the prettiest darned bridesmaids you ever saw. I'm pleased to say the girls took to me in the end, even if it was just for Pepita's sake. Doña Frescura's neighbours all turned up and we partied until dawn, we all had a fine time.'

'Did you go back to Sonora?' I asked.

It was way into the night about then, nearly dawn as I recollect, and I don't recall being tired through any of it, though I sensed Jimmie Granger was nodding off. The empty plates and beer bottles lay scattered across the cell floor, it was messy, but no one cared.

'No Cletus, not directly,' Sam replied. 'That major fellow from the Presidio found out where I was and turned up a week or so after the weddin'. Said he had orders for me to return to Fort Leavenworth and be damned quick about it. Jubal and Billy were gone, so there was no point in staying.

'We hitched another lift on Leland Stanford's train as far as it would go, and went on horseback from there to Fort Mohave. The cavalry and Pinkerton agents must have caught those bandits because we didn't run into trouble and the stage was operating again. It was getting damned hot across Arizona then and we stopped off at Lord Duppa's spread for a few days. He and Frederick were over the moon to see Pepita hadn't been killed. They both had a real soft spot for her. We didn't go back to Pierce, but via Fort Marcy and Santa Fe. It took over a month, but we got there in the end.

'Back at Leavenworth Colonel Grierson didn't rightly know whether he was glad to see me or not. Turnin' up with a brand new wife wasn't quite the Army's way either. You know what it's like, Cletus, you still need permission from your CO to get hitched, ain't that right?'

'I believe so, Sam,' I replied, although I'd never had the opportunity to put it to the test. 'What did they say about you losing Jubal?'

'I think they were kinda pleased really. Sergeant Hawken of *A* troop still swore Kincaid pulled the gun and it was an accident, but there was no changin' the stories of the fellers at Pierce. It'd have caused more problems than enough if I'd brought Jubal back. He would never have gotten away with the murdered guard, and he wasn't ever going to betray Shadow Woman. No one resolved the facts and it just blew over in the end, best forgotten I suppose.

'The only plus was that Henry Cook got all my troops back safe from Mexico and that young medico at Fort Pierce fixed the wounded up just fine. They confirmed Henry's promotion and gave the troop a bravery citation to boot. Henry went on to be one of the first black men to be commissioned — no easy thing in those days. Nor now for that matter.

'But, my Army career was all shot the pieces. I'd disobeyed a direct order from Major Devlin by going in to Mexico after all. In the end it was Petorio who suggested I resign and join the scouts. He reckoned I'd learnt enough from him to make a go of it. Colonel

Grierson was all for the plan, 'cos it got him off the hook, and that worked out fine. Not that he wouldn't have backed me up, it wasn't his style to abandon his men, but it just made things easier all round. George Schofield said I'd get pretty fed up with bein' a lieutenant all my career anyway, and he was a sharp sort of fellow who knew the Army well. Petorio and I teamed up plenty after that, not just in the Apache wars, but up in Wyoming, Montana and the Dakota territories as well.'

'What became of Teresita and Alameda?' I asked.

'Them gals never went back to the Hopi Nation for their thoroughbreds, but they sure made names for themselves, I tell you,' Sam smiled at the though. 'If they thought Tucson was fun, they sure partied in San Francisco. Doña Frescura showed 'em off right away and they were the toast of the town in no time. I reckon Miss Teresita kinda held a torch for Billy Songbird, but that just weren't to be. She didn't pine none though, and sure broke a bunch of hearts in her time.

'Married late in the end, to a feller who took photographs, made a packet at it too. They moved just outside of Los Angeles and started makin' moving picture shows, why they're more popular than anything these days. They got a young cowboy called Tom Mix workin' for them now. Miss Teresita wants to make moving pictures about her adventures with Jubal and Billy.

'Miss Alameda fell for a rancher up Napa way, just north of her Aunt Frescura's spread. Led him a merry dance for years, then married and settled down. They took to growin' grapes and winemaking. Brought some experts out from Europe and now they're supplying all the fancy restaurants back east from New York to Chicago.

'Did Zeb Turner get to see the 20th Century?' I asked.

'He sure did. He went down to Sonora and started sparkin' Pepita's Ma for a spell. The place was all fixed up by then, although Don Margil missed his girls so much he spent more and more time in San Francisco. I don't think Benigna minded the attention and canoodlin', but realised Zeb weren't the *do-your-chores* kinda guy, so she shooed him off back into the mountains after a bit. Petorio and I ran into him a parcel of times over the years.

'He finally hit pay-dirt and made a pile from a West Texas gusher that spewed crude for years — still does maybe. He even bought his own automobile, killed hisself driving back home all liquored up after celebratin' the birth of the century. Rolled off the side of the road, most folk reckon he was so boozed, he didn't feel a thing. We buried him with his watch and chain.'

'I guess he had a good run. He must have been over ninety, but maybe if he'd heeded Lord Duppa's advice he'd have lived a little longer.'

Sam nodded.

'But he'd seen his time out in grand style, I doubt that a man could have had a better life or lived it more fully than old Zeb Turner,' he said.

'What about Petorio?' I asked, more curious than a racoon in a trashcan.

'After he finished with the army he took his kin up to the Grand Canyon, he was so impressed by it. Got a permit from the Navaho Nation and runs camping trips for tourists now. I still go and visit on occasion, take the whole family. You know Pepita and I had four fine kids, three girls and a boy. Our boy rode in Buffalo Bill's Wild West Show for a while. He's still thick with Bill Cody and they're experimentin' with aeroplane engines. It's costing Old Wild Bill a pretty penny, but he's rich as Croesus anyway. My boy also works as an engineer for the Coors Brewery in Golden, Colorado. Makes you proud, don't it?' Sam smiled. 'Brings me a couple of cases when he comes to visit. And, our gals turned out just a sweet as their Ma.'

'Did you ever hear of Jubal or Billy again?'

Sam reached across the cell cot and opened a small suitcase that contained his personal things. Inside was a faded, yellowing newspaper.

'Major Schofield brought this back from the Montana Territory in eighteen and eighty-one. We stayed in touch over the years. He gave me one of his first revolvers that the Smith and Wesson Company made for him. Came in a fine presentation box, and I've used it plenty since.'

It was the copy of the *Kamloops Daily* which George Schofield had picked in an Alberta barber's shop. He was working up on the Canadian border with the North West Mounted Police, trying to sort out what to do with the Sioux and Cheyenne tribes who'd fled there after the Little Big Horn debacle. George Schofield reckoned Custer had it coming. He'd seen him in action during the War and thought he was just a darned fool who'd had a lot of luck and a runaway mouth that the papers liked to hear from. Although, of course that luck ran out spectacularly, but Sam reckoned he wasn't one to judge when it came to diving in boots and all. And Indian fighting could just be so damned unpredictable.

I guess I can remember the headlines well enough. I've looked at them plenty of times since then.

McLean Boys and Alex Hare Swing for Heinous Murder.

Kamloops was one of those gold towns in British Columbia Province as I recall it, but folk were settling into farming and commerce like everywhere else. It's probably better that I just quote the newspaper article.

> *January 31ˢᵗ 1881*
>
> *Today British Colombia is rid of four viperous young individuals who have terrorised the Kamloops area for too long. The desperadoes were hunted down by a valiant posse six months ago after the vicious murders of Sheriff John Assher and Farmer Kelly and the critical wounding of Assher's deputy, Jubal Quinn.*
>
> *Craven, half-breeds, Charlie, Archie and Allan McLean and their evil compatriot, Alex Hare were hanged today and have finally received a just punishment for their murderous rampaging.*

Now that sure got Sam thinking, but he wanted to know for sure. He rode up that way one fall, and a mighty pretty trip it was too with the aspens and maples in their autumn colours. He took Pepita the next year just for the romance of it. He discovered that a black fellow named Jubal had indeed farmed the area for a bit. Took himself a handsome Nez Percés wife too, but they moved on after the shooting and no one could say where.

Of Billy, there were only whispers, rumours and hearsay. Some folk said he was dead for sure, some said he went back to Mexico, but no one, including Sam ever rightly knew. Even Petorio couldn't track him down. But Sam kept his ear to the ground and knew plenty of folk in the Southwest, so word got back to him. It was Snake's family that had finally camped near Fort Pierce when Sam and the patrol rode out to check on them.

'And the dead man was Billy?' I asked.

Sam replied he sure was. Apparently the rumours were true, Billy moved all over the west, but he spent most of the time in the Sierra Madre with Snake's tribe. He took a wife on occasion, but could never settle to it, and most womenfolk tired of his wandering after a piece.

So Sam sneaked into the camp and warned old Snake that he'd better skedaddle if he didn't want to wind up on the Fort Sill Reservation. And that's when he discovered Billy and while Snake's people slipped away into the night, Billy told him the story. He'd learnt plenty from Pepita, Teresita and Alameda, but Billy put the final pieces in place.

Billy often visited Jubal in Canada and finally taught him some guitar chords as he'd promised way back in Claude Valentine's camp. But, Jubal never shook off his guilt, and volunteered as a deputy sheriff to help uphold the law he felt he'd let down so often. The McLean boys were half-breed kids, reminding him of Billy when he was young and he hoped to help them mend their ways. So he joined John Assher when the scoundrels stole a thoroughbred stallion and headed up country.

The trouble was that Alex Hare was pure evil and murdered a farmer who was just unlucky enough to cross their path. Then he persuaded the boys to bushwhack the sheriff and his deputy. After he recovered from the shooting, it seemed that Jubal and his wife lived a happy, nomadic life for a while, before moving to the Klondike when gold was discovered. Jubal established a saloon and general store in Dawson City. Supplying the stampeders made him a very rich man. But the Yukon's winters were long and cold, so he moved his business down to milder Victoria on Vancouver Island. He and his family are still living there as far as anyone knows.

Billy remained secretive about Shadow Woman, as he still believed she could be brought to trial for murdering the guard at Fort Pierce, even though Sam suggested it was unlikely, especially as she was now over eighty. But, Billy was taking no chances.

'Is that when you shot Billy?' I asked.

'I didn't shoot Billy,' Sam replied rather sadly. 'Hell knows I've thought about it long enough, but when it came right down to it, I wasn't going to kill him in cold blood. I don't even know if I wanted to bring him in after all, but I reckon that's what he thought I intended to do.'

However Billy was a sick man, he'd developed a tumour in his brain and it pained him more each day. He judged the cause to have been hit over the skull so often. He knew he was dying, and it wasn't going to be pleasant. When he heard the soldiers advancing he drew his Remington pistol. Sam went for his Schofield revolver as well, but he'd already proved he was a might slower than Billy.

Even after all these years Billy could still out-draw him. Sam's gun was just out of its holster when Billy placed his revolver under his own chin and pulled the trigger. In all the excitement that followed no one ever bothered to check whether Sam's revolver had even been fired.

'So why didn't you just say so?' I asked. 'It'd have saved me a trip, although I don't regret coming for a moment. You could have sold the story to the papers.'

'That's the last place I'd go. I wanted folk to know the *truth*. That sure ain't going to happen in any newspaper I ever read. I needed someone reliable, and I determined that was you. I said I'd know when the right person came along.'

That was a fair enough comment, although sitting around in a jail cell for six weeks seemed a bit extreme to me. But Sam explained that Corporal Beaufort was more like a host than a jailer, and they often sat up late playing dice and checkers, and reminiscing about their days in the Apache wars. It hadn't been such a hardship.

'You can rest assured that I will personally take the full story to Colonel Grierson,' I said, and I meant it.

We had been up all night and the sun was lacing through the guardhouse window. Silhouetted against the frame was a tall, rather severe officer. It was Major Bevan, the post commander.

'I believe it is military protocol to report to the officer commanding on arriving at a post, Captain Mellow,' he said.

I jumped to attention and saluted and was damned snappy about it because he was right, and I must have looked like a very sloppy soldier.

'Begging you pardon, sir,' I replied, and it sounded pretty lame at the time too. 'I thought I'd only be an hour or so and report to you at the mess hall.'

'Okay, settle down, mister, there's no harm done. In fact I've been here longer than you think. You finally got this old goat to open up and tell us what really happened. Have you formed an opinion, Captain?'

'I don't think there's a case to answer, sir. Sam claims it was suicide and there is no one to gainsay his statement. I believe him anyway.'

'Quite so, Captain. I agree with you. Jimmie, will you fix up the paperwork, and as for you, Sam…'

He didn't finish because just then there was a hammering on the guardroom door. Corporal Beaufort opened up to admit a woman in her mid-fifties. Her hair was still raven-black and she was as trim as any twenty year old. She was still a beauty if ever I saw one, and would be for many years to come.

'Ah, Señora McAlister, you have come just in time to take your husband home. He has finally told us everything we need to know. He is free to go.'

'Why, thank you, Major Bevan,' she said with an engaging smile. 'My Sam can be so stubborn at times. I do not believe how I have put up with him all these years, but that is love. Do you not find love beguiling, Major?'

'Alas madam, I fear that like so many of the Army's frontier soldiers, the opportunities to find out are rare.'

'Then I must say I am sorry to hear you say that, Major, for you miss life's greatest joy.'

She had stayed with friends in the village outside the fort over night so that she'd be up early to visit Sam. She knew about me as word of my arrival and purpose had quickly spread. I was introduced and she curtsied politely.

'I am pleased to make your acquaintance, Captain Mellow. I assume my husband's explanation is to your satisfaction.'

'Indeed so, ma'am,' I replied with relief, because who knows what she'd have done if it had been otherwise. She was a fiery woman for sure.

'You have certainly had some adventures and must have been pleased when Sam settled down,' I added just for the conversation of it.

'*Settled down*, Captain Mellow?' she said, arching her eyebrows. 'If you believe Sam, Petorio and that old rogue Zeb Turner settled down, then you are very much mistaken.'

'Then I would truly like to hear more of your story,' I said, turning to Sam.

'Anytime, young feller,' he invited. 'We love visitors and the view is truly fine from our place in the high country.'

'Thank you, I will take you up on your offer.'

'But that is quite enough talk for now,' Pepita said. 'I have bought the wagon, my dear. So please take me home. It has been six long weeks, and I do believe I am in a juicy frame of mind,' she added with a wink and seemed to enjoy Major Bevan's obvious discomfort.

Sam gathered his things and Jimmie returned his revolver. Pepita thanked Corporal Beaufort for the kindness he'd shown her husband and they left.

So there you have it. Jimmie and I packed up the papers and headed back to his office. I took the news to Colonel Ben without delay and I was real pleased I did, because he took sick with a stroke soon afterwards and I don't know if he'd have been able to take it all in then. He sure was happy to hear one of his boys wasn't a cold-blooded killer after all.

In the years that followed I rode up to Sam and Pepita's home in the mountains whenever I could. It was just as stunning as he claimed. I always took Sam a case of *Coors Golden Lager Beer* and some Napa Valley wine for Pepita. It was a bit sweet for my taste, but she liked it.

And, as for Sam's adventures as a scout in the Indian wars...I've written them down too.

The End

The Author

Richard Marman was born in Swindon, UK. His father was a RAF pilot who had served with distinction during WWII. The family moved from base to base after the war, including four years in Germany. They immigrated to Fremantle in 1962. Richard attended six primary and three secondary schools, so he is familiar with the 'new kid on the block' status.

After school, Richard joined the Royal Australian Air Force and trained as a pilot. He served for nine years, including a tour in Vietnam and a significant time flying in New Guinea. In 1975 Richard left the RAAF to fly with Ansett Airlines until the company closed in 2001 at which time he was a Boeing 767 captain. Afterwards he trained Singapore Airlines pilots on Lear Jets until 2007.

Leaving aviation behind, Richard completed a Diploma of Visual Arts at Tewantin TAFE and a Bachelor of Arts at the University of the Sunshine Coast, majoring in creative writing and design. Most of Richard's book ideas have stemmed from University projects.

Richard lives on Queensland's Sunshine Coast with his wife Judy. They have twin daughters who live interstate.

The McAlister Line

The McAlister Line Reader Reviews

'...Masterfully handled and quite eloquent...wonderful.'

'I like this book [McAlister's Way] it covers issues that need to be addressed.'

'Waiting for the sequel'

'*McAlister's Spark* is a fast-paced, action-riddled amazing read you will struggle to put down.'

'A great action read for teenagers and great graphics...a great literary effort.'

'...with pirates and secrets set amongst the northern tropics, you're in for a delightful read. With a good sense of place and the voice to the detail it's [*McAlister's Way*] a very fast-moving action story that will have you wanting more.'

'*McAlister's Way* is a fast-paced, page-turning read — the kind of read where you lose track of time. Absolutely enveloping! Highly recommended!!'

'Through the non-stop action and the integration of history, new cultures and wars the reader is kept engaged from beginning to end on a literary roller coaster ride they won't soon forget.'

Illustrated Books for All Ages

Other Adventure Titles

Approaching his sixteenth birthday, Henry is thrust into a perilous quest when his village chief's wife is abducted. Joined by three companions and his pet wolf, he vows to track down the mysterious kidnappers.

With no magic or special skills, they can only rely on their courage, determination, wits and friendship to survive in a cruel realm which makes no concessions for youth or innocence.

Danger mounts with each challenge until ultimately they face a seemingly unconquerable foe at the gates of a hostile, alien city.

A mighty dragon called Brimstone is terrorising the quiet village of Oak Tree. Prince Roger and his sister Princess Crystal set out to hunt the fiery beast.

They are ably assisted or hindered — as the case may be — by an evil knight, a mysterious good-guy, the local sheriff, loyal men-at-arms, forest brigands, ogres, trolls and Oak Tree's villagers with a bunch of attitude.

There are thrills, spills, romance and heaps of rollicking fun to be had by all.

Illustrations for other Authors